CYRUS CYRUS

Adam Zameenzad was born in Pakistan and spent his early childhood in East Africa. He is the author of three other novels: *The Thirteenth House*, winner of the David Higham Award for the best first novel of 1987, *My Friend Matt and Hena the Whore* and *Love, Bones and Water*. He now lives with his family in Kent.

ADAM ZAMEENZAD

CYRUS
CYRUS

Minerva

A Minerva Paperback
CYRUS CYRUS

First published in Great Britain 1990
by Fourth Estate Ltd
This Minerva edition published 1991
by Mandarin Paperbacks
Michelin House, 81 Fulham Road, London SW3 6RB

Minerva is an imprint of the Octopus Publishing Group,
a division of Reed International Books Limited

A CIP catalogue record for this title
is available from the British Library
ISBN 0 7493 9915 5

Typeset by Falcon Typographic Art Ltd,
Edinburgh & London
Printed and bound in Great Britain by
Cox & Wyman Ltd, Reading, Berkshire

In remembrance of Cyrus Cyrus* –
after all, it is his story, his life, and his book

CONTENTS

APOLOGIA

The author realises that most British readers who pick this book off the shelf will be only too familiar with much of the information contained in the Foreword. However, public memory is short and, like most contemporary historians, he feels that he has to record these events, albeit briefly, for the benefit of future readers and overseas patrons, as a prelude to the entirely new and exciting revelations of Cyrus Cyrus himself.

DISCLAIMER

I, Adam Zameenzad, take no responsibility for the veracity or otherwise of Cyrus's version of facts, nor do I necessarily agree with his vision of truth. I am too personally involved, and biased, so to do. I can, however, simply state that his brief mention of our first encounter and various references to our subsequent meetings are quite accurate from a factual point of view, even though they have been hijacked by his rather imaginatively coloured perception and somewhat hyperbolic prose. I take no exception to the few unkind cuts and back-handed comments he makes about my person. As a writer it is his privilege. Besides, overall, he has been very generous towards me. Much more than I deserve, considering that I was never really able to do anything for him except encourage him to start writing his book, and then help in publishing it – both of which he could have managed on his own, I have no doubt.

The editor, greatly to my distress, chooses to describe *Zoetrope* as *Images of sex and survival, death and after-death, madness and genius, as relived within the dark, unfathomable recesses of the black hole of his mind by Cyrus Cyrus, one of the most notorious men this century has produced.* I eventually agreed to let this blurb be printed as I was made to see the commercial wisdom of it: very different, I have been advised, from greed.

My final suggestion to alter the blurb to: *Images of birth and revival, death and after-death, reality and nightmare, from the colourful cornucopia of his mind, by Cyrus Cyrus, one of the most maligned men of the century*, was turned down by the editor, politely but firmly. I quote his letter to that effect in full, barring names, except my own. Despite the fact that I have been accused of being an unqualified idiot when it comes to official matters and business know-how, even I am sure that there is no chance of my suing myself.

Dear Adam,

I was delighted to receive your letter the other day. You are a great writer, and one day you will write a great book. As for your letter, all I can say is that I was delighted to receive it.

Now to another one of your suggestions about altering the blurb. I think it is nice. Very nice indeed, but it simply dilutes the original, castrating it almost, without adding any new dimension to it, and leaving it bland, neither biting nor exciting. Now if you had come up with a totally different and original idea, I would have been more than willing to give it a chance. I am sure you would understand.

Keep in touch. Longing to see you again. Liked colourful cornucopia.

Yours,
*****

PS I showed your suggestion to *****, and to *****, and to ********* All of them happen to agree with me. Sorry.

What really maddened me was the fact that up until then I *had* been giving original and different suggestions, and was specifically told to try and stick to the existing line, modifying it if necessary. When I do that, I am accused of not being original! But there you have it. That is editors and publishers for you. Can't live with them, can't live without. Perhaps he was right about lack of originality.

FOREWORD

The name of Cyrus Cyrus has been associated with sex, drugs, murder and satanism ever since his protracted and complicated trial some three years ago. While passing sentence upon him Judge James Parkinson called him 'the most truly evil man that I have had the misfortune to try in a court of law'. He further took the unusual step of recommending that his three life sentences 'ought not to run concurrently, but each, for an absolute minimum of twenty-five years, to follow the other, to ensure that this vile creature is not let loose among decent citizens of the civilised world ever again'.

On the first of January last year Cyrus walked out of the solid stone wall of his solitary prison cell in the maximum-security gaol near Hastings, as if from an open door. Seconds later his naked, exsanguinated body was discovered by a urinating tramp in the Levergate Cemetery in south-east London – some ninety-three miles away from the location of the prison – next to the graves of his three children. He had always expressed a desire to be buried alongside them, a desire which had sent shudders of revulsion and disbelief through newspaper readers and television watchers: it was for the brutal and bizarre murders of those children – among a host of lesser offences – that Cyrus had been convicted!

5

The various crimes proven against Cyrus stand as under: shoplifting (twelve packets of fine latex condoms, multi-coloured); disturbing the peace during a peace march; wilful submission to buggery by a minor; possession of illegal drugs and other harmful substances and perverted objects for the purposes of personal use and of sale to the general public (not excluding minors); aggravated robbery; enticing young children away from school, young executives away from offices and the stock market, and mature businessmen away from important business, in order to hold parties of a morally repugnant nature; being drunk and disorderly; sexually assaulting a male police officer during the discharge of his normal duties; travelling on British Rail without a valid ticket or a permit to travel; organising the desecration of Santa Claus and the mugging of three old ladies (near a Bingo Hall in Southend-on-Sea) within the space of half an hour; crossing the road without due care and endangering the life of other road-users; kidnapping and murder of three children: Sal, aged four years, three months and three days, his first son with his common-law wife Jennifer; Hagar, aged nine years, five months and fifteen days, his first child with his deceased wife Belinda; and Jason, fifteen years exactly, his common-law wife's son with her first husband.

Pleas of epileptically-induced hallucinations and para-noid schizophrenia, of mental disequilibrium and diminished responsibility were all dismissed by the court. The court also disregarded the assertions of three of the country's top-ranking psychiatrists that Cyrus's staggeringly high IQ had led to serious problems with personal relationships and social adjustments, making it impossible for him to bridge the gap between his abilities and expectations on the one hand, and the troubled realities of his appalling life on the other.

This conflict was further exacerbated by a facility of total recall which did not allow him to forget anything, thus making the corridors of his mind far too over-crowded and dangerous to live in. This last claim was met with unconcealed scepticism on the part of the court. Cyrus had previously claimed that he could remember nothing at all of certain actions and activities attributed to him or of which he was alleged to be the epicentre. The psychiatrists argued that memory, even the finest, even Cyrus's, could have blank spots, or be selective; especially concerning periods directly before, directly after, or during drug-induced states. At this point Judge Parkinson simply arched his eyebrows, suppressed a smile, and looked at the jury. No firmer directive to treat those claims with utter contempt could have been given by one above contempt. For once Cyrus almost agreed with the judge. He maintained that he had no memory of the said events simply because they did not happen: not to him, nor through him – implying though not amplifying that some others may have been the real culprits – and not because of any memorial eccentricities.

Apart from such muted assertions, during the trial, Cyrus refused to say anything at all about the central charges of abduction and murder of the children, neither admitting nor denying guilt, leaving his helpless advocate to take whatever line of defence she thought best in the circumstances.

Once sentenced and in prison, he extended this silence to all contact with inmates and staff for the entire duration of his stay in the establishment, doing no good at all to his popularity rating within the system, until the morning of his astonishing escape when he blessed the entire prison, an act of outrageous audacity which has since been referred to by all who heard it as 'The Blessing on the Balcony' – to the great annoyance and shocked disapprobation of the popular press and media moralists of all colours, complexions and persuasions. Prior to that he had uttered not a single word under the most truculent of provocations and the most violent of confrontations, not even while being subjected to the most sophisticated of psychological approaches. He spent most of his time in solitary by invoking rule forty-three: in writing.

The fact that he did converse, if sporadically and when he chose, with Father O'Neil and myself made his glassy taciturnity towards the rest all the more irritating to staff and prisoner alike, proving it to be wilful and not pathological.

Unproven charges against Cyrus ranged from stealing a child's brolly to planting a bomb at Harrods; attempted murder of Jonathan Develin, owner of chic London nightclub Style, the son of the country's most prestigious judge, Lord Cornelious Develin; attempted murder of Darren Plummer, better known as Biggun Dangler, stripper/singer at Style nightclub and personal friend of Jonathan Develin; murder of Professor Ralph Jacobs, one-time English tutor of Jonathan Develin; murder of one eighty-seven-year-old retired schoolmaster by the name of Desmond Smith; holding satanic rituals in a disused church in a small village near Rochford in Essex; running a sadistic brothel in which a fifteen-year-old prostitute was gruesomely beaten to death by a fourteen-year-old prostitute; and interfering with a seventy-one-year-old dead man.

Thirty-six other offences were taken into account, including urinating, at twelve noon precisely, upon a fruit stall in Soho Market on a Sunday.

Cyrus left behind him the completed manuscript of a book which he had been writing during his time in prison. It was tied round with three ribbons, one aureate, one viridescent and one rubious. They glowed eerily even in complete and utter darkness. Laboratory tests have proved that they are made of no known material or substance, biological or synthetic. On top of the manuscript lay a flaming asphodel, its tongue-like petals rising above the central bulb with velvety smoothness, its heady aroma sending the senses reeling overboard into some ever-ever land of commingling doubts and certainties. The asphodel is still fragrant today, well over a month on, its petals fresh and dewy.

To some people the final episode of his life was the final proof of Cyrus's involvement with witchcraft and satanism. To others it was incontrovertible evidence of his complete innocence; of no less than Divine intervention on his behalf.

I make no comment, even though I, along with Father O'Neil and two prison officers, was a witness to Cyrus's disappearance through the four-feet-thick wall. I say witness, but in actual fact I witnessed nothing. One moment Cyrus was there, looking at us with his large black eyes, and the next he was not there.

Neither did Father O'Neil see anything. We were both busy looking at the ribbon-tied manuscript and the radiant asphodel which Cyrus had entrusted to both of us, his last known act on this earth. The prison officers *were* keeping a sharp eye on him. They, George and Barry, tough, time-hardened men and chief tormenters of Cyrus, have been incoherent masses of jelly since then. Whatever they saw, no one will ever know.

Rumours abound. There are those who say that a door, narrow but sharp and clear, opened up within the wall to reveal a blindingly illuminating light through which and upon which Cyrus walked from his cell. Some say the Devil Himself, with burning red coals for eyes and rigid but bent phalli for horns, melted the wall with his profane fire and pulled his most unholy accomplice from out the cell and took him to the very gates of Hell and beyond. Still others claim that a cross-shaped, man-sized entrance appeared within the wall, and Cyrus walked out through it, arms spread wide.

The fact that Cyrus's cell was in a corner all by itself on the fourth and top storey of the prison made his sudden departure even more remarkable.

But of course there are, as there always are, a hard core of disbelievers who say it is all a hoax, some sort of an elaborately contrived smokescreen to cover up for the fact that Cyrus had either managed to escape or been brutalised to death. This last is, alas, only too close to what could have happened were it not for the efforts and vigilance of Father O'Neil, and to a modest extent, my own protests on Cyrus's behalf.

I don't suppose that anyone will ever know the real truth behind the façade of fact and fantasy. However there is something that I can do which should help clear up many of the foggy uncertainties that surround the life and death of Cyrus. Actually it is something which Cyrus himself did. I am only passing it on, as it were, acting on his behalf.

I now introduce and present *Zoetrope: Reflections and Memories* by Cyrus Cyrus, published by publishers of unimpeachable reputation and integrity, as Cyrus requested me to do, without letting any part of the manuscript get into the hands of unscrupulous, unsavoury, money-hungry tabloids. I would have thought it was a bit too late for that, considering that he had already helped each one of them to sell millions of extra copies over the years as they revelled in righteous rage, with every lurid detail specially created to appeal to the pious. Anyway.

Cyrus Cyrus, Satan or saint? The most evil of men, or the most wronged? Just another loser, or someone who triumphed over everyone and everything?

You know the official verdict, you've read what the papers say, you must have caught the rumours. Now hear his side of it. Then make up your own mind.

In the meantime Cyrus's body, after several inconclusive post-mortems and umpteen futile forensic tests, lies unburied in a secret location in the north-west of England, as far away as possible from Cyrus's favourite haunts. Or so the authorities believe.

ZOETROPE

Reflections and Memories

by
Cyrus Cyrus

Zoetrope

Images of sex and survival, death and after-
death, madness and genius, as relived within
the dark, unfathomable recesses of the black
hole of his mind by Cyrus Cyrus, one of
the most notorious men this century has
produced.

Offered in utmost reverence to Father O'Neil,
with deep gratitude
for the peace he poured into my soul,
and the lust he roused in my body.

And to Adam Zameenzad.
He will be changing the world as soon as possible,
but he means well.

Contents

Part I
THE FULCRUM AND THE HUB

One Birth

One of my earliest memories is of being born. A hugely revolting and horrifying experience, ghastly and grotesque. In fact, a more ghastly and grotesque experience it is not easy to conceptualise. And I have had encounters with a kaleidoscopic range of ghastly and grotesque experiences, I can assure you. I know what I am talking about.

The wages of sin is birth.

One moment I was afloat in a sea of tempestuous peace – a throbbing vibrant peace: the only kind of peace which competes winningly with the challenges of war and for which it is worth forgoing conflict; the peace which does not suffer from negative growth rate, which does not engender boredom nor produce its own niggling second-rate protagonists. The next moment my sea is pulsating with agony, as if being boiled by Mephistophelean fires, rising to ebb away, dragging me along with horrendous force, ripping me from the comfort and security of my moorings.

Tearing flesh, gore and blood. Blood on my face. Blood in my mouth. Blood in my eyes.

How I fought and struggled. How I begged and pleaded. How I prayed.

In vain.

I resisted with every gene of my tiny being as I went through the terrorising process of being pushed down, head first, sucked the wrong way out of the suffocating one-way passage, squirming, tortuous, oxygenless.

In vain.

I felt with appalling horror the searing pain I was causing my protector and sustainer as I tore through the centre of her body. I cried in empathetic pain, augmenting my own.

Oh how I cried.

In vain.

How I prayed.

In vain.

There I was, *plop*, in the middle of a world of which I knew nothing, and from which I wanted nothing; snipped in the bud, and knotted up.

How I cried.

How I prayed.

I could not understand why a hitherto loving and caring God had suddenly deserted me through no apparent fault of mine. The bitterness of His betrayal in my heart was worse than the bitterness of blood in my mouth.

I stopped praying.

I cried bitterly.

Mother wiped me clean, wrapped me in a clean shawl – it was a cold morning, being the first morning of the Year of Our Lord 1954 – cleared up the mess, washed herself with Sunlight soap, dried herself with a tattered but clean blue-ribbed towel which had a lingering hint of musk on it, and went back to milking the goat.

The goat, pure white, with a strong lithe body which rippled under your hands, was the family treasure, the healthiest and best-fed member of the household. It was given to my mother by one of the local zameendars after he had raped her – raped my mother that is, not the goat, though I wouldn't put *that* past him either. Mother was really pleased. The goat was the best thing she had ever got after being raped. In fact it was the best thing she had ever got, after, during, or before *anything*. The worst, at least after being raped, was a black eye and three broken ribs. But then what could you expect from the local police chief? Mind you, my Aunt Verna did get more: two black eyes, five broken ribs *and* a broken nose. She looks like the world heavyweight champion to this day. At least she did the last time I saw her, which was some years ago. She fared better than my Auntie Neelum, who

22

killed herself after she was raped. But she was only fourteen, and in love. Terrible thing, love. Also, hers wasn't a normal rape. There were five of them, including two superintendents from Lucknow, the city of Mogul splendour about fifty miles to our north as the jet flies, come to our little town of Chandan to help the poor people after the rains brought many houses down. They were helping my Aunt Neelum get her charpoy out of the mess. A mud house can be very messy if it comes down in the rain, especially if it wasn't set up properly in the first place. Not enough straw and little cow dung, and you can be sure of saying goodbye to it sooner or later. But it isn't easy to come by cow dung if you haven't got cows, nor straw if you haven't got access to a field.

I must explain. All these rapes in the family. You must think we come from a very common lot. We do. We are Choodahs. In India, the lowest of the low, the shit cleaners. We survive in older, poorer parts of big cities, or in small towns; modern parts of big cities have modern toilet facilities, and people in villages use the open air, or have pits dug in the case of rich zameendar families. We are the most untouchable of the untouchables.

I don't suppose that explains too well, does it? If we are that untouchable, you might argue, how do we go about getting our mothers and aunts (to mention only the female side of the family) raped every other day, almost as a matter of habit, since the process must involve some form of touching by others and betters, however brief the carnal act? But you have to understand India a bit better to better understand, especially the India of villages and small towns. And don't tell me about the outlawing of untouchability. Try telling it to the people in our town, living practically on the banks of the Ganges and under the shadow of the holiest of cities, Varanasi, better known in the West as Benares. Try telling the British there are laws against racism.

Our untouchableness is absolute, but only in so far as *we* want to touch something we ought not to, or worse, someone we ought not to, someone better and superior to us in every conceivable way, according to our birth and the will of Brahma. It does not prevent our superiors and betters from touching us, if the fancy takes them, provided they wash in the Ganges afterwards; or, should the Ganges not be meandering close by to their rape location, at their water taps or handpumps; even the local canal would do, mud, urine, shit and all, provided they go to the temple to get properly purified afterwards. Mind you, many didn't bother with all that. Rape, and straight home to dinner, which is a shame. I believe there is a great deal to be said for tradition and ritual.

We got the brunt of the rampant cocks. We were the only Choodah family left in Chandan, so there wasn't much choice available. (Modern plumbing had started spreading its devious pipes round our little corner of the world forcing others of our kind out into bigger cities for employment of similar social orientation.) The peasants and other menial workers in our town had gradually become better organised and more difficult to deal with since one of them turned a Marxist, making it prudent to leave their sexually desirables alone, unless they happened to be too sexually desirable, in which case it could be worth the risk. They got beaten up more often than us lot, though, and had more goods stolen. Goods that later adorned the local coppers' houses, or those of the landowners' henchmen. That left only us for the naughties. The other families in the area were known and respected, some even feared.

Ours was a small – within a radius of about five miles – but important little town. It had its own railway station, and was surrounded by villages with very fertile land. All the grain and agricultural produce was first brought to our Chandan, to be later transported to places like Lucknow, the capital, Varanasi, the sacred cow of cities, and Allahabad, the famous University town, rival to Aligarh. We had our very own police station, controlling an area of thirty miles all around. Anybody wanted trouble, they had to send for our police lads. Not many small towns in India can boast of that.

The particular zameendar who indulged in my mother, the kind one with the goat, was a Muslim anyway, and Muslims needn't even bother with the post-untouchable-rape sex cleansing rituals. They have to have a bath, of course, as they do even after holy intercourse in marriage. But they do not believe in this untouchable nonsense. Neither do the Christians. That is why our family, like many of the Choodahs since departed, had converted to Christianity years ago. Didn't help much. We were still treated as Choodahs; and what's worse, called Choodahs.

I remember my great grandmother, one of the first to be called to Jesus, telling me of her First Holy Communion. She said that once she was inside the church all she could see, through a haze of glorious heavenly light, was Jesus and God and the angels, Mary and the baby and the halos, shepherds and kings and saints. She came out to find the same old bucketful of shit in the same old place where she had discreetly left it, covered with the shit scraper and carrier tray. Next to it sat the wicker basket, shaped like a giant cereal bowl, with the two straw brooms – one hard and spiky and brown, the other soft and fluffy and golden – alongside. Everything was just as she had placed it, some distance away from the grand holy structure made of specially carved stones, tall as a mountain, its presence as imposing as the presence of God Himself. She could not believe her eyes. Shutting them tight and then looking again did not help.

Actually she had wanted my great grandfather to do her round for her that day. She had explained to the families concerned and obtained their permission, so that she could be one hundred per cent for Jesus. But he had the malaria – Great Grandfather, not Jesus – and only just about managed to do some wood chopping to which he was previously committed and which if he hadn't done could have resulted in a roughing up, which wouldn't have done his malaria any good. Great Grandmother was left with no choice but to get on with her work.

After she had collected the shit from the last home on her round there wasn't enough time left to go down to the canal just outside the town to dispose of it and wash up her bucket, so she rushed straight to the church. She was much too excited and nervous to think of an alternative. Her whole being was in a state of spiritual preparation, as if for take-off to heaven. She was somehow hoping that her life would be permanently changed from then on. She would be reborn, and rebirth should mean a new life. Obvious, it would seem. Once she was actually in the church, and sitting alongside five *white* people, the missionary family that had brought her to the Lord, she had no doubts whatever. It was no longer a matter of hoping, or even of it being a logical imperative. It was a moral certainty.

Upon emerging into the sunlight from the holy light she found the same old bucket, full of shit, waiting patiently for her to come back, pick it up, place it on her head above the knotted roll of cloth, tuck the wicker basket under her armpit, hold the straw brooms in her hand and start her long walk home, as if nothing at all had happened! She was too stunned for words. The sheer nerve of it all. She would never have thought a bucketful of shit capable of it. She had thought all it had was shit. Clearly not. It had her whole life in it, mapped out to the very nth detail.

When the white family – Father Robert Parsley, Mary Jane Cowie, his widowed sister, and her children, Jacob, David and Jo – promised to see her in church the next Sunday, and hurried away well before she could get to her daunting bucketful of shit, she was still too stunned to speak her humble thankyous.

I asked her why she continued to believe. Her reply was strangely convincing, if a little baffling at first. I was so sure that a miracle would happen to change my life, she said, so utterly and truly sure, that when it did not happen, it was a miracle. After all, what is a miracle but the happening of something which you were certain could not happen. I was so certain that my life could not remain the same that it was a miracle when it did. That shit bucket, its old metal winking away in the sun, sitting there when it had no right to be there, was as much a miracle as the burning of the bush or the parting of the waves or the seeing of the blind. It took me half a lifetime to work that out. I kept going to church and praying to Jesus all along, but my heart was never in it. Not until I understood the real nature of the miracle of the shit bucket. Only then did I realise that Jesus truly was the Messiah, she said.

I said nothing, contrary to my usual loquacity in the presence of my great grandmother. I was set to thinking.

I was three at the time, and a real mouth, given half a chance to express my opinion, but she was the only one prepared to carry on a normal conversation with me. Everybody else thought that at that age I should not be talking 'like a grown man', and therefore avoided speaking to me, certainly at any length. Father wouldn't have minded, but he was half dead from tuberculosis by that time, and did not have much wind left in his lungs to carry on a conversation with anybody, much less me, who had brought nothing but bad luck to the family since the day I was born. The family fortunes, and you may laugh, had been tumbling downhill since my birth, there is no denying that, whatever the cause. '*Manhoos*' they called me, the ultimate condemnation: the bringer of ill luck and death. Possessed by the Devil, I was thought to be, talking like a grown man at the age of three! And that was not all. I was the blackest child in the family. An utter and total disgrace. Even without the hairy mole or the devil riding my back.

All that on top of being male! In the Choodahs – though not to such an extent as in the Kanjars, the 'dancing families' – it was the females who were the main breadwinners. Males were often no more than encumbrances, mere appendages for the production of more females, only managing to get some seasonal employment now and then, like chopping wood in the winter. They weren't allowed anywhere near the corn at harvesting nor anything to do with food production or any household work or work in a shop. They weren't 'clean' for that. Shit clearing was restricted mostly to women, as the presence of outside males, even for shit clearing, was offensive to the ladies of the house.

Going to the big cities has altered much of that, I believe. Men change their family name and can get most work now, if it is going. I can't be sure, though, not being anywhere near that part of the world any more. But then I was, of course, and in a small town where male Choodahs were not much in demand. To be black as well, blue-black, was just not on. Of course most Choodahs, unlike most Kanjars who claim descent from Moguls and Nawabs, are quite black – like Bengalis, Madrasis and others from Eastern and Southern India. But in my case, having a near cream complexioned sister, the one that resulted from the Muslim zameendar's attention to Mother, made my own very dark hide look particularly repugnant. But alas, I was much like my father, Mother's husband, and he wasn't much good to anyone for anything. Just a coughing, blood-spitting wreck of a man who neither lived nor died. A constant unwanted weight round the family's neck. Mother's in particular, who had to do all the hard work, in between getting raped and all.

Two Murders

I have seen hundreds and thousands killed and murdered in my life. I cannot even give an approximate number as to how many. This is not a wanton exaggeration, nor does it indicate any lapse of memory.

I will tell you about two here: the first, because the first is always important, and this one was more than just any old first, I can assure you; and the second – it also happened to be the second chronologically – because it was the one responsible for formulating two of the most powerful aspects of my character for the rest of my time on Earth. It also confirmed my status in the family as being the *manhoos* one, the bringer of ill luck etcetera. You've already heard about that so I won't elaborate.

The first first.

It must have been about twelve noon on a burning hot day in June, June the 21st it was. The place was just past the meeting point of our town and the first village to our south. I was twenty-five and three then, weeks and days. Mother had left me on a little green mound underneath the shade of an ancient peepal tree that spread its branches like a gargantuan umbrella of thickly woven leaves over the seasonal canal which went brushing past Chandan, and where Mother washed and cleaned the accoutrements of her trade: buckets and scraper and suchlike. She had gone, I know not where, except that it wasn't to wash up the accoutrements of her trade, as they sat next to me, already cleaned up, shining resplendently in the light filtering through the gently

29

trembling leaves; and it wasn't to get raped, as she usually had someone with her on such occasions.

She had tied a soft belt of cloth round my right ankle, then run a rope through the belt and wound it round the peepal tree, which had a trunk as broad as the dome of a mosque, so that I did not wander away and drown myself in the canal or throw myself under the wheels of the first bullock-cart that happened to idle past that way in search of something to search for. The heady smell of wet grass and water-heavy sod in the fields (it had rained all night) combined with the sound of intense silence broken and enhanced by the occasional crowing of an errant crow, and the buzzing of greedy flies looking for some signs of leftover shit in the bucket, had led me close to a state of sleep-induced hypnosis when it happened.

The sound of heavy footsteps squashing the earth – still juicy with rain despite the harsh sun – broke through the stillness of the atmosphere and cut into my consciousness. I could feel: the weight of charging feet, the speed of running bodies, the beat of pounding hearts; feel: fear turning to panic, anger rising to rage, hate becoming death; feel it all, feel overwhelmed by it all, but unable to do anything about it, being small, naked, belted and tied to a tree larger than all the people I knew put together, older than the lifetimes of everyone I knew added up.

A face appeared first, the face of a young man. A young man ageing years by the second. A beautiful face, its beauty shining through the distortion of fear. His eyes were greyish black, the pupils contracting and expanding with each beat of his racing pulse. His mouth was open showing even white teeth framed by full sensuous lips; his strong nostrils billowed with the spasmodic rapidity of his breathing.

His shirt, torn all over, revealed a pale skin spread over strong firm shoulders thrown back against the growing breeze, glowing with health and sweat; a filled-out chest with one tall nipple clearly visible, rigid with excitement of a kind, standing up, reaching out.

He was followed almost immediately by seven men: three shirtless, wearing chequered dhotis that flew open with every stride, offering momentary glimpses of heavy, hairy genitalia; two wearing fine muslin kurtas and pyjamas; the remaining two in cotton trousers, one with just a vest on top, the other in a shirt. Two of the seven were a bit runty; the others ranged from normally built to three giants: two in dhotis and the one with trousers and a vest.

The seven now caught up with the one and jumped on him, right in front of where I sat next to the washed and dried but still vaguely odoriferous bucket, a little to the side of the wicker basket in the shape of a giant cereal bowl, my fingers entwined in the soft and fluffy golden broom, my naked backside ticklish with the spikes of the hard brown broom, my feet touching the empty shit tray with the scraper sitting neatly to its right.

One of the giants straddled the young man's chest, facing his feet; the two others caught him by the crook of the knees and lifted his legs up in the air, the remainder set about tearing his clothes off his body. I could not see the young man's face as it was blocked by the huge man sitting across his chest, but I could hear him breathing, each breath preciously taken, in the knowledge that it was among the last, if not *the* last. After the initial cry of hoarse pain and blind terror when he was thrown on the ground, he had not made a sound, uttered no cries, begged not for mercy nor called for help or shouted abuse. Whether he was incapable of speech, or was silently praying to his God, or was just resigned to his fate, I could not tell.

When he was made naked the two runty ones pulled at the young man's penis, pointed to the circumcised glans and shouted in Hindi: Musla (meaning Muslim), just as we thought, mother-fucking sister-screwing bloody Musla! One of the men pulled a silvery sword from the side of his dhoti and, while the others tugged the young man's legs in opposite directions till they were as far apart as East and West, swished the blade powerfully, chopping off the entire genital apparatus in one stroke. A fountain of blood splurted out and caught his assailants in the eyes.

They let out screams of agony as the hot viscous liquid, red and blinding, invaded the sanctity of their organs of sight. Cursing and abusing wildly they began to hit, kick and pummel the young man. When they were absolutely exhausted, and after they had cleared and wiped away the blood from their eyes with various articles of their clothing, they lifted the young man up, and swung him and threw him as far as they could into the canal, cursing and abusing all the while. He fell with a splash which carried a thud of finality with it. He hadn't uttered a sound through it all. One of the dhoti wallahs picked up the young man's torn and bloodied genitals, wrapped them in the remains of their owner's shirt, and put them in the part of his dhoti which went round his waist, like a pouch of money in a belt.

Only when they were turning to go did they see me. Their faces changed completely. Ooh, kootchie koo. Look, a baby, said the one who had sat on the young man's chest, Isn't he cute! Ugly, but cute. More ugly than cute, said one of the runty ones, black as sin. He has seen everything, said another, don't you think we should . . . He made a sign across his throat. Don't be silly, said another giant, he is just a baby. Choo choo chooo. Choo choo chooo, kiddo. Don't touch him! warned another with a shrill cry, Can't you see, he is a Choodah. He pointed to Mother's business gear. There was general silence. Then, So what, said the first giant, and bent down and tickled my chin, it's not his fault. He is just a baby. Even if he is ugly as a donkey's ass. He chuckled good-humouredly.

After some hesitation one other, the one in the vest, joined in, saying, Look he's got this funny mark on his back – this as I turned away in controlled fear – like a . . . like a . . . He tried to think of appropriate words to describe it, while running his fingers over it and laughing. That's the devil riding his back, whispered one of the kurta pyjamas in awed tones. Unlucky that, very unlucky.

That created a greater silence than the Choodah bit. Don't you think we should go now? I am tired, said one of the trousers. So am I, said the other. After a few farewell tickles, the giant got up and walked away with the rest, giving backward glances to me, smiling and waving goodbye, though not without a certain apprehension in his eyes. Throughout, I had remained as silent as the young man, who was no longer a man. He was no longer anything. He had ceased to exist. Except in my mind, where he would never die, but would grow old.

When Mother came – she had only gone for a shit in the fields, but was delayed as she started admiring the butterflies flitting around between the wild flowers, Mother loves flowers and butterflies and all things beautiful, pity she was landed with me for a last-born – she nearly burst a gut seeing me covered in blood. She looked around in terror, and saw blood everywhere. She made no attempt to discover the cause of it but clutched me to herself and ran homewards, leaving her precious bucket and all that went with it behind. No one would take a Choodah's things anyway. Indeed, they were later recovered when the entire family came together for that purpose. There was safety in numbers.

To her dying day Mother thought I had something to do with that bloodshed, even though the story of the young man's murder came to be generally known, largely through the open boasting of the killers. The true cause remained a mystery. Among the possibilities: It was purely sectarian; The young man had raped a Hindu zameendar's daughter; He had just made a pass at her; It was a quarrel among men; He was a thief. When the story reached Lucknow, from where the young man had come to study village life, there was a mini-blood bath between factions of Hindus and Muslims.

† † †

Actually it was the second murder that set Mother thinking I must have had some responsibility for the first. Not by doing anything, of course, but just by being who, or what, I was. To be fair, it wasn't Mother at all but Aunt Verna who started my fall from grace. There is something peculiar about that boy, she said on every given occasion, beginning with when she first saw me, aged two hours and five minutes. Mark my words, there is something very peculiar about that boy, she said. And who could blame her? After all, I had been born with my eye-teeth fully grown, a hairy mole on the left of my ass, and the devil riding my back: a sort of lop-sided cross, regarded by the populace to be a disfigurement of the sacred swastika and hence dreaded as the mark of the devil, which stood out clearly, getting clearer and sharper and better-defined by the day, on my left shoulder-blade. The left side is not the right side, on our side of the world. Anything 'unnatural' anywhere is bad. On the left side, it is twice as bad. At least. Even left-handed children are shunned. I did grow up to be left-handed, in case you are wondering. To further prove my unnaturalness, I started walking one morning, suddenly, without any warning and without any crawling beforehand. Just stood up, from sedentary, and took my first nine steps. The horrified Aunt Verna counted each one of them: three times three – she had difficulty with numbers above three. And to make matters even worse, I said my first word, 'owl', not in English but in vernacular, 'ulloo' (with the *u* as in *put*) the very next day. The owl is considered by all in India an ominous bird, a sly creature who hides himself during the light of the good God's day and comes out only in the night, along with thugs and murderers and adulterers and others with guilt on their minds and no good in their hearts. That was just one week before the first murder. Mere coincidence, or a sign from the Almighty of great unnatural things to come?

Now to the second murder. It is still not easy to talk about.

Ali and Hafiz, two of the local constables, Muslims, came to our house early in the morning two weeks later. It was Eid, one of the major Muslim festivals. Families like ours look forward to Eid. Always some charity fell our way from Muslims on that day. Some actually came to the house, bringing sweets, money, even clothes. The coming of the police generally spelled disaster. When these two coppers came in on the day of the Big Eid – there are two, Eid ul Fitr, the one after the thirty days of Ramazan fasting, and Eid ul Azha, the Big Eid, on which animals are sacrificed according to the will of Allah – we didn't know what to think. That they were police pointed towards the road to despair; that they were Muslims raised hope.

We should have known better. What have you got for us

poor coppers, dearies? said Hafiz, standing inside the small open verandah facing the two little rooms which contained the entire belongings and all the remaining members of our branch of the Choodah family: myself, aged twenty-eight weeks; sister Nazli (the *gori*, the 'white' one), aged two; sister Edwina, aged six; brother Junior, aged nine; Father, aged thirty; Mother, aged twenty-eight; Aunt Verna, age unknown; Aunt Neelum, aged twelve; Uncle Dano, of Aunt Verna, aged thirty-seven; Grandmother, aged fifty-two; Great Grandmother, aged seventy-one; Umrao, the goat, aged nine. Ali grinned, showing big teeth, paan-discoloured, making them look bloody. You Choodahs make much more than us poor coppers, now don't you? Which was nearly true. The copper's salary was a meagre one, providing good incentive for corruption. But count the 'blessings' that result from that incentive and they make more than their share of a good living.

I really do not want to talk about it, but I feel I must. Without it no story of my life would be honest, or complete.

After some buffoonery and clowning they made straight for our goat, standing handsomely in the corner of the verandah to the right of the outside door, next to the charpoys stood against the wall, beside a plastic bowl of water, a few niblets of fresh grass surrounding her – she had eaten the rest – making the most perfectly formed droppings you have ever seen, like biological marbles, a curiously black shade of green. They started dragging her along saying they had no money to buy an animal for the holy sacrifice, and that this would do, and that we should be grateful that Muslims do not have any prejudice against the untouchables otherwise they would not have so much as laid a finger on her. Their laughter and joking turned sour as the goat firmly refused to go along with them. The family sat silent, motionless, expressionless. They all knew what crossing the police would mean. A chain of ugly rapes, beatings and accusations of theft and of plotting against the state. Yes, we have been accused of that.

OK, sister, if you don't want to get out of this house then so be it, said Ali. We all felt the blood coming back to our brains, but we should have known better.

Hafiz pulled out a big knife. Ali got the goat between his legs, held her head by the horns and twisted it to one side. Hafiz called on Allah three times and slit the stubbornly bleating throat. Then began the wait for the old girl to bleed to death. She didn't go without kicking.

As they were leaving, Ali threw the heavy offal at us. This is what you Choodahs eat, don't you? Keep it. There was truth in that. Everyone threw us offal whenever there was an animal killed. Hafiz said, You didn't even get us a glass of sherbet in this heat, we'll get you for that. He smiled at Aunt Neelum as he said so. It was not a cheerful smile. The old goat's blood dancing on the verandah looked no different from the young man's splurging by the canal.

It was Aunt Verna who first found voice. It's him, she shouted above the sudden weeping of Aunt Neelum, pointing a shaking finger at me. He is the *manhoos* one. We have had that goat for eight years and no one . . . and now . . . and now . . . She was now sobbing hysterically. Father had always maintained that Aunt Verna was merely jealous of me because she could not have any children of her own after her first rape, but that day even he did not come to my defence. Mother's eyes were clogged with tears and her throat choked with guts. She could neither see nor speak. Nazli, Edwina and Junior were dry-eyed and frozen.

As for me, that murder, following so soon upon the other, developed in me a total and utter abhorrence of all violence, and a deep love for all things living, especially animals. My greatest fear in life is that one day I may be given the choice between saving a human life and the life of an animal. What would I do? I pray to God I never have to make that decision.

Father got up, picked up the milk pail, went to the handpump in the centre of the verandah, which also served as the bathroom, and began pumping the water, no doubt with the intention of removing the blood while it was still alive and playing around. If it died on the mud floor, it would stay there for ever. We should have kept the babies, we should have kept the kids, he kept muttering to himself, we should have . . . Till a spasm of rattling coughs made him stop talking and pumping. He doubled up in pain and began splurting blood out of his mouth. He had gone to clear up the blood off the floor, not add to it, but that's my dad for you, never got anything right. Everything he did began and ended with, We should have . . . Spoken or unspoken.

Losses and Tragedies, Gains and Benefits

The two years that followed were difficult, the high points being the destruction of our house in the rains, and the suicide of our Aunt Neelum after the police lads helped her in getting her charpoy out of the wreck of the house. You know about that. We lost most of our worldly belongings then.

Our house was one of the very few in the town made of mud, but then we were not exactly in the town, more on the fringe, bordering the village of Gulpur, among the jhuggis and shacks of the very poor. All went in the rains. We made a makeshift jhuggi of dearly-bought corrugated iron, but that kept flying away with every gust of strong wind, the wind then scattering the rest of our possessions wantonly about. This went on for another two years or so.

But good came out of it. Sister Erin, a nun of indeterminate age, ran a free clinic for the likes of us and had vacant servant quarters within the compound of her house. Since we belonged to her church, she finally allowed us, upon approval from the Lord Himself, to come and stay there free of charge. Not only that, she employed Mother to do the cleaning for her and Junior to run errands and generally help in doing odd jobs at the clinic, and she paid us for that. Only a few rupees, but what with free accommodation and left-overs of food daily, we had never had it so good. There's more! Sister Erin personally undertook to have a good doctor examine Father, and then arranged a regular supply of medication for

39

him. She even got him a job sweeping the Chandan railway station twice daily.

Things went really well from then on, until tragedy and misfortune caught up with us again, this time leaving us with no option but to flee the town. In fact, we decided to take the big leap and flee the country altogether. The road to East Pakistan, Bangla Desh, looked inviting, so we took it.

But there is a lot that went on before then, between 1959 and 1964, which I must talk about first.

Visions and Manifestations I

Mother objected strongly to two of my favourite sports: picking my nose and pulling my willie, both played simultaneously while staring meaningfully into space with a half-grin in my eyes, as if toying with the purpose of life, digging at the truth at the heart of matter. The first, picking, with the little finger of the right hand; the second, pulling, with the index finger and the thumb of the left. The latter particularly worried Mother, and for two reasons: one, because it involved the use of my left hand, which was becoming increasingly active and a cause of great concern, despite reassurances from Sister Erin that it did not necessarily imply criminal tendencies or possession by the devil; two, because my willie was already showing signs of growing too fast for my age and any further pulling and tugging at the lengthy foreskin, which continued quite unnecessarily beyond the point of the knob, could only aggravate the matter in hand. Everything about me was wrong for my age, or just wrong anyway, so any further extension of an overlong prepuce over an overlong membrum virile was not to be encouraged, at least not at such an early age: five.

Sister Erin blushed pink and purple trying to explain that pulling at the . . . thing . . . was not going to affect its . . . size . . . Not in a child, nor in anyone else for that matter, otherwise the well-off willie wallahs would be employing professional willie-pullers with greater frequency than they employed pankha wallahs. She didn't exactly say all that, but you could tell that she was dying to say it. Mother remarked, to herself, that what would *she* know, having given her virginity over to Christ, who was not around to take advantage of the offer and her not willing to have anyone deputise for him. One had to be raped a few times to know what an over-extended organ of lust can do to one's soul. But of course she did not say anything to Sister Erin. She decided to take action instead. That is the only way the likes of us survive, by having practical mothers. They might do some jolly stupid things in their pursuit of practicality, but if they were to sit down and let things take their own course, we would get steam-rollered, with collectively fatal consequences.

Mother tied my left hand to my waist with a ribbon, pure nylon and a lovely shade of boy blue, and put a langoti – a sort of home-made jock strap with strings to adjust and tie according to size (of waist and thighs), somewhat on the principle of a *proper* bow tie, as against those with hooks or elastic – over my crotch and underneath my pyjama bottoms, which were holed across the buttocks with a heart-shaped hole to allow the free passage of faeces without filthying the garment. Urinating, after the langoti discipline, meant either calling for outside help, or just wetting myself and waiting to dry, which at most times of the year did not present too many problems. That took care of the willie-pulling, and the over-active left hand: more of a Muslim taboo than ours or Hindu, but in a truly multi-cultural, multi-religious society, people like us ended up with the worst fears of everybody who happened to be better than us, which in our case was everybody. The nose-picking, after some soul-searching, was left alone in the hope that it would die away on its own. In fact it was looked upon as a blessing, albeit mixed, as it was expected to keep the right hand too busy to wander down to the unmentionables.

As it happened, with the end of the willie-pulling, the nose-picking automatically and instantly stopped. It was a sort of synchronised duet in my mind, or like a song-and-dance routine: one lost its flavour without the other, became meaningless, pointless, tasteless.

Without my hobbies life became hollow as an empty and

desecrated burial vault, shallow as a piss-puddle. I desperately needed something else to occupy myself with.

It was then that I began to play the most dangerous game in the world, discovered the thrill of the deadliest weapons in the world, learnt to love the most explosive objects in the world. Obviously I refer to reading, the written word, books.

And the ultimate mischief on God's part (serves me right for renouncing him at birth) was that I began not with Hindi nor Urdu but English, the language which offered more pernicious literature to choose from than any of the hundreds of languages that proliferate in our part of the world. What's more, a stockpile of literature was right in front of me, to pick from with greater bogies as prizes than my nose ever offered and to play at with more tumefying headiness than any pulling away at the little prick's skinfolds could provide. Sister Erin's library was a treasure-house of books: books for children, books of stories for old people of all ages, fiction, general interest, books on philosophy, books on religion, books on politics. You wanted a book, you could get it from Sister Erin's library, or at least something quite close to the one you had in mind.

Many of the books, especially children's books, probably dated from the time Father Robert Parsley and his widowed sister Mary Jane Cowie used to live there with her children, in the time of my great grandmother's youth. Others may have been brought in before and after by various missionaries, according to their tastes and inclinations; some had been donated, still others had been stamped out years ago by libraries of many different countries. The house had seen book-lovers of all sorts and from all corners of the world. Or perhaps it was just one book maniac who was responsible for all of them. Howsoever they got there, they were there, and that's the point.

Not long after being shown the alphabet – I had already picked up spoken English from Sister Erin and the Harijan doctor who helped her – I was busy browsing through a whole catalogue of all sorts of books, though I must confess I understood little of what I read, barring some story books. But the words remained even if the concepts eluded me, and when I encountered them again in later life it was like meeting old friends.

My favourites, at least in the early days, were books on the mythologies of all nations, especially Graeco-Roman. I found myself performing all sorts of deeds of Herculean valour, with, obviously, him; or challenging the might of Zeus along with Prometheus, the true friend of man, the immortal among mortals, joining him in the pages of Theogony and becoming immortalised myself; or hunting ghost deer (I would never hunt real ones) with that most handsome of giants, Orion, in the darkest haunts of Hades down below, while at the same time forming a constellation in the heavens above – in other words, enjoying the best of both worlds.

Religion fascinated me as well. More and more, the more I read of it. Krishna, playing his bansuri and seducing pretty girls with his music and his what-have-you, was a special favourite. It came as a revelation that one of the best-loved of Hindu gods was as blue-black as myself, and as sexually active as me, that is if tugging at your cockskin could be designated a sexual activity. Mother seemed to think so. Sigmund would agree. So I am well backed up on that.

One of the reasons why mythology and religion so compelled me was that beautiful engravings and pictures often accompanied the text. Perhaps that was why the puritanical monotheism of Islam left me cold, in spite of the fact that our province, Utter Pradesh, had one of the largest concentrations of Muslims in India, and that on the whole they were quite kind and generous to our sort, particularly on festivals and special occasions.

I used to sit under the largest table in the library. It had a cloth on it which came right down to the floor and hid me from view should anyone suddenly walk in. The blue nylon ribbon tied round my left wrist and then taken round my waist, my langoti wet and stinking, I turned the pages of a book often as heavy as myself, which I had carried with great difficulty not just because of its weight but because I was hopelessly left-handed then. I have improved considerably since, almost to the extent of being ambidextrous. I have Mother to thank for that, as indeed I have for many other blessings. If she hadn't kept my left hand tied so tightly to my waist for one whole year, I would still have been hopelessly left-handed today.

Often I found myself in a half-asleep half-awake reverie while reading, out of which I was usually jolted by the hysterical cries of Mother that I had gone missing, *again*! I would then crawl out from under the table and mysteriously turn up right behind her. The number of times she jumped up in fear and screamed before she realised it was me! Did not endear me to her much. Or to anyone else. I was not a popular child. No one found out where I went. Aunt Verna was convinced that there was no natural explanation for it. I am paraphrasing her in polite words. Can't see why she should have been so rude. Wasn't my fault if no one bothered to look under the big table, all set with seasonal flowers, in Sister Erin's library.

It was during one of these trance-like states of exhaustion and fascination that I had my first vision. There were two after that, in quick succession. Then nothing. Not for a long long time. Then came actual manifestations. I was seven at the time, rid of my langoti and ribbon, and in respectable short trousers. I still pulled my willie and picked my nose, but no one knew about that. I suspect that Aunt Verna did, but she couldn't prove it. After all, she had no business keeping such a close eye on my willie.

† † †

Neither the visions nor the manifestations are to be confused with the illusions and hallucinations which preceded and followed. Though I must confess that in some cases I am somewhat unsure of the distinction. In others there can be no doubt.

There could also be no doubt that I would not again be donning pyjamas or any other garment with a large, heart-shaped hole in its posterior to surprise an unsuspecting world with the sight of my bare nates.

No doubt at all, and yet I was proved wrong.

Realities

The past is another place, not another time. Even if it is the same place you happen to be in now, it is still another place, for every place is in the process of unceasing change. Same as our bodies, which after all are only places which have been leased to us, for a limited period, to live in, to spread out, and to develop – until we are ready to move on to a new home, leaving the discarded shell, the body, the temporary abode, behind. Time is no more than one of my illusions. I often talk to her in my solitary cell. Even if what you say is true, says she, I am still the sea upon which the ship moves. A frozen, unchanging, unmoving sea at best, I retort. Still liquid enough to permit motion through it, she counters. More gaseous than liquid, I sneer. Be that as it may, matter has to pass through me to alter its relative position and character. She is unabashed. I am unconvinced. I still believe her to be an illusion. The fact that she is an illusion collectively experienced by mankind does not make her any less an illusion. Only greater. Animals see only places, and no time. I know for I have reduced myself to being one before I further reduce myself to being nothing, in the way a true poet or artist reduces his work to the barest minimum for the maximum effect. And being nothing is the barest minimum, above not being at all. Animals possess this knowledge through a higher understanding of the nature of the universe, an instinctive understanding that transcends the intellectual gropings of the word–bound homo sapiens. Sapient my sphincter! A greater misnomer it would not be possible to find were one to traverse the lengths and breadths of every known and unknown galaxy and discover each to be overflowing with life and words. Words as concepts, words as precepts, words as patterns, words as possibilities, words as names.

On the subject of names, the one that stands out like a flower among turds is that of Doctor Prashad.

Doctor Prashad's face was like an earthquake in progress. But once you got over the shock of it, beneath was a personality solid as a rock that no earthquake could shake and gentle as the waters that lie beyond the reach of disasters which afflict the cruder landscapes of our planet. He had fought long and hard against the disadvantages of his Harijan origins to educate himself and become a fully qualified doctor in India, and then travelled to England to become a Fellow of the Royal College of Surgeons. Then he had to go through another and greater struggle, this time with himself. He had to decide whether to stay on in the relative affluence and comfort of the United Kingdom, or pursue the much greater monetary recompense available to doctors in the USA, or return to the hardships of his village back home in Rajasthan near the glorious pink city of Jaipur and try to help others like himself, fighting a losing battle against social injustice and disease. The traces of those fights and struggles were etched in his features, as were the signs of the angry spirit which ultimately persuaded him to return.

Back home his ideals took an expected knock in their stride, but could not cope with an unexpected one. His practice was shunned by the better folk – he was praying it wouldn't happen, but was prepared for it; but it was also avoided, guiltily and with much embarrassment, by his own people, lest they be accused of grouping together to form political pressure groups, like some Marxist menials. This he had not provided for in his scheme of things. Black depression set in, which, coupled with financial bankruptcy – he was not hoping to make money, but was expecting to eat and not parade around in the nude, can't see why, personally, he had a beautiful body – made him end up as a patient in an ill-stocked, ill-run state hospital for the nouveau poor (the pedigreed poor could rarely afford to get there). Here he met Sister Erin. She was on a mercy mission, visiting various hospitals and clinics for the poor across northern India.

From then on it was a happy story. Doctor Prashad made a remarkable recovery, and accompanied Sister Erin to assist her with her latest long-term project, the one in our little town of Chandan. The umbrella of the white woman helped to provide him with the respectability and acceptance he had longed for, and the plight of the poor gave him the opportunity to help ease the suffering of their bodies and so to soothe the anguish of their souls, first cousin and loyal friend to physical anguish, as any Christ will tell you.

Doctor Prashad took to me from day one and, after spitting on each other's palms and rubbing them together, we became true spit-brothers. I was quite willing to cut across my wrist and become a true blood-brother, but Doctor Prashad was scared of the sight of blood. I believed him for a while, but later realised that that was his way of dissuading me from taking the knife to my wrist. Now I know that he was telling the truth. He *was* afraid of the sight of blood, but in a more significant sense than being squeamish about wrist-slicing.

It is strange how little truth has to do with facts. When people insist they are telling the truth, or exposing the truth, or wanting the truth, what they mean, at best, is that they are giving the facts, revealing the facts, or wanting facts. Truth is something else again. Not just different from facts, but often at variance with them.

In fact, facts are frequently the greatest obstacle not only to the truth, but also to truth, or even Truth. This last is absolute anathema to facts. Or, to put it another way, facts are a by-product of its violation. When Adam violated Truth (sinned against God, as most say), the world of Fact was born, and with it, bad (to be preferred to badness, though only as a word; as a concept bad is worse, with apologies to M. Jackson and other neo-American linguists). For bad belongs to the world of Fact, good to the world of Truth. Naturally there are problem areas. There always are. Life has a habit of developing percepts which defy or negate concepts though sometimes the two link up. The perceptual conception of beauty, for example. An *object* (as opposed to a *thought*) of perceived beauty, such as a lightning-stricken tree, even though it belongs to the world of Fact, transcends its factual origins and becomes one with truth in a conceptual sense, as John would have us believe. But I would never go so far as to say that truth is just beauty, nor that this is all we know or need to know. That honour belongs only to Love, the only of life's percept/concept links to override all bad and elevate it to para-good, para-spiritual status, at the nerve-centre of the being of the supreme being itself. But that is because life did not create this link in the first place, but was created by it.

Our clinic was dead centre of the town, surrounded by narrow lanes of chipping red brick with open drains running down both sides, dirty, smelly and slimy; foul enough to make a genteel visitor throw up her, or his, entrails in one elegant retch. Several residents too poor to employ the services of Choodahs like us simply washed their waste down these drains, thus adding solid colour to their liquid drabness. The whole atmosphere was disease-ridden, just what Doctor Prashad wanted. After all, what would doctors do without diseases to cure, their business being to ensure the health of the continuum of birth, life and death. The whole area was infested with exploiters exploiting those weaker than themselves in the service of the Self, just what Sister Erin wanted. After all, what would do-gooders do without having do-badders to undo their good so that they, in turn, can undo their bad, thus keeping the wheels of morality going round in static motion.

Whatever spare time I had left after my long secret sessions of private study I spent trying to help Doctor Prashad, or Pasha as he wanted me to call him. Mostly I was just in his way, but he was too fond of me to say so. Besides, *in truth* I really was helping him by appreciating him, more, by loving him, even if *in fact* I was just being a nuisance and getting under his feet.

Aunt Verna hated the man, for no reason that I know of except that he once gave me a great big kiss in her presence. And any friend of mine is no friend of hers.

And as you will have guessed by now, she did not exactly specialise in the art of camouflaging her feelings. The only way she could shut her mouth was by putting her foot in it. She had been heard, and overheard, several times voicing her opinions of the doctor in yes certain terms. And one day, when he found a dead rat beneath his chair after she had cleaned out his surgery and he complained, in I must confess a somewhat ungentlemanly manner – a noteworthy contrast to his usual courteous style – she went outside and expressed an urgent desire to put a cushion on his face and sit on it until spring. It was summer then.

This reminds me of only yesterday. George and Barry covered my nude self with cushions and walked all over me, lingering upon the crotch – they had taken to my crotch and butt ever since I came under their custodial supervision – to light a cigarette. Since neither of them smokes, it took a while to manage. At one point Barry dropped a lighted match, accidentally, setting the cushion on fire, the cushion resting on my you-know-whatnots. They were careful to see that I got no more than singed pubes and heat, real heat, before putting out the fire by stamping upon the cushion upon my crotch. They were quite gentle, relative to some of their other innovatory approaches to my person; and after their promenade, followed by close examination of my body, a little rudely at times, to see that there weren't any tell-tale stress marks – they never used to bother, but since repeated complaints by Father O'Neil and Adam Z they have become a little cautious – they led me back to my solitary cell. Although by now they have got used to the complete absence of physical resistance or verbal responses on my part, they still feel cheated on that account, and rightly so, for that does reduce the quantum of their pleasure. But I do hope that one day they will find it in their hearts to forgive me.

Back to Aunt Verna and her expressed desire to sit on Pasha's face, fully dressed, I am sure, and upon a cushion, as you know – I say this lest you form some funny ideas about the sexual inclinations of Aunt Verna. Mother laughed. Dad looked under his right armpit. And Mohan, the boy Aunt Neelum loved and who loved her back, recoiled in disgust. He had not yet recovered his sense of humour since Aunt Neelum's death; nor had he forgotten the desperate efforts made by Doctor Prashad to save her life, even though it was well past midnight and he had just gone to bed after a hard day's work, was practically naked, and had to run through high winds and a monsoon downpour to get to the surgery where the half-crazed Mohan had brought her after discovering her, naked, writhing, contorting and foaming, by the banks of the big canal, the perennial one across the railway tracks where they normally met at midnight.

Hers was a strong and vigorous death. She had taken a tumblerful of dhatura, one-time popular ingredient of dishes set before Indian husbands unpopular with their wives. Modern society, with its greater investigative curiosity, had rendered the making of such culinary delights more difficult for the average housewife. And it was supposed to make life easier for women! Proof, if any were needed, of the inherent sexism of progress. Aunt Neelum's body convulsed in prolonged agony, went into electric spasms, arced like a taut bow, and shook and vibrated as if plugged into a battery charger.

That night cut its way through my cerebral cortex to imprint itself indelibly upon the innermost core of my brain.

That night I discovered how delightful the naked human body, both male and female, can be. The naked Dr Prashad – he did wrap a cloth round his waist, but it kept coming off so he gave up trying to put it back and concentrated entirely on the job in hand – forced emetics down the throat of the naked Aunt Neelum. Mother, eyes covered with her left hand, pulled a safety pin off her bra and pinned the cloth above Pasha's hips with her right, but not before I had enjoyed the full-frontal beauty of his nakedness, rivalled only by the delicately chiselled nubile loveliness, even in the throes of death, of Aunt Neelum. As her naked body raised itself off the ground, her feet and head digging themselves into the floor, her pelvis arched, her knees apart, she seemed to be making the ultimate offer to her impotent saviour, who, though equally naked, was unable to accept the offer of death or return it with an offer of life. Their pudenda faced each other: hers torn and clotted with blood and semen. His firm and coated with a soft and gentle shyness.

I had woken up and run after Mother as she ran after Mohan as he hollered past our temporary shelter on his way from the canal to the surgery.

The whole scene, from this distance, seems as hilariously tragic, as sexually charged with death and as fiercely full of life, as it did that night of power and madness. I can clearly see the geckos gathered up on the ceiling, above the naked 60-watt bulb, sticking out their tongues with as electric a rapidity as the convulsions of Aunt Neelum, orgiastically feasting upon the hundreds of gnats and mosquitoes which had come to dance their dance of death round the light, itself wildly dancing to the whiplashing of the wind and in step with its howling notes.

† † †

It is said that true love never dies. Pity the same is not true of true lovers. Mohan died about seven months after we moved into the servant quarters of Sister Erin. Said he could not bear to see Doctor Prashad every day; each time he looked at him, it brought back Aunt Neelum's death with startling vividness. He took a large handful of dhatura for a nightcap one night. There was no one to admire the vigour of his death. He was not even discovered till he was half devoured by wild dogs, by the banks of the perennial canal where he and Aunt Neelum used to meet at midnight. Who knows, they might still be meeting there. I often saw them. Still do – same time, same place. Whenever I get the chance to get out there. Does you good, in solitary, to get out and about a bit.

Visions and Manifestations II

As any child who has skimmed through the pages of *Tractatus Logico-Philosophicus* and grasped but the barest bones of Ludwig's picture-theory and its exploration by exceptions and negations will tell you, in the face of the inexpressible it is best to remain silent, and serious problems, not only of logic and language but also of perception and meaning, occur when we try to utter the unutterable. But moving away from philosophical certainties, however uncertain, to the vagaries of life as she is lived, it is the expression of the inexpressible and the uttering of the unutterable that make the mysterious apparent and the unreal real. And the reality of the unreal is a far more fascinating reality than that which can be discovered, uncovered, or recovered with the help of a carpenter's bag. Even the carpenter's son had to chuck away his tools to construct the scaffolding needed to build the kingdom of heaven on earth.

Ludwig may have brought in Art and Functionality at this point, but my understanding at age seven was not advanced enough for all that. I was content with visions and manifestations, however inexpressible or unutterable. Not only that, I shall now commit the ultimate philosophical heresy by trying to express and utter these in the simplest possible terms. I will let my language take a holiday, and welcome ye brickbats from intellectuals and purists.

My visions were clearly symptomatic of God reaching out to me, trying to break through the barrier of my seven years of silence – remember that I had not spoken to Him since the barbarism of my birth – via terms of reference within my experience, namely the Holy Trinity of Broom the Spiky, Broom the Fluffy, and the It Bucket (the last being the comforter and the main source of passing on the message and keeping the circuit open). As such it was only natural that it was It that first appeared to me. That was under the table in the library of Sister Erin. At the time I almost did not recognise it as a vision.

But when, after about three months, Broom the Spiky and Broom the Fluffy made their appearance, one after the other, there was no doubt left in my mind. I was being approached from the Higher World.

Actual materialisations soon followed. I would wake up and find myself with my arms around either Spiky or Fluffy, and I would talk to them, and they would talk to me, revealing secrets to which only angels are privy.

It was about that time that Aunt Verna's brooms started going missing, and her suspicions and accusations took an ugly turn. The woman never did love me.

Illusions and Hallucinations

It was one of those days. We all have them, some of us more than others, some of them worse than others. I have more than some, and this one was worse than most.

Aunt Verna's brooms had gone missing again. And you know what *she* thinks! And not just because she heard me talking to Pasha about 'my Brooms' one day. She would hold me responsible for her amoebic dysentery if she hadn't had it since she was only old at heart and not old all over. Well, she's not exactly pre-Flood, but you know what I mean.

She refused point-blank to believe that mine were made of the heavenly equivalent of coppery gold (Spiky) and mercurial silver (Fluffy), and were part of the Divine Trinity, the diamond-studded (heavenly equivalent) It Bucket being the fulfilling third. She manufactured a necklace of rude words when I tried to explain all that.

The Aristotelian irony of the situation lay in the fact that she had always been quite willing to accept, indeed offer and accord with, all sorts of the absurdest supernatural explanations and expatiations re my person and activities when it suited her, and when the said explanations and expatiations were designed to malign and undermine me and to bring me into familial and social disrepute. But when the paranormal was presented in my defence, she says: What do you take me for? A kettle-head! This is the politest she says. Take my word for it. I dismissed the idea of trying to point out the inherently fallacious logic of her stance. You may think it ungenerous of me to prejudge Aunt Verna's judgement, but if you had known her for as long as I had (my entire life) you may well have felt the same, unless your faith in human nature, somewhat like Adam Z's, outstripped your wits by a mile and a yard.

There I was, accused of purloining Aunt Verna's brooms, yet again; in disgrace, yet again; and drenched in guilt, yet again. Why was I so guilt-wet, if innocent? The answer is quite simple. I may have been lily-white in my innocence of any misdeed concerning the allegedly missing brooms of Aunt Verna – I say allegedly, because . . . but I am sure you know why I say allegedly – but I am pot-black (pre-electric) in my skin; have a hairy wart on my left buttock; the mark of the devil on my shoulder; nostrils like the caves of Ajanta; eyes you need extra eyes to see; a chin like the second highest mountain in the world turned upside down; eyebrows that meet in the middle, go back to their starting positions and then come back and meet up again; a willie like . . . not a pretty sight. And I was *manhoos*. My poor family! Forgive me, I told you it was one of those days. Wallowing in self-pity was not my usual.

Mother was out making professional calls; Aunt Verna had gone to buy new brooms (more guilt: the poor woman is poor, I mean poor); Pasha was busy with his patients; Sister Erin was in the library, so no go there. I decided to get out of the house simply to get out of the house, not in the least aware that it would turn out to be one of the most remarkable and portentous days of my life.

Our little rooms, brick-built and concrete-roofed, were at the far end of the large enclosure within which sat Sister Erin's temporary temporal abode. I say temporary, for she was reputed to be always rushing about from continent to continent, and who could say when and where she would find a place worse off than our Chandan to do good at. Also, the future of missionaries was a precarious one in post-independence India.

Ludwig would have disapproved of the structure, perhaps even screamed at the sight of it. No higher mathematical harmonies there, or none that my untrained eye could detect. No symphonic compositions of architectural music, or none that my coarse ear could discern. No symmetry of line and form to elevate the consciousness above the mundane into the realm of true Art, or none that my primitive sensibilities could relish. But even he, Ludwig, would not have quarrelled with its functional efficacy. Or maybe he would have. I really cannot say: the workings of the superior intellect have always eluded my simple mechanical responses to the variations on the enigma of existence. Of course I do lubricate the mechanism with Elysian oils, occasionally, to keep it going, and to enable me to play the fool to the Lords of Wisdom, to survive without bursting a brain vessel.

The external wall prevented unwelcome visitors from suddenly descending upon the incumbents, while providing a barrier of sorts against wafting odours of an odious character that abounded outside its perimeter. The compound itself contained a circular garden – complete with grasses, flowers, and trees – surrounded by a brick-laid patio – complete with two sets of garden tables and chairs – and a hammock, given gratis by a local dignitary, despite protests from Sister Erin who took care never to go anywhere near it. I loved it, and in the middle of the night when no one could be looking I would climb in, curl up, and daydream. It is always nicer to daydream at night than during the day. More than once I fell asleep, but when found in the morning denied all knowledge of how I happened to be there. Nothing anyone could say or do would budge me from my stance of injured innocence and total surprise at my hammocky awakening. A garden, and a hammock, in the middle of our Chandan. What next? you might ask.

I will tell you what next. Our own toilet, *that actually flushed!* Can you imagine that? A family which kept lungs heaving by clearing out other people's droppings had its own aristocratically gurgling down to Stygian oblivion, or even to the paradisiacal Ganges and eternal turdiality. A great comfort to our Aunt Verna, that, our very own flushing toilet, with her amoebic dysentery requiring frequent defecatory trips. I was not allowed to use it, just because once, only once . . . But it is a messy story and I'd rather not discuss it now. I, would you believe it, had to go right down the street, behind the houses at the near end of the town, against the wall of the local granary.

I crawled up the outside wall and then jumped down on to the street. I could have opened the door and walked out, but it wasn't half as much fun as crawling up the wall and then jumping off. Also, it helped to take my mind away from things.

I jumped straight into a puddle of cow piss. *Splash*. All over my nearly-new khaki shorts, worn for only three years by Junior before me and patched up in the very latest style, and all over my not-so-new shirt, mostly in tatters of various geometrically unrelated shapes and sizes. My feet slipped out of my shoes, too big even for my big feet, and I was well and truly baptised by the sacred bovine's body fluid. At least it wasn't human, a not inconsiderable consolation.

I successfully resisted the temptation to go back inside and wash up. Not because I had anything against washing myself. Contrary to popular belief, I hadn't. I enjoyed water and its tactile effect upon the human body. But that day I was just keen to get away from it all.

Without any conscious decision, my squelchy feet directed themselves towards the railway station. Might catch up with Father there, and even though we didn't often hold conversations of great international import, it was good to have his presence close to me, especially when I was feeling down and out. He knew what it meant to feel down and out, and I knew that he knew, and it helped. There were many routes to the station, and I often spent a large part of the day going back and forth through different narrow lanes and taking different turns and corners, but that day I just walked there without at all bothering which way I took.

Along the way I did not even count, as I sometimes did, the number of people who put handkerchiefs to their noses and moved aside as I walked past, squashing themselves against squalid house walls and risking filth-jammed gutters that ran along either side of the narrow lanes in order to avoid social and spiritual contamination through physical contact with a Choodah boy.

Even while I was still some distance away from the

station I could tell that something unusual was going on. There seemed to be much more activity than normal at that time of mid-morning, when everything is winding down for the mid-afternoon lull. July can be a very hot, very humid and very debilitating month, except, of course, when the wind freshens up, the clouds start to gather, and the moist smell of summer rain assails your nostrils with the promise of regeneration and revival and rebirth. Yes, in spite of all the devastation that they can bring, rains are always welcome, and the most looked-forward-to season of the year: the season of young love and old romances; of singing and dancing and merriment; of simple folk songs and sophisticated film music. The paeanised months of Sawan and Bhadon, roughly coinciding with July and August, carry their gifts of joy and happiness and laughter to vast sections of this sub-continent. To the West they are known as the dreaded monsoons. The wealth of the harvest they create outbalances the misery they may cause.

And the treasures of the rains are not just for the well-off landowners with thousands of acres of fields teeming with raw banknotes. The poor farmer with a tiny holding, the landless tenant slaving away to fill the already overflowing coffers of a zameendar – both would starve without the rains. Even the survival of the town poor, who do not farm themselves, depends on a relatively low price of grain; costly flour, and they might as well be on death row. But more than even that, the sheer magic of the rains, the strong heady breeze, the madly swaying fields, the black thundery skies, the cool needles of water: all are the stuff of Art and Music as expressed in universal terms. One of the most difficult and painful things I had to learn after coming to England was to hate the rain.

But, back to that day when the skies were clear, the air was hot, the sun in full strength, my shoes heavy with cow piss, my mind squelchy with thoughts, and my heart pumping away unclean Choodah blood at a slower pace than usual.

I was now out on the wide metalled road that led straight to the station, and on which travelled heavy lorries carrying grain, broken-down buses carrying passengers, and cars belonging to the few big houses on the outskirts of the town, or to the zameendar families in the interior; not to mention the horse-driven tongas for the not so poor, bullock carts, cycles, pedestrians (human and cattle), and of course stray cats and wild dogs, jackals and foxes, the occasional wolf, and various varieties of rodent and reptile, whenever they could venture out safely into the hostile and overcrowded world which had overtaken their simpler more open-spaced one. There was something strange about the traffic. It seemed both more and less. I didn't have to be Albert to understand that it could either be relatively more or relatively less, but not both at the same time. It took me a while to understand what was going on. Not much. That was it. So there must be something going on. The traffic was hardly moving in places on the side of the road leading to the station, while there was little on the other. The temporary illusion of there being both more and less was easily explained.

† † †

The second and more significant illusion of the day I could not explain till years later, after coming to England and seeing Jason for the first time. For it was him that I saw that day, both as a god-child – or perhaps I should say god as child, for god-child has a different connotation in the West – and as my own child; and also as my own true self. The trinity of my own life. One of a set of three trinities of my life.

† † †

As to the third illusion of that day, the illusion of my father, it was the most difficult to understand at the time, and in many ways still is. I dealt with it for a long time by dismissing it as an hallucination, a false perception with no basis in reality at all, as opposed to a false perception of some present reality, like an illusion. Rather absurd, that, now I come to think of it.

For what my father was doing is an established fact, witnessed by many others present. Yet it remains one of the most unreal episodes of my life. And the happiest. Perhaps that's it.

In fact, I am sure that is it.

Zeus! Sometimes you spend aeons trying to explain something to yourself and nothing happens; then you try explaining to someone else and it clicks. Just like that.

Now I understand. It was the *happiness* of seeing my father behave like that which I could not cope with nor accept, not his behaviour per se. *That* was simple, clear-cut, witnessed and authenticated. Some people talk about it to this day. But the fact that he was happy and laughing and making other people laugh and be happy and making me laugh and be happy was a fact so removed from the truth of his life that I just could not reconcile one with the other.

I have just had another flash. The most vital one. What I experienced was not only not an hallucination or illusion, it was no fact either. It was the truth. The rest of my father's life was fact. I had been looking at it all from the wrong perspective. Suddenly it all hangs together, makes complete sense. That laughing, joking, happy man, alive, aglow, and pulsating with life and the joy of living – he was the true man, my true father; not the half-dead carcass, barely self-propelled, that I daily saw carrying the burden of existence with awkwardness and in darkness.

I'll tell you what happened. Now that it is all clear in my mind I can talk freely about it, without feeling all choked up. It was very simple. You will wonder what all the fuss was about when you hear it.

But first to explain the traffic and the rest of it. I am not being perverse, it is just that it is essential to know the basic facts without which what happened would not have happened – up to a point. Beyond that, what happened would not have happened if I had stayed at home and not brought my *manhoos* presence to bear upon an already tragic situation.

There had been a multiple accident on the railway track some twenty miles east of Chandan. A goods train had been unable to stop in time when a herd of cows started running across it apparently for no reason, probably panicked by the very train they hit. The train overturned on its side, on to the other track, and hit a passenger train coming from behind. Limbs and blood of cows and humans lay inextricably intertwined with broken twisted steel and overflowing diesel. As a result, all trains leaving Chandan from two of its four platforms were stopped indefinitely, or until the wreckage of lives and machines could be cleared from the scene of the accident.

No one in Chandan was as yet aware of the details of the tragedy. It was only known that there had been an accident involving a goods train and some cattle.

Platforms 2 and 4 were unusually quiet, except for a few hopeful travellers. No trains were expected there 'until further notice' – which in India could be anything from a minute to a lifetime. Platforms 1 and 3 were more crowded than a dozen wedding processions put together. Two trains, overloaded beyond credibility, were stranded there awaiting clearance signals. Passengers had overflowed out of the doors, climbed down from the roofs, and given up hard–fought–for seats in compartments packed as tightly full of human cargo as cart-loads of hay, in order to stretch their legs, get some fresh air, cool down and, if possible, obtain some information as to what was going on. Perhaps have a drink, or something to eat.

A host of vendors of various varieties of the same fish, pakoras, chappatis and bhujya, cigarettes, lukewarm hot tea and lukewarm cold drinks, rattles for little babies and cloth and wooden dolls for older ones, were shouting out their wares, calling out for customers, forcing their way through the crowds of people, parading their goods, hoping to make some good hard cash out of the unexpected rush of prospective consumers which had come their way.

The middle section of Platform 1 was cleared out and guarded by four policemen. Some very important passengers were resting in the Ladies Waiting Room. They were said to be the wife and three children of some ambassadorial personage, white, along with two guards, Indian, going to Lucknow on some very important business. All white people travelled for very important reasons, or for no reason at all.

It was there, close to the middle of the platform, where there were enough people to constitute a sizeable audience yet the police barrier prevented a mad rush of trampling feet as along the rest of the platform length, that Father was doing his act.

Like a piece of Panopean clay become Man beneath the fingers and through the fire of Prometheus, and brought to radiant life with Athena's breath; like the essence of the benighted Rartri infused with the flamboyant spirit of Agni; like the cognisable cognate of *ignis* as deified Vedic; like a clod of black rock, a lump of dull, dead coal inflamed into a red glow of passionate heat, or a half-baked diamond traumatised in a full-blown furnace – my simple father stood metamorphosed, every limb of his body vehemently eloquent, his flesh exuding vaporous energy, his eyes burning with an intensity that would have put Charon's dogs to flight in frenzied fear, words pouring out of his mouth with expressive abundance and in a voice that was not just a musical instrument but an entire orchestra in the way its pitch, its tonal variation, indeed its entire character altered with every hint of a change in syllable or content.

He was only telling jokes.

The difference between the approach, the appeal, the syntax and the complexity of the above two sentences stating essentially the same basic fact is the linguistic equivalent of the perceptual gap between the observed event seen as a fact by a stranger, and as seen by me: an illusion or an hallucination as I then believed, a revelation and a truth as I now know it. The analogy is, of course, unavoidably inadequate and imperfect, keeping in view the limits (numerical) and limitations (etymological) of words as opposed to the limitlessness of thought and experience – not just mystical and occult, or merely analytical and deductive, but even cognitive and empirical. None the less, it can further be extended to the difference between Father's existential demeanour within the context of his household, and his enhanced performance at Platform 1; or, yet again, to the difference between the reaction of his family to his daily activities and pronouncements, and the reaction of his fascinated audience beside the stranded train to his stand-up comic routine.

It was then that I saw the child. And the fact that I saw him at all – entranced as I was with Father's comedic talents, more unexpected than a snowstorm in the Sahara, more enchanting than a snowstorm in the Sahara, more life-instigating than a snowstorm in the Sahara – was a witness to his uniqueness which, at least at that point in space, overrode the uniqueness of my father's quintessential transformation.

About three years old, with eyes as pale blue as the pale blue of a very hot summer day, yet much sharper, with a deeply penetrating look which seemed to give them a diamond-edged hardness in sharp contrast to the mobile liquidity that floated within the pupils; hair as golden and soft as to rival my heavenly broom, the fluffy one; skin as white as the milk of Umrao; and mouth as soft and full and red as Aunt Neelum's bloodstained labia majora.

What happened afterwards would have been the stuff of Greek tragedy, jointly lamented by the holy Grecian trinity of Sophocles, Euripedes and Aeschylus, perhaps even later re-lamented by our own (I speak as quasi-British) William, had I been a king's son, and therefore worthy of having my sufferings and experiences recorded, rather than my father's child, the type, both genitor and boy, for whom suffering is well-deserved and well-earned at best and at worst is not suffering at all, for they have not the sensibility or the ability to suffer – the argument more openly and less bashfully used for the 'lesser animals' – being created from dross and hence irrelevant to the edifices, literary or otherwise, that proclaim the greatness of the truly human empire. The likes of us are excluded even from those monuments built round the scaffolding of their bones, fleshed out with their tendons and muscles, kept whole with the damp of their blood, pointed with the marrow of their bones – for the very plausible reason that we did not belong there in the first place. It may have been our dead bodies that hewed the rocks and carried the stones, but the dead bodies that lay within such monuments of human endeavour were of the Pharoahs and Moguls.

He looked at me, and I at him. We both instantly recognised

each other, as father and son – though which one was which I am not to this day sure – and as one and the same. I advanced towards him, he towards me. I lifted him up, he elevated me.

Shouts and screams. *Haramzada behnchode maa ka lauda. Gora butcha uthanay chala*, all in one breath: bastard, sister-fucker, mother's cock, he's going to abduct the white child . . . A lathi caught me on the left side of the head and I fell on top of the screaming boy even as Father rushed to help me and fell on top of me with the force of the blows rained upon him. Father upon child upon father, or child upon father upon child, or any of the permutations you might like to play with. From then on it was blood and kicks and sticks and abuse. The illusion had vanished, the boy was gone, reality was back in full sail and high wind.

When I regained consciousness I found myself in the police station charged, along with Father, with the kidnapping of the white boy and his mother. Note: *kidnapping*, not attempted. It took me a while before I caught on. It transpired that in the mêlée that followed the orgy of violence on our bodies, the child, his mother, and his two sisters *were* actually abducted. It was believed that we had deliberately created the diversion while our accomplices got away with the memsahib and her children.

We were kept there for weeks, regularly beaten, with the best possible intentions, of course, i.e. to recover the poor memsahib and her family. The furore in diplomatic circles soon reached a crescendo of anger and despair. I also had my first sexual experiences in those days of custody. Can't say I found them half as exciting as some of the books I had read had led me to believe.

Sister Erin's intervention – she had a lot more influence than at first thought – and the apprehension of the actual culprits, all of whom happened to be out-of-towners, off the train, and with whom we could have had no possible connection, notwithstanding the best efforts of the police to prove otherwise, eventually gained our release. But Father's job was gone forever, and his health sank to its lowest ebb.

The memsahib and her two daughters were recovered,

unharmed. Or if they were harmed, the fact was not made public.

He was not found. The kidnappers said that he managed to run out of their grasp at the station and got lost in the crowd. The memsahib could neither confirm nor deny the story as she was blindfolded at the time. She did say that she never saw the boy again, though that proved nothing, for she was kept apart and did not see the girls either until the day of her release. No one ever found out what happened to him. I think I know. In truth, I am sure I know. But no one would ever believe me.

Secrets

Adam comes to see me today, face like an out-of-focus picture of a deceased platypus, duck-billed. Not that I have anything against platypuses, deceased or boisterously alive, duck-billed or not. (Are there any who are not? I am not sure I know.) I don't want to be accused of racism, the ultimate, and the worst, of which we are all guilty, namely, the unqualified assumption re the superiority of the human race over other animal forms. It is just that the face of a platypus suits a platypus fine, but does not go too well with our Adam, despite the sore temptation to say that anything would be an improvement upon the original, and notwithstanding some suspiciously monotrematous peculiarities of his person.

Anyway, in comes Adam. By now he has access to me at twenty-four hours' notice, on the pretext of helping me with 'the book'. In the beginning my request to write was met with derision, insults, and an outright refusal by the authorities. *If you think we are going to let you make filthy lucre by selling filthy porno fucking shit* . . . However Father O'Neil, with a cunning of which I had not thought him capable, dropped a hint or two that my outpourings might contain important and vital information regarding this and that. And you know how important this and that can be. That, and the assurance that any and all monies made from the author's royalties would go to a children's charity, eventually managed to lubricate the rectal passages of the admin deputies. Permission was granted, and so was a cartload of stationery. Also granted were much freer visiting rights to Father O'Neil, over and above his pastoral role, and to Adam. All in the hope that I would eventually reveal a network of devilry and drug racketeering and the workings and locations of multitudinous centres of sexual perversion, enabling the salvation of hundreds and thousands of innocent people from all of the evils to which flesh is heir apparent. And who was I to disappoint them?

They even promised not to 'vet' the book as it went along, so as not to hamper my style or curb 'the exhibitionistic tendencies common to all common criminals'. I made no comment on the voyeuristic and vicarious urges of the law-enforcing fraternity. However, I am still careful to make any derogatory references to the prison and its staff in simple but effective code words which make perfect sense on their own but have signals written into them, which either Adam or Father O'Neil can decipher later, upon verbal instructions, as they are probably doing now with some sections of this chapter. The rest I write as I damn well please, and the screws and punters can make of it what they will and what they can.

I still haven't told you the reason why Adam comes to me today looking like life is sitting on his face, giving it the appearance of a platypus, deceased, duck-billed – or an out-of-focus photograph thereof. He is suffering from grief. Had I known earlier I wouldn't have mocked him, nor compared him to a resting-in-peace Antipodean egg-laying mammal, duck-billed. One of his new crop of baby cats, a tabby girl called Nino, went missing yesterday evening. He spent most of the night searching the roads and the fields, and found her dead on the grass verge at dawn when it was light enough to see. Another unrecorded road accident statistic. His torch had not been able to locate her body in the darkness.

'If only I had found her earlier . . . I should have let her stay in my bed in the evening. She *had* come up, and I . . .' Adam continues and I stop listening. It is all too painful, and for once I can feel what he is feeling. That is why he has come to me. To most people a kitten is just an animal; to him, and to me, just an animal is another life, no less precious than any other life. My mind went back to Umrao. And to Father. Adam often puts me in mind of my father, all those years ago when I was a little child, with his frequent *I should haves* and *if onlys*. Except that Adam's ambitions run higher than my father's. If things had gone better, my father would have been a better father and been able to provide his family with a better life, and so forth. If things went according to plan, Adam would change the world: the kingdom of his choice would be upon us forthwith. I dread to think of the day that happens – not that I need worry much on that score – I mean what would the likes of me do in this kingdom? Be bored to death, I suppose. But Father would have liked that. He too was a hankerer after Peace. Even peace. I sometimes wish I could have shaken him and shaken him until all his regrets fell out of him and left him with some of the peace he so longed for.

One of his greatest regrets, and one that virtually destroyed him was his sexual encounter with me.

It happened while we were being held in custody for our 'involvement' in the conspiracy to abduct the white personage's white wife and his white children. I told you that the police kindly arranged to provide me with my first sexual experiences during that period. One of their most ambitious plans in that direction was to organise my initiation by Father. They thought it would be a splendid idea and would work on many levels. Their only fear was that Father might not be able to rise to the occasion. However, to ensure his erection they brought some woefully second-rate 8mm sex films and a projector, and showed them to Father. No problem with erection at all. The problem arose after I was impaled on Father's limb, and held down on him while he was held down on the floor. As the films played on and drinks were passed round and giddy laughter circulated through the smelly little room, Father could not get off! The more he screamed and shouted and begged for me to be released off him, the thicker and stronger grew his erection, with no release of pent-up semen. It just would not shoot. It came to a point we were stuck like dogs, and even if the officers had let us go, we would not have been able to come apart so tightly was I screwed upon him. It was long after Father fainted and everyone else around me dropped senseless with drink and merriment before I could ease myself off him. I was horrified to see his penis covered in blood, but there was nothing I could do to ease his pain and distress.

Father swore me to secrecy about the incident, and this is the first time I have talked about it in twenty-seven years. I still do not feel like talking about the sexual adventures that followed, until the police had to set us free, unconditionally. They did so because they were left with no option. The case had gained so much notoriety by then that we could no longer have been put away in a cell and forgotten. Too many people had come to know about it, and us. However, they were not happy about it and vowed vengeance. *If you think shit bloody eaters fucking Choodahs can get away and leave us looking like mother-fucking idiots . . .*

Another Death, Another Life

They waited for a whole year. They were not so stupid as to show their stupidity by acting any earlier. But in getting at us Choodahs, they got the Harijan first.

One cold winter's night Pasha was found savagely knifed to death. The bloodied knife lay in the unconscious hands of Father, who had apparently knocked himself cold against the sharp upper edge of the medicine cupboard while attempting to make a quick getaway. Pasha's wallet was in Father's pocket.

But the best laid plans . . . Sister Erin found them both, as must have been anticipated, one dead, one half dead. Strange how Father was almost perpetually half dead, yet managed to survive; it must have been that hidden comic talent of his, and the fire that came into his eyes when displaying it, which kept him going. However, instead of calling the police, as she should have, she rang – yes, she had a telephone – for Mirza Nazim, the kind zameendar of the goat.

Although she was so badly shaken that she was having difficulty in forming words (the whole future of her clinic was now in doubt without Pasha, not to speak of her sense of personal loss) such was her resourcefulness and faith, in us as much as in the Lord, that she managed to formulate a plot worthy of a cheap Bombay movie – and equally successful. She realised that the police wouldn't hang about too long waiting. If they did not hear from her within the hour, they would drop by on the pretext of patrolling the area, and then 'sense' something was

73

amiss, or claim a passer-by had heard screams, or something.

Time was short. Her strategy was simple. Mirza Nazim was to send a few peasant farmers with half-filled jute-sacks of grain to the back of the house. Father, after quick first-aid measures, and all the rest of us were to be hidden in a sack of grain each, carried to the granary, and from there loaded on to the first cattle truck of the day, driven to Patna, and then put on a train to the border town of Dhulian where the sacred Ganges entered the unhallowed land of Pakistan. From there on we would be on our own and could make our own choices. Mirza Nazim thrust a wad of banknotes into Mother's clenched hands and squeezed them gently, but there was no time for anything else. We had barely fitted into the sacks before the lads on the beat arrived.

Our flight 'proved' our guilt but saved our lives – all our lives, not just Father's, for the rest of us were bound to be implicated in some way or other. Also, it spared some other poor innocents from being made scapegoats, which would have been necessary were we to have remained there and then somehow been proven not guilty.

One phase of my life, in many ways the most important, was over; the next was on its way.

Part II
ALONG THE RADIUS AND OVER THE SPOKES

Vade Mecum Vade in Pace

I begged him to go with me. But he wouldn't. I prayed that he go in peace. But he didn't.

Father disappeared one day.

It was the 9th of June, Father's thirty-ninth birthday. We had prepared a special supper for him of onion bhaji with potatoes and brinjals, mustard leaves, ground maize chappatis, ground rice feernie with pistachio and almond topping – all his favourites. He was not expected to live to his next birthday (but then he hadn't been expected to live to this one, either, or to the one ten years previously) and Mother, Aunt Verna, Father's cousin (under the supervision of Grandmother, Mother's mother) and Great Grandmother (Father's grandmother) had really laid it out for him. Especially as, for the first time in our lives, we could afford to splash out like that.

Father had not adjusted well to our new-found prosperity. Various reasons. I couldn't tell you exactly which one worried him most, and which the next most, and so on down to the last most; but I can tell you they all worried him a great deal. At a guess I would say that the fact that it was zameendar Mirza's money which had helped to set us up in Joshanabad, and the hard labour of everybody else in the family which had made it a success, was the source of his greatest shame. Father had not only not been any help, but a 'heavy burden' for the rest to bear. Even had the family tried to dissuade him from that belief they would probably not have succeeded. That Aunt Verna and, I must confess, Mother made a point of pointing out his inadequacies to him once in a not so infrequent while did not help.

I tried to tell him that if he had not been found with the knife in his hand beside Pasha's body – and believe me, it is not easy for me to talk about Pasha's body as a dead body; it was a beautiful body, with a beautiful heart and topped with a beautiful mind; all three beautifully alive, and which for me always will be alive – all of this would never have happened, and therefore all we had then was due, in truth, to him. But he wouldn't have it. Also, he missed Chandan, and his 'secret' friends, secret in that even I – and I am an inquisitive piece of junk – knew nothing about them until I saw Father in action among them on that day full of illusions, hallucinations and truths. These friends listened with rampant enthusiasm to his jokes and tall tales, and probably gave him the energy and the will to live on despite the bad odds.

There were other reasons: too much rain, too many trees. He would not admit it to anyone except me, but Father was afraid of trees, especially in the dark. The sea frightened him, too, and so did high winds. Nature by the Bay of Bengal was altogether too powerful and abundant, too fierce and angry, too passionate and prolific for his sparse frame and basic nature to cope with. Making up silly stories and telling them to mere humans, mostly simple folk even if of a higher class – everyone was compared to us – was one thing. Facing up to daunting realities of the external world with the loneliness of his soul was quite another.

Just when Father was sitting down to eat, Aunt Verna said something about a free meal tasting better on a birthday, being better deserved, and Mother said it wasn't free but well paid for, and giggled a little.

Father went into a coughing fit and rushed outside to spit out his blood. I rushed out with him, but he told me to go back in as he wanted to go for a short walk by himself. I said let's have our food first – I was dying to eat it, it looked so wonderful and smelt so delicious – and then he could come with me, for I was planning on a long walk up to my magic woods. But he said he wanted to go on his own. I knew then that he would not come back. I knew it with more certainty than I knew my name was Cyrus. He enjoyed going for walks with me, and had never refused an offer – not even if he could hardly walk for pain.

I told him to go in peace, not out loud, but in my heart, and came back in. But I did not eat. I said I would wait for Father.

That was a fat lolloping lie, but I couldn't think of anything else to say.

✝ ✝ ✝

It took me seven years to find him. I ate regularly all the while, but I did not relish my meals as much.

But first I should, according to Adam, tell you more about where we were, and how we got there to begin with.

The Sun's Penis

When I say the sun's penis, I really should be saying the sun's penises (penes, for those who prefer penes), for he has a quiverful sticking out like prickly poseurs from every atom of his being – an abundance that, were they quills, would be the envy of every self-respecting porcupine.

Shiva may be content to propagate the world with only one lingam, albeit an ever-hard stone erectioned one of towering proportions; Priapus might find his singular penile grotesquosity sufficient to lust after, if not into, Lotis, and to exercise his wrath on the equally well endowed ass – lingua Britannica and not Americana – that brayed; Krishna, Casanova and Errol Flynn also managed heartily with the one rompustuous (sic) one, if one is to credit the credibility of the legends surrounding legends; but the sun, perhaps because of his dismal failure as a lover in the form of uni-phallic Phoebus, keeps one concealed – or revealed, to those with oval yonic eyes covered with hair and sometimes watery – in each ray, contrary to the schizophrenic's singular observation and the Mithraic mythology. *Quod erat demonstrandum* collective continuity, inherited tradition, and so forth. Apologies and credit to our Carl.

Ideas with consequences; concepts with vision; wisdom with love; God with certainty; suns, like their homonyms, with penises.

As for dreams, mine I leave you to discover among my words as you travel upon these pages. And to dream your own along the way. Overlook not mine just for being too obvious or too remote; cast not your own aside just for being too abundant or too ambitious.

Interpret them as you will. Your own way, or that of Madam Katrina, or fall back upon good old Carl, or even Sigmund if you dare. In the end they all, like reality and life and love and salvation, signify nothing – as has already been expositioned by our Will. But their progression towards nothingness is something else again. Well worth the sacrifices and the pains, and productive of the most intense pleasures. And hopes. Even fears! And there is nothing makes you more alive than fear. Pursue them with the unforgiving ferocity of the passion which women call love but men know as death.

I deviate. I postulate. Dilate, procrastinate. Forgive me.

† † †

I was telling you about the sun's penises.

Have you ever fondled a ray of the sun? Stroked it, massaged it? Caressed it, lingered upon it? Kissed it with your eyes while tickling it with your eyelashes? Swallowed it whole with the orifice of your soul while frigging it with the muscles of your body? Allowed it to penetrate the very depths of your porous being? That is what air and water and earth do, in perpetual and communal concupiscence, each recipient of the tumescent solar shaft doing so in its own inimitable fashion and with its own special equipage and by its own inbuilt techniques: aeons older than Man, yet as young as God Himself.

The result of that rampant copulation is the life you see all around you.

And never was it more copious than in the Gangetic basin of Bangla Desh, then East Pakistan. The sun's ubiquitous penis was at work everywhere and anywhere, coupling with the most juicy and willing and prolific cunnuses of matter-producing life-forms of the most awe-inspiring nature in such profusion that confusion of the senses was an inevitable consequence. That, or the deadening of the senses. Or fear or wonder or pride.

In the case of Father it was fear. In my case, utter confusion.

It was difficult to tell with Aunt Verna. One day she would shout and scream in rage at the incessant beating down of the wind and the rain across the tumultuous waters upon which floated the Gypsy river boat towing our own small craft (rented from the Gypsies with a small part of the money thrust into Mother's hands by the zameendar of the goat) down the murky waters of the sacred Ganges towards the southern forests of our newly-adopted country. The next day she would stand in rapturous awe, admiring its calamitous beauty with sighs galore and wordless exclamations of shuddering delight. I would almost begin to feel a kinship with her in those moments. She was my relative, after all, and not just a foundling deserted by some discerning goblin at our doorstep an indeterminate number of years ago. *She* still thought I was an obnoxious alien of sorts sent from far-off galaxies to bring shame and disrepute upon the great good name of the Choodahs; or just simply an evil little pest, the root cause of all our collective misfortunes.

Mother found it inconvenient, the river teeming with fish and gharyal and frogs; its banks hiding creatures with furtive footsteps and coy calls or those with unafraid footsteps and unashamed calls; the troops of trees marshalled all around displaying their virility and colours, harbouring the pulsing wings of prehistoric flying reptiles – or so believed Aunt Verna; the moving interplay of light and shadow upon the never-still, ever-muddy, perpetually-mobile, passionately-fickle highway of the gods; the thundery vapours ganging up together to blot out the very functions of human vision, splitting open to expose the ballsy sphere of white fire with his ray-pricks continuing their eternal fuck of universal matter, with or without the condom of clouds. All were no more and no less than inconveniences, as far as Mother was concerned, since they disrupted the smooth running of family life.

Not much smooth running of family life was possible while being towed on unsurfable waters in a crumbling old craft by a dying Gypsy boat.

Getting to the town of Dhulian – despite two changes of train and numerous delays – and crossing over the border to

East Pakistan by river was simple. So simple that its very ease was frightening beyond anything we had feared.

As we stood by the eastern bank of the sprawling waters, wide as a continent, trembling even in the pleasant January sun, the man who had sailed us across walked over towards us, squirting viscous, chewed paan-spittle the colour of clotted blood out of whistle-pursed lips at a scuttling grey beetle some ten yards away from his feet and close to Mother's ghagra. He came and stood next to us, grinning. And staring. Just grinning and staring.

Eventually it was he who lost his cool first, and spoke. Not because of our resolve and strength in the face of his brazenly amused and blatantly cynical ogling. Quite the contrary. Utter lack of resolve and the draining away of all strength had left us bereft of speech. Even some expression of annoyance, or perhaps friendliness, which might have been natural under ordinary circumstances from ordinary people, was beyond us.

My my, now what have *you* been up to, to be so desperate to leave the land of our forefathers and come to these Bhagwan-abandoned birth-cursed monsterritories. Clearly he was not a Muslim, and clearly he could tell that we weren't. But there was a lot more he couldn't tell and wanted to know. Every visible part of his body was an interrogatory comment, his posture assuming the shape of a crude question mark: hand on bent hips, back and neck craning forward, legs straight only below the knees.

Father's trembling turned to shaking and he went into a paroxysm of coughing his guts out. It couldn't have been better timed if he had rehearsed it. Took the heat out of the moment. Even Mother looked kindly at him – though she still didn't move to help as he stumbled blindly forward, hands on bent knees – and refrained from bursting out into a happy laugh, as she usually did when, as then, squeaky jerky farts escaped from his anal cavity (despite his heroic attempts to control the same) in a disharmonious accompaniment to the hoarse retching raging out of his oral orifice. The man rushed to support him, held him by the shoulders, and moved his hair out of his eyes.

He ended up selling us a crumbling old boat with tattered sails. Just needs a little looking after, he said, a little looking after. But who would do the little looking after? I thought to myself. But no one was listening to my thoughts. This is the quickest, the most direct, and the safest way to get down south to the fertile mouths of the Ganga, he said, where nobody will find you, but where you will find a good living and a good life. Oh yeah! I thought to myself. But no one was listening to my thoughts. Can't blame them. They hardly listen to my words.

More money exchanged hands and we were promised new second-hand sails, fitted and ready. Of course we would have to wait, for a day or two, but that would be no problem as a distant cousin of the man lived not many miles away and would be willing to suffer the inconvenience of our presence in his small but clean house for the paltry sum of fifty rupees only. It may be a paltry sum now, but it wasn't in those days. However, we had it, and the man knew we had it. I wondered if it would make any difference to his offer were he to know that we were Choodahs, or would the fact that we had the cash overcome the unovercomeable. I didn't dare say anything, but I made a big thing of sniffing around Mother's ghagra, and Aunt Verna's ghagra, and Grandmother's sari and Great Grandmother's ghagra – I wasn't tall enough to reach their cholis. I even pinched my nostrils and waved my hand about a bit; but got nothing for my troubles except a thick ear from Uncle Dano, a slap from Mother, a push from Grandmother, *the* look from Great Grandmother, and a tight hair-pull from Aunt Verna. Junior made the terrifying 'I'll see to you later' sign, Edwina lifted her nose up in the air and pretended I didn't exist, Nazli kicked me in the groin. The man registered no emotions and made no comment.

Instead of two days and fifty rupees it took one week and a hundred rupees before the sails were done, and they didn't look much different to me. The only promise made that first day and truly kept was Junior's 'I'll see to you later' one. I thought I'd never walk again. At six foot, eighteen years and fourteen stones Junior was no idle threat. But the man was kind to Father and even gave him some of his cousin's tablets and syrup. He had died of tuberculosis no more than three years ago, so the medicines weren't too old.

When we were out on the water in the river, it was like being on the sand in a desert. It stretched everywhere, up to the limits of vision, and beyond. The waves were like shifting dunes, despite only a mild breeze, and our progress through them couldn't have been slower had we set sail in the Sahara. As far as we could tell we weren't moving at all, just buffeting about while staying fixedly in the same place.

That's not to worry about, said dear little Nazli, the one with the pretty face and the cream-white skin, cheerful as ever. Start worrying when the wretched thing *does* begin to move. Dear Nazli, at age eleven plus, had the eyes of a day-dreaming six-year-old, the mind of a bottled-air salesperson, and the visions of an embittered old granddad in the throes of a nightmare. And, most important of all, the tongue of Aunt Verna. The difference being that Aunt Verna's mouth, being wholly unsupported by the brain, though managing to cause great annoyance never really hurt deep. What she uttered was usually so ridiculous that after a while it ceased to rankle and became amusing. Little Nazli could shoot as straight at the heart with a word as she did at the crotch with a kick.

If someone – she always said 'someone' when she wanted to show her superiority to everyone – does not know how to point the sails in the right direction, then if someone were to fold up the wretched – 'wretched' was her new word, she had a new word every week or so, and it killed you hearing it – things we might start shifting down river. Which I guess was the idea in the first place. All the wretched things are doing now is holding against the wind, she said, so we can neither go forward nor wretched backward. That's what Nazli said, and waited, and sighed, and blew her hair off her forehead, and waited, and sighed, and blew her hair off her forehead, and waited, and sighed . . . Until Junior went up to the mast and rolled up the sails and behold, the boat began to slowly move down stream, the slight wind in the opposing direction preventing over-rapid acceleration in the fast waters; and Nazli stopped sighing, looked at everyone, and said nothing.

Everyone shuffled about with embarrassed relief, Junior bloated his big chest arrogantly as if it was his very own idea, Great Grandmother made the sign of the cross (which Mother had expressly forbidden her to do, you never knew what the religion of anyone you met was, so it was safest to remain neutral), Aunt Verna looked proudly at dear Nazli (the more she hated ugly black me, the more she loved the pretty white darling), Father smiled vaguely into the air, Uncle Dano looked as harassed as ever, Grandmother burst out into a song with her hoary croaky voice that nearly tipped the boat over, and Mother patted Nazli's silky head, gently (even she didn't dare ruffle her long hair). I did nothing. I had learnt to ignore the petty cleverness of the spoilt brat. That is why she shot a well-heeled foot between my legs whenever remotely possible. That was the only way I took any notice of her, couldn't help but, and well she knew it. I was far enough away to be safe then, so there was nothing to perturb my dignified and distant stance of studied nonchalance. I could feel her gnashing her cutely perfect teeth and my heart swelled with joy. I was certain I was in for a real whopper of a kick up the balls at the most unexpected of times, but till then the pleasure was mine. I had prevented her triumph from being absolute.

I needn't have worried. The triumph of the brat was doomed to disaster, her pride to shame, her name to slime – sooner than even I would have dared hope in the most unbridled of my fantasies. But then I was not aware of the temperamental nature of nature in those foreign parts.

The wind picked up with calamitous suddenness and we were turned round in one fell swoop, then round again, and ended up sideways going nowhere but up and down. More down than up. Another blast, and it was round and round again. The river turned from a flaccid desert to a rampant ocean. The sighs and moans of the gentle breeze turned into the wails of grief and screams of agony of a maniacally disturbed being, confused and angry at having been so wantonly let loose in an iniquitous world. Maybe that was not the case and she had reasons of her own for behaving so badly and so irresponsibly as she was; or at least appeared to be. I can only say what occurred to me at the time. I am no mind-reader. And even for a mind-reader, it is not easy to read the wind's mind.

Had we had our sails up, we might have had some control. Between you and me, we might well have been worse off, but I let the thought float out just to see it germinate in all their heads so infatuated with the charms and wit of the wily creature that passed for my sister N, and for once give HER *the* look, instead of reserving it for me all the time. Actually, she might have gotten more than a look – words even, such as no one dared to utter in front of her, much less to her – had we not been in imminent danger of losing our mental balance along with our bodily.

Junior's attempts to struggle heroically with the sails, unfurl them, and use them as some sort of a protective guidance for the boat nearly ended in his fat rump sinking like a rock (an enormous rock, enormously cleft) into the depths of the sacred waters – he cannot swim to save his pubes – cleansed for ever from its carnal sins. Venial, Great Grandmother would say. Perhaps, but carnal also. For surely you must be wondering how Junior got to be the size he was on any diet WE could afford?

I'll tell you how. And it's no secret either. The only secret, and that not much of a secret, is the secret pride Mother had in him for it. He can look after himself, our Junior can, she always said, eyeing me from the corner of her eyes. I could tell what she was thinking straight off. Who would have *him*. And she was right, though not entirely. After all, Father had had me, if only under duress and in the police cell while being held down by four rather dashing coppers; but he had; and the coppers did too. So there to her thoughts. I often had more than half a mind to tell her about it, but then my promise to Father got in the way and I let it pass. Besides, I am sure she'd have turned round and said: Well, but you didn't get paid for it, did you? Not with a tarnished dhela (not even legal tender any more!) and a dry loaf of bread, much less with silvery rupees and pure ghee parathas, such as filled our Junior out in more ways than one. She wouldn't have said the last bit, but she would surely have mentioned the pure ghee parathas. She loved them so. But she also knew how to do without – pure ghee parathas or anything else. Mother, as I have said before, was a practical, down-to-earth person. The likes of us wouldn't survive were it not for mothers like her, and all praise to Allah for that. That is why if Edwina, or dear Nazli, were to have started up on their own, Mother would have well nigh killed them. They were girls, the future mothers. And girls, the future mothers, have honour, which they must cling to, at least until they are married. They may indulge in the occasional fling after that, provided it is all discreet and below board. As for men and boys, they didn't have any honour to start off with, so there was nothing to lose. Besides, they did not get pregnant however many pricks jetstreamed up their whatyumacallits. There was nothing else to worry about.

If you haven't yet guessed what I am talking about vis-à-vis Junior, you must be either remarkably thick or remarkably pure. I will give you the benefit of the doubt and opt for the former.

It all started when Junior was about eight. The local grocer gave him a handful of sweets in exchange. It might well have ended there, but our Junior is not just an asshole, even though that may be his most obvious feature. He went back to ask for more. And he wouldn't budge until he got a candystick as well. From then on he became a real businessman, or businessboy, and never looked back. Even if he had he wouldn't have been able to see much because of the waiting queue. He'd opened up a regular shop in his asshole, and hooray for him. Especially since from that very first time, he enjoyed the whole damn thing more than some of his paymasters, and would willingly have let himself be had for nothing – if, that is, he had been a pure asshole. But he wasn't, not when it came to mixing business with pleasure. Come to think of it, can there be such a phenomenon as a pure asshole? Yuk. Certainly not one used as a trading premises.

He liked women too, and women him. Sometimes I am not even sure of Aunt Verna . . . But then again, I have a suspicious mind and you will have to excuse me for that.

Thinking about all that brought back the urgent craving to

tug at my willie – I suppose I should stop calling it that now as I was fast growing up, and developing even as Aunt Verna had feared. I rolled over in one corner of the boat, took my knees half way up to my chest, my hand all the way between my legs, and began to enjoy the convulsions of the boat. Get up, you lazy bugger, and do something, shouted Uncle Dano above the roar of the wind and the waves. I *am* doing something, I shouted back, just loud enough to be heard but not understood.

We were more lucky that day than we realised. One boat run by experienced boatsmen sank that day not far from us, and two more besides. We were just thrown ashore, but back on the Indian side of the border.

We should have seen the guiding hand of God in it, but didn't. Father did, but who listened to him? Anyway, the boat came with us, and if one were to read signs and portents in the happenings of that day, the survival of the boat could have meant that we were intended to go on and try again. So go on we did, and tried again too – this time with the help of a large, power-driven, if ancient, Gypsy boat. That was a true piece of good luck. Or perhaps it was not so much good luck as the good hearts of the Gypsies who found us, half drowned and half dead, lying scattered on the shore with a half-drowned look on our faces and a completely-dead look in our eyes. Luckily – there was no end to our luck that day – our money, though wet, was still safe in Mother's bra inside her skin-tight choli, even though we had lost everything else we had brought with us or bought on the way, except the boat.

We were taken into the big old boat, dried and warmed, given clean clothes, and tea annnnnnd parathas to eat. Pure ghee parathas.

Our boat was tethered behind the Gypsy boat. They happened to be going into East Pakistan, and sailing southwards, and promised to tow us along as far as they went, which could be a mile or could be forever and a yard. Father offered them some money, which he didn't have and which Mother had to fork out, none too happily; and which they happily accepted after making sure we had enough, not knowing that we had a lot. Even Father was not foolish enough to let on how much.

For a little extra consideration, monetary, they even agreed to share their food with us, and that was to prove a big help, for we had lost all our provisions; and even if we had managed to get more, cooking and cleaning while being tossed about in the boat would not have come easily to us landlubbers. All this was amicably sorted out within an hour of our first encounter.

After that it was a matter of waiting for the sun to expose himself, again.

First Love – Revelation Auspication

It was during one of the many stopovers we kept making, while drifting downriver in the typically unhurried style of the Gypsies – they did not use the motor of their boat unless absolutely necessary – that I met my first and my greatest love. The truly true and undying everlasting love that only the luckiest of this or any other world are ever privileged to experience.

Mama Gypsy, Saira, around forty-five, twice the size of our Junior, dressed in what appeared to be a cross between our choli ghagra and the Western blouse and skirt, was busy putting the clothes out to dry on the deck; Papa Gypsy, Bhuddan, around fifty, twice the size of Mama Gypsy, dressed in Muslim-style shalwar kameez, was busy counting the white stars upon the surface of the river as they twinkled in the blindingly reflective light of the midday sun; daughter Gypsy, Hema, about thirteen, the size of our Junior, dressed in a proper white blouse like Sister Erin's and a red knee-length ghagra, was playing the harmonica and rocking in an old rocking chair, its weary creaks acting as an eerie accompaniment to the girl's playing; son Gypsy, about twenty-seven, Junior and a half, dressed in tattered khaki shorts, was chopping some wood, whether to mend the boat with – he had all his heavy tools out – or for the cooking fire, I was not sure; and then, last but not least as they say, the other daughter Gypsy, Nalini, about nineteen, slim, shockingly beautiful, and wistful like a daydream (she neither looked nor acted as part of the family and greatly excited Aunt Verna as living proof that rumours of Gypsies abducting attractive young girls to turn them into 'you-know-whats' were true after all) this Nalini was unplaiting her long brown hair so that it fell in sharp tiny waves down her back – a style our Nazli was quick to pick up – with a strange far faraway look in her large brown eyes. She dreamed of being rich and famous as a glamorous film star and setting her whole family up in a huge mansion in Bombay.

(There were three more children, we had been told, two boys and a girl, but they had left their family's dying lifestyle, dying boat, and dying trade – tinkering/carpentry/entertaining – and gone over to the 'other side', by which was meant land and the 'stagnant' ways of the city. Grandma and two grandpas had also left with one or the other of them. The shudders which went with the telling and re-telling of these facts showed the depth of feeling with which Mama, Papa, son and daughter – I use the singular because Nalini never spoke of them, further evidence, said Aunt Verna, that they were not her 'true' family – regarded such acts of betrayal on the part of so many of their own flesh and blood. I had a feeling Nalini would soon follow their example, if not their route.)

My family were all huddled together at the stern, I think it was, of the big boat, having come to consume a meal with the Gypsies and then not daring to walk down the plank to our own for fear of bringing it up. All, that is, except Junior, who was standing by the side of the boat, clutching on to the railing and eyeing the son's muscles in action. It was so long since Junior himself had had any action that I was deathly scared he might bring the whole family into disrepute by trying to ply his trade to the strapping future of riverside tinkering, carpentry and entertaining – whatever that entailed. Certainly not entertaining the likes of Junior, I hoped. I was sure Junior hoped differently. Worse, he might go for tempting his hugeness, and that could provoke an incident resulting in our imminent departure into the depths of the river. Even he would be sensible enough to realise that he wouldn't cut form with the future of the Bombay film world. Or would he?

Whenever I saw that yearning, craving look in our Junior's eyes, the one that seemed to say 'For love or money', it all sort of set my own flesh a-tingle in a strangely uncomfortable yet not wholly unpleasant manner. It was not just excitement, nor just concern over the family honour, for when it came to Junior's for-love-only stand – there was some justification and plenty of excuses for the for-money attitude, but to do it just for love, which in effect meant just for nothing, was an utter shame, an unmitigated disgrace! – there was also the fear that the big Gypsy boy might turn on him with his big chopper, the one for cutting the wood with rather than the one Junior might have had his inner eye on, and threaten to chop his chopper off? The thought didn't bear thinking. I spent some time thinking it.

But even that got tiresome after a while.

Don't get me wrong. I loved being on the boat, drifting along the now placid river watching the ripples on its surface change from flickering shades of gold to flickering shades of amber, or bobbing up and down the now not-so-placid river watching all my near and dear ones turn from varying shades of brown to varying shades of green, facing the rising sun or the rising winds, feeling the spray splashing up and hitting my eyes, nose, lips and the rest of me with such bracing briskness that every pore of my being began to dance with uncultivated delight alongside every drop of the assailing waters.

But there always is a but or two, no matter what the situation, isn't there?

Firstly, I missed all the books at Sister Erin's, missed them with a ferocity I wouldn't have believed possible. Secondly, it was confusing and hurtful trying hard not to miss Pasha, my spit-brother. And lastly, much though I loved the boat and the river, I was aching to get ashore and do some exploring. This I was strictly prohibited to do. A few sneaky attempts to slip away on the odd occasion were immediately spotted and rewarded with the stick from Uncle Dano or the elbow from Junior or the kick from sister N or a jab in the eye from Aunt Verna or all of these goodies together in quick succession under the indifferent gaze of sister E. What would I not give to know what she was thinking all the time her eyes were half open without seeing, her lips half open without speaking. Could she too be dreaming of stardom and greatness? With *her* face!

The time was about eleven in the morning.

The Gypsies had a different routine for meals, which we had to follow: one big meal at about ten in the morning, tea and toasts or some snacks at around four in the afternoon, and another big meal at about nine at night. I didn't like the system – I like being able to nibble something every now and then, if I can manage it – even though the meals on the whole were the best I'd ever had.

Before we went over to live with Sister Erin we ate what we could when we could, which wasn't much and not too often. At Sister Erin's there were regular meals, but the portions were much too small, with thin slices of bread and a tiny piece of meat and a potato or something. I don't think white women, especially British white women in India, know what a hearty dinner is, particularly if they happen to be married to Jesus on top of everything else. If they are married to an ambassador sort, it isn't too bad. But married to Jesus! Not a good omen for the flesh when it came to food, or to any of its other weaknesses. An absent husband couldn't do much for the table, or the bed, no matter how much you waved your fingers about and thanked him every time you opened your mouth to pop in a morsel, or how long you knelt and prayed by the four-poster before sliding into it. I remember saying as much one day and nearly getting slaughtered by Great Grandmother. She is not normally a violent woman.

On the plus side there used to be no problem getting something out of Sister Erin's larder for a sneak preview, if only a measly biscuit or a dry piece of bread. There was no chance of any such indiscretions round the big boat. Mama Gypsy would have strangled me by winding her little finger round my throat. Aunt Verna didn't like the system either, for no other reason than that she did not like anything which was not her idea or her practice. Nazli did not like it because she believed it was always more fashionable and elegant and upper class to say you didn't like something than to admit that you did. Mother thought it was eminently sensible, and the others didn't mind, especially since, as I have already said, the food was good and plentiful.

The sun was blazing away, saturating the dampness of the atmosphere with humid heat. The river was not really rough, but choppy, hence the changing colours of near and dear ones. Somehow, rather than getting acclimatised to the pleasures of liquid locomotion, they seemed to be reacting more adversely to it by the hour. Traumatised as they were by their first disastrous encounter with the water, Papa Gypsy said it would grow worse and worse, then go one day, so suddenly they wouldn't remember what it was like, provided they remained on the boat long enough for one straight, accident-free stretch. In the meantime they weren't a pretty sight, not even dear Nazli, so there was a bright side to it. More than one bright side: Aunt Verna was often too ill to be her usual loud self, and that, I can assure you, was no small mercy.

It was then that I decided to slip down to our own boat, and from there off to the bank and away. It seemed the only course of action, inevitable as love. And love indeed it was that beckoned me out, though I did not know it then. And love it was that kept my secret: for though I left in front of all and stayed away long enough to travel back to the origins of the world (for it is there that lie the origins of the love that awaited me), no one noticed my absence for a second of Time, and when I returned it was the same Time as when I had left, proving my point that she is an illusion. But then again, she might well believe that I am an illusion. And maybe I am. Maybe an illusion is no less than a glimpse of truth flashing its light from the dark, impenetrable confusion of facts.

It was good to feel the solid earth beneath my feet. Bare feet. I cursed myself softly. I should at least have put on Edwina's sandals, having been made fully aware thirty-seven times of the various dangers lurking in the overgrowth surrounding the river bank, not least of which were poisonous snakes of five or a hundred thousand different varieties, depending on the knowledge and accuracy of whoever happened to be giving the warning and imparting the information. But it was too late to turn back.

I did turn back to look.

I could see the family looking back at me. Like a painting in a frame, they all sat or stood in such a way so as to proportionally fit within its confines, looking at me – but, like in a painting, without seeing. Their eyes, though alive with the touch of a master, were nonetheless glazed; their bodies, though caught in movement, were immobile as fixtures in a divine theatre. Even Junior, whom I had left on the other side of the boat, was now clutching on to the railing this side of it, looking – not at the near-naked body of the Gypsy son, nor at the lovely Nalini, nor at the fat Hema, but, with the same yearning lust in his eyes, at me. Looking, but not seeing. His left elbow was raised in an awkward posture, as if on its way to settling down after having performed some necessary act, but it stayed up at that awkward angle. I remember being mildly amused at the discomfort it must be causing him. Nazli's long hair was lifted up by the breeze and was surrounding her face and head like the drunken rays of a hungover sun, and that's how it remained, etched in a coppery sky of unnatural hue. Father was reclining in an attitude of utter peace, as if he had finally chosen to die. Aunt Verna's mouth looked pale and crooked, like a slice of lemon in a glass of cold tea twisted in by a sadistic, humourless person. Uncle Dano's right hand was very close to the centre of his ass, its fingers stretching out for a vigorous scratch, just on the point of contact. He suffered from worms and was often constrained to scratch his rectal opening vigorously. Sister Edwina's nose was up in the air and, strangely, from this distance I could see what I had never been able to see close up, despite many attempts at trying: an indiscreet bogey, thick, oblong and wet, sticking loosely at the upper end of the right nostril, ready to be picked, reprimanding Edwina for being too well-mannered to do so in public. Grandmother's eyes looked tired, her hands looked tired, her soul looked tired. Great Grandmother was smiling. Her lips seemed to move, contrasting weirdly with the utter petrification of the rest. Mother's face was turned away.

I had to tear myself away, otherwise I too might have been frozen in active inertia, dooming my family, and with them the rest of the world, to a forever of nothingness.

I was soon in the thicket of the jungle and coursing through its hardened, ancient arteries and swollen, varicosed veins, still throbbing with life that seemed larger than life itself, and pulsating with the treads of animals and friends, predators and preys, foragers and gatherers, those travelling and those just commuting, inhabitants and visitors; and, of course, intruders, like myself. It was at once more dense and more open than it had appeared from the river: more dense in that the size and the number and the types of trees were far larger and greater and more varied than I could ever have mind-seen; more open in that the spread and the heaviness of the trees at the top, not allowing much sunlight to filter through, left large areas beneath them free of growth. Completely bald patches were interspersed with grasses and shrubs of differing hues and shapes and thicknesses – some shooting forth flowers and fruits of dazzling colour, others self-contained within their foliage.

Caution mingled with curiosity, desperation with elation, fear with joy.

The urge to run and forge ahead struggled with the desire to turn round and run.

But destiny decides before man. I didn't have to do either.

The tiger jumped, from the top of some tree on to my back and sunk its teeth in my neck as I fell to the ground crushed beneath its body. Either because of the lay of the ground or because the weight of the tiger was concentrated on my neck, my torso and legs were jutting outwards and upwards at an awkward angle. Therefore, when the claws of the tiger ripped my flesh apart and my blood poured out, it streamed downwards towards my face and entered my mouth as I opened it to let out delayed screams of terror and pain. Almost at the same time, or so it appeared to me, bits of my body which the tiger had torn off slipped out from between its teeth as my blood dribbled out of its mouth – its face almost directly above mine – and into my own teeth and mouth, my own meat chasing my own blood.

I was able at this close proximity to admire, even as I ate my meat and drank my blood, the fierce, inexplicable and inextinguishable fire of the tiger's eyes, exactly as I would have imagined the eyes of a god to have been. A primitive fierce god of a selective persuasion when it came to loving his created ones. But against all my fears and expectations, the eating of my body and the drinking of my blood was not only painless in itself, it brought to an end all the pain that I had been experiencing up until then.

A peculiar unplanetary peace descended upon my mind, body and soul. I lay back in a state of passive but nonetheless rapturous ecstasy as the tiger continued to follow the dictates of its divine need for survival and devoured me piece by piece, with a methodical lack of haste, certain of his commanding role and no longer in the throes of fury or hunger.

Entering the tiger's body was, and remains to this day, the most ecstatic and the most aesthetic and the most moral of all my experiences. I was completely whole, despite the fact that every muscle and every bone of my body had been ground into my blood and marrow and become the body, blood and marrow of the tiger.

Inside was a complete void and an utter darkness. I knew then, without the use of my senses – having lost all my organs, and there being no stimuli of any kind to titillate those organs even were I somehow to repossess them, which I did later, I know not how – with absolute certainty, that I was in the beginning. This revelation, alas, was not to be followed by more, at least not then, for when there was light, I passed out. It was like being in the eye of the sun, and my poor being was not strong enough to withstand the power of its naked brilliance.

I regained consciousness in a heightened state of being, somewhat like waking up just a milli-second before the culminating spasms of a forceful wet dream. A long sticky tongue was licking my face. My face! you might well ask. I know. So did I. But yes, I had my face back. The same one I had always had, I am sorry to say. But it was back. And so was the rest of my body. Yes, the same old one. Not an item missing from the inventory, not a dice of flesh less, not a scratch or a mark upon its surface other than what nature had placed upon it at birth or what life had left upon it afterwards. This is not strictly true, but I did not know it at the time.

The long sticky tongue was really a bifurcated fang spitting out of the open mouth of the nigrescent, numinous Naga, the magnificent, munificent mover, the all-wise, almighty Ahura Mazda, the death-dealing, death-defying dyadic-divinity, the causative, cataclysmic cobra. Blacker than the chaotic night, and longer, its timeless body was coiled round me in circles of centuries, holding me up, providing me with its cold-blooded warmth, its mountainous head swollen and erect pointing itself towards my face, directly above my face, just where the tiger's face had been before, its ever-open eyes looking straight into my half-open eyes. I looked up into its. It was love at first sight.

Older than God Himself, though God's bastard, the child growing and ageing faster than the father, it revealed to me secrets which neither book nor man, neither life nor world, neither experience nor meditation could ever have done. In a flash of eternity I had become eternal myself, if only for a fraction of a moment.

We decided to auspicate our love. The Naga reached up to the skies with only a fraction of its length and brought down the holiest of the holy temples and we floated inside it. There we burnt incense and offered burnt offerings to the High Priest who was robed in robes of silk embroidered with gold and inlaid with jewels. The High Priest, whose tongue was several feet long and lolled right down to the floor, incantated. The choirboys – whose eyes had been pulled out of their sockets so as to protect their innocence and prevent their lust from being roused at the sight of the naked acolytes with circumcised phalluses in full erection and lighted candles sticking out of their anuses – and the naked temple virgins with their shaved pudenda sang; and the naked acolytes danced round the naked temple virgins who danced round the altar and the High Priest, who was robed in robes of silk embroidered with gold and inlaid with jewels and whose tongue was several feet long and lolled right down to the floor as he ogled the choirboys whose eyes had been pulled out of their sockets so as to protect their innocence and to prevent their lust from being roused at the sight of the naked acolytes with lighted candles sticking out of their anuses and circumcised phalluses in full erection, and the naked temple virgins with shaved pudenda who danced round the priest in fits of violent ecstasy and impassioned abandon. But the lust of the choirboys was aroused nonetheless.

Then came the Man, and the virgins covered their shaved pudenda and the acolytes bent over double to hide their naked erections, thus raising the lighted candles high up in the air and throwing more light on their shame. But the Man smiled past them without chiding or reproach, went over to the High Priest and tore off his robe, rendering him stark and naked: beneath his robes his penis was shrivelled and flaccid and his testicles cold and smooth. The Man moved forward to the choirboys and handed their eyes back to them. Their lust immediately subsided when they saw the beauty and the holiness of the temple, and they went down on their knees and worshipped the Lord.

The Man then came towards us, put his sustaining arms round me and his Brother, and carried our naked bodies out of the tiger's womb.

I was back in the jungle, and alone.

The first proof of the actuality of my love, evidence that what I had experienced was physical and real, came just before dinner time.

Mother practically tore off my torn shirt, as she was prone to do when annoyed by something, in order to give my neck and back a good scrub before I could be allowed to eat. The angrier she was, the cleaner I emerged. Half way through she gave a gasp, stifled a scream and jumped back. Aunt Verna came rushing along and started babbling on about what the hell had I been up to *again* and so on and so on, until she realised the cause of Mother's agitation. Then she shut up. Not a word. Not one single word. Now both these reactions were extraordinary, unique. Mother seldom got visibly upset, and never had hysterics. Aunt Verna had never before been so successfully silenced. I ended up feeling terribly insecure. What on earth could be so unusually wrong with me that people normally quite used to finding everything wrong with me could be so taken aback by this . . . whatever it was.

I soon learnt from the cool voice of sister Edwina. The devil riding my back had ridden away. My infamous mark had disappeared. Gone. Vanished without so much as leaving the slightest trace, no hint of an indication that it had ever been there.

I remembered that that was where the Man had placed his palm on my naked shoulder.

When all had quietened down in an eerie sort of unresolve, we all went to the big boat for our meal, after being made to swear that not one word of this unnatural occurrence was to be breathed to the Gypsy family. It may well have had something to do with Gypsy magic, in which case the less said the better or worse things could happen. That was the considered corporate conclusion.

The special dish that night was shabdeg, a true connoisseur's dish: a Kashmiri speciality requiring slow overnight cooking – hence the name, 'shab' meaning night and 'deg' meaning a large pot, usually earthenware. Its main ingredients are diced leg of beef and turnips, and it is eaten with generous helpings of plain rice. I had only had it once before and longed to have it again. Even dear Nazli, so anxious always to show her disdain for mundane activities such as eating and sleeping, was having difficulty not letting her drools drip. Greedily and eagerly I sought out the largest piece of meat that I could find and swooped it up with one resolute motion of my fingers and shoved it into my wide open gob.

Instantaneously I could feel and taste my own meat in my mouth. The body of the cow was my own body was the tiger's body was my lover's body was the body of the Man was Umrao's body was the body of all life. The hypocrisy of my own professed belief that all life was sacred, not just including but *specifically* including animal life, and my practice of eating animal flesh became manifestly clear in one blinding flash of light, like the one after the pre-primeval darkness. I ran to the edge of the boat to disgorge. Aunt Verna was silenced for the second time that same evening.

Ten-to-the-Power-of-Eighty
Ten-to-the-Power-of-Eighteen

Am I doing time or is time doing me? You know my relationship with her, in the abstract as Time, not in everyday parlance as time, is shaky at best. But lying here rolled up like a rag doll, stripped naked in a bare beige room on a bare beige floor, she is anything but an illusion. However, if she is real, and has been on this earth in terms of seconds at a rate of ten-to-the-power-of-eighteen, as opposed to Matter in terms of atoms at a rate of ten-to-the-power-of-eighty – thus making the possible configurations in the system of atoms higher than the actual number in which they exist and so limiting only by Time the ability of Matter to outstrip time – then how come there is so little matter around here and so much time?

It wasn't like that in the huts and villages, towns and streets, jungles and mangrove forests where I searched for Father. There was little time and too much matter. Perhaps science has more to offer than philosophy. Perhaps I am being a literal idiot, as opposed to being an idiot literally or a literary idiot. Perhaps all three.

I used to disappear from home for days, come back to the inevitable beatings from Uncle Dano and brother Junior, not to mention some good smackings from Mother and Aunt Verna and Grandmother, and a few well-aimed kicks from dear sister Nazli, and the turning away of sister Edwina – and then disappear again. It was the turning away of sister Edwina which hurt the most and to which I could never get used. Each time I returned I didn't care who beat me up but wished Edwina would say something, however nasty, hit me, tear my hair or my eyes out. But nothing. She just looked away.

And no Father, no matter how far I went or how wide I roamed. Frankly, I didn't really expect to find him. I did in the beginning, but after that it was more a matter of hoping . . . and of getting away from the dhobi-ghat and the laundering of clothes by the riverside, which, after Mother's investment of zameendar Mirza's money, accounted for the great prosperity of the family, great in our context anyway.

I think of those years as the second phase of my growing years, or the second set of my living years, depending on whether I am looking from down upwards or from up downwards: the years that marked my transition from learning via books while hiding under the table and experiencing life often at second hand through the family and its multifold problems, to learning via nature while hiding under the sky and experiencing life primarily at first hand in the world out there with *its* multifold problems. And its awesome beauties and its terrifying pleasures and its excruciating agonies which no book could have ever rivalled or equalled or even approximated to with any degree of success.

On the other hand, real life was way behind on what books had given me: a sense of direction, a meaning, a purpose; a feeling of a beginning, a middle and an end; the choice to go backwards in time, or to skim and move forwards and reverse again; the ability to select or to reject, to assimilate or to disgorge; and, above all, an overall belief that justice and goodness and right have, at the very least, some inherent worth even if they do not always triumph. Life seemed to ignore, bypass or flatly contradict all this and I was left shaken and unsure of myself, and of everyone and everything around me. Most of all I was frightened. And lonely. Without books, without Pasha, without Father.

Of course I had discovered my Naga. And although I did not know how or where to find Father, I knew perfectly well how and where to find it. But I did not have the courage.

I saw the tiger many a time. In the paddy fields skimming

over the waterlogged shoots with the speed and grace of a tiger, sat on weather-gnarled branches of time-nourished trees with the stillness and the strength of a tiger, swimming through the crookedly upright roots of the mangrove swamps with the beauty and the power of a tiger, running upon the tangled wild grasses with the ease and the urgency of a tiger, flying through the air with the magic and the wings of the wind. It looked at me with challenging eyes and surging limbs, but made no attempt to attack. Not physically. But it did attack me with all the mockery and derision of a demi-god. It knew, and knew that I knew, that if I wanted to meet my Naga again it would not make it easier for me by making the first move, by lunging forth and killing and devouring me. I would have to go up to this tiger and offer myself, my body my blood, my flesh my skin, my bones my marrow; and only then would it condescend to tear me apart – bite, masticate and swallow every particle of my physical being and thus present me to my revelatory lover and friend.

But my will was weaker than my desire, my desire weaker than my passion, my passion weaker than my fear.

My love was not love enough yet.

The Woman's Penis

Five years thus went past in wanderings and launderings and beatings and some sort of schooling in between. The schooling was not so bad. The Master knew nothing, which was a big help, and cared still less, which was even better. The lessons lasted for less than half the day, and attendance checks were not taken seriously so you came and went as you pleased, which was the best. Almost everybody ended up learning much more than they would have under more stifling conditions: any time spent there was spent willingly and happily and with the desire to make the most of it. I am not sure whether I learnt anything there or not, but I enjoyed myself, masturbating beneath the takhtis. I had entered my teens and was obsessed with my penis. So much so that I nearly forgot Pasha, began to forget Father, and avoided thinking about the Naga, except in terms in which I shouldn't have. Our love was of a different sort altogether, even though we had been naked for that as well.

As if tensions weren't strong and volatile enough between me and my penis, Junior had to get involved in the sticky mess.

It wasn't really his fault. It was I who intruded – quite unintentionally I assure you – into the realm of his encounters with esoteric erotica, though I can't say he hadn't been giving me peculiar looks ever since he caught me bathing in my skin at the dhobi ghat (expressly forbidden) a couple of months ago and said, My, you have grown since I last saw you. To which I replied, Another six inches, in such a tone of voice as to leave open the question as to where those extra six inches had been added to my person. At the time, as ever, it was sticking out a mile and I was slapping its head left and right and up and down with all my strength, to see how long it would take for its tight oscillations to cease and for it to come to rest in its usual gravity-defying position. My favourite was pushing it down with full force while standing with my legs apart, down to the very limit, and then letting it go to see how hard it would hit my stomach, and how often rebound. Or to push it down and try to hold it between my thighs to see how long it would take to jerk itself upwards against the strength of my thighs, and quite strong they had grown too, since I started getting good food here in our new land and spent most of my time running round and climbing trees and using my legs in all sorts of other ways I'll tell you more about later.

It was good of Junior not to tell on me – Mother would have taken the washing rod to me, and I tell you that was bigger than mine and Junior's put together, and that is saying something – but I couldn't help feeling that he would bring it up later in a conversation, along with the words 'or else'. As it happened, it was I who ended up getting the upper hand on him. Not a common occurrence in our household, for me to have the upper hand on Junior, or anybody else for that matter. And it was great fun too, for as long as it lasted.

It was one of those beautiful mornings when it is both pleasantly warm and pleasantly cool. A soft breeze kept the humidity from being stifling; friendly teams of dark fluffy clouds and silvery flat clouds were playing football with the sun, allowing its still gentle rays to filter through with varying degrees of intensity and light, making the interplay of shadows beneath the trees more intriguing and exciting than usual – leaves and branches assuming grotesquely exaggerated shapes, either uproariously funny or terrifyingly monstrous; the cries of angrily quarrelling crows and happily laughing crows, of anxiously lonely sparrows and merrily mating sparrows, and the songs and dances, arguments and debates, friendly conversations and admonitory pronouncements of hosts of other birds that I couldn't identify put a name to or even see filled the very real and earthy atmosphere outside – as it filtered through the paneless schoolroom window beneath which I squatted – with an atmosphere of fairy tale unreality and magic.

My mind started to order a world of its own out of this chaos of music, beauty and light. Characters and beings of my imagination began (glory be!) to walk and dance and sing in this new heaven and earth; trying (alas!) to obey my laws, which were not for the created but all for the creation, for physics not metaphysics, for the body not the mind, for well-being not righteousness; and trying (oh confusion!) to follow my whims, which were striving to reach out beyond the ultimate point of multiplicity and which I had still not learnt to control.

They started developing personal and individual whims and caprices of their own, many of which I found scandalous, others I merely disapproved of in moderately strong terms. Some were quite fancy, and I enjoyed these rather against my will.

Matters got out of hand. Out of my hands. Worse, out of my poor creatures' hands. In desperation and ignorance they soon began to deconstruct the magic of my land by selecting and deselecting and electing races, places and faces; by laying down rules, creating obligations and, most heinous of all, promulgating laws for protecting what didn't need protecting and thus endangering, impoverishing and ravishing what needed protecting but was protected anyway without the laws which were meant to protect them but were the means of their destruction. All this in defiance of my authority, the true authority, the authority of law-free free-love.

But they also succeeded in developing a magic of their own, and even investing it into my magic, managing to surprise and astonish me with the excellence of their creations: works of such astonishing beauty and splendour that I felt left behind, cheated; as if I was being robbed of my own powers, denuded of my own creativity; as if my position as the ultimate lord and master was being eroded, usurped from right under my ass, with the ultimate in crassness and the penultimate in subtlety.

Saddest of all were the restrictions and barriers on the most joyous of my gifts – the gift of abundance and procreation and proliferation. On the other hand, the greatest of my curses – the scourge of denial and defunctness and devastation – was allowed the most liberal expression. Such promotion of the instruments of death and destruction and defilement! Such denial of the pleasures of sex and birth and life!

Instruments of Death. Pleasures of Sex. Instruments. Pleasures. Sex. Death. Sex. Death. Sex. Death. Sex. Death. Instruments. Instruments. Instruments. My fist moved faster and faster upon my Instrument. My Instrument of Sex, my Instrument of Pleasure, my Instrument of Death. Faster and faster. Faster, through the Rites of Sex. Faster, through the Temples of Pleasure. Faster, approaching the Fields of Death. The Throes of Death. Faster. Faster. Faster . . .

O thou first born of a pederast's anus, screamed the Master in chaste classical Urdu, why shakest thou so? Shaking, shaking, all the time. Why canst thou not sit *still* like thy brethren here. Thou wilt spurt thine ink all over thine clothes, and thine takhti, if thou keepest shaking in this fashion of a mad harlot. More likely spunk than ink, I said, but not loud. Speak clearly, thou unloved son of Ifrit, thou ulcered ass of Iblis, *clearly*. Why mumblest thou like a wind-stuck fart?

He moved towards me with quick, short, nervous steps, shaking his rod menacingly in the air. What art thou up to there with thine eyes half shut and thine ears fully closed? Shaking shaking shaking . . . Dost thou hear me? I say, dost thou? Dost thou? Dost thou? Dost thou? He was upon me by then, and landing one good one upon my back with each dost thou. I took thee for the great scholar of the ghazals of the great Mirza. Why then art thou not paying attention to his words, thou great scholar of Mirza?

Not true. Certainly not fact. I knew little of Urdu poetry. It was the only subject I learnt at this school – there were no Urdu books in Sister Erin's library. When I was introduced to the magic and music and rhythm of the language and the medium, I soon became absolutely fascinated – especially by the ghazals of Mirza Ghalib, which the poor Master just about managed to half misunderstand. Once I had grasped the essentials of the language and the complexity of the script and enriched my vocabulary by stealing the Master's most valuable dictionary, I began to fathom the meaning within meaning of the poet's play upon words, ideas and concepts. I managed to steal most of the school books on the subject after that. No one used them, so why not? One morning I made the mistake of correcting the Master's largely vague and specifically incorrect interpretation of a particular sustained quartet within a particularly rich composition, and aroused his everlasting hatred. To do him justice, I was not an especially lovable pupil, or person. But his somewhat extreme treatment of me often exceeded my merits.

I reacted to his physical attentions in one of two ways, depending on my sexual state of the moment. If inactive and dormant, I jumped up at the first blow and ran out of the half-built school shack to freedom and security. If in erection, and active, I kept squatting stolidly and took the beating patiently, with my own head unrepentant and unbowed and with my hand still functioning beneath the takhti.

The Master, though a simpleton, was not simple. He had cottoned on to the fact that if I did not immediately bolt I would keep on taking it. It was my folly altogether. If I had had the sense to plan a better counter-strategy it would not have been difficult to confuse him. But he enjoyed getting the better of me that way. He knew he couldn't rival me educationally, even though I never let on what I had read; and I was so used to being beaten up by all and sundry it didn't hurt much to let him have his fun, especially as I was having mine at the same time. His was a dreary little life and he could do with some relief of pent-up frustrations. Having a lower IQ does not lower one's desires and expectations, and life can be hard. As for me, I'd rather be beaten up or bodily abused any day than verbally insulted and morally ignored. Any day the fists of brother Junior and the palms of Uncle Dano rather than the turning away of Edwina.

I don't know how much of this I consciously thought at the time and how much I am reading into it now, but that is how I look back on it: with hindsight clearing the picture and the distance blurring it. But that I cannot change, nor would change if I could. After all, what is the use of all one's living as it is being lived if it is not allowed to play its role in reliving what has already been lived?

But going back from now to then.

Did God masturbate? Sometimes? Never? Always? Only when he daydreamed? Daydreamed about his creatures. Their pleasures, their sex, their death. Certainly their death. The violent passion of death was surely strong enough to give anybody an erection, especially so passionately involved a creator as God. Allegedly speaking.

But of course God does not masturbate. I know the answer to that one now, learnt it that very day after I left the schoolroom in disgrace. I learnt that God possessed both the male and the female penis, and therefore had no need to masturbate. He had full intercourse with Himself. That was how the world and everything in it was born. But I didn't know this that morning. I did not even know that women had penises. And although I was aware of Shiva's lingam, and had seen it displayed in its hard-rock splendour at the back of our local temple back in Chandan, I did not know what else He had, or did with it

Was I created by God, or by Iblis, the other one? Or, as the Master said, was I no more than his ulcered ass, the unloved son of Ifrit, the troublemaking, vagrant djin. I hated my father being called names, even if I was the sole object of derision. In this case I believed there was more to it. I *was* the unloved son. The Master knew that only too well. He had also fathomed that as I often sat tight and took the rod with my eyes half shut and a delirious expression on my face I couldn't be suffering much. His choice then lay in either adding a few leather strips to his weapon, or using hurtful words. He'd made the right choice. Hurtful words hurt like nothing else. Verses from Sister Erin's favourite book, *the* book (from the left-out sections saying rude things about the ladies), came back to me:

> *The lash of a whip raises weals,*
> *The lash of the tongue cuts to the bone.*
> *Many have been killed by the sword,*
> *But not as many as by the tongue.*

The unloved son of a vagrant! The Master knew my father had left home years ago. But Father was no Ifrit, even if I was the unloved son. Unloved by all the rest, that is. Father loved me. Of that I was sure. Or pretended to be sure. Did he really? And if he did, why did he leave me so?

Self-pity invaded my soul, eroded my creativity, but still did not smother my erection.

But I was past caring. The memory of Father came pouring back into the pores of my being, tears welled up in my eyes and, forgetting all decency or prudence, I jumped up, bole of flesh and all, and made for the door.

The whole class was stunned. And enthralled. They had seen me sit and take it with calm, unsulking passivity, and they had seen me run out laughing and light-hearted. No one had ever seen me with my face contorted with pain, my eyes swelling with tears, my lips trembling with emotion. No one had seen me with my massive cock sticking out of my dhoti, which Mother had taken to making me wear, in custom with the local Bengalis and in preference to my preference for shorts or trousers, which were expensive to buy or make and had to be renewed every so often for a growing lad, adding to the expense.

In a clumsy hurry I stepped on the loose cloth of my dhoti thus disengaging and unravelling it, to the delight of all the boys and the horror of the Master. It fell to the floor while I was half-way through the door. Luckily by that time the class and its conductor could only see my disappearing backside; but, as I have said, I was past caring what they saw or thought.

I ran about half a mile down the open fields, my rod lashing itself wildly against my thighs and wrists and stomach, to the nearest tall tree, and climbed up, regardless of what or where I got scratched during my rise to its sheltered leafy top.

There I collapsed like the crumpled, waste-paper A4 of a dissatisfied writer, and my erection followed in sympathy, subsiding completely like a pricked sausage balloon and hanging shamefacedly between my jack-knifed legs, looking as miserable as it could for being the prime cause of all my trouble and the sole cause of my final humiliation that day.

Both of us remained motionless for a long time before it began to raise its head again to peer one-bleary-eyed at my two bleary eyes.

It was then that I saw the tiger.

Draped along the tallest branch of the tree like some eternal Lucretia avowed to avenge her dishonour at the base hand of man, clothed in the inimitable messaline of her skin, mouth provocatively half open, long, luscious tongue, pink and moist, hanging out ready to lick your very essence into screams of ecstasy, eyes mesmerically staring down at me and radiating the unsated lust of a million generations like the unseen but powerfully felt heat of the midsummer sun.

Upon the nappy of the Evil One, I thought, what have I left to lose!

Trembling with cold on what had turned out to be a stiflingly hot day, bursting out in sticky sweat yet feeling dry and parched to the point of asphyxiation, on the edge of agony and death while on the way to resurrected glory and love unending, I half stood, half bent forward and offered my head to the beast's open mouth. It jerked its chin back with a contemptuous snarl, raised itself on all its legs, distributing its weight with delicate precision upon the supple branch, swished its tail, and walked out of the tree on to the air . . . and kept walking in mid-air, tail pointing vertically with its upper end brushing against the silvery clouds and its lower end exposing the entrance to the magnetic warmth of her womb – the secret of which I was about to fathom, at least partially, through the unlikely agency of none other than fat-assed, thick-skinned brother Junior – and disappeared into the midday sun.

That was the ultimate rejection. Apparently even offering myself to the beast was not enough to qualify me for another audience with my Naga. What else could I do? Neither my love nor my body and blood were enough. What else was left?

It was to take me many a sacrifice to learn the answer to that, but I'll tell you it for nothing. A broken spirit.

That's what was missing. Either that, or your Naga could come to you for absolutely nothing, but only when it chose. It was the Naga's free choice, or the offering had to be nothing less than the fragmented pieces of your very being.

And you want to know why I have told you this precious secret for nothing? Because it is not a secret at all. Everyone knows it, like everyone knows everything. But knowing the answers or secrets is nothing unless you *experience* the answers and secrets. And for that you have to make your own sacrifices and go through your own Heaven and Hell. Or it could happen just like that, through no act or suffering or quest of your own. Experience or revelation. Knowledge based on reason and information alone is no more than shit without the shit bucket. There is nothing you can do about it. Nothing at all. It just sits there, moist and alive and smelling, for a while; and then starts to die and crumble into dust.

So there you have it, the shit without the shit bucket. My compliments and all. Make of it what you will while I carry on with my story.

† † †

After the tiger's dismissal of my offering and the shock frustration of my yearning to meet my Naga came an intense and long period of an intense and long depression. During this time atop the tree not a fragment of time progressed and the sun remained static in the horizon. However, places and people move if time doesn't, and I decided to do something to put some life into my life.

First, a return to some sort of modesty of person: removing my shirt I tied its arms round my waist and wrapped the tail round the nates before bringing it up between the legs to shroud the organ and its grinders, forming a Sabu-type langoti.

Second: a where-to-go and what-to-do decision.

Third: going there and doing it.

I decided to go find Junior, badger some money out of him if I could, plead with him to get my dhoti from school – Mother would kill me if it got lost, and I didn't dare to go back to the scene of the crime for a month or so. Then I would wrap it on and set out for another search for Father till I was ready to show my face in public again.

† † †

At this point I believe I should fill you in with a brief fact sheet of what had been going on in our family for the past five years since we fled Chandan.

Many changes had taken place after Father left. First, Mother and Nazli went Muslim – at least they pretended to be Muslims and claimed they had always been so. Nazli even learnt to read the Koran. The Faith, and financial well-being, and her good looks helped to find her a 'good husband from a good family' by the time she was fifteen, which was last year. You may go *Ugh, poor girl*, or exclamations to that effect, but for an erstwhile, poverty-stricken Choodah family it was a monumental achievement. Even now, one whisper of our true origin and the poor girl could be dumped at our doorstep, fair skin and all. Untouchability may not be the Muslim way, but family pride is. Besides, East Pakistan at the time, unlike the West, had a large Hindu population and was still heavily under the influence of the Hindu way of life.

Edwina, having once refused a marriage (because she did not think the boy was good enough for her) on the grounds that she hated the idea of marriage, now felt duty-bound to refuse any other offer as well and at twenty put herself on the shelf.

Uncle Dano would have also liked to be called a Muslim, but was afraid his uncircumcised dick might give him away and bring down the wrath of the Faithful not only upon him but upon Mother and Nazli and the rest of us as well. And although he took great care never to wear a dhoti which could fly open at any time revealing the parts that other garments do not reveal, and even wore an undergarment beneath his trousers, he was still too frightened to make a

118

declaration of Faith. So he joined forces with sister Edwina and Grandmother, who had never much cared for religion and who had gone to church only as a social occasion, and pretended, along with them, to be lapsed, or agnostic, or a mystic; or he just mumbled when asked. In those days you could just about get away with that sort of an attitude provided you kept a very very low profile. It wouldn't have been possible now.

Great Grandmother and Aunt Verna remained staunchly committed to Christianity, and refused to alter their faith in Christ. My respect for Aunt Verna shot up so steeply in her moments of defiance that I almost came close to loving her at one stage. However that stage soon passed. Was it her integrity or her stupidity that made her take that stand? On reflection, I suppose it was neither. The woman really believed. I saw her as a different person from then on. Great Grandmother was eighty-five at the time and very frail and in no position to pose a threat of any sort. Aunt Verna, though choosing to announce herself openly as a Christian, was as frightened as the rest of being called a Choodah, and therefore not likely to expose the family history. To ensure greater security, Mother claimed that 'the woman' had been corrupted by some missionaries and since then had lost the balance of her mind and didn't know what she was talking about. Looking at her and hearing her, it wasn't hard to credit that, so the family position remained reasonably tenable.

That left Junior and me. Our black faces had a suspiciously Choodah look about them, so we were declared foundling brothers. Father's presence would have made that claim difficult, but with him gone it was easy for people to believe that we couldn't be the real brothers of the fair and beautiful Nazli, or the haughty and comely Edwina. Junior enjoyed any and every kind of deception and loved lies, so he was happy to go along with the idea. I was told to keep my mouth shut or else I'd be doctored. Everyone knew I loved my prick and its hangers-on much too much to risk that eventuality.

Ironically, Junior could have passed the male test of the New Faith, having been circumcised as a child because of a sticky prepuce. Both he and I suffered from exceptionally long ones, only mine didn't stick. I never really gave it a chance to stick, pulling and tearing at it all the time during my periods of concentrated study under Sister Erin's library table.

Mother was now called Begum, and Edwina, Bano. Junior and I continued to be called Junior and Cyrus, because *These were the name tags round their necks when they were found, and it would have been unfair to the memory of their poor parents, whoever they were, to change them.* Actually, Junior was a harmless cross-cultural nickname, so it didn't matter anyway, whereas I kicked up a big shindy and refused to answer to any other name. I even unfurled my dhoti and dared anyone to cut it off. My name I was not prepared to change. Father had loved that name. He used sometimes to take me up in his arms and say, O Cyrus, O Cyrus, I love your name my Cyrus, my Cyrus. Perhaps that was his way of saying that he loved me. I would never know, but I hoped it was. So Cyrus I stayed, to become famous now in the great United Kingdom, and even beyond its shores.

Had we been really poor, our stories might have appeared suspect, but a bit of money in the pocket made them, and us, happily acceptable.

Junior, too, had got some sort of religion. I could never quite make out what. Something to do with Hinduism or Zen or Buddhism or Tao or Confucius. Or all of them put together. It was strange, not a bit like Junior. Once I found out what was going on, it wasn't a bit strange – though very peculiar and very much like Junior.

He started spending a lot of time away from the house and the rest of the family, which was surprising as he had always been quite a mama's boy. He also spurned attempts to get him married off, which was not surprising as his inclinations ranged and his passions lusted and his body circulated far more extensively and generously and with a greater catholicity of spirit than a mere monogamous marriage could have possibly satisfied.

Now what could a throbbing cock and a pulsating asshole and a gaping mouth and a salivating tongue like Junior have got to do with getting religion? The answer to that is, of course, everything. The lust of the body for sex and the quest of the mind for God are two aspects of the same passion. On the positive side of the coin: monks try and unite the two into one, often quite successfully – they do not 'give up' sex, they pour it into their love for God as nuns become the Brides of Christ. On the negative side of the coin: the lust for money and the quest for power.

The first two, sex and religion, aim for the Kingdom of Heaven on earth; the second two, money and power, for the Kingdom of Mammon on earth. The first two are based on God's gifts of the body and the mind, and are enriched with love, the true passion. The second two are the two temptations of Satan rejected by Christ, and cursed with pride, the third temptation. The first two are represented by prophets and by the followers and disciples who spread their word; the second two are represented by politicians, and by the media and economists who spread their words.

The Eastern faiths see them less as opposing factions and more as co-operatives in a sort of universal dualism, as the Taoist yin and yang. Or back to Carl and the collective unconscious, rambling its way up and across from pre-history and the East to post-history and the West, as anima and animus. Male and female principles. Male and female penises. The female in the male, the male in the female: acting, inter-acting; creating, procreating; uplifting, humiliating; conquering, vanquishing; killing, destroying, maiming and hurting; creating, procreating; acting, inter-acting.

But I, in spite of all my book-worming and my clever-above-my-station ideas, was still too young and too inexperienced to understand that at the time.

Once, during one of my running-away-from-home periods, I had seen Junior go into a broken-down temple, old and disused, far out on the other side of the river mouth. This place was believed to be haunted by evil spirits after a group of 'non-believers of the worst kind' desecrated its resident gods, immortalised in stone and paint, by peeing all over the deities while reciting extracts from the 'wrong sort of book' – the book of 'another' religion. The temple was later drowned by floods, in spite of the fact that it was built high up on an artificially created hill especially to avoid such a catastrophe. It was believed to be an attempt by the gods to wash away the blasphemous words of the minds and the unholy water of the bodies of the desecrators. When the sea retreated from its portals, most of its ancient structure had been permanently damaged. Some people who were in the temple, to tut-tut piously at the work of the vandals, just before the tidal wave hit it, were never seen again, nor were their bodies ever found. No one went anywhere near the temple for fear of retribution and eternal bad luck.

Now Junior is not the sort to venture forth into areas where no other dares. He loves his fat ass too much for that. I confronted him with it. At first he turned pale, as pale as anyone as black as me can turn. Then he denied ever having been in the temple, denied even knowing about it. I just kept looking at him. Inveterate liar though he is, I know how to break him down. He insists I have the evil eye. Maybe I have. But if so, it is only my evil eye that can penetrate his evil mind. Finally and most reluctantly he confessed to having found a great and wise teacher, a white man would you believe it, who was not afraid of such superstitious nonsense and who was instructing him in the 'true' religion, the only religion which delivered what it promised: everlasting peace and happiness and satisfaction. He was still not telling me the half of it, I was sure of that. I was also sure I would get the rest out of him. He is quite good at catching hold of me and beating the shit out of me, but is no match for me when we sit down face to face and talk about anything. But Mother called out to him then, and he ran away in great relief.

I didn't get to talk to him again about it for a very long time, mostly because I was on the run myself. However, when I did get the chance to try and pin him down for more details, he evaded the issue with skill and a cool nonchalance. I had never before known him to be capable of such poise. Perhaps there was something in that religion of his, and the methodology of his great and wise white teacher. I did manage to find out who he was: an American who had come over to the East in search of peace and Nirvana – it was the sixties, remember – and had stayed on, along with a white girl he later married. He lived way on the other side of the river and travelled about in a rambling old jeep. He had been David Dunlop when he had arrived, but now called himself by the Hindu name of Jagdeep, meaning light of the world.

So, decently clothed once more and full of purpose, I decided to go over to the temple and personally see this light of the world switched on and Junior basking in its glory. I was sure I would find him there and hoped he might be a little more generous with his money in front of his white teacher. He might even agree to fetch my dhoti for me.

That was all I had wanted. I got more.

I reached the temple after bouts of walking, running and swimming. Recently the river had been getting fuller and fuller and speedier and speedier and more difficult to swim in, but I couldn't be bothered to go to the rickety old bridge further up. I took off my shirt and tied it round my head before getting into the water, not caring about the cries of 'Besharam, besharam', meaning shameless, that emanated from certain envious mouths around the river bank, nor about being so obviously uncircumcised, with a prepuce like an ant-eater's snout. Being unceremoniously exposed in full swing in front of the class in the presence of the Master *was* mortifying, especially when I was hurting inside and showing it, along with showing *it*. Here, I couldn't care less. I might have another day, but not that day.

By the time I got to the temple, on top of the man-made hill yet hidden from view by tall trees, I was quite exhausted. The façade of the building was built very much like the lower half of a huge woman seated on the floor with her legs jack-knifed and her knees raised and well parted. The enormous wooden doors at the centre were shaped like two halves of an oval. These doors were firmly shut, and either locked or so tightly jammed that my tired limbs couldn't so much as budge them a fraction of an inch. There was another smaller door at the back, but that too was locked, or jammed. No windows either. The only possible means of getting in would be to climb up one of the walls and in through the sections of it which had fallen away. Unfortunately all such broken areas were fairly high up.

But I am not the one to give up easily, tired or not.

After a bit more reconnoitring I saw the sturdy branch of a giant sheesham tree hanging almost above the roof of the temple. Nothing could have been easier after that. I did get scratched and grazed a bit, here and there, but that was all in a day's work.

On the roof you could see why windows were not considered necessary by the architects. There were large openings, some with glass panels still intact, to provide light and air below. They also provided a crystal clear view of what was going on down inside.

I was so stunned and overwhelmed by what I saw that I forgot to move back out of view and stayed where I was, transfixed like a gharyal basking in the sun. Fortunately, the gathering down below were so thoroughly absorbed in paying rapt attention to the Sermon on the Mount (of Venus – *Mons Veneris* or *Pubis* to the Latin types) being delivered by their phallic messiah that their eyes never once strayed upwards.

The roof slanted downwards towards the front of the temple, although the walls were all the same height. This indicated that there might once have been another roof on top to create a separate chamber. Once I had recovered the use of my faculties, I started sliding down until I was virtually on top of the front door. This shielded me from view, as well as providing a much better sight and sound panorama of the dramatis personae, as if from a front-row-centre seat in an imaginatively built auditorium.

There was a white woman seated centre back in the posture suggested by the temple building upon a high pedestal. Next to her was a white man standing on the main floor. Facing them stood seven strapping lads: four Europeans, one African, two local – of whom one was Junior. No one need have worried about the costumes for this production, as none were required.

All the boys were in full mast; but the white teacher's organ, though full-bodied and firm and healthy looking with a good head on it, was hanging down apparently fast asleep and quite oblivious to the tension and excitement which was vibrating through the atmosphere.

And that, it appeared, was the whole point of it.

The only way to get even with the immeasurable and unfathomable and insuperable power of the female penis, the teacher was explaining, was for the male penis to retire within itself and not rise to the bait; or else it would be swallowed and destroyed in no time, and the female penis would start another greedy and insatiable wait for another victim, another male penis, to grind to nothingness between its toothless jaws. If the entire male penis population of the world could be thus trained – the Buddhist monks could let their bodies burn in fire without twitching a muscle so the male penis should at least be capable of burning in desire without letting its flesh twitch – then all trouble and strife of this world would come to a permanent and peaceful rest. Once harmony was achieved between the male and the female principles, as overtly manifested in the male and female penises, then a state of universal harmony would automatically ensue.

Once the power of the female penis was neutralised, or paralleled, by the male penis, the two could come together on equal terms, as and when felt necessary by both partners, and the cycle of birth and life and death would resume. This healthy balance of power would eliminate the necessity of men trying eternally to subdue, molest, rape, confine and oppress women in an attempt to get even with them for the unmatchable superiority of their penises.

Ever since the emergence of human beings on this planet, the current unequal struggle between men and women was and has been extended to the unequal struggle between opposing factions of mankind all over the world for all sorts of apparently different reasons. The real reason was always the same, with its root in one factor and one factor alone: penis envy. Sigmund had obviously got the term right, but he had confused the sexes, thus perverting the very nature of the issue. It was not the female who believed herself to be castrated and hence envied the male for his penis. It was the male who envied the unlimited potency, the perpetual unabating erection of the penis of the female. The human female was the *only* being among ALL God's creatures with the ability and the potential to mate at any time all the time.

It was the male who feared castration each time he entered the woman's penis – fear which proved only too justified on every occasion. Not only that, the man's ego, his id, his super-ego – indeed his entire psyche – was at the mercy of the power of the woman, a power based entirely within her penis.

This unequal struggle led some men to compensate for their ridiculously low penis power – and that peaking at just nineteen and drastically ebbing away after that – by turning to religion or philosophy or science or literature or music; or to any of the many other forms of temporary and inferior expression and gratification. Others, less capable and so more vulnerable, took to physical violence: upon other men, against the environment, against women. Or turned to rape, rape being the only form of inter-gender intercourse, not just sexual intercourse, in which the male had true ascendancy over the female, albeit for a minimal period of time. Men's bodies, though originally meant to service the women, were their only and last bastion of male superiority over women, and they exercised that superiority like cornered rats. They transferred the fear and hatred of their own weakness to the fear and hatred of all women, and the cycle of violence and inequity continued and continues to move through this troubled world.

Women had no need either for such vile diversionary tactics, or for any of the so-called higher pursuits. But when they did decide to follow them, it was from choice and a position of strength. Their relative lack of success or participation in these areas was due to lack of sufficient motivation, and not through lack of ability in those or any other fields: quite the contrary. If a woman set her mind to it, she could do anything better than a man. But she had little reason to feel the need for it.

She was confident in the knowledge of her own indispensability to the scheme of creation. Men were dispensable. Like throwaway nappies they could be used and discarded. They were superfluous, at least in any number, unless as slaves. A thousand men could be used to service one woman for her pleasure; one man was enough to service a thousand women for procreation. Like bulls, the few best could be kept as studs, the rest ruthlessly butchered without any loss to the world.

Women were precious. The world would die without their abundance. And they knew it.

For their perpetuity women demanded a price from men, a covenant. They let men live instead of strangling them at birth, provided they acted as their born slaves, went out to hack at rocks to build them shelters, went out to chop trees to give them fire and warmth, went out to dig the earth for gold and diamonds to bedeck their bodies, went out to kill the beasts to provide them with food and skin and fur, catered to their every need and whim and fancy, offered all possible comforts and luxuries. On this condition women kept the human race going, and even let men exist – all men, not just the chosen and necessary few. And if any of the men faltered in the deliverance of these pledges, then shame and guilt would be piled upon them and piled upon them and piled upon them until they were crushed beneath its intolerable weight, unless . . . And the epicentre of the power that could achieve all that lay, you guessed it, in the woman's penis.

But (apparently a big but had cropped up in these post-modern times, a but that gnawed at the very heart of that covenant) post-modern man had built such an infrastructure of mundane power for himself, largely based on economic and military strength, that for once women were beginning to feel threatened. And if they did decide to add temporal power to their eternal power, then the violence and struggles that would ensue – because of men increasing *their* efforts to regain some sort of control over their petty little empires – could have catastrophic consequences for the entire universe.

I understood most of what he was saying without really understanding what he was getting at. At the time I wasn't even sure whether he genuinely had a theory to express, or whether he was just playing golf: different sized clubs, all those balls, one central hole . . .

However, I was so hypnotised by his speech that I even stopped fucking myself, after the first hasty ejaculation, and hung on to each word he uttered. I can still recall every syllable, if I concentrate enough.

He spoke in a calm, unhurried voice, frequently moving, sometimes to grasp one or other of the men by his straining prick, or to squeeze another's swollen testicles; sometimes to reach between the woman's thighs, separate her labia and finger her insides or tug at her clitoris in order to drive home a point. Now, I knew that that funny little thing, the clit, seen so clearly by me for the first time – the glimpses of Aunt Verna on the toilet seat hardly count – raw pink on a blotchy white skin beneath stringy blond hair, was often referred to as a rudimentary penis. But that was not what the man was on about.

In current parlance, he was trying to liken the little button to an imploded penis, like a collapsed neutron star, thus giving that chickpea-sized object nothing less than astronomical proportions. It even had its own accompanying black hole, which was not really a hole at all but pure concentrated mass, like the solid mass of the penis only a million billion times denser. With its intense and irresistible gravity, it sucked everything and anything into itself. A bit like our Jean-Paul's existential hole, only to the power of whoosh!

Then he was trying to liken the power of women to the power of cooking by radiation. There was no sign of the heat, no browning or crusting of the food, no damage to the dishes; and yet it was faster, deadlier, stronger than all other forms of heat. The woman's violence left no marks on the body of her victim, was not noticed by those at whom it was not directly aimed, yet managed to disrupt the very molecules of the being it attacked. The poor man could only retort clumsily with his fist, or his cock. How abjectly pathetic, and how miserably weak.

That, I believe, was what he meant by the woman's penis. I remember Edwina's turning away from me, and Mother's treatment by silence of Father, and wonder. I remember Belinda, remember Jenny, and wonder. Wonder wonder wonder . . .

Was he just a sex-mad trickster, having it away with sturdy young men and using his wife to help provide the unkosher meat? The exercises that followed his lecture added weight to that obvious proposition. I shan't go into details. I am too much of a prude for that. Suffice it to say that the alleged purpose of those exercises was to rid the mind of all conflict and passion through Transcendental Meditation (what else?), but to do so by way of a living experience rather than by the kind of barren emptying-out which always tended to backfire, being based on hollow foundations of withdrawal from the world rather than on a meeting and overcoming of its challenges.

Before the ultimate control, i.e. no erection, could be achieved, the men had to learn to confront the female penis with their own penises, and yet refrain from penetration for as long as possible. Then there should be a meditative stillness, while the male penis was in the female penis, again for as long as possible. Then should come the stage of stillness in movement – pumping intercourse which could, with practice, last for hours, even days. That was the only way to neutralise the power of the female penis, to match it by developing the power of the male penis through man gaining absolute control over his desires.

The pitfalls of digression were practically illustrated. When the man impaled himself repeatedly on one and all of the men, his own penis distended itself beyond belief. That, he said, was the punishment for his deviant behaviour – even though it was meant for purely instructional purposes, a sacrifice of self for the education of the species.

He kept referring to this Shree Ramnath, his teacher and guru, and urged the men to go out and sell as many copies of his collection of prophetic writings as possible each time they went to the cities; especially if they could get anywhere near airports. The great message must be spread and the cost of running the mission met.

The men were also urged to practise first among themselves before practising with the woman. She was too powerful for them at this early stage in the training of their power, and would utterly destroy them. For she could, like any woman, take them all, one by one, suck out their manhood, and then go on to take hundreds more. Which one of the men could satisfy so many women like that? Control through active meditation would enable them to do just that. In the meantime, practice was the watch-word.

I couldn't contain myself any longer and jumped down into the middle of the throng to practise myself, straight upon the penis of the mildly surprised woman, bypassing all deviations, however necessary.

† † †

When I was really and truly sated, I went to sleep between the thighs of the white woman.

I woke up suffering from a heavy bout of post-coital depression, perched on top of the tree where the tiger had so brutally rejected me, and neither the Man nor my Naga had interceded on my behalf, thus completing my betrayal.

It was getting dark and I decided to get back home that night and start out on my search for Father the next morning. I felt hot and clammy and unclean and wanted to have a bath. I wanted to wash the white woman's secretions from off my cock, from out of my mouth and eyes, to disentangle her stringy blond pubes from my coarse black ones, to pull them away from my lips, my tongue. I vomited all over the floor when one clotted one stuck to the roof of my mouth and I couldn't get it out.

† † †

After constant nagging on my part, Junior at last introduced me formally to his white teacher, and his white wife. They took to me immediately, and we used to have long discussions whenever I was around and they had time free from their lectures and their demonstrations and their disciples. They did not officially accept me as a disciple for they said I was too young at fifteen, sixteen being the lower limit for proper initiation.

They were absolutely amazed to find what I had read and knew. The woman, who had been renamed Shakti – meaning power – by Shree Ramnath, just couldn't believe it. I just can't believe it, she kept saying, which is saying a lot, since she and her husband had been taught by Shree Ramnath always to remain cool and collected and never to go over the top, especially in expressing surprise, for nothing that happened in the world was in any way surprising, but only natural, and part of the greater scheme of things. And this was also the teaching they passed on to their disciples.

Actually, I had a feeling that it was after discovering about my interest in books and learning that they decided I was too young. They had appeared quite willing to accept me at first – at least, that was the impression I got. What a big boy you are, they said, big enough to learn. When I got excited and told them that was what I had always wanted, to learn, and explained what I had already read and learnt, then they decided I was too young. They seemed quite cool about my quest for knowledge, amazed, but cool. Still, we got on tremendously well, and I did learn a lot from them, if only in private intercourse rather than at their formal tutorial sessions.

Water Water Everywhere . . .
Nor Any Drop to Drink

The year was 1970. The year I was seventeen, and of an age to be part of PLM – the Power and Light Movement of Shakti (Power) and Jagdeep (Light-of-the-World) – but somehow I never got round to joining. I believe they expected me to ask again; while I thought that since they knew of my desire they should make the first move and invite me in now that I was old enough. Anyhow, I was still mostly on the run – though unlike most runaways always coming back to home base, vaguely hoping that Father might have returned on his own – and they were busy touring round the country as well, so it didn't really matter that much.

The year that began with the auspicious news which the nation had been awaiting for the greater part of the last decade: President Ayub announced on 21 February that he would not be contesting the Presidential Elections that year, and actually resigned the following month on the 25 March. It ended with the historic victory of Zulfiqar Ali Bhutto in the western wing of the country, and the less surprising but more portentous victory of Sheikh Mujib-ur-Rahman in the eastern wing. This outcome was soon to plunge East Pakistan into a savage civil war, which included the attempted genocide of several million Bengali people by the armed forces of the Pakistan government, and culminated in the breaking up of the sovereign state of Pakistan into two separate halves. East Pakistan emerged as a nation and a country in its own right, as Bangla Desh – helped along by a timely and astute intervention from the always on-time and greatly astute Mrs Indira Gandhi and her armed forces from neighbouring India. All this within one short year. It is quaint, looking back, to realise that all three protagonists – Mujib, Gandhi, Bhutto – of the blood drama that was so cold-bloodedly directed and so passionately and cathartically enacted upon the horrified soil of that land ended up meeting bloody, violent ends themselves, rather similar in nature to the ones they helped arrange for hundreds and thousands of their fellow creatures. As, indeed, did those who arranged *their* violent and bloody ends: President Zia of Pakistan; some Sikh gentlemen of India; and President Ziaur Rahman of Bangla Desh.

The year that couldn't wait for the deaths and disasters of 1971, and brought death and disaster of its own by rendering millions homeless and killing well over a quarter of a million with the great tidal wave of November and the floods that followed.

The year that saw water water everywhere while people searched desperately for water to drink.

The year that Mother lost everything she had built up and acquired in that little world of hers she called home.

The year that we lost Nazli. Smart, beautiful Nazli with the near cream skin and the haunting dark eyes and the long curling lashes of an aristocrat's daughter. Drowned. Body never found.

The year that we lost Aunt Verna. Aunt Verna who hated me with all her heart and had difficulty counting beyond three and who loved Jesus without even knowing who he really was or what he represented, or understanding the deeper significance of resurrection, and who only blushed shyly at the mention of his Passion. All she believed was that he was the best, and that was what counted. Body found, half bloated, half eaten by crocodiles, but still eerily recognisable.

The year we lost Grandmother. Bitten by a water snake.

The year we lost Uncle Dano. Mauled by a tiger while trying to fish. He'd never fished before in his life, but was driven to it by lack of food. First time unlucky.

The year we lost Great Grandmother. Cause of death: grief.

The year I found Father. Floating on water, belly up.

† † †

The year Edwina cried on my shoulders, and Mother put her arms around me and held me close to her for one whole night and one whole day, while all three of us perched on top of a very unreliable-feeling tree as roaring waters raged and lashed angrily round its ancient trunk. Junior had been gone three days in search of a boat. We had given up hope of his return, and I realised, with the suddenness of a divine revelation, how much I loved him, despite all the terrible beatings he had given me over the years. I also realised how much I had loved the taunting and annoying Nazli, the silly fool of a man Uncle Dano, the never-pleased Grandmother and, of course, my very own very dear Great Grandmother, my only true friend. I am not even going to mention Father. I think I even loved Aunt Verna. When it was all over – I was still too young and foolish to understand that 'it' is never all over for the likes of us, 'it' just appears somewhere else in a different shape some time when you are least expecting it – there wouldn't even be any graves to cry and repent over. But does repentance need graves? Perhaps the waters had pulped my brain and made me soft in the head? Or perhaps I was just beginning to grow up – a feat which most of mankind never manage to achieve from birth till death, no matter how long they live. Maybe I was going to be the lucky one after all, in spite of Aunt Verna's conviction to the contrary. I was sure she blamed me for the cyclone right up to the very last moment of consciousness. Perhaps I was being unfair to the poor departed. Mother blamed herself. It was all because of her abnegation of her faith. Jesus was extracting vengeance. Nothing would convince her otherwise.

Aunt Verna was a staunch supporter of Jesus, I said, you would be hard put to find a stauncher supporter than her, I said. More sensible, easy, but stauncher? Very difficult indeed. And look what happened to her, I said. Even Edwina

135

agreed with me. For the first time in her life, even Edwina agreed with me. But nothing would convince Mother. It was all because of her abnegation of her faith. Jesus was extracting vengeance.

What about all the hundreds of thousands of other people who had been killed or lost their relatives and friends or become homeless? asked Edwina. Do you believe they were all lapsed Catholics, apostates? she asked. Even I agreed with Edwina. For the first time in my life, even I agreed with Edwina. But nothing would convince Mother. It was all because of her abnegation of her faith. Jesus was extracting vengeance.

They weren't even Christians, ninety-nine-point-nine per cent of them, I said, trying to advance upon Edwina's argument. That was a mistake. Exactly, said Mother. They weren't even Christians so it didn't matter, said Mother. I was horrified. You mean, if they weren't Christians it doesn't matter because . . . That is not what I meant, said Mother, without even giving me the chance to say what I meant, which was that they were not Jesus's responsibility. Of course they were – are, I insisted. If Jesus is God, then surely . . . Shut up and don't upset Mother, said Edwina, more like her old self, which was a relief. But Jesus is not . . . I tried again. Shut up, said Mother, and don't upset Edwina. It was back to Edwina now, Begum and Bano forgotten overnight. Was I glad that I had not changed my name!

It is all due to the abnegation of my faith, Mother continued. Jesus is extracting vengeance.

First Love – Consummation Continuum

Junior did return, and with a boat. We ended up in Chittagong which was less than a hundred miles away and where most of the relief supplies were concentrated, apart from Dacca.

Once the waters had well and truly subsided, we built ourselves a little jhuggi at the lower end of the town, near the port – overcrowded, dirty, smelly, and dangerously close to the water should it rise again, but that was all we could manage. And to think we had got used to living in a proper house with proper rooms, three in all.

Junior and I fetched mud and straw and bamboo from wherever we could lay our hands on any, and Mother and Edwina worked at the structure.

Once it was ready, the first thing Mother did was to sell some of our food to buy a large wooden cross, which she hung in the centre of the main wall next to a picture of Mary and the baby Jesus. Then she bought an old rusty bucket from a tinker, rummaged through the city dumps to find a couple of brooms, and set to work. But not before going to the nearest church, and begging for forgiveness with all the eloquence and tears she could muster. She also managed to smuggle the bucket and brooms inside, by hiding them in a long, white, shroud-like chadar, in order to sanctify them. Edwina thought it was sacrilegious and would bring more bad luck, but Mother said it was all right since they had not been used, which was a joke for they had been used to death by whoever owned them before. But we knew what she meant.

I found work as an 'outside houseboy' and driveway cleaner-cum-gardener's helper in the bungalow of a local paper mill boss. My luck really had turned. Such good jobs were very hard to come by, and the competition was fierce. Millions of people lived in the city, and most were willing to sell body and soul to keep body and soul together. But it was hard work. The bungalow was enormous, and the driveway itself curved around for half a mile. By the time I had finished clearing all the leaves and rearranging the gravel if it got messed about a little, it was time to start again. And the boss was not the kindliest of men. Still, I was very lucky indeed.

Junior was lucky too. He got a job as a municipal road sweeper during the day. At night he hung around the grand hotels in the fashionable parts of the city in the hope of finding a white tourist or a local businessman looking for a young fat ass or a sturdy young cock; and often he succeeded in finding one. Or two. He had the advantage there in that, apart from being very appetisingly built, he wasn't ashamed to ply his trade with a certain brazenness which went down well with the punters; whereas the competition, of which there was plenty, both sexes, were careful not to be seen to flout the local morality codes. Of course he had to pay for his roguish panache by giving free fucks as well as a good part of his earnings to some of the more energetic and enterprising members of the local constabulary. However, by lying about what he made and by stuffing most of the higher denomination notes in a plastic bag and swallowing it before the officers concerned got to him, he managed to save a good amount on a regular basis. The only question was, how long would he last with that heavy a workload? After all, there is a limit to how much a body can perform. In particular, a merely male body.

Junior was giving no thought to tomorrow as far as his body was concerned. As far as his life was concerned, he was full of tomorrows. He was hoping to go and settle in England, once he had the fare, and then call Mother and Edwina and me over as well. Mother and Edwina were really looking forward to it. I was the only one who didn't want to go. Can't say exactly why. Perhaps I just wanted to be different, as I often did. Strange that I was the only one who was destined to live, and die, in that country.

General elections came and went, 1971 came and stayed on.

Political excitement in the country, already at maniacal pitch, continued to rise. Hope in a new, fairer future with democratic control over their own destiny in their own half of the country gave new vigour to the energetic Bengali people. Their own Bhasha would at last come into its own, with its own heritage of literature and music which permeated the very soul of its speakers, writers and singers – from the humble fisherman to the great Nazrul Islam, the true national poet and archetypal hero.

Our family, being neither Bengali nor Muslim nor really Pakistani, and certainly not political, could not possibly share the depth of feeling of the general population, but we too were quite excited about the excitement, and vociferously and heartily agreed with whoever expressed an opinion, however much that opinion differed from the one we had agreed with a moment ago.

For differences there were. Beneath the façade of unanimity, various beliefs and political propositions vied with each other for ascendancy: from the strongly patriotic and nationalistic vis-à-vis the cause of Pakistan and the nationhood of Muslims, to the strongly patriotic and nationalistic vis-à-vis the cause of a Bangla Desh separate from Pakistan and the nationhood of the Bengali people.

The divisions started to intensify, by the minute rather than the hour, as Islamabad began hedging over its avowed intention to accept the people's verdict and hand over power to the democratically-elected leaders. Sheikh Mujib's resounding victory and tough stand raised the spectre of secession even in the most liberal of West Pakistani leaders, such as Zulfiqar Ali Bhutto; while at the same time the fear of perpetual 'colonisation' of their homeland by the superior military power of West Pakistan began to haunt the minds of the Bengalis.

139

Bhutto asserted that just because the Bengalis were in a majority, that did not mean the rest of the country had to be subjected to their tyranny, for tyranny of the majority was the worst kind of tyranny. Mujib retorted with his tirade against the tyranny of the minority.

Divisions then started appearing within the electorate of East Pakistan itself. The Biharis and other Urdu-speaking people were strongly in favour of a united Pakistan with its centre of power in Islamabad; the Bangla-speaking people wanting the centre of power to move to Dacca. As tensions heightened, even those Bengalis who had previously been for a united Pakistan, allegedly including Sheikh Mujib himself, openly started voicing demands for an independent Bangla Desh. To some the motive force behind these demands was the upsurge of a long-suppressed love for Bangla Bhasha and all things Bengali; to others it was a CIA plot to break up Pakistan, with the help of Mrs Gandhi of India fame: the always-on-time, greatly astute, true daughter of the very important Nehru; or the scheming, conniving, ruthless, totally opportunist and utterly frustrated wife of an unimportant Gandhi – depending on which side you were on.

Junior and I played our part in this passionate eruption of political awareness: joining marches, shouting slogans, carrying banners and placards, and pledging our life and limbs to the service of whichever party happened to be going our way. The Awami League and the Muslim League were the major ones, the PPP having completely failed to make its mark on the Eastern wing of the country.

Tempers and tensions reached breaking point when General Yahya Khan announced on 1 March that the Constituent Assembly was suspended indefinitely. Sheikh Mujib spurned the invitation to come to Islamabad for talks, saying talks should be held in Dacca in the majority province of Bangla Desh, the newly fashionable name for East Pakistan. Bhutto declared it an outrage, and just stopped short of calling it an act of treason. Mujib retorted by calling a general strike throughout East Pakistan, Bangla Desh, and received unprecedented total support. Even those against him participated, some out of a sense of expediency, some out of fear for their lives. But there was no doubt that the vast majority was strongly behind him. Even the judges refused to acknowledge the authority of the President of Pakistan.

General Yahya's attempt to resolve the deadlock by a mid-March visit to East Pakistan proved worse than futile, and upon his return he declared Sheikh Mujib and his followers to be traitors. On 26 March Mujib announced a Unilateral Declaration of Independence for the new state of Bangla Desh. General Yahya immediately launched a massive military operation to 'recover' 'East Pakistan'. A full-scale war soon developed between the supporters of Mujib and the Pakistan armed forces, and although India did not officially enter the arena until the December of that year, its unofficial action was there for all, except the foreign press, to see. What the foreign press also failed to see was the massacre of the Biharis and the Urdu-speaking, pro-Pakistan citizens of Bangla Desh by the Bengalis, though it rightly saw and rightly reported the genocidal waves of attacks by the Pakistani Army upon the Bangla-speaking people. These were led by the notorious General Tikka Khan, even though it was his successor who was mainly responsible for the worst of the butcheries committed in those days of blood and sorrow. By this time Mujib had been arrested, and thousands of Bengalis were fleeing in terror to India on a regular basis as the 'Liberation Army' was forced to move out of Chaudanga, badly battered and in chaotic disarray. All this on top of the devastation wreaked by the cyclone of a few months before, and its horrific aftermath, from which the people had still not properly recovered.

The frenzy which seized the people of Pakistan, civilians and soldiers, was the frenzy of another 1947: the frenzy of the politically suppressed, the sexually deprived, the ideologically stuffed-right-up-to-empty-craniums-from-overflowing-colons. Inhumanity was matched with inhumanity, the Bengalis desperately trying to make up in depth what they lacked in scope and volume.

India made full and judicious use of the situation. Not even her best enemy could deny that she did her worst.

Her propaganda machinery manned by people of far greater intelligence than Pakistan would dare employ proved that right was wrong especially if it was left. Indira Gandhi, like some wild maenad with Gorgonic hair and eyes and the blood of Salome in her veins, danced for the head of Pakistan, putting on rather than casting off veils. With foes like General Tikka Khan she hardly needed friends, but anyway found plenty in the West. Gloating over every murder, histrionically hysterical over each atrocity, she wept in public with artistic fervour and politicised passion. She lost no opportunity to preach, with smug nobility, what she had never practised – e.g. giving the majority their rights, as in Kashmir – nor had any intention of practising. She spaded in when the soil of Pakistan was wet with blood, sowed the seeds of war, and reaped kudos from the world. Her role as the instigator remained unrevealed, her reputation as a saviour established.

Patriotic Pakistanis were not to be outdone, and Mrs Gandhi's passionate hypocrisy was matched with awesome hebetude and breathtaking benightedness. Taxis and rick-shaws owned by the faithful carried 'Crush India' posters stuck all over them like fake medals on a magician drowning to death in his own watery escape chamber. Unfunny clowns and intellectual dwarfs and moral freaks followed suit in their newly acquired cars, and it came to a point where you could not strip a good, solid, patriotic Pakistani, for whatever pur-pose, and not find a 'Crush India' poster sticking gracefully out of his posterior, so firmly and deeply entrenched as to deny any access to those parts of the said patriotic Pakistani that you might have intended to reach in the first place, not that I am suggesting you did. On the other hand, why else would anyone want to strip a good, solid, patriotic Pakistani? I wonder. Never mind.

Jama't-i-Islami was not to be left behind, and turned its organised efficiency, developed at great personal and global expense by the Creative Insurgency Activators (known by some as the Criminally Insane Agitators, by others as the Confidential Insurrection Advisers: Capitalist, Ithyphallic and Armed) and meant primarily to prevent good, honourable

Pakistani citizens from embracing the blasphemy of Marxism, was now put to excellent use, and overnight public and private walls were painted with 'Crush India' slogans. So much so that any time the self-same solid, patriotic Pakistani squatted to piss beside one, he was roused to fight by the spirit of Jihad while holding his weapon firmly by the hand, like a cannon that would blast the Indians right out of existence, and the rebellious Bengalis along with them for good measure; or like an inexhaustible fire hydrant that would flood away the enemy civilisation in a manner to be remembered by the surviving world with the same holy awe as the rains in 'After the Rains'.

The results of all this political madness were manifesting themselves with stark horror all around us for anyone to see who had eyes to see. But did they! Had they! Why not? you may wonder. Does nationalism ever? I wonder. But whatever the reason, there you have it. In the meantime, death lived on.

I was without a job now. My employer, the paper mill owner, was a Panjabi – as indeed were most businessmen and industrialists, a major cause of the unrest and the uprising of the Bengalis – and had fled to Lahore at the first sign of serious trouble, along with his family and some chosen servants. His house was now occupied by some activists of the Liberation Movement, and the last thing they wanted was a houseboy with the appetite of a baby elephant. Used to wandering aimlessly, despite strict instructions from Mother to stay at or near home, one day I latched on to a wildly chanting Nazrul-Islam-songs-singing crowd of about fifty thousand, roaring through the heart of the city where some of the most popular cinemas and shopping arcades were located. Without any warning we were beset by soldiers in battle camouflage and fired upon with somewhat excessive zest. It was rumoured, by the pro-Pakistan lobby, still strong in some quarters, that three planeloads (or one or many, depending on the monger's imagination or knowledge) of injured and mutilated Pathans and Panjabis and Biharis had arrived at Karachi Airport the day before, and orders had come from above to take a thousand for each man, woman or child, but not to worry if the count was lost, and simply to start again.

It was a hot day, so humid that your sweat stuck to your body like motor oil. The blood ran freer. I just managed to escape slaughter by running with accustomed athleticism over the butchered remains of some faces I knew and others I did not that littered the road about me. I ended up in some squalid little street. I had no idea where it was.

It was nearly dark, getting darker. A strict curfew was being enforced, and apart from the heavy military presence, more sensed than seen, no one was about. Absolute stillness descended. Not a leaf stirred, or would have stirred had there been any around to stir. Not a dog or a cat dared put paw to tarmac, not a crow cawed over the deaths of the day. Feeling afraid, the type of fear you experience in an obsessively haunted house rather than in a ravaged land, I cowered into an alcove tucked away behind a sharp bend in front of a crumbling old house alongside many other crumbling old houses. I knew that I could expect nothing less than a bullet straight in the heart if a soldier were to chance upon me. I could hear the gruff whirring of a helicopter up above and flattened myself against the coarse wall.

My sudden scream cut through the air like a madman's axe through an infant's skull as my flesh was torn apart with the savagery of a madman's axe cutting through an infant's skull. I remained conscious until the very last morsel of my meat was devoured and the very last bit of my bone was crunched and the very last drop of my blood was lapped up by the tiger. The tiger lusted insatiably with the lust of the questing soul for *the* body and blood that would redeem its quest and let *its* body finally rest. In peace. In stillness, so that God could finally be God. So that God could finally be. That God could be. That God could. That God. God.

Even within the tiger's being, within the coiled lap of my Naga, there was no peace this time. No ritual, no rite, no ceremony. No holy temple, no maidens dancing, no choirboys singing, no acolytes carrying candles, no priest incantating. The Naga's infinite body twirled and swished restlessly with controlled rage infused with some uncontrollable passion which a mere mortal like myself could neither understand nor put a name to – except to say that its power seemed to rest in some form of a duality, like the duality of the Naga's own power, with its inbuilt, unresolvable conflict containing within itself the inbuilt resolution of the conflict. Both the certainty of resolution and the inevitability of conflict were equally valid and part of the same one and indivisible reality. This indivisible reality, as indivisible reality, simply comprised the two, but as indivisible reality it transcended both with its own separate identity of being.

The Naga's skin of luminescent night shone with a blackness that could outshine the white heat of the sun and cast it into blinkered nothingness. Its rich body, formed of all the substances in Heaven and Earth fused and infused into one another with irrevocable creativity, which was the doing of being, writhed endlessly with the grief of a lover who has lost his love forever; and with the ecstasy of a lover in eternal union with his love.

This time its tongue was not going to lick my face with the gentleness of a mother. I could tell it the instant my troubled, half-open eyes looked up into its serene, ever-open eyes. I could not tell what it had in mind instead. I got no time to speculate.

Like lightning it lashed out with its fangs and buried them deep into the innermost recesses of my heart, introducing its eternal-life-giving poison into my mortal blood to flow in it forever more.

There was no ritual this time, no rite, no ceremony. Just the Eucharist, the ultimate communion. The consummation of love.

The consummation of our love.

And for as long as its poison remained the blood of my blood, which was always, the continuum of our love was guaranteed.

† † †

The man – I wasn't certain whether it was the Man or just a man – ran his fingers through my hair and peered anxiously at my face. Don't worry, child, don't worry, he said in a voice which could have been the Man's voice, you will be all right. I heard you screaming and pulled you inside before anybody could find you outside during the curfew. You are safe now. You must have had a fit, an epileptic fit. I can tell, my son used to have them. There is nothing to worry about. He died of one. You'll be all right. There is nothing to worry about. I'll get you something to eat. You look starved. There is nothing to worry about. You will be all right.

Epileptic fit! My apocalyptic foot!

I knew what it was. But I was not telling him, even though he meant well. Just like the Man.

I stayed with the man for the night. In the morning, when the curfew was over, he explained to me how to get to my house, having first made sure that I had one.

Blood Blood Everywhere . . .
and Many Drops to Drink

As I got closer to home I felt a stillness and a desolation in the air and on the streets even more strongly than during a curfew, in spite of the fact that there were people about, if much fewer in number than usual. By the old lamp post in front of the all-purpose kiosk I met Nathu from next door, but instead of returning my greeting he looked at me with alarm, as if at an unwelcome ghost, and hurried away in the opposite direction.

On our front door were three palm prints in a blacker shade of coagulating red.

Inside our one-roomed jhuggi, Mother, Junior and Edwina were hanging upside down, with one foot each tied to the lone beam in the ceiling, and the other falling free. They weren't wearing any clothes. Beneath the pendulous head and lolling hands of each of them was a huge wok to gather in the blood as it flowed out of the severed arteries of their wrists and necks. Most of Mother's white hair – black with a little help just a year ago – had turned scarlet as it lay swimming in the wok below. Edwina kept hers short. Half of Junior's head was drowned in blood. He was a tall lad, and when he stood with his head held high it nearly touched the ceiling. Upside down it nearly touched the bottom of the wok. Edwina's and Mother's breasts, as well as Junior's penis and testicles, were not in their usual places on their bodies, but secreted away about their persons wherever an opening could be found to accommodate the same, if partially.

Missions Omissions Emissions Decisions Expulsions and Flights

Hey, leave the poor man be, shouted a voice which I would have instantly recognised at one time. That day it didn't even sound familiar, just foreign.

When I could just about focus my eyes I could tell that I knew the man, though I wasn't fully sure who he was. Whoever he was, I blessed him in my heart for he was trying to help me. And he called me a MAN. I *was* a man by then. Eighteen years old, with a straggly beard sprouting all over my unwashed face.

Some beggar boys and girls had taken the few coins out of my bowl and kicked it into the gutter. Again. They were only little, half my size – even though you could now see more bone than meat on me – and half my age, but they messed me about something awful. I could have got up and strangled each and every one of them had I wanted to, even in my condition, but I couldn't be bothered. They laughed round me, and mimicked me if I spoke, and pulled at the hair on my head and on my face, and spat and urinated on me when no one was looking or it was getting late and they still hadn't gone home or their guardians hadn't come to collect them. My home was there beside my bowl. I lived and slept there, through curfew, riots, sirens, bombings, gunfire and all. Aunt Verna was right, I was unlucky. Too unlucky to die. Or be killed. Or perhaps it was the fermentation of the poison with which my Lover had penetrated and impregnated my heart on the eve of my greatest trial which kept me going – the poison of life, which is death, and of hope, which is life. My Naga was acting not just as the two-fold principle of creator and destroyer, but as the triadic preserver as well.

The police had got used to me being there all the time. One of them even gave me something to eat once or twice a week, and another would give me a mite of the sticky brown lifesaver called opium if he had managed to force some out of someone that day, seeing how desperately I needed it. He didn't even want me to suck his dick for it any more, said my mouth was too filthy. He had also stopped frigging my dick, said my emission looked yellow and unhealthy and he didn't want to risk disease and death just for my sake. Actually I was quite pleased about that. I didn't enjoy it that much any more – never did, to tell a fact. Not with him, to tell a fact. But he let me have some opium all the same. Every now and then. It was really very kind of him.

Hey man, don't I know you from somewhere? continued the foreign voice. Aren't you . . .? Yes, he is, said the woman next to him, mildly surprised, he is Cyrus. I recognised her immediately. Well, not immediately, but soon enough. She was Shakti. The man therefore had to be . . . you know . . . had to be . . . him . . . light or something.

They put me in their car and took me home, put me in a hot bath (my first time ever), shaved me, both up and down, gave me something to eat, and took me to bed. It was really very kind of them. They saved my life and gave me a future I would never have had, as you will soon find out.

In the morning they gave me the most scrumptious breakfast I had ever had, something called cereals, with milk and honey and orange juice and fried toast and coffee. They went out and bought me some clothes as well, though they said I didn't have to wear any around the house if I didn't want to, but I said I'd rather and they said that was OK too. They said they usually had some boys and girls to help them with this and that, but good, *trustworthy* help was getting more and more difficult to find. Also, they were ready to leave the country any minute and didn't want anyone hanging around as their turn could come any time.

Apparently the airport – no longer under the control of the Pakistan government – was scheduled to capacity, what with many ex-officials being expelled from the country, and foreigners being airlifted out by their embassies, not to mention the thousands wanting to flee. So all they could do was wait.

They said their first stop would be Lahore, en route to the States, where they planned to set up a Shree Ramnath Ashram and Mission Centre for the evangelicalisation of PLM. Shree Ramnath himself had gone ahead to make the necessary arrangements, and they were authorised to bring over a few faithful helpers with them. They had already selected two and would be willing to take me as well if I was willing to go along. The decision came easy. In fact, there was nothing I would have liked better.

They were pleased for me. They said they would pull a few strings and get me an emergency passport and some papers to help me get out of the country and into America. He said that under ordinary circumstances it might have taken longer, but because of the emergency it could be arranged quite quickly, especially as they knew some right people in some right places.

They said my incredibly remarkable mind and almost equally incredible physical assets (a combination perhaps overstrong for the gentle East) would come in very useful for recruiting and convincing and converting the more volatile and sceptical youth in good old Motherland. I was thrilled beyond belief. I was going to be the lucky one after all. So there, Aunt Verna! And good luck to you too, wherever you are.

When they asked me about Junior I said that I hadn't seen him for a long time. Which was fact, the only fact of which I was sure. Of what had happened to him, or to any of the other members of my family, I had no memory. I had completely forgotten not only the blood deaths of Mother, Junior and Edwina, but also the flood deaths of Nazli . . . who else? Did I have a father? I used to know and like a very old woman once . . . I distinctly remembered Aunt Verna. She had me sussed all right, wherever she was.

What an incredible mind! I could barely recall my name. What incredible physical assets! I could just about stand, same as it. What gentle East? Where had these white folk been living the past few years? Or weeks? Or days?

Part III
ARCS AND SECTORS

An Avowal An Appraisal

A woman's boobs are her Achilles heel.

Adam dared me to put that in, in connection with Shakti's downfall.

She would be furious if she ever got to read it. 'A small but significant weakness' says my dictionary about Mr A's heel. Weakness! Shakti would have fumed. Small! she would have screamed, pointing upwards and inwards, elbows sticking out aggressively, at her prominent what-nots. But in the heart of her heart, as yet a medically uncharted territory, she knew that her breasts, though not small, *were* her weakness and would prove her downfall. What's more, in the same heart of hearts, she must have wished that they had been small. Smaller, at least. If they had been, they wouldn't have drooped so. Or rather dropped. She would not admit to a droop.

Once, when I did use the word droop, rather tactlessly she said: Not droop, not yet, *drop*. I would have thought dropped was worse than drooped, but she just gave me a surly look and refused to go into the linguistic niceties. I was more persistent. Drop? Drop where? At least if they drooped they stayed roughly where they were. Basically. Foundationally. She looked at me open-mouthed. She liked having her mouth open, even when speaking. A woman's boobs *did* remain rooted to their foundations, she said, basically and foundationally. But when a man's brain begins to drop, she continued, it goes straight down to his testicles. And the process starts much earlier, complete by the male's sixteenth birthday. And there is no plastic surgery available

155

for *that* fall. No surgical skills can lift a man's brain out of his testicles once it's firmly lodged there, she said, which it inevitably does, she said. This time it was my turn to give a surly look, but I kept *my* mouth shut. I mean, once you sink to that level of logical perversion, what else is there but silence to counteract it with!

I really shouldn't be writing all this, for I still have a very soft spot for Shakti. After all, she was my first mortal love. But what the heck. If she were to think of suing, she'd find there are too many people to be hurt, too many graves to be dug, too many hearts to be staked, and in the long run I am sure she would decide against it. I think I know her well enough for that, though how can a mere man ever claim to know a woman well enough, even someone as sexually open as Shakti, and therefore more generous and more honest and more simple than most women? It is the sexually pure and faithful-to-one kind of woman, like the sexually chaste and faithful-to-one man, who are the dangerous ones. Be that as it may or not, I cast caution and good taste to the winds and begin this section with that somewhat puerile remark about the mammary glands of the human female, with special reference to Shakti. Especially as Adam dared me to.

Father O'Neil, being younger and wiser and knowing that such childish taunts by overgrown men always produced the opposite response to the one intended, looked at each of us in semi-despair and shook his head at the hem of his cassock. But only for a moment. It wasn't a matter of great concern to him. In the sophistication of his liberation-theology-minded priesthood he realised that a mere literary metaphor, however bromidic and however crudely mixed, *and* naming parts of the male and female anatomy not recommended publicly to be seen, was not a cardinal sin, even by the standards of some conservative-minded cardinals. His mind was busy with more serious, albeit still venial, transgressions on my part, such as harbouring thoughts of the flesh regarding his holy person. He had to think of a way of rejecting me without turning away from me. He was quite fond of me, actually, and in other circumstances might even have . . . There I went again . . . looking at him and turning him cardinal.

I had to turn my mind back to Shakti. Shakti was dropped from her position of prime importance in the TLM (new name for PLM, the Temple of Light and Movement) as the squatting house woman during HMEs (Higher Meditation Exercises for the chosen few); and her name – Power – was excised from the nomenclature of the Movement and the Ashram – both following a perceived and alleged drop in her boobs. At least according to Shakti. Charlie, Shree Ramnath's business adviser, tour manager and chief PR man, declared that her relegation was due to her surly attitude, and had no connection with the dropping of her boobs, real or perceived. Shakti maintained that the surly attitude followed, rather than preceded, her fall from grace, which was the result of deliberate and malicious pre-planned attacks upon the firmness and lift of her etceteras. It was a very serious matter, I can assure you, almost of life and death. Jagdeep retained his position of prime importance as valuable teacher and chief demonstrator at HMEs because he could retain the flaccidity of his prick in the most trying of circumstances – an expression of volitional ability through a suppression of natural surges not to be found in most white males.

It is strange going back to those far-off days, days of excitement and fear, disappointment and hope, love and despair, running to nearly three years of my reckless youth, between the time Shakti and Jagdeep picked me up from the streets of the country going through the labour of giving birth to itself, and the time I fled to the USA, a country that had done the same not much more than a couple of hundred years before. The land, in both cases, had been there some while before that; and the people too, though not the important ones. Just people, and not worth much bothering about, though of course they had been satisfactorily and permanently dealt with. The poor beleaguered country was now trying to deal with other types of unwanted creature, of whom I was one, along with spics, coons of various descriptions, and those with not enough get up and go to make the most of what that great land of opportunism had to offer; and, of course, those with the unmitigated gall to fall ill when they could ill afford to do so, developing demands and diseases best left to those who could so afford.

It is like remembering some other man's life from the odd, disjointed and often conflicting information passed on to you by his friends, or by his enemies; by those who knew him well, and by those who didn't know him at all; through a haze of distance and unreality that at once confuses and clarifies the essence and the meaning of every experience without necessarily adhering to its logic or sequentiality.

I do know for certain that it took us almost a year longer to get to the United States than I had originally anticipated, even after a lot of groundwork and contact-establishing in India, Pakistan and various European capitals. In the United States itself a suitable site for the Ashram had to be found – large enough to be able to house a growing community of faithfuls; far enough away from a major US city to be affordable, yet near enough to reach the youth centred in and around major US cities. Eventually a compromise location was chosen, somewhere between Santa Fe and Albuquerque in New Mexico.

The Movement, renamed, as already mentioned, and revamped – a new image and a new perspective to reach the seekers of the West, who might not be ready to grasp the female penis and its ramifications just yet – set about the business of esoteric philosophising and achieving eternal peace and harmony in the world through the harmony and balance of power between the sexes. The excesses of female power were now given refined definition as: (a) the power of perpetual penetrability; (b) the power to order urgent male erection at her will; (c) the power of multi-orgasmic sex; (d) the power of non-orgasmic sex; and finally, (e) the power of total abstention from sex.

Meta-yogic HMEs were demonstrated, taught and practised only after long periods of preliminary exercises designed to release culturally restricted thought processes and open up socially blocked emotional avenues, and then only to those who were 'truly ready'.

Once this male/female balance of power was achieved, the new teaching went on, the world would then be prepared for the Ultimate Balance of Power – between humans and God. Man and woman harmonised and at peace would be able to challenge anyone, even the gods, even God. The result would be an idyllic working relationship, bringing the Kingdom of Heaven to Earth, and taking the Kingdom of Earth to Heaven: peace and harmony, not only in the world, but the entire universe. Sex, with a capital S, was the most potent force in the cosmos. Once all infighting over it was banished, it could conquer even death, bringing the promised eternal life within the reach of you and I.

Thus spake Shree Ramnath.

However, in order to prevent the faithful from running away with unrealisable hopes and dreams of an everlasting, everhappy, everfulfilled life, the Shree had a grave warning to give to all mankind, but males in particular.

There was one area of Sex in which the male could never rival the female, and that was the vitally important *creative* area as opposed to the *penetrative* area. The latter could be tackled through meta-yogic HMEs, if at first by only the few. But the woman's creativity, often denigrated as procreativity, was virtually unmatchable. Not all the art and music and the literature and science in the world could equal even one single life to which a woman gives birth. And saying that it was the result of man's insemination was just like saying that Shakespeare's sonnets were the result of a woman's inspiration. Nothing more, possibly less. The fulfilment that a woman derives from creating a life can never be equalled by man through any of his achievements; whereas the woman is capable of achieving those as well.

As long as this great unbridgeable gap lay between the miraculous creativity of woman and the mundane creations of man, eternal harmony and eternal life could only be an ephemeral dream. If man completely controlled his aggressive and violent impulses, his warmongering, his rapes, killings and murders, his heinous butchery of animals, his callous brutalising of the planet, his massacre of youth in Occupied Territories, his burning of Beirut, his blasting the legs off of children in Namibia, his treatment of blacks in Soweto, his graffitoing of the New York Subway, urinating in public phone booths, littering the streets of London to the anguish (great) of the Woman (great) to come, his tacit acceptance of famine and starvation in this age of glut and surfeit, insider dealing on the stock market – all impulses of a destructive nature, in fact . . . If man controlled and channelled such impulses into creative areas, then there was just the possibility that a creative balance between the sexes could be achieved along with the penetrative balance, making eternal life etcetera a true possibility – soon, if not within the designated term of the currently elected democratic government.

Actually he didn't say the last bit. He didn't say the bit about London streets either. And one or two other bits. Sorry, Shree.

I apologise out of good manners, not because I'm afraid that you will sue. You can't. In fact, I dare you to sue.

Oops. Two dares in the same chapter. Two much. I hope he doesn't take this one on. That really would be too much, even though his challenge would not amount to much. After all, I can prove what I say. He has far more to lose than I have.

To continue.

I, and others like me, were to use whatever mental, physical or sexual powers we had to bring as many young or old, but particularly young, to the fold; and to go forth and collect much needed funds by getting donations, begging, and selling leaflets, handicrafts, gifts, souvenirs – or failing that, ourselves. Great would be our reward if we did so. Even greater our punishment if we did not.

I realised quite early on that I would have to pay for my fares and travels in some form or another, but I had not bargained for the extremes to which I would be required to go to do that, nor the total absence of choice it entailed. My passport and identity papers and social security number were all locked up in the Administrative Offices under the control of one Jaggu, an Anglo-Indian, and his henchmen, all of whom were characters you would not lightly antagonise. The likes of us, referred to as drones, were not allowed to keep any money and were kept under strict scrutiny when out and about collecting funds. Our closest friends were always in the custody of one of the henchmen for 'due reprisals' whenever any of us was in any position to make a run for it.

In the Ashram itself we had relative freedom. There was nowhere to go. We were in the middle of a desert with nothing around us for what seemed like hundreds of miles, except a sea of sand and one road, too far away to reach in the heat of day or the cold of night. Besides, you could be spotted right to the horizon on the lonesome expanse, even at night. Five minutes or less in a powerful jeep and they'd be upon you. It happened more than once to some of the unfortunate drones, two of whom were never seen again. Whether they eventually succeeded in escaping or were 'dealt' with, none of us knew. When the Shree went to lecture or address meetings in the big cities, mainly in Los Angeles, those who could not be trusted were either left behind or kept under rigid surveillance.

In the circumstances it was greatly comforting to have someone as powerful as Shakti, even if fallen from her original heights, on my side. *By* my side, for by then we had fallen deeply in love.

Although I was not too young (twenty) and she not too old (under forty was all I got out of her) she was still vulnerable to 'old enough to be his mother' and 'cradle-snatcher' taunts. Even Jagdeep was younger than her, which put her further on the defensive. The affair had to be kept utterly secret anyway, which helped, but made life difficult in other ways. At least for her. For me it was a plus. It gave me a sense of identity, retrieved my self-respect, and provided me with a reason to live and look forward to the future with a degree of hope I could not possibly have envisaged without her.

To her, my youth and the firmness of my pectorals were as much of a pleasure as a painful reminder of her lost youth and the laxity of her pectorals. On her walk of life I was just another cross to bear.

I was to learn later than when a woman carries her cross, she first nails her man to it.

Makes it very difficult for her, but ruddy impossible for him.

An Arrival An Analogue
An Exhibit An Exhibition

I remember the feeling of ballooning excitement as the plane began its ceremonial circling and nosed downwards before landing at Albuquerque. When it became possible to see the city beneath more clearly, and details of houses and of people started to emerge, I held my head up tautly with sharp and delirious intakes of quasi-homesick, semi-patriotic breaths. When we got off the plane, those initial reactions stood confirmed.

It was nothing like Europe, or what I had been expecting. It was like being back in Pakistan: the stifling, startling heat that you could almost touch and see, the flat-roofed, open-plan houses, the richly brown people and, most of all, the muddy, uncultured looking river making its way across burning plains of sand.

I say 'quasi' and 'semi' for it was not much like Chandan and nothing like Bangla Desh, the places of my early consciousness and growing up; but like the desert surrounding Karachi; or, if you realised its deceptive height above sea level, like the mountain plains of Baluchistan, which weren't home, but made me homesick nonetheless.

When I actually spoke to some of the friendly brown people, they turned out to be friendly brown people, even the white ones, not in the least like the cold, blue people of Northern Europe, the glassy-eyed-fish variety. Then it got to be more like home. Not like India or Bangla Desh or Pakistan.

Just home. I felt myself being greatly and pleasantly surprised by each new encounter, visual or personal.

I still couldn't recall what happened to Junior or the rest of the Choodah family. I would try really hard to work and save up enough money to call them all over there. They would love it. My heart swelled with pride. Junior had been renting himself out in the hope of bringing us all out to England. But it was now up to me to get them out of . . . wherever they were – it shouldn't be too difficult to find out, the gardener at my ex-boss's place would certainly know, he used to sometimes walk home with me at night – and bring them to the USA. Mother would surely be proud of me then, for once. Even Edwina would look at me, if not up to me. Actually meet my eyes.

A sudden chill ran down my spine, despite the heat. Somebody was dancing on my grave.

† † †

Fog of time; smog of Los Angeles; shimmering of New Mexico roads; intrusiveness of young daydreams; heat-haze of Arizona deserts; density of New York; frailty of memory; mist of the Alps; rain-diffusion of British summers; obtuseness of self-inflicted ignorance; the edifices of Parisian elegance and pride; the endemic arrogance and salacious prudery of the English; the political piracy of the Americans; sun-distortions of the sands of Sind; anamorphic visions of uprooted night-mares; astrally asphyxiated hopes and anally assaulted ideals; pains of regret; pleasures of prison life: one, some, all, or more combine to throw up, throw out, make appear, make disappear, distort and sometimes, in a peculiar way, help put in perspective pictures of a time that came and went like a demonic love affair which should never have been but without which my life would have been that much poorer.

The sun shone stronger than ever through the glass dome above our heads. After the freezing cold of the previous night the searing heat of the day stretched our contracted bodies to the limit where they appeared just about ready to explode. Mine did. I couldn't be certain of Shakti. She had more discipline than I had. But by the way she looked she did not seem to be faring any better.

We were tied to these stakes which went under our long white robes, the one and only garment worn by disciples of TLM – made all sorts of ambidextrous activities so much easier – so that from the outside it would appear that we were standing with the freedom and by the strength of our will. In the beginning, being tied up had made the situation even more frightening. Now we were grateful for it. Without it we would have collapsed on the burning hot sand and literally fried in our own fast-drying body oils.

My tongue was blistered and parched, feeling both withered and swollen. Shakti's face was cracking up, making her look old enough to be her own mother. Her lips were bubbling up, part red, part yellow, part purple. My eyes could only focus fractionally on all the eyes firmly focussed on us – eyes growing hungrily out of the faces of those walking leisurely past the dome, which was the size of a generous auditorium, fanning themselves and drinking ice-cold lemonades and Martinis or what have you. Eyes full of admiration, and awe and envy. Eyes that kept moving, so that no pair was upon us long enough to see that we were in distress.

The dome was at the far end of our twenty-five-acre area, the restricted end, and you could only enter it after passing through a single, well-guarded gate in a high wall that blockaded that section off. People were now being allowed to stroll in, and then gently but firmly coaxed out the other end.

Their eyes, and the brains behind them, believed that we were beneath that dome practising self-discipline for the harmony of the sexes leading to the harmony of the world leading to the ultimate harmony of the universe.

That balance was supposed to have been climatically created within the dome itself. The glass permitted the life-giving light of the sun to filter freely in, while the air-conditioning inside prevented the heat of it from becoming excessive and disrupting the equation of light and warmth.

Actually the air-conditioning inside had been turned so low that it only served to stir the air within into a sort of haze, making it even more difficult for the passers-by to notice our real plight. But it did help to keep the heat just a little bit lower than it would have been, so ensuring that we and our suffering would last that much longer.

There were some eyes who could see all that. Eyes who knew. Had been specially enlightened. Told the fact that we were being punished.

Yes, we were being punished.

The evening before we had been caught making our third attempt to escape. Exemplary treatment was urgently required. All the possible escapees were duly informed, and made to assist in the preparations – dig the stakes into the ground, deep enough and secure enough, and tie the knots in the sharp ropes going round those stakes and our naked bodies beneath the robes. Word was then sent out that Shakti and Cyrus were going to perform a marathon stand-up, without food or water in the cold of the night and the heat of the sun, albeit tempered, to further train their bodies through the power of their minds. I was their youngest, most able pupil. She, their most experienced, most worthy elder. This would be my second time, the umpteenth for her.

Shree Ramnath was off on tour, along with Jagdeep, and in his absence this feast of courage and conviction was laid out in front of those eyes. Those ever-moving, ever-open eyes . . .

We were exhibits, designed to inspire the growing community of members with awe and admiration, and to instil the doubting drones with holy terror.

In the process we were being punished. Or so we were told. And so I believed, until that morning.

Now I believed we were being killed, right in front of all those eyes, none of whom were allowed to remain long enough in front of us to suspect anything other than our devotion to world peace and harmony.

A chance remark made to one of the faithful during our 'preparation' came back to me and hit me in the guts. After this extreme form of disciplinary exercise, the devotees were sent to their dream place for rest and recuperation, Jaggu had said.

Our dream place was likely to be six feet under the ground,

perhaps under the very ground we stood upon, beneath the sunlit dome.

Yes, we were being killed. Written out of the big soap of TLM, NM, USA, EARTH.

If that was so, it was not a bad way to go, watched and admired by all those eyes. I always was a bit of a ham at heart.

Poor Shakti. I wished I could do something to save her. She had so much more to live for than a second-rate Choodah boy like me would ever have, or deserve.

The Choodah name cut like a knell through my brain, and with it flashed the memory of what had happened to the rest of my Choodah clan.

My screams rent the dome and shattered the glass to pieces. Clouds gathered in the horizon and blackened the white-hot sky like the night of a thousand sins. Thunder and lightning and rain. Rain. Cool cool rain. Wet moist rain. It drenched my body and deluged my soul. I was saved. We were saved. My Naga came and coiled its body round me, cradled me in its lap, and lifted me up to the land of my dreams where a cool cool breeze from the Elysian fields was fanning my body as the houris of Paradise fan the believers as they sleep the sleep of the redeemed.

I saw a man's face, high above me, above a lot of other faces crowded on top of my face, trying to bend over me. I recognised him as one of the new members I had helped to recruit.

I am a doctor, he was saying, as he was being pushed away, I am a . . . Do not worry, Sir, he's a doctor too, among the best, one of the voices pushing the first voice away was saying, pointing to Jaggu . . . Everything will be . . .

You had a fit in there, an epileptic fit, said Julio, one of the drones. You will be all right . . . The control switch had been turned off, interrupted Tony (another drone) excitedly, we had to break open the glass door. If we hadn't, brayed the hard voice of Jaggu, even harder than usual with anger and sarcasm, the good doctor there was going to break the glass by shooting at it. Guns should never be allowed in here . . .

I was hearing but not listening.

Mother, I cried, Mother, Mother, Mother . . .

Don't worry, said another voice, as I was pulled along and out, she's all right. Just needs a little . . . My mind reeled under the shock of that statement until I realised, even in that befuddled state of mind, that the voice was referring to Shakti. How on earth could anyone ever take that beautiful white woman for the mother of an ugly black creature like myself? It was funny. Well, actually it was very annoying, but at the time it sounded funny.

I started to laugh. And laugh and laugh. Just couldn't stop myself.

An epileptic fit. What utter nonsense. Never had an epileptic fit in my life.

The laughter would not go away.

Calm down, Cyrus, calm down, said the voice of a fellow drone. Hold on, hey, what's that big mark on your back. My robe must have come off my shoulder. Don't remember seeing it before. I knew without even looking.

The devil was riding my back again.

This made me laugh all the more.

Even the feel of Junior's bloodied genitals in my mouth could not stop the spill of my laughter, nor the wasted breasts of Edwina, nor the scarlet hair of Mother, nor the bloated body of Father, nor the half-eaten corpse of Aunt Verna. No, not the entire fucking Choodah clan was going to stop me from enjoying myself that day.

An Escape An Imprisonment
An Opening A Miracle

Shakti and I are once again standing on the burning hot sand. Only this time it is out in the open, no dome, in our ordinary clothes, two suitcases sitting idly by our sides.

This time we have really escaped. Been allowed to escape. Sent out, thrown out, cast out, discarded. A danger to the good name of the Ashram and the TLM.

This is not what we had expected.

At first we had expected slow torture and death. Or rather, quick torture and death, for the slow variety had misfired last time. Then we were granted a royal pardon, a paid holiday in Denver or Vancouver, followed by the freedom to do as we chose. We ended up in the middle of the desert with two suitcases containing soiled clothing and human droppings. We were told they contained our best clothes – which to be honest they did, only not in the best of condition – our passports and some money. The last two items were conspicuously absent.

Shree Ramnath returned soon after the glass dome escapade. I have no idea how soon, my mind was in no fit state to register the so-called passing of so-called time. Jagdeep stayed back, 'on business'.

The Shree was furious. Absolutely positively furious. Enraged beyond belief. I had never seen him like that. Nor, judging by their expressions, had anybody else. His slight figure rose to its full height, his beard fluttered ferociously in the winds generated by his words. His eyes rained fire.

How dare anyone treat two of his beloved children like that. He had no idea any of us wanted to leave the folds of the Mother Ashram. However, if we or others did, all were free to go wherever they wanted to go, do whatever they wanted to do, with all his blessings, all his love, and all the fruits of his wisdom which they had been able to gather in his humble attempts to enlighten them even as they enlightened and enriched and ennobled and humbled him with their very presence in front of his love-thirsty eyes and in the bosom of his knowledge-hungry being and in the heart of his peace-and-harmony-seeking soul.

He was opposed to any punishment for anyone, no matter what their offence – that is why there was to be no punishment for those who had played this heinous game (he had been told it was all a game) with his beloved children – how could he possibly even consider having his beloved children punished for wanting to lead their life the way Bhagwan directed them in His Infinite Wisdom!

We were offered luxury facilities for rest and recuperation, promised a holiday in some cool mountain resort and the freedom to go where we chose and do what we chose.

The next day we found ourselves taken to the heart of the desert and abandoned. By Jaggu and his gun.

But the Shree . . . I began. He's not here, is he? was the reply I got. And a sneer. And a kick in the groin. God, how I hate rhetorical questions! And the snide people who ask them. I am none too fond of sneers and kicks in the groin either. Or the gross people who deliver them. Ugh, triple ugh.

So there we were. Free from the Ashram. Imprisoned by the desert.

I had developed a great love for the desert ever since I first experienced one in Pakistan. Now I was to become an integral and eternal part of one. Along with Shakti, with whom I had often desired eternal union.

So why all the carping? Are humans never satisfied? Is there no end to the quest of one's psyche to find a brain? Can one ever find a meaning in the meaningless search for meaning? Is *Dynasty* on tonight? Stupid rhetorical questions. Except one.

† † †

The desert has wings. It flies ahead of you when you walk.

After our first panic run in search of the road, any road, we decided to rest, conserve our energies and sweat, and try to plan our next move. Remaining where we were meant our bodies were certain to become burnt offerings at the mesa altar. Walking about without any sense of direction was sure to bring dehydration and death closer by the step. But what other course of action was available?

We made good use of the suitcases as mini tents we could carry above us to give our heads, eyes and faces some essential protection from the direct rays of the sun. Even the woman's penis was no match for the sun's. Fortunately the suitcases were made of some flimsy nylon material, and could be plonked on the head occasionally without feeling too heavy when our arms got tired, as they did only too often. Of course we had first to throw out the shitty clothes and wash out the insides of the cases with hot dry sand, but that was easy. The hard part, for me, was getting rid of the clothes. I wanted to sand-scrub and keep them as well – when you have been brought up wearing tattered cast-offs it is hard to throw away good strong clothes, nor do I have any special aversion to handling shit, even the wet kind, much less the turdy type which is easily got rid of, but I could understand the look Shakti gave me when I suggested preserving the clothes, and abandoned the idea. But not without a sense of loss and tragedy. Did me good, though – got me worrying about the good strong clothes instead of myself, at least for a while.

We did a lot of calculating: the position of the sun, where north might be, and hence where east – the nearest road to the Ashram ran generally east-west – and the shortest route towards the possible road. We needn't have bothered.

After coming to what seemed to be the right conclusions and after wandering for what seemed to be forty years we seemed to be no closer to a road but much closer to collapse.

However we did manage to get near some clustery rows of those fabulous gigantic cacti that had fascinated and enthralled me since I saw my first Western not long before I was born. Father, Mother and one of her rapists went to see a Glenn Ford film when I was thirty-three weeks post-conception, or five weeks pre-birth, as some prefer to reckon it. Can't recall the name of the film. Father used to get a free pass for four at the late-night show once in a while for cleaning up. Mother found it hard to forgive him for finding work in the only cinema that screened English films at that time rather than in any of the three others showing Indian movies all the time. I remember seeing another one shortly after birth, something to do with a thousand hills, and being so on edge with suspense I bit Mother's tit off. Not entirely, but very nearly. Didn't get fed again till the night, and then from a bottle.

I don't know how I could sit and think of Mother then, having re-lived what had happened to her only days before, but there I was doing just that.

A hundred years to sprout just one arm! And now they spread outwards and upwards like so many silent AUMs (or OMs as they are known in the West) proclaiming the incontestable godhead of consciousness.

I had never stood so near them before. Here were marvels of creation I had loved since childhood, yet I had been living in their territory and sharing their environment for nearly a year without bothering to visit them once to pay my homage, to admire and worship them from close, to fall prostrate at the base of these pricks of pricks and to suck at their seminal fluid, savouring its secret of eternal life. How insignificant mere man felt and looked in their awesome presence!

Further in the distance we could see different sorts of desert grasses sticking their grainy, pointy heads up in the burning stillness above the tops of varied green and purple bushes and some arid-looking trees. Sharp, cliffy mountains showed up blue and brown behind them, so far off as to virtually blend with the horizon. All this was encompassed within the sizzling yellow of the sandy, rocky soil where we stood. In the beginning was the Word. In the end, a painting. Had we reached the end?

Our hands were getting less effective as instruments of tactile comprehension and physical apprehension. This is worse than the boobs and the Achilles heel bit, but never mind. When you are being slow-cooked on sand beneath the white-heated wok of the sky – another bad one – metaphors run dry, and what emerges is a sort of perverse literalism. As under any situation of extreme stress, you would imagine. And I would agree, for I know. Maybe you know too.

To continue. Our arms were getting heavier and heavier and the feather-light suitcases lighter and lighter: so light that we could hardly feel they were there. Earlier on, if a foot faltered, an eye ran out of focus, or a body lost its balance and a suitcase dropped, we instantly knew about it. Now we began to drop them more frequently, and didn't become aware of doing so until seconds later. And then we had to stagger after them, followed by those balls of crazy bushes out-running us every time. It was like being in an out-of-sync, surrealistic, chili-con-carne movie.

We decided to rest for a while. The best shelter available was in the crooked shade of a Giant Saguaro Cactus. I did not know it was a Giant Saguaro Cactus, Shakti told me it was a Giant Saguaro Cactus, in a hoarse croaky voice. I was impressed. It was then that I saw the hole: a small opening in the weatherbeaten Giant Saguaro Cactus. I had once seen a picture of a tiny owl sitting in one very similar. Apparently these elf owls made their home in these cavities, created by woodpeckers while whacking away at the cactus for food or a place to nest.

That day there was no elf owl in it nor could any woodpecker be seen poking with his long beak at his young ones. Just a hole. An empty hole. An empty, inviting hole.

Let's get into that hole I said, excitement and life returning to my voice. Don't be such a stupid little child, Shakti sighed. Not that stupid and not so little . . . I would have added 'either', but I was interrupted. Don't give me that stupid little child's answer back. No matter how clever, you are still stupid, and no matter how big, you are still little . . . She had me figured to a T. Strange how women have the ability to do that to men. Oh why oh why did I have to get involved with such a stupid little child! This time she was practically wailing. I was seriously hurt by this third denial of my adulthood and maturity and intellectual and physical development. Well then, why did you? I sulk-shouted back, why did you? Eh? I told you I was unlucky, everybody knows I am unlucky. Aunt Verna said I was unlucky. So if *you* are such a clever sensible mature person why did you get . . .

I am sorry, child, she said suddenly putting her arms round me and hugging me like death, I *am* sorry. You may or may not be unlucky. Perhaps you are to get saddled with me. But I am very lucky to get . . . to have you by my side. Honest? Honest. Even here? Even here. In the middle of this smouldering desert? In the middle of this smouldering desert.

All this was making us hotter than ever. Then let's get into that hole, I said. All right, what the hell, let's, she said. And in we climbed, me first. Then, turning myself round within the massive prickly tube, I put my head and arms outside and pulled Shakti up, over and in.

I thought Shakti might have greater difficulty in getting in than myself, what with her impressive front and a generous behind, but not at all. She got in easier than I had. I believe it was a miracle, considering the opening was no bigger than her left breast, and certainly smaller than her right.

I have the same problem myself – not with breasts of course, though my left nipple is *not*, alas, a perfect match for the right, but lower down – with my testicles, I blush to say. There appears to be a proportionate difference in the sizes of the left and the right. I don't mean exactly or mathematically – we haven't calculated or measured or weighed or anything, naturally. That would be silly. Just going by appearances, which of course *can* be deceptive, they are not the same size and weight, that's for sure; though in my case the left is the heavier and looks the bigger of the two. Come to think of it, my left eye is not a perfect match for the right . . . nor, indeed, is my left nostril a perfect match . . . That is quite common, Shakti tells me, universal even. Transcends the barriers of race and culture: Aryans and non-Aryans, the chosen ones and the rest of us rejects, the lot.

A Unity A Diversity
A Trinity A Miracle

Inside was Death. An atheist's Death. Nothing and nothingness, with more nothing to follow.

We had been tricked. I had been tricked. Tricked by the big D. I should have listened to Shakti and not allowed myself to be tempted inside the ever-gaping, ever-hungry hole that was the mouth of Death. No wonder we squeezed so easily through its ever-gaping, ever-expanding jaws when it was in the process of devouring its prey. If we can be born through an opening as small as a woman's vulva, we can surely die through an opening as small as a woman's breast.

But it was too late now.

If Woman had tempted Man out of Paradise on to Earth, I, Man, had tempted Shakti, Woman, out of Earth to . . . Where? Was this Hell? It was certainly no Paradise! But if Hell, was it really so terrible? Was nothingness a double negative and hence a positive hell, or just a positive negative and therefore nothingness in essence as well as being?

I needn't have worried. Neither of the above possibilities needed to be addressed or tackled. I had got it all wrong, once again.

It was not Death that had tempted us in, through Man, Cyrus, but God. As indeed it was God who had tempted us out, through Eve, Woman. God, the Supreme Creator, the Ultimate Tempter, the Great User. After all, what is Creation for if not to be used by the Creator, be it car or computer for Man, or Man and Woman for God.

Yes, it was God who had tempted us in. God, in his unity and in his diversity, in his spirit and in his spirits, in his tranquillity and in his turbulence, in his matter and in the many forms of his matter; and also in his trinity and in his miracle, which were to be our release – another previewing of mankind's final release, a part of his grand plan since the beginning and in the beginning. I bet you had figured it out all along!

But perhaps I was right, too, perhaps it *was* Death tempted us in. For through Death comes our release. In which case Death is God. Perhaps the cry of twentieth-century despair, God is Death, should be changed to a shout of joy: God is Death. For who more potent, more powerful, more inevitable, more irreversible, and more liberating!

And who more creative? For if nothing dies, everything dies. All creation ceases, all birth and rebirth is stifled. Death is the Great Creator, the God of all things, their final refuge. And what is final has to be primal, the end lies always in the beginning. The end is the beginning. God is Death. Death is God. And shares His authority, His creativity, even His love. For who can deny the love of Death? The spectators of death, perhaps; those participating in its glory, the recipients of its love, never. Anyone who has been embraced by its pain-relieving, shelter-giving, home-offering arms will testify to that.

† † †

I can't see anything. I am stumbling. I am falling. I can't breathe. I can't feel. Where have you brought me, child? Why do I let you lead me into these situations. I can't see. I can't see. I'm stumbling. I'm falling . . .

I can't see either. I'm stumbling. I'm falling. But here. Hold my hand. Hold it tight. We'll get out of here. I promise you we will.

I've heard that before.

Well, we did, didn't we?

And ended up here.
Just give me a . . . Hey, I think I see something!
So do I.
And I could stand steady for a moment there.
It was green and dewy.
No. It was yellow and arid.
White and fluffy and hard, like a snow-peaked mountain.
I am steady again.
Like a blue lake.
Like a forest in the night.
Help me. I'm drowning.
Hold on tight.
I am, but . . .
I'm hungry. There is nothing to eat.
I'm cold. I need a blanket.
I'm hot. I need water. Cold cold water.
I want to die.
I want to live.

† † †

I've figured it out! Shakti, Shakti, I've worked it out. Listen, it works. Don't interrupt, it works. Yes that's it. Can't you see? Can't you? I can. I can walk as well. It is the desert, I can see it all around me. The desert from which there is no escape. Like God. The . . . boy. I understand now. I understand everything. Life. Death. God. I understand . . .

Will you stop babbling on and tell me –
Don't let go of my hand, Shakti! Don't. Don't pull away . . .
I'm not pulling away, you are. You're walking ahead . . .

That's what I'm trying to tell you. I can walk. I can see. And so can you. Just shut your eyes and step on nothing.
Shut my . . . Yes, so can I.

That's why we could see a glimpse before, that was when we blinked. Keep your eyes shut, and you can see. Open them, and all is gone. Step on nothing, and you can walk, look for a foothold, and you stumble. I've figured it out Shakti, I've figured it . . .
Stop screaming in my ears, fat lump.

177

Look who's talking, dome boobs . . .

✝ ✝ ✝

It was wonderful. It was marvellous. The earth shook and the stars flew all around our heads awaiting our slightest command.

When God reveals himself in all his complexities and offers himself to you, stripped, to be your servant and wash your feet, then the rest of creation must also be at your service.

I knew then the many faces of God.

When we are in the desert, of life or of hope or of land, we are actually in God, for there is no escape from Him. Like the desert, He has wings and flies ahead of us and retains us within Himself. In the desert, God is one.

When we are in the forests and trees of childhood or the world, God is many spirits, hiding behind each ancient trunk, trembling in each budding leaf flying with each rustle of the breeze.

When we are on the mountain of age or of rock, with the vast vault of the sky above and the thinning atmosphere and snow and whiteness and nothingness all around, then God is silence and meditation and emptiness.

When we are cold and wet and uncomfortable, at the mercy of weather and landscape, or longing and desire, God turns into a blanket to keep us warm, into a chair to let us rest, and builds himself into a room for our protection.

Where there is nothing but famine and hunger and loneliness and love withdrawn and hope desecrated and the cold hearts and cold fingers of observers with pious tongues supported by economic theorists and wise politicians, then God is Death.

But Man, in his selfishness and pride, manages to corrupt all these manifestations of God.

When God became desert, those in it appropriated Him as their personal property, to the exclusion of the rest of mankind, thus denigrating the very essence of His being.

When God appeared as the many spirits of the forest, people began using those spirits for the purpose of inflicting evil upon their fellow men and wishing grandeur upon themselves, thus corrupting His universal spirit.

When God turned Himself into meditation and prayer, those who received him became oblivious of the rest of the world and contented themselves with a part when the whole was at their disposal.

When God turned into matter to shelter and warm and protect those in need, matter was all, and the flesh and blood that went into the making of that matter was cast aside with philosophic cant.

This left no option for God but to turn into Death.

Or was there still one option left? Could becoming Man help? Could a ghost be called upon to comfort and save mankind?

† † †

The sun was hotter than the limits of heat, the sand stretched around us beyond the boundaries of the universe.

I was working out my trinity of salvation, as I used to when a child: Broom the Fluffy, Broom the Spiky, and the Shit Bucket. Always helped.

Sun the There, Sand the Here, and . . . I couldn't seem to complete this trinity. And salvation lay only in its completion.

We are never going to get out of here until I can complete my trinity, I moaned. It was like working out what the train is saying to the railway track, or what the clock is ticking away at. Unless you figure out the answer, you never get off the train, are eternally bound by the clock.

Cactus. How about the cactus? suggested Shakti. Of course not. Cactus is just a manifestation of sand, it cannot be elevated to the trinitarian status. Sky, how about the sky? There is no such thing as the sky. Now you are being pedantic. No I am not. It has to be something which moves, which can reach all men, which can effect change. What is wrong with God, then? Hang about. God is already booked, overbooked. I don't want anything already in use. Well, so is the sun – the sun god is one of the oldest . . . But he is no part of any trinity, is he! I am thinking of . . . the equivalent of the Holy Ghost. The sun and the sand are two manifestations of God, I'm looking for the Holy . . . How about the road? The road goes everywhere, brings help and comfort. But where is the road? I want something which is here. Besides you have to get to the road, it does not come to you . . . But road is not bad,

I must admit, a possibility, if we can find one. The air, what about the air? Too airy fairy. What do you mean too airy fairy! You're just being bloody difficult. Don't swear, I don't want to go to hell just for swearing in my dying moments. You're not swearing, so why the fuck are you worried? I'll swear as much as I want, bloody bloody fuck fuck fuck . . .

Greyhound bus! *That's it.* Yes. I can see it, too. Sun the There, Sand the Here, and the Everywhere Greyhound Bus – the perfect trinity for our –

Stop babbling, you fat ass, can't you see that was a Greyhound bus just gone by?

We're saved. I told you we'd be saved when I complete my trinity.

But it's gone. All the time you were babbling on . . .

But honey, darling, can't you see, where there is one Greyhound bus there will be another. There will be a road with another one going the other way or something. We couldn't have got to that one anyway. Let's lift our backsides and trek. The road can't be too far off. We might even get a lift. Come on, hang out your boobs! Of course not, you hang out your balls. OK, here goes. Oh do stop being an idiot and put them away. No, I've done what you said, now you do what I say. I will do no such thing. But we made a deal. We did not. We did we did we did . . . Oh, all right, stupid boy, just this once.

And we walked together in search of the road, suitcases held over our heads, balls and boobs hanging all out, in the middle of the burning, endless, pointless desert of existence, stepping on the heart of God with each reeling foot.

A Surfeit A Hunger
A Glut A Nothingness

I had, for various little reasons – such as her habit of drinking a glass of yukky cold tea, American style, during normal sexual intercourse – often suspected Shakti of being slightly pixilated. A short period of unhurried, unworried togetherness convinced me beyond any doubt that she was well and truly off her rocker.

Shakti had, for various little reasons – such as my habit of letting out suddenly a shrill, sphincter-splitting scream, especially when discussing Plato's assertion that 'to be' and 'good' are multi and not univocal, dialectically speaking – often suspected me of being slightly pixilated. A short period of unhurried, unworried togetherness convinced her beyond any doubt that I was well and truly off my rocker.

So far so good. But trouble lay ahead of us in that I wanted more of the same. The crazier the life and its experiences, the more I relished them. Shakti had had enough. She wanted to revert to a sort of normality, indulge in the luxury of sanity, become 'average'!

It had little, if anything, to do with age, and I was being neither 'kind' nor 'stupid', as she put it, when I told her so. If I had to look for conventional excuses I suppose I would put it down more to gender than age. She was a woman, so she wanted to settle down and have a baby or thirteen before it was too late. This idea angered her even more, but I still believe there was some truth in it. I also believe, now as then, that it had a lot to do with colour, culture and class. And of course wealth, which is just another way of saying class in the US of A.

For Shakti was rich, not fabulously but comfortably. I had no idea of it until that day when we got into the Greyhound bus, indecent parts decently tucked away, and she gave the driver her telephone number and home address to bill our fare. I couldn't blame the poor man for being sceptical. Somewhere close to Rodeo Avenue, between Beverly Hills and Santa Monica – we had often visited that area on our way to Westwood, and the UCLA, to beg for money and look for seekers. Her folks owned a villa out there! I couldn't believe it.

She had managed to keep her secret, I'll give her that. If only Jaggu had known he would have polished her toenails with his long slimy tongue instead of throwing her out in the desert.

However, after one passionate and explosive encounter, we did not stay there but went to live – temporarily of course – with a 'poor' aunt of hers way up in Altadena, beneath the mountains. Poor! She lived like a queen in a palace as far as I was concerned. Admittedly she did not own a single limousine, just a VW Beetle and an old Pontiac; and her privet hedge was no more than fifty feet from all four sides of the five-bedroomed, four-bathroomed house. This was slightly in need of repair and its furnishings were showing their age; and the kitchen looked up towards the mountain peaks instead of out to sea or across a vast hot-and-cold pool with built-in seats and hammocks and multi-level patios.

And now, I think, we are getting close to the real reason for Shakti's changing attitudes. It wasn't just her money. It *was* her money, by the way. Both the houses, and one more besides, plus a few hundred thousand dollars, give or take a few hundred thousand more, were in her name, left to her by her deceased father. Her mother had died earlier. Both her current parents were step: her father, having married her stepmother, died shortly afterwards, and her stepmother married again a couple of years later. She had five brothers and sisters, three step, two half.

Her real father had been Chief Financial Administrator of an evangelical Christian charitable trust, and was among the early pioneers of the American far right and the impending Moral Majority. Her mother held Bible classes for ennui-ridden wives who had bought everything they could buy for that week – consumerism did have some limits still in those days – arranged flowers for the Sunday congregation, gave parties for the rich and the pious, and prayed every evening and twice every morning that the evil Godless monster of Communism should not pounce with its vicious tentacles upon the poor unthinking people of the world and thus deprive the rich thinking people of the world of their wealth and property – which they were holding in trust for the Lord and for his Second Coming, to anoint him with and to prepare him for a second burial, from which he would arise resurrected for ever more in their midst, making sure not to repeat his earlier errors of judgement and to bless the *right* people this time. Christianity must get them – the poor unthinking people of the world – before Marxism did. Even Islam would do, since that monster Nasser was threatening the piety and the poverty of one fifth of the world's population with his bent towards the Soviet camp.

Her stepmother was equally pious and full of Christian goodwill and hope and joy, and worked tirelessly along with her father in the cause and the name of the Lord, giving even bigger parties and surpassing her real mother in the fine art and science of a perfect barbecue. She could play the piano and sing hymns as well. These were the real reasons why her father had married this woman, his secretary's sister, and not for carnal pleasure. The fact that she happened to give the impression of being carnally pleasurable – being possessed of blond hair, large blue eyes and a well-filled-out figure, was irrelevant. Her stepfather to follow worked for an organisation with a very high low profile, and had just been put in charge of a new division with the responsibility of providing Bibles to the Christian and pagan world, and copies of the Koran to the Muslim world.

Her aunt in Altadena was the black sheep of the family. She worked with the alcoholics, drug addicts and young runaways who came in their droves to Hollywood in search of fame and fortune and ended up waylaid, laid, made and dismayed.

Shakti, then called Martha – she had hated Martha, and now hated Shakti even more, poor kid, talk of an identity crisis – had opted out by rebelling against everything the noble family stood for, beginning with cleanliness, being so close to Godliness. After her ninety-first day without a bath she paraded her unwashed body naked alongside a march of future hippies demonstrating for black civil rights. How could she! Trying to undo what God had done! Could mere Man take away the black mark, or face, of Cain and raise it to a level equal to that of the untainted Abel? Her body, however unwashed, was clean underneath it all, and white. Could *their* blackness be washed away even by the waters of another flood, and even if the new Noah did decide to have one of *them* as one of the seven?

Had I been brought back to her home to prove a point, even at this late stage?

Shakti's craziness was a reaction, a rebellion, a protest. It wasn't really her. Once she felt she had made her point, she could safely revert to a 'normal' lifestyle, such as she had been brought up to learn and respect and accept, and against which she had kicked and kicked hard. I wouldn't know what a normal, peaceful, quiet life was if it hit me in the testicles. I was born crazy, and would remain so till I died. I wasn't trying to shock a morally cunt-bound upper-class family. Hadn't I hidden away under tables to prevent shock, despite the little trick of suddenly appearing behind Mother? My family was weird enough without my help. I had nothing to prove or gain, no one to impress or reject. Shakti had, and she had had her fling at it, and no mean one at that. She wanted to call it quits. She had a choice. I had none that I was aware of, no other life to compare or contrast with my own or to evaluate and adopt.

Pseudsville! said Shakti indignantly when she heard my psychoanalysis of her predicament. You may be happy to pay homage to Adler and explain away your life as an inferiority compensation neurosis, but I pay homage to no man, certainly not to Freud, so would you please keep him well out of my pubes. Shakti had a thing about keeping things out of her hair.

I screamed. I always screamed when anyone mentioned my inferiority compensation neurosis. And I always screamed when I thought I was losing an argument, or when I felt my guts stepped upon by the well educated and the better spoken. Somehow, since learning that Shakti came from a rich background, I had become more self-conscious of my origins and started screaming more than ever before. Her aunt had stopped coming in running. If I had had a real accident I bet I would have died screaming before she came to help me out.

Of course I am pseudsville, I screamed. I am not a genuine anything. Not a genuine poor ignorant peasant because my poor pure innocent ignorance was raped by words and books and thoughts above my station which should never have been allowed to penetrate the asshole of my shit-rooted brain. I am not a genuine intellectual because I have no education, no culture, no real roots in the right sort of soil. I am just a pseud all round. You know it, you have always known it, so what's new and why bring it up . . . I went on and on as I sometimes do. I no longer scream, though. What's the point? There is no Shakti around to take any notice. My poor poor boy, said Shakti, coming up to me and putting her arms round my head. I used to hate her saying and doing that. You just wait here while I make myself a nice cool glass of fresh tea.

That meant only one thing, and I didn't feel up to it. Theoretically we should both have been at our sexual heights: I, though no longer nineteen, was close enough; she, though over thirty-six, was not far off. Practically and technically I was no match for her, but then which man is for a woman who really likes it? That is why wise old mothers in the wise old days sat round telling good little girls they should endure it and not enjoy it. That was the best way to avoid disappointment.

It was at moments like this that I missed Jagdeep. I had learnt some of his technique, but I had to be in the mood. The Shree's true disciples were supposed to be above the vagaries of mood, and Jagdeep certainly was. And that was another thing. Shakti would just not talk about Jagdeep. I thought that was wrong. After all she couldn't have lived with him for nearly ten years without feeling something for him, even though the relationship was not entirely monogamous on either side. But she just would not talk about him. I told her what Freud would have said, but she wouldn't rise to the bait, and that is saying something. At the time it made me very jealous and very angry. I should have been grateful. I have since met a barrage of women who do nothing else but talk of their ex, either run him down to the gates of hell, or make him out to be a candidate for ascension.

She brought in a *whole jugful* of freezing cold yukky lemon tea. I shuddered as I began to untie my shoelaces.

Oh well, if that's how you feel about it, she hissed, and went out. I was sure she hadn't seen me shudder. I wondered, and worried.

Much later on I found out that she had discovered that when I began by unbuttoning my shirt I was in a romantic mood; when I began by unzipping my trousers I was just randy; when I began by taking her blouse off I was wildly passionate; when I began by putting my hand up her knickers I was again randy but not fully prepared; when I let her remove my clothes I was lazy and sensuous; when I began by biting her ears I was in a reflective and thoughtful state of mind; and when I began by untying my shoelaces I was bored and reluctant. Heavens, what that woman knew. Even I did not know I had so many moods, and so many manifestations thereof, and all of them relating just to diurnal drawing room sex! She had worked out a much more subtle and complex signal system for when we were already in bed at night. She might have let me in on it earlier! Would have spared us so many needless quarrels and arguments.

You must have gathered by now that Shakti and I were having a wham bang of a time in Los Angeles. Our life was a series of volatile encounters: sexual (graded), intellectual (acrid), or hysterical (plain), with periods in between of blissful emptiness, communicative silence, and a rest-giving, peace-giving togetherness of the kind which holds and points the building blocks of any relationship in the strongest and most effective manner. What went wrong then? Perhaps the blocks themselves were weak, of defective material, made with faulty workmanship.

In many ways we represented the contradictions within the turbulent life of the city itself. I know that sensitive intelligent and beautiful people are not supposed to refer to good old LA as a city, but a collection of bla bla blas, but to a common lout from a backward country any place with a properly metalled road or two, a few groups of houses and a couple of large shops is a city. By those standards LA certainly qualified. The size of the population bore me out. As to whether it had a cathedral or was the seat of a bishop, I was still making inquiries. I couldn't be sure if it had a centre, a heart, a core or not, but did I have any of those myself? I called it a city, and a marvellous city at that. Don't pay any attention to those who whinge and whine about the smog and the characterless, congested freeways. Anyone who does not find the combination of a barren desert and luscious greenery, of rising and falling hills and interminable stretches of sand and sea, of a staggering variety of the human species all just about tolerating each other, caught between man-made paradisiacal extravaganzas and man-made hell-holes, between Disneyland and Watts, between artificial glitzy lights and the squalors of poverty, between the glamour and glory and disintegration of Hollywood triumphs and the horrors and desperations and disintegration of Hollywood failures, between the glut of riches and the glut of misery, the emptiness of riches and the fullness of misery, the cluttered nothingness of material affluence and the hungry clutter of material deprivation – anyone who does not find all that utterly and repellingly fascinating, and describes it as nothing more than smoggy dreariness, has no heart or centre or core. Perhaps I have the whole country in mind, seat of a bishop or not. Perhaps I have the wrong country in mind. But never mind.

A Darshan A Bhakti A Nirtak

Death is another day. That explains its fascination for those who are having a rotten today. I should know, having fallen for its magic, lived through it, and returned to the day before.

But why does it frighten people so, even those of us not having a heck of a time just now? Why does it frighten me, someone who has witnessed a parade of deaths, from the death of total strangers to that of parents and children; someone so experienced in dying and death – devoured by the angry tiger, stung by the almighty cobra, sucked in by the timeless cactus, killed by life or lack of it; someone who has more than once craved death, longed for it with the sickness of a mother longing for a lost child?

It is my thirty-fifth birthday today. As I stand with my back against one cold stone wall, painted a pale cream, looking at the cold stone wall opposite, painted a pale cream, framing the tiny barred window that lets in the early morning rays of a pleasantly warm first day of the first month of the new year, I can see the shadow of my Naga forming itself over my naked body, blacker than the blackness of my skin, more vibrant and more alive than all the cells in it, beckoning, calling, demanding, sucking its poison back out of my heart. And I know that this will be the last birthday on which I will see the sun rise and then see it set again. A strange, unaccountable sadness envelops my being, like a cold white shroud wrapping itself round the warm body of a child even as he plays beside the favourite river of his imagination in the cherished field of his desire.

It is depressing anyway to look back upon a time that is no more, especially a time which, for all its pains and problems, had a certain romantic, once-in-a-lifetime glow surrounding it, like an aura of sanctity that gives some sort of meaning and substance to an otherwise profane and hollow existence. If, while looking back at such a past, you look up and quite unexpectedly find yourself staring at a future which promises certain death – not at once, which might be welcome; nor after an unspecified period of time, which is everybody's future; but on the next birthday, neither near enough to signal relief nor far enough away to be ignored – the combination can leave you feeling weak and sweaty.

I slithered slowly down the cold stone wall till I came to squat on my haunches and heels, rested my elbows on my knees and my head in my hands, and began to sob. Like a foolish, frightened little child. And on my thirty-fifth birthday! Just as I had done on my twenty-first birthday. Only then I had an erection, and the angle of my member matched exactly the angle of my squatting thighs as it lay proudly parallel between the two, its stupid knob, also in tears, aspiring vainly to be another knee between knees. How awkward and foolish I must have looked. I wouldn't have blamed Shakti if she had burst out laughing, but she just left the room.

That was the day I was finally convinced that it was all over between me and Shakti.

Today is the day I am finally convinced that it is all over between me and life.

Shakti's walking out of the room hurt – still hurts. I should have seen it coming. Instead I was busy planning for a lifetime together, having decided in my mind to make the ultimate sacrifice: offer myself in marriage to Shakti. What an utter idiot I must have been. I was so sure she would be thrilled. What were my motives? I tried to think that her money was not an important reason, that to a wanderer at heart and a vagabond in mind and body a couple of houses in LA and a few hundred thousand bucks in the bank would only be an encumbrance. But if that was what Shakti wanted, then I would be willing . . . What a brainless, vacuous, unoccupied asshole.

Strange how everything suddenly becomes clear when death stares you in the eye for one sunlit shimmer of a moment's wing.

I picture myself getting dressed up in my best gear: a white crocheted vest, my prize possession, knitted by Mother and once Junior's, which had somehow managed to travel with me all these years; wide bell-bottom trousers made of a soft, light blue denim; a rather tight, short-sleeved bush-shirt hanging loose above them, bright red in colour; and huge platform shoes, off-white, adding another six inches or so to my six-foot plus. I had washed my collar-length hair three times over to get it as grease-free and light as possible, and would look into every glass window I passed to see if it was bobbing up and down or not. The fact that I had an ugly face, and knew it, didn't stop me from being terribly vain. And I can't blame it on my youth at the time, for I still am. Even when I was half dead, half dying to die, half living, half wasting away on the piss-washed pavement of the Embankment in London I remember trying to clean my crumbling face and comb my straggling hair.

I was going to walk down to the intersection of Lake Drive and Altadena Avenue to catch the RTD 423, get off at neighbouring Pasadena and buy it there, it being an engagement ring. Or I could hop on to another bus bound for one of the shopping centres downtown where I felt more at home, Broadway or thereabouts. Or maybe I would carry on to Long Beach. I had never been there. The name sounded good. There were sure to be some jewellers there.

It was hot and humid and I was uncomfortable in my tight shirt, but glad that the trousers were loose and flappy. The feel of three hundred dollars in my pocket was good, the best feel of money I had had since the first fifty paisa I earned carrying packs of bricks for one whole day back in Chandan, helping to rebuild the wall outside the local granary after the rainstorm in which we lost our house. I had earned these three hundred dollars as well, taking the van round to people's houses and doing odd jobs, mainly gardening. Of course the van had been bought with Shakti's money, and so had the tools, but I had worked hard. That day was going to be all the fruit of my own labour, which was why I was not going in Shakti's van but walking and bussing it using my very own money. Would I have made it without Shakti's money? Well, I could have got work somewhere. Even though I didn't have a green card I did have a social security number, and I knew many who managed on just that. As Shakti's husband I would get the right to work legitimately, and the right to US citizenship. I tried not to think of all that. I wanted my motives for the marriage to be as pure as possible.

The geometrically intersecting roads were completely deserted, except for the occasional car. Why did walking seem like a crime? I tried not to hunch my shoulders and look guiltily down at the rapidly moving tarmac between my strides. On either side the deep green hedges, tall and thick and leafy with tangled branches, sent out a hot, steamy scent which mingled with the hot, steamy sweat of my defensively aggressive body as it asserted its right to transport itself from point A to point B without the use of man-made wheels. I kicked a loose pebble or two about and hop-skipped a bit. A thin black woman, small with greying hair tied in a taut, curly bun above the nape of her neck, looked at me with wide white eyes, arms crossed over her shrinking bosom, one foot ahead of the other and cautiously tapping on the gravel in her driveway. I grinned a big grin, jumped twelve feet up in the air and waved my arms about. For a split-second she jerked back, not sure what to make of me. Most people weren't. I have black Negroid skin with features which are neither obviously Negroid nor really Indian; I am neither brown nor red, neither mulatto nor any other determinable mixture, and certainly not Hispanic or Mexican. But she rallied soon, grinned broadly back, jumped fifteen foot in the air and waved her arms about shouting, Lord bless you, my son, have a rib-tickling, gut-cracking day! Oh *Mom*, I heard somebody shout from behind her, and then came the sound of footsteps. I didn't wait to see who turned up beside her to pull her inside. I don't know whether the Lord blessed me or not, and I certainly didn't have a rib-tickling, gut-cracking day, but I shall always remember that small black woman with gratitude and pleasure for as long as I shall live, be it just another birthday or a hundred more.

The humidity was broken slightly by a rather pleasant breeze, which started up gently but soon accelerated, bringing clouds, then a light shower, then a heavy downpour. What better way to hail in the New Year?

I had left Shakti, or Martha as she was called by then, sleeping off the effects of the previous night's partying, and I was only half way to the bus stop when a sudden fear cropped up in my heart that all shops might be shut. I needn't have worried. I was in America, not Europe. Nothing here could be allowed to come in the way of making an extra buck or two.

The night had been my best New Year's Eve ever. I spent all the time watching 1975 being hailed in over and over again in the different time zones. It felt strange still to be in the old year while New York was well into the new. Shakti said I was being really boring and stupid, not to mention childish, nay, babyish – she almost said baboonish. It was a slip of the tongue but she blushed a very red blush, mistakenly believing that, being black, I would be angry and hurt at any reference to monkeys. Actually I love them. Besides, I was too excited by the repeated announcements of a Happy New Year dawning to care. I sat glued to the set, changing channels, waiting for the next new year which would be the same new year. I know there were only three or four, but at the time it seemed like a hundred to me. I suppose drink has a habit of multiplying images and sounds. I just couldn't get over the thrill of it all. I ignored all the guests and didn't even dance. Normally I love to dance.

Now was as good a time to dance as any.

The floor beneath me is getting wet today, on my thirty-fifth birthday, just as the road beneath was on my twenty-first. I look down, somewhat surprised. Where can this wetness be coming from? It isn't water, but milk. The milk of Umrao. The milk Mother had been milking just before I was born.

Not only is the floor covered in Umrao's milk, the floor is Umrao's milk. And her blood. The blood which had once covered the floor of our verandah and which poor Father had so desperately and unsuccessfully tried to wash away. Pure white and pure red, side by side. Milk and blood, mingled but not mixed, each retaining its character and viscosity and colour.

With a reverberating crash the roof burst wide open and a black thundery sky appeared above my head. It started to pour down with the heaviest of rains I have ever experienced in my life; stronger than the ones which brought down our house and brought over the helpful police who enjoyed the tight virginity of Aunt Neelum. The day was turned to night, illuminated only by crackling flashes of streak lightning. But not all the water that flooded down diluted Umrao's milk and blood which were the floor upon which I danced.

I was no longer naked. Jewel-studded scarlet and gold garments girded my loins and draped my shoulders, leaving my arms, thighs and feet bare and exposed. My head was ringed with a gold crown, its lustrous yellow surface burnished and bright, bursting out with huge pimples of diamonds and rubies. Clusters of bells were strapped round my ankles and wrists.

My feet pounded the floor as the Dance Master pounded the beat, on the taut tabla and with his taut voice: *One two three four. Tha thayya tha tha, tha thayya tha*, I danced. *Tha thathayya tha, tha thathayya tha*, I danced. *Dha dhir dhir dhir dheray na, dha dhir dhir dhir dheray na, thayya tha, thayya tha, thayya tha* . . . The balls of my feet and the heels of my feet alternated with electric rapidity as I moved in powerful rhythmic steps all over the milk and the blood which extended from horizon to horizon. My hands opened and shut in quick-slow motion, like musical notes. *Sa ray ga ma pa dha ni sa, sa ray ga ma pa dha ni sa, sa sa sa sa ray gaaaa ma padhanisa, padhanisa, padhanisa*. The tabla strokes went wild but the Dance Master's voice held pace with it, the bells clamoured for freedom but my feet kept the beat oblivious to their pleas. Soon I had broken through the confines of the horizon and my ecstatic steps were encircling the world, the rhythm and the beat following rather than leading me. *Tha thayya tha tha, dha dhir dhir dheray na, sa ray ga ma padhanisa, padhanisa, padhanisaaaa . . .* I was now surrounded by a host of dancing girls, their arms undulating like waves, like my arms, like a pillowy breeze blowing through ruffles of satin and silk with the grace of the serpent.

It was then, even as the first notes of the insistent melody of the pipe and the flute spun me into a god-like trance, I saw that I was the king cobra, and they were dancing the snake dance for me as I danced the human dance for them. The power of the Naga's poison coursing through my heart was now maturing, its development time nearing its peak. It tied up with my impending death. I would have no further need for this life and its pains, mine would be life immortal and pain everlasting.

I could have done anything then. Flown out of the prison, for there wasn't one any more, turned into Hanuman, or remained Cyrus Cyrus, convict and Satanist, murderer and child-killer, evil incarnate. I chose to be the last. The time was not yet ripe. Suffering had not yet been crowned with thorns nor nailed to the cross. Great Grandmother sat in Shiva's lap. Man the son, Man the father, and the spirit of Brahma stood guard over her, while the muezzin called the faithful to prayer and Aphrodite swayed rhythmically, surrounded by bacchae in the temple of Apollo. Shakti Borgia lay naked on a silver and pearl couch scratching at Jagdeep's ritually exposed penis, raking out blood and semen from that beleaguered weapon of flesh.

I continued to dance.

And dance.

My eyes danced my fingers danced my toes danced; every muscle of my body every pore of my skin every drop of my sweat every corpuscle of my blood every gamete of my semen danced.

Martha Devi appeared by my side, dressed in a rainbow cotton sari, sindoor glistening orange-red through the parting of her long black hair, and began to dance as Cyrus removed his vestments and went over naked to Shakti Borgia and offered his penis to her claws of steel.

My neck began to swell and flare out until it encompassed my head and formed a deadly black hood, the brutally severed head of my Naga, which swayed with lethal grace from side to side and backward and forward to the trance-inducing rhythm of the pipe and the mesmerising music of the flute. My Naga's body, glistening black beneath my royal adornments, followed with an ecstatic bravura of its own.

† † †

Shakti, heavily made-up and over-dressed, was sitting on the couch, legs tightly crossed, reading *The National Enquirer* and watching television.

I was Cyrus once again, lying on the cold stone floor, naked and exhausted and ashamed.

What makes you think I would want to marry you? Or any man! I could hear Shakti's voice breaking through the barriers of time and space. But you said you wanted to settle down, I hissed back, hardly believing my ears. What's that got to do with anything? She seemed surprised but not as surprised as I was. I thought it had everything to do with it, but at the time I knew nothing about women and marriage. But you said you loved me, I whined. Of course I do, can't you see that's why it is so important *not* to get . . . No, I can't see. Could it be because you think you can't get a divorce from Jag . . . She gave a curt laugh. Could it be because you . . . still . . . *love* him? Shakti gave a long hurt laugh. Couldn't see what she had to be hurt about. Couldn't see anything. Eyes filling up with tears. You are such a baby, you need a mother, not a – But I haven't got a mother, she's fucked up and cut up and . . . and . . . I cannot have a mother, not another . . . I was both screaming and sobbing by then. I know you can't have one, but you *want* one, you want commitment, a sure sign of immaturity and harking back to childhood. You want the commitment of a mother to a child. Maturity, growing up, means freedom

– freedom to choose, to travel, to experiment, to live, to fuck. Commitment means going back, back as far back as the womb . . .

That brought back memories of my birth, and of the pain of separation and of the hurt of rejection and of the fear of choices and of the dread of options; and, most of all, of the loss of commitment. I knew she was right.

But you said you wanted to settle down, was all I could mutter under my breath. Now, she said, *now* I want to settle down, what I'll want tomorrow I do not know. Besides, I said settle down, not die and be buried. She laughed a hoarse laugh. So getting married to me is dying. Not to *you*, getting married period. Understand? Comprehend? It's because I'm black, that's it, because I'm black . . .

We were both shouting at the same time now: Don't be pathetic . . . Your precious family . . . Fuck my family . . . Couldn't get a hard-on . . . Telling me . . . Money . . . You think I want your . . . Pathetic, pathetic, pathetic . . . Black black black . . . Poor little black boy wants a mother, poor little . . . Shut up, shut up, SHUT UP . . . Poor little black boy wants a mother, poor li'l black boy wants a motherrr, poooor li'l black boy . . .

† † †

How could she say that to me if she loved me? Did she love me any more? Did she ever love me? Did I love her?

† † †

The insistence of the pipes and the lure of the flutes and the hammering of the tabla and the commands of the Dance Master crescended.

I was left with no option but to get up off the floor, put on my crown, don my gold and jewel inlaid garments, and dance.

The harmony of the music clashed with a different set of sounds, cacophonic sounds, as of ghosts clattering and clanging in deserted dungeons looking for their long-lost souls.

Barry unlocks the cell, kicks the door open and bursts in, swearing furiously. In the split-second before George follows him, Barry's pink-white face turns to chalk-white putty and his eyes drop to the floor and his mouth opens wide to scream but remains open wide as a blown-up mine without any scream emerging.

So what the fucking hell is going on here, screams George, not noticing his mate's petrifaction. Come on, come on, where have you hidden it? Where the fuck is it, and no nonsense otherwise I'll plug your asshole with my truncheon and lose this key here and leave you to rot till kingdom come!

Seeing his mate's composure, Barry recovers his. Yes where is it, mo . . . mo . . . motherfuck . . . fucker. He is still having difficulty with his consonants, but he does remember that though I never react to their taunts, the ones that disturb me most have to do with sexual adventures involving my mother.

All that racket, continues George, bagpipes and drums and that, everybody in the hall can hear you, where in cunt's name have you . . . Come on, bend over, bend over I said. I bet it is that fucking priest.

Watch your mouth, says Barry, speaking coherently. It's more likely the other one, the weasly poofter. Never trust these writers, doing nothing all day long, laying around with a pen stuck up their assholes.

And put some clothes on, you fucking black savage. George forcefully boots the part he has been rummaging through for the radio. I'll fucking have to have a holy bath now, he says, twisting his face as I hit the wall opposite. Barry is busy turning the room over, only too glad to be busy doing something so as not to have to think.

You'll have nothing to eat but meat and more meat – which basically means I'll have nothing to eat – till I say otherwise, hisses George under his breath, even though he knows he can't really carry out the threat, or not for long, I hope.

Barry suddenly gives up the search, throws his arms in the air and turns to George. There's no point in all this, he is the Devil, I tell you, he is the Devil. His voice is a question, a doubt, a fear, despite the certainty of his words. I can feel his soul quiver inside his body. I have never seen him like this before. I would put my arms round him and hold him close, if I thought he'd let me.

The Man came over to me and put his arms round me and held me close. I could smell Great Grandmother. It was a nice smell. I wished he'd take me back into the tiger.

A Chance An Inevitability

Six months later I was on the freeway hitching a lift east to New York. Shakti was in her room, silent, motionless, tearless.

I should have taken the shiny red VW Beetle she had bought for my birthday. I might not be lying on the cold prison floor today if I had. If you change one little thing in your past, it can change your entire future. I wish I had taken that shiny red VW Beetle. I'll never be able to do that now. I'll never find another woman like Shakti now.

She was to be mother of my first-born, one of her many children, though I was not to know.

I suppose it was inevitable that we would part, though it was a chance encounter which brought it about.

I was at one of the stalls in Olvera Street, trying out a richly colourful poncho and a broader than broad Mexican hat. Shakti was around somewhere looking for an eating place which would do some vegetarian stuff for me while she enjoyed her chili-what-have-you. It was a hot, dry day with the threat of a wind gathering up in the atmosphere. I could smell myself and other people and the buttons and the tassels and the colours on the clothes and the concrete beneath my feet and the stillness in the air. An oddly familiar smell filtered through the drifting breaths of the gaggling crowd around me and assailed my nostrils, softly, gradually, strikingly: a smell of flesh and sweat and desire, a smell of hunger and anger and hate, a smell of urgency and tension and waiting. A smell of pungent after-shave and vapid beer, a smell of both long and short hair, a smell of lips and testicles and armpits. A sexual partner? It was. Partner and rival, Jagdeep.

You stinking black hole of Calcutta, he smiled pleasantly, bringing his face close to mine, your days are numbered, the end is nigh, and it will not be a pleasant end, I am pleased to say. His lips were practically touching mine, Shree Ramnath is going to India for a month, and Jaggu is just waiting for the day, waiting to get you and take you to White Sands and explode the latest atomic bomb up your black ass.

I had never seen him look like that or smile like that or talk like that. He used to be my friend.

What about Shakti? was all I could bring myself to say. The flickering fire that came to light itself in his eyes at the mention of the name explained his attitude, not that I needed the explanation.

What about her! he nearly screamed, fists clenched and raised. Restraining himself, he released his fists, let his arms hang tensely by his side, turned his face away and said, Depends on . . . where she is when you . . . you get yours. If she has the good sense to be well away from you by then, which I hope she has, then . . . But if she is anywhere near you when, then . . .

What if I go to the police and tell them how you hold people against their will, try to kill them, threaten them, and all the rest. I bet your Shree wouldn't be pleased about the investigations that would follow. The fact that he didn't interrupt me rather took the wind out of what I was saying.

Go ahead and do it, he replied after about a minute's silence. See what Martha — this was the first time ever I had heard him call Shakti by the name Martha — has to say about it first, though. His point was well taken. I *had* mentioned it to Shakti once or twice before and she had gone all silent on me. Besides, he continued with sinister mildness, we have such a huge turnover. More people leave than join. You haven't a leg to stand on. I'm not talking of just any people, I said, I'm talking of people like me, slaves – This time he did interrupt. Don't moan about it then, go ahead and try. I'm sure your friends will be very pleased to get the opportunity of having their passports and papers checked. With this he walked away, turning back and looking straight into my eyes for one final time before disappearing in the crowd.

I didn't have much time to think about either his look or his words before Shakti turned up.

Was Jagdeep here? she said.

How on earth did she know! I suppose the *very* close physical contact that members of the TLM have with one another, coupled with the meditative silences, eyes closed and ears out of the reach of any noise, leads to the development of a high degree of olfaction. We begin to experience the presence of people and objects with our noses without even realising it. The hearing too gets more acute as less and less reliance is placed upon the eyes for cognition. The brain gets sharper . . . I am beginning to sound like one of our publicity brochures. Not ours any more, theirs. Can you sense a pang of remorse somewhere here, a feeling of loss, of damage done?

Was he? she repeated. The look in her eyes decided it for me. It was made up of the same flickering fire that I had seen in his eyes. Whether or not she was married to him, she was certainly in love with him. She had not fallen in love with me, she had just had an affair. She had not wanted to leave him, she had just wanted a change. More than that, she had been so afraid of being cast out for being old that she had decided to run off with a youth and whatever was left of her youth. She was proving something to herself, to him, to them – not to me. I was just a means.

I would have risked a nuke up my ass for her, but there was no point in endangering her life when she didn't even love me. A number of things which weren't making sense suddenly began to add up. They were all part of a picture, and I wasn't in it, even though I had been instrumental in its creation.

I left a note by the bedside in the tradition of the truly tragic Hollywood heroine and walked out of the house in Altadena one middle of the night not long after.

Aunt Verna was more than right. I was *manhoos*, even after all those years and beyond all those distances, and would continue to remain a mortal danger to anyone foolish enough to love me – in howsoever temporary or temporal a way – or cast their lot with me. My family had no choice, Shakti had. I had no right to ruin her life or mar her happiness or play with her future.

I wanted so much to hold Doctor Prashad's hands and tell him how sorry I was for what happened to him and how much I missed him and ask his advice about this and that. He always knew how to comfort you and what to say or do to make you feel better.

A Confirmation A Denial

I had always imagined New York would be like Chandan, and it was.

More like a dream-and-nightmare Chandan than the real Chandan, but Chandan nonetheless. I felt there the same heady excitement and the same dreaded fears that I felt when I was an infant and a child within the tight, overcrowded streets of Chandan; the same energising yet enervating confusion of emotions and sensations at the overspilling hustle and bustle of wheeling and dealing big business centred round the shops and the granaries and moving outwards towards the station and into the rest of the world – or what I thought of as the rest of the world; the same resurgence of sensual and intellectual poetry in the blood, the same abundance of actual and mythical imagery in the atmosphere, the same wave of carnal and carnival revelry that deluged my senses, invaded my soul and rained upon my brain while crouching under the table immersed in the dramas and tragedies and turbulences and joys and ecstasies experienced through the books in Sister Erin's library in Chandan.

It was a magical dream come true, cut with nightmare visions of a city built on putrefying flesh and cancerous bones, and inhabited by humans made of tarnished steel and spalled brick.

After some unsuccessful attempts at hitch-hiking I decided to take the Greyhound bus. It was freezing cold inside, burning hot outside. Even the thick glass of the never-ending windows, heavily into blue like the temperature within, couldn't disguise the white-hot heat through which we cut at red-hot speed. This heat spread all around the shooting bus like boiling steam, over and across the limitless expanse of the once free and still marvellously majestic and impossibly beautiful land – land conquered, colonised and ravished yet proud, unbowed and unbeaten, unlike its erstwhile children.

I was sliding low in my seat, leafing through a bunch of *Newsweeks* and some other magazines I had picked up by walking casually into and discreetly out of a few selected waiting rooms and reception areas. I had hunched my shoulders in an attempt to conserve the warmth of my body, and was wondering whether I would look too much of a fool if I took my pullover out of my bag and put it on. Nobody would have given a damn, or if they had, I shouldn't have given a damn, but I still wondered.

We were passing through the vast plains of Texas, somewhere between El Paso and Dallas, and heading towards Arkansas. I hadn't yet made up my mind whether to drop off somewhere, look around, kip on the road or under a railway bridge or in one of the Greyhound bus stations, and restart the journey the following day – I had one of those open tickets which allow you the freedom – or to continue right up to Dallas and enjoy the place which marked the turning-back point in American history. It really depended on whether or not a particular town or landscape caught my fancy. Frankly, it was all too much. Every stretch had its breathtaking grandeur, every turn its myriad of surprises, every 'flat and boring' one-gas-station town its own still and silent mystery. I could have spent a million lifetimes lost in each square mile of this great Kingdom of Heaven which still stubbornly refused to yield entirely to the Kingdom of Mammon so rigorously and remorselessly imposed upon it.

It was just past the hour of noon, as far as the sun was concerned. Clockwise, Mountain Time had just turned to Central Time, and I was not sure which was which. We were supposed to be stopping somewhere soon for lunch and refreshments, either at one of those sloppy bus places, or at the posh truckers' stops. I preferred the former. Felt more at home there.

The seat next to mine was empty – in fact the whole bus was practically empty. This made me feel exposed, and the feeling that every available eye was fixed on my every move seemed to take a more and more determined hold on my gut. At least one pair of eyes was certainly directed towards me, of that I was certain. You know how it is when somebody is looking at you, somehow you can't help becoming aware of it. It is as if the gaze penetrates your flesh and touches some primitive nerve centre which sounds a warning bell saying, Predator approaching! Or something to that effect.

I could not control my curiosity or my nerve any longer, and craned my neck slightly to the left and upwards, towards where I could feel the signals emanating. No one was even sitting there, much less sitting there watching me. Both disappointed and relieved, I was in the process of adjusting my head back to an angle suitable for reading when I met these two over-large hazel eyes staring out at me from a thin bony face surrounded by a mass of thick brown hair and with two very full, very orange lips slap dash in the middle of it. She could have been under twenty or nearer thirty, it was difficult to tell. All you could see were eyes, hair and lips – there was not much else to see – and all three can be trained to take away or add on years.

I got back to my magazines, feeling quite pleased with myself for being an object of interest to an attractive white girl; but also uncomfortable, not sure how to react. It would have been stupid or arrogant, probably both, to read too much into it. I was nervous and unsure of myself anyway. These were my first days on my own in the white man's world, without Shakti or anyone else to back me up and to guide me on how to act in given or unexpected situations. There was also a certain nagging doubt in my mind, as if something was not quite right. Perhaps she had mistaken me for someone else. The more I thought about it the angrier I got with myself for thinking about it. After all, there was hardly anything to think about. I am sure I would have been able to dismiss the whole trivial matter without too much difficulty or anguish were it not for the fact that I continued to get this strong signal reaching out to me from somewhere through the top of my skull.

At least I didn't feel cold any more. In fact I was beginning to sweat.

But I was determined not to look her way again. I didn't want to make a fool of myself and be a bad ambassador for my colour and my country, though I wasn't quite sure which was my country – India, Pakistan or Bangla Desh. Most people here thought I was a black American or an African of some sort. I was beginning to get a bit confused myself. Did it matter? I mean, did it *really* matter!

It was then that Shree Ramnath and his techniques for emptying out the mind came to my rescue. I had never before felt the desire to apply them to the everyday problems of existence. In fact I had given up all practice since leaving the Ashram, though on occasions I missed the becalming, uplifting influence of the meditative process, despite having developed a deliberate and cynical resistance towards it based on my understandable aversion for the whole period of my life associated with the TLM. Strange, that, for in many ways it was the best period of my life, and remains so to this day. Strange too that I sought refuge in what I had learnt over such a meaningless matter as being looked at by a pretty girl in a Greyhound bus, whereas when I was going through painfully troubled times in my relationship with Shakti I did not once call upon those inner resources of mine for strength and sustenance. But then Shakti was all too deeply involved with that whole business, and I couldn't learn to separate one from the other, although I did try.

It came as a shock when the bus wheeled itself into this grand car park surrounding a shopping and showering and eating complex – truckers' stop – and came to a halt. All started scrambling to their feet to get out into the open and onto solid ground, and to stretch the limbs, stuff the oesophagus, air the ass and relieve the bladder.

No matter how wonderful the facilities on the bus, nothing beats the pleasures of urinating openly in a public convenience surrounded by the free flow of the goodwill of one's fellow men. Whatever the superiorities of the woman's penis over the man's, it can never rival the mere male tool when it comes to this primary yet pluralist function: physical, mental, personal, social, and unerringly moral; not to mention olfactory, aural, visual and tactile. The feel of the firm smooth tube in one's hand; the random glance, casual yet furtive, at the neighbour's member – massive, minuscule, or just boring, a possible threat or a source of amusement, held out openly and brazenly or covertly hidden beneath outstretched fingers or cupped within the hand; the sight of the steaming jet of the golden fluid, aimed high, low or medium; the sibilant diffusion of hissing, swishing, gurgling sounds; the terse acidic odours vibrating past the navel vibrissae to the nasal vibrissae; the final tug at the skin and the pressured flicks and jerks before tucking the jet-propelling shaft back in and away and adjusting the crotch. No woman could ever experience the elemental joys of this exclusive social event. Solemn and sacrosanct, it is yet relieved occasionally by offered or received fellatio (frail to fierce) or buggery (bungling to burgling) by the odd cock-coveting or hole-hungry homologous soul, thus completing the gamut of senses – the fifth exercised and the sixth required for the successful accomplishment of this finale of phallic feats.

I don't know why I am saying all this. I hate going into public urinals. So embarrassing and uncouth. Totally uncivilised. All those men so shamelessly and unceremoniously arrayed and displayed. Private parts and private functions need private quarters, not social collectivism but personal space – internal through meditation, external in the wide unending expanse of the country, the two kinds of space forming the essence and spirit of India. Open air ventilation and heat disinfection. To be able to contemplate as well as urinate – none of the rush rush, wait your turn, in and out madness of the thoughtless West. A secluded spot of your own choice, often green, leafy and pleasant, under the shade of a banyan tree if possible.

I always hang around waiting for a lavatory to be vacant, and some of *them* are exposed! Not to speak of being utterly filth-ridden. Yuk, and double yuk.

Now I remember why I am saying all this. I desperately wanted to go. In my meditative trance I had forgotten all about bodily needs. Now it was too late to go in the bus, so I would have to go in one of those places.

It took me a while to emerge from the trance and adjust myself to the here and now. I couldn't see the girl among the passengers making their way out. She must have left fast. By the time I got to the door, the enormous driver had just started to roll himself out of his little cubicle. He was around seven feet tall, and must have had at least a sixty-inch waist. I bet he was looking forward to his free lunch. And it is not true that all Greyhound buses are driven by the same man.

Just as I was getting off, I happened to glance back . . . felt impelled to glance back. On the third row of seats behind the driver, by the window, where I had encountered the gaze of the big-eyed girl, sat a golden-haired, blue-eyed boy of about fourteen years of age. His eyes cut through mine with an intensity which comes only from intimacy over a period of centuries, however intermittently experienced during the intercourse of one's respective karmas and dharmas through the cycles of incarnation. Whether he had been there all along, and I had not seen him because he was too small for his head to stick up above the level of the seats, or whether he had joined the bus at some later stage when I might have dropped off to sleep or was in a self-induced trance, I could not be sure. But I was now sure that it was he, and not the girl, who had been looking at me, whether on board the bus at the time or not.

He was my son, or my father; my wife, or my husband; my lover, or my brother; or just me. He was the boy I had so wanted to hold in my arms that fateful day at the Chandan railway station.

I did not look back again. If we were destined to meet, we would. I was not going to tempt providence again, for his sake if not for mine.

I divided my time, after the unedifying essential visit, between enjoying the absolute stillness and silence of the white heat outside the built-up area, and wandering around in the cool within, having snippets of conversation with fellow passengers and eating heavily buttered bread and one of those interminable American salads, preceded by a large glass of fruit juice and followed by an even larger glass of milk. I could not see the girl anywhere.

There were still about fifteen minutes of our rest time left when I saw the girl come out of a glitzy gift shop, freeze for an instant on seeing me, and then, with a restrained urgency in her eyes and the muscles of her face belying her calm and laid-back movements, started walking in my direction.

She was so close to me that I thought we were going to collide. We did, before I could move out of the way. She pressed something in my hand, before I could react. She moved quickly away, before I could protest.

It felt firm and heavy and greasy. I looked down. It was a large, black leather wallet, full of hundreds of notes, tens and twenties and fifties and hundreds! Like a fool I kept it in my open palm, ogling it idiot-eyed for I do not know how long before hurriedly forcing it down the front of my jeans and running after the girl. She was nowhere to be seen.

A sound of running footsteps behind me made me jump, but they ran past me – they being a tall man in his thirties wearing a blue suit, a young man of about eighteen in shorts with a badge stuck to his shirt, and an official-looking person with greyish black hair in a greyish black uniform. I thanked my star (Saturn, for Capricorn – or Umrao as I called her – the goat) but still found it difficult to ease my tensing muscles.

After another moment of paralysis I decided it would be unwise to stay in the shopping area any longer. Moving with as much cautious speed as I could I made my way out and started searching for the coach. I was joined by a strange young woman who interlinked her right arm with my left, smiled pleasantly and said, Not that way, over here.

Too bewildered by the speed and turn of events to resist, I allowed myself to be dragged along for a minute or two before stopping, and forcing the woman to stop. Strange though the world and the ways of the white man, and particularly the white woman, may be, there was just so much I could take, however docile a member of an inferior species like myself should be.

Excuse me, I began. Just keep on walking, she said. Partly it was the urgency in her voice, and partly the surprising strength in her small bony arms, but soon I was again being dragged along towards the opposite end of the car park from where our bus was waiting. To a passer-by it might have been a mildly amusing or perhaps grossly shocking spectacle to see a young black man, tall and sturdily built, being unceremoniously dragged along by a short, thin, dark-haired and near blind white woman.

Of course by then even I had come to realise that it was the girl from the bus. Her eyes, now without the thick black eyeliner that had made them appear so large, now looked small and even squinty behind a pair of spectacles with huge pebble lenses. Her mouth now had a pale, luminescent lipstick on, making the lips disappear rather than stand out, the cheeks were painted much more daringly in a scarlet blush, the hair was almost black, and gamine-ish. She was wearing a black halter top and white shorts, most likely what she had been wearing underneath her loose flowery blouse and long flowery skirt, both of which would be lying in a trash can somewhere in the ladies' toilet, along with the thick brown wig and the six-inch stilettos.

We'll hitch a lift on one of the trucks to Dallas and catch a flight from there. No problem with money now. She smiled, a trifle anxiously. Or Amtrak, if you don't like flying. She didn't sound like most Americans I had met, but she later explained she was from Boston. It was apparently meant to clarify all, so I accepted it as such. My own accent and idiom and understanding of different sorts of English were more confused then, what with Sister Erin's gentle Irish rhythms and Dr Prashad's Indian BBC, a childhood diet of American and British and strangely dubbed Italian films, my recent tour through Europe, my time in laid-back New Mexico, and the months spent in LA among representatives of every race in the world, all talking different languages in all different accents.

They'll start looking for us in the bus, she continued, emphasising the *us*, and they're sure to catch on sooner or later. They might send out warnings to other buses in their fleet, so buses are out, for a while. It will soon be forgotten. Not important enough. So don't worry too much. No big deal, no big worry.

My body, already somewhat prone to producing more than the average supply of sweat, was pumping it out fast and thick, the large sticky drops turning immediately into little icicles despite the heat. I would never make a good James Bond.

How can you see through those thick glasses? was all I could bring myself to say. Oh but I need them, absolutely, can't see a thing without. My contact lenses are in here. She tapped a little red purse with long skinny fingers.

I must get my bag. I disentangled my arm from hers. You must be crazy, you can't have much in that . . . Not much, but what I have, I want. Nobody suspects me, despite your *us*, so wait here. For the first time I could see her getting nervous. The money was still with me. I could just disappear. But she did not argue. I suppose that helped to make up my mind. If she could trust me, I should trust her.

Besides, the boy was there. Fate was telling me to leave him alone this time but I still hoped to see him one last time, desperately . . . He wasn't there. I boarded the bus, quietly removed my bag from under my seat – it had some old photographs and some letters and Junior's crocheted vest which were dearer to me than any worldly possessions I had ever had or was likely to have – and walked back to the girl.

She was talking to the driver of a truck which was so heavily decorated with paints and lights and baubles and bits that it looked like the inside of a mobile temple dedicated to twentieth-century rituals and sacrifices. The driver, untypically slim and youthful, was grinning happily, though his mouth fell open a little wider when he saw her pointing towards my approaching figure. But on the whole he was quite good natured about it all, and even offered us some beer along the way.

† † †

We were on the plane to New York. The wallet had been dumped, the cards destroyed and the money divided up. I got a third. I was divided between not accepting any and asking for a full half, but settled without argument. My own supply of cash, not much to begin with, had been sadly depleted by Greyhound riding.

She was snuggling closer and closer, rubbing her head against my shoulders, her face against my chest, tickling any exposed skin with her tongue. I was going up and down. On the one hand I was roused, on the other I didn't want to. I didn't think it was quite right. We hardly knew each other and Shakti was still very much on my mind. Besides, I couldn't understand it. Why should she want to? I was ugly, and sweaty, and unlucky.

I needed some time and some space. I said Excuse me, and started scrambling to my feet. I hate window seats in planes, you get so blocked in. What now! she said in a pretend-hurt voice. Just need to stretch my legs, I said. She pulled up her knees to let me out, then let go, nearly tripping me over. Hey, listen . . . She held me by the sleeve in mid-exclamatory ejaculation and whispered excitedly, You go down to the bathroom, and I'll meet up with you there. Leave the door unlatched. Don't worry, she continued, reading my face, no one will notice. There's hardly anyone here. The plane was nearly empty, but that was not the point. Don't worry, she repeated.

I suppose I should have point-blank refused to comply, but I was still a bit overawed by white women, especially peculiar ones. Also, I was tempted.

It is very difficult to get rid of a certain Indo-Pakistani variety of puritanism, part racial, part cultural; part Hindu, part Muslim, part Christian: a large part Christian in my case. You have to have a reason: in marriage; or for self-knowledge, self-development and ultimate self-control, as in the Ashram; or as a means of gaining favour or earning a living; in desperate cases, even love; or perhaps being on violent heat; diminished responsibility even. But just like that seemed a bit extreme, especially in an aeroplane toilet, although the fact that the plane was bound for New York could be considered a mitigating circumstance.

We hardly fitted in the toilet. *I* hardly fitted in the toilet.

Half way through she pushed me away against the wall and made me pull it out, reached for her little red purse, fumbled something out of it which I could not see, put it in her mouth, then forced me down on the seat, squatted astride me, brought her mouth to mine, hungrily pried my lips open with hers, forced her tongue between them, began to wiggle it over my tongue. I felt something soft and powdery dissolve in my saliva, and a sharp bitter taste reached down to my throat and up to my nostrils.

It was strangulating and suffocating. I had to get it out of me. I had to get me out of there. Had to fly out on my own. The confines of the toilet, of the plane, of the entire world, were too restrictive. I had to get out. I needed freedom. I needed air. I needed me.

One superhuman effort, of the will and of the heart and of the soul, and I made it. I got rid of my human body and became a bird, a formless, weightless, substance-free bird. I flew free, out of the solid steel enclosure and out of the little porthole window. I flew free over the known world and the unknown, terra incognita and aqua untraversed. I flew free over all the peoples of the world, the chosen ones – pre-ancient, ancient, modern, and post-modern; the rich, the Jews, the whites – and the rejects – the poor, the Gentiles, the non-whites. And I danced.

This was the first time ever I danced.

And I mourned.

I danced and I mourned that the prophecy be denied fulfilment.

> '*We piped for you and you would not dance.*
> *We wept and wailed, and you would not mourn.*'

The pipes sang out and children wept and mothers wailed.

It was easy to mourn.

It wasn't easy to dance.

I did not think I *could* dance.

I don't mean a little bit of flash rock and roll with the girls on a bright floor of a night.

I mean Kathakali and Bharat Natyam and Manipuri, high

up in the skies, jostled by the clouds, buffeted by the winds; on the heads of millions of delicately arranged Cambodian skulls; and millions more beautifully blanched black skeletons; and hundreds of thousands of Semite bodies, alive and maimed, dead and dismembered, yet to come. All rejects and Gentiles, as indeed it should have been and should be and should continue to be and will continue to be for as long as the earth shall spin and the sun rise and men have erections and women labour in childbirth.

It wasn't easy to dance.

I did not think I *could* dance.

But I was left with no option.

The whip of lightning made me jump as it caught my feet. The thunder rolled its drums and forced me to its beat. The hurricane twirled me round and swirled me about.

I danced.

And danced.

And danced.

And I mourned.

Way up in the skies, over ocean and desert and mountain, above town and city and village, I danced. And I mourned.

Dogs too have children.

And swine feel hunger.

The Man danced and mourned with me.

Our lamentations tore through the earth's atmosphere and shattered the stars above and burst the clouds below.

And when the flood waters rose, Noah locked himself into the musical loo. He was English, the loo was Venetian, Mrs Noah was drowned. She had been out searching for a new kitchen.

The waters abated while Noah masturbated and the loo floated for nine months until it came to rest on the crowned head of a very tall lady of stone, severely denting her tiara which was carved out of a sawn-off shit bucket. She was waving a fluffy broom about – either in welcome or admonition, it was difficult to tell – while standing on a tiny island nearly getting her feet wet. She was Aunt Verna. Under her arm she carried a stiff broom and two scooper-shaped tablets containing the two ultimate commandments: Thou shalt not be poor, and Thou shalt not be a communist. For the terrifying and immediate wrath of the righteous God and his righteous governments will visit those who are foolish or stupid or lazy or evil enough to be either or both – visit them with hunger and homelessness, sickness and Contras, death and Mujahideens, holy books and guns, not to mention reporters and television cameras.

And Noah opened the door of the loo and looked out and called for help and was seen by a bald bird with sharp eyes which swooped down to the loo and pulled him out to safety and laid him at the giant lady's stony feet.

There, for three hundred and eighty-three years, eight months, eleven weeks, seven days, nine hours, five minutes and thirty-three seconds, approximately, Noah spent his time in constant copulation with the lady of stone with the body of stone and the heart of stone and the eyes of stone, who was Aunt Verna, resting not even on the Sabbath. And although she had no children of her own when she was flesh and blood, with the new strength of her incarnation as imported rock she gave birth to the entire population of that island and most of the (free) peoples of the (vast) hinterland as well.

And God appeared to them repeatedly in television broadcasts and said: Ye are my new chosen people of the new Holy Land in the New World, and so will be your kith and kin in distant lands, as were your ancestors before ye, and so shall be your descendants after ye. All the rest shall be the new Gentiles from henceforth, and ye know what *they* deserve. And as long as ye shall put gold in my temples, sponsor the right programmes, get good ratings, and finance the right companies and the right countries, I shall honour my part of this post-new covenant and give ye dominion over the other peoples of the world as I gave humans dominion over animals and men over women in the old. And I don't give a prepuce what ye do with yours. Do what ye will with it. Surely if ye want to tell yourselves apart from the rejects ye can do so without taking each others' knickers off and putting the blame on me?

And they listened, for such was the will of the Lord, and they argued, and will continue to argue until the next coming, be it awaited but delayed, or quite unexpected, or unwanted and feared, like the first.

† † †

I danced on regardless.

An Affirmation
An Opportunity An Escape

More flying, but back in a plane this time, heading out of New York. A real flight, too, an escape – to London, England. The opportunity coincided with the necessity, so for once I was lucky. Well, if I hadn't been unlucky in the first place, I would not have needed to escape at all, so the bad luck was still primary. But still . . .

Now that you know about the opportunity and the escape, I come to the affirmation. That took place somewhat earlier, and according to Suzi was mainly responsible for the aftermath. Even I have to admit – though I hate to because of my deep mistrust of anything rational or time-related – that there was a murky sort of logical and chronological progression from one to the other.

It was an affirmation of the innate and (essentially) indestructible beauty and purity of the human condition and the human being – whether you credit it to the unconditioned Brahma and the manifestation of the universal atman in mankind as in all creation; or to the conditioned Brahma and his manifestation as maya or the individual atman in mankind and in all creation; or to God the Father, and the Holy Spirit as present in and available to mankind alone through the intervention of God the Son.

I tended to favour the first option. It is perverse that as a child of the East in the East, and despite the capture of my inner being by the sacred Naga, the bases of my faith and belief rested primarily on Western philosophies and Western mythologies and the Judaic Triology of Middle Eastern religions, while since coming to the West, and after spending time in college libraries in LA and a few weeks of daily visits to the public library in NYC – so objected to by Suzi – my mind and my faith were turning more and more Eastward. Of course, I still could not detach myself absolutely from dualism. (I should explain that the dualism I speak of here is not the dualism which relates to monism or pluralism or even monotheism, but specifically contrasts with non-dualism, and is the dual dualism of Christianity: the dualism of the Creator and the Creation, and the dualism of the power of God and good, and the power of Satan and evil.) And I still clung on to the idea of a personal God, if in a hybrid Hindu/Bharati fashion which left room for both Vishnu and Shiva, Kali and Shakti, Jesus and Naga, me and the Shit Bucket. But the deeper recesses of my personal atman were being dragged towards non-dualism of the absolute sort.

I began to see myself, and God, reflected indefinably yet clearly, as much in a malformed turd as in the glory of the Arizona sunset. Suzi said if I carried on like that I'd end up overdosing myself. I said she was the one supplying, to which she retorted by screwing her face and jabbing her forefingernail into my chest, face and head, and saying, It is what you are putting into your head which is doing it and not what I am putting into your mouth. We never progressed further than that on the issue.

Still, I was only twenty-one, and there was a lot of life (and living) and change (capacity for) in me yet.

Suzi was getting fed up with me sitting in the library 'feeding my head up and blowing my brain out' while she was busy picking pockets and turning tricks to feed our bodies and pay the rent. Not that some items for ingestion provided by her were any less brain-blowing. You might consider her resentment entirely fair, but it wasn't. It was she who had not wanted me to look for a 'normal job' in the first place because it was against her principles to aid and abet 'this rotten society by performing its menial chores so it can go on exploiting the weak and the vulnerable, especially women and blacks'.

Now she wanted me to hustle, but not women, as she did not want any 'rich superbitch getting her bejewelled mitts round your poor supercock and swinging you around Manhattan until it's drained dry and limp forever'. I would have liked to give it a go, but Suzi was dead against. She wanted me to 'roll guys'.

'After all, I do, and don't tell me it's because I'm a woman. If it's good enough for a lady it should be good enough for a man. We're not second class citizens, you know.'

Suzi knew her mind, even if no one else did, and knew how to speak it. I was not too keen on the idea and said I wouldn't know where to start. She sighed deeply and rattled out a number of street numbers, with special reference to certain corners and alleyways. I still managed to look blank and helpless. It sometimes pays to put on the stupid savage act, not that she was fooled. Or even if she was, she did not relent. She sighed again and said she'd show me an easier way, personally. She took me by the hand to a cinema, and said, Go in just before the show. They always need dancers there, and I know you *love* dancing. I had made the silly mistake of telling her about my dance. It said on the wall outside: FLESH AND CHAINS. ALL MALE CAST. YOUNG MALE DANCERS. *LIVE*! And underneath: *Young male dancers required, apply within.*

So I was sent in to apply.

She certainly regretted that moment, and it is not often that Suzi regretted.

I came out of the cinema not long after, white as a buffalo in a flour mill, affirming the beauty, purity, etcetera of the human being, etcetera – you know about it all so I am not going into it again – and declaring myself totally unworthy of the job and the moral and spiritual responsibilities it entailed. For a moment Suzi was dumbstruck, a phenomenon rarer than the appearance of Halley's Comet. Her jaw moved, her lips parted, even her tongue moved, but no words came out. Then her eyes squinted and the brittle hardness asserted itself. Now what in the name of Mary Antoinette's cunt . . . If I had said that she would have called me a sexist pig.

I explained. Or tried to.

I am too tainted by guilt, I said, to do my clients justice. To give them what they really want, one has to be pure and innocent and open and joyous and above all guilt-free. Or else the whole relationship is sullied, its purpose destroyed. What on earth . . . she interrupted. No no no. Let me finish. To give pleasure, no, not just pleasure, happiness, to give happiness, to another human being is a big responsibility, in some ways the biggest. It is not sin that kills, but guilt . . . Suzi cut in again: Oh my God, she wailed, what am I going to do with you? If you don't want to work, why don't you simply say so? Men men men. Never an honest one among them. After publicly fucking around for all these years . . . I had told her about the Ashram. However, 'publicly fucking around' was not quite fair. We did have demonstration evenings for the initiated, but I had no personal responsibility there, that was the point, and I told her so. Have you no personal responsibility for your own happiness, or at least for your own food and clothing? she hissed.

I was going to tell her more, about the boy, about how I had come out a different person than I had gone in, how I had had this experience, underwent a transformation, made the affirmation. But I shut up instead. She wasn't listening.

It was easy to see her point, I wasn't sure if I could quite see it myself, or whether I had a point at all. How could I explain? That there was this child I met as a child, or rather, this *infant* I *saw* as a child. He was white, blond and blue-eyed. But he was me, or my son, or my lover, or even my father. And that I saw him again in the bus the other day – only it wasn't him, not in a *factual* sense. And I saw him again just now, in the cinema. He was dancing and prancing up there, on the stage and in the aisles, soliciting around and fucking about with other dancers and assorted customers, sodomising and being sodomised, openly. And yet . . . in my entire life I had never seen anything or anyone quite as pure and as innocent and as undefiled as his small slight figure, very fragile, very pale under the brash stage lights, smiling with his soul and radiating a glow of the most awesomely divine happiness, which seemed to touch the hearts and minds and bodies of all he came in contact with, transforming them with his own exuberant spirituality into transcendent beings.

You try telling that to Suzi. To anyone. Suzi is a hard nut to crack even with a substantially more credible argument than that in your weaponry. Sum up by saying that you'd resolved not to enter that career because you felt you were not chaste enough for it, and darling Suzi would probably prune your privates with a rusty pair of garden shears, put the spoils in your hand, and say, There, that should help, chastity will come easier now.

I offered a compromise. I'd pay my way provided I did so by doing any ordinary job I could get. This wasn't the first time I'd suggested this, but this time I said it like I meant it.

Until you feel you are good enough and pure enough for the other? She slapped her knees and gave an exaggerated nudge-nudge wink-wink ho-ho laugh. I ignored that, but an agreement was reached, and that was that. She wasn't too pleased about it, mind you, and kept repeating something about sauce, geese and ganders, but I ignored that too.

I got a job shifting boxes and helping with deliveries at one of the big department stores.

It was there that I met this bloke one day who asked about Suzi. Said he'd seen me with this chick and she was real cute and looked real hot, real classy, all bones, eyes and mouth, if a bit short, but he didn't mind, in fact he preferred them petite, more passion, just the way he liked them, and could I fix it for him to go with her? Didn't think much of his vocab. Didn't think much of him. Shiny black suit, shiny black skin, shiny black shoes, shiny black hair, shiny white tie, shiny white teeth, shiny white scarf, shiny gold rings. Why don't you fix it on for yourself? I ain't got much time no more, lover boy. Going back in a couple of days, and a real busy schedule till then. I couldn't have cared less. I was about to turn away when he flashed his shiny white teeth, which would have left me colder than dead were it not for an accompanying flash of green.

I stretched out my hand just to give him the pleasure of

jerking his own back, but to my surprise he let me have the twenty he was holding out.

I'll speak to her, I said, folding the bill and putting it away in my hip pocket. That should teach him, I thought to myself. It didn't. See you tomorrow, OK? Don't keep it any later. I know, I said, you haven't got much time. Got it in one. He winked, and left. I had never made such easy money in my life. Maybe he was someone who got his kicks by handing out twenty-dollar bills to fellow blacks, even though I wasn't African or Caribbean or whatever he was.

I told Suzi about him that night and she said, Why not? Send him over. I would have said no, but then it was her . . . body.

Next day arrived, no surprise there. I was half expecting him, half not. Half of me was hoping to be sent away on a long-distance delivery that day so I wouldn't be there when he came, if he came; half of me wanted to work round the store so as not to miss him.

He did come and I didn't miss him. I gave him the address, though I didn't guarantee she'd be there. He gave me another twenty.

I got back a little late that day. My mate in the pick-up got lost for a while during one delivery, he too being a stranger to the US of A and the avenues, streets and ways of New York.

I met Suzi on the landing, running out. Hey! I shouted as she tried to push past. When she didn't stop and shot down the stairs I followed and grabbed her by the shoulder. Where's the fire? Or is it flooding from the top downwards? I wondered. It's all your fault, she panted, I'm going, getting out. Where . . . Why . . . I was being as original as I could under the circumstances. Home, to Mom, to Chelmsford, that's where. I *hate* going home. It's all your fault. Chelmsford! I had never heard of Chelmsford before, Massachusetts or Essex. Yes, Chelmsford. And it's all your fault. Why my fault? I didn't build the place. I've never even heard . . . Ha ha, very funny.

By then she had calmed down a bit, so I coaxed her into coming up and explaining. All right, but I'm not staying. Not for more than a minute. Deep inside I think she was pleased to have some time to think and talk. But she was still a desperate woman, and I was dying to find out why.

I soon found out. And it *was* my fault.

Apparently the flash customer I had passed on to her from the store had died on her. In fact, at that very moment, he was lying flat dead in the pokey hole we called our apartment.

I queased at the sight.

Are you sure he's dead, I whispered. I don't know why I whispered, he sure wasn't listening. Looks quite . . . warm . . . to me. Which he did, though mind you, with his complexion it would have been difficult for him to look cold encased in ice and wearing a Jerry Hall bikini. I was trying to look at him without really looking at him.

Of course he's dead! Why else would he be lying flat out on his back with his balls rolling around and his prick hanging out? I don't know, he's not the first in this room to be lying flat . . . All right, all right . . . She stopped mid-sentence, a bright light coming into her eyes. I always dreaded that. I used to say, What now? with a sigh of resigned consternation when I saw that bright light coming into her eyes, but that day I dared not ask. She enlightened me anyway. Suck his cock, she said. What! Suck his cock, you heard me. (I shared an apartment with this girl!) Suck a man's cock, she persisted, and if he's the least little bit alive, it will come to life. Even impotent men get a hard-on if you suck their cocks. Come on, don't stand there wasting that open mouth, use it. Even if it just swells a little, it means . . .

I'd had enough. I am not sucking his fucking cock, you do it. I've already done it. In fact, it was during sixty-nine that he . . . sort of . . . convulsed . . . She made a face. Come on, your turn now.

The heck it is.

Why not? He's black, isn't he? Her logic was at its peak.

So! I was at my most articulate.

OK, OK, take it easy.

Something in my look must have told her that I wasn't sucking no dead man's cock, even if he was alive. And black.

Do what you like, don't do what you like, he's all yours. I'm splitting. So saying she started pushing towards the door again. Hey, what about me? I pleaded. For one bad moment I was a nine-year-old again. I almost expected Aunt Verna to come out of the closet and give me a dressing down. She stopped, looked at me for a second, then suddenly put her arms around my neck, pulled my face down a foot or two, and kissed me smack on the lips. You are a dear, even if you don't know it. Here, you can keep his wallet. She reached into her handbag and took out what didn't look like any wallet I had seen. It was a money belt.

Before I could respond she was out of the room. I could hear her high heels on the broken surface of the corridor, then on the stairs.

Hardly aware of doing so, I unzipped the money belt. The man did not believe in travellers' cheques. He did believe in money, though. Six thousand, four hundred and eighty-nine dollars; nine thousand, seven hundred and six pounds; not to mention thousands of deutschmarks and Swiss francs; and a few pesetas in a little plastic moneybag.

Also in the belt was a British passport and a return ticket to London, Heathrow, with a seat confirmed on a BOAC flight leaving Kennedy Airport late that night.

The man was about ten years older than I was. The photograph on his passport was about ten years younger than he was. I was never one to miss an opportunity.

I didn't look too much like him, but then we all looked alike to them. At least I hoped so. My hair was Indian and not African, but I could always wear a hat. He had – it was there along with his shiny suit, this time a shiny white one. Could have been tailored for me. Shark skin, I was later told. Went in the Thames, hopefully back to the sea whence it came.

I wished I could go back to the land whence I had come.

† † †

On the way to the airport I stopped the cab and telephoned the police, the fire department and the paramedics. That would add to the risk, but also to the excitement. Besides, the bloke deserved a chance. He was black, and a human being, perhaps even a living being. Or even a dead living being. I wasn't too sure. Neither was I sure whether I thought he was alive, hoped he was alive, or feared he was alive.

I half expected the plane to be recalled in mid-air on account of a dangerous murderer and an imposter being aboard, and I more than half expected armed police to be waiting for me at Heathrow. But none of that happened.

I was allowed to enter the United Kingdom, the country where hordes of my countrymen had come as immigrants, and from where, historically, people had also often emigrated in their hordes; the country where Shakespeare, Fielding and Marx had lived, loved, died; the country which was now to be my home on Mother Earth. The word 'mother' struck more than a single chord. It came to me in a fuzzy sort of a way that there was a certain inescapable similarity between my escape from the USA into the UK, and my family's escape from India into Bangla Desh. A cold shudder ran through my blood. What Mother had proudly termed her new nesting place had become her final resting place. I wondered once again what eventually happened to her body. At least she had Junior and Edwina for company.

Part IV
UPON THE WHEEL

Leicester Square

I was sure I was not being followed.

I looked behind me just the same.

I was being followed by a crowd.

A crowd of pink, white, brown and black people, all blue with unnatural cold, grey from lack of oxygen, and yellow with pent-up bile.

All climbing up the stairs in one mad rush to get out of the hell-pit of the London Underground tunnels, having escaped from the claustrophobic, strangulating, suffocating hold of a Tube train – one marginally cleaner but less picturesque and graphically ornate than those of New York.

They couldn't all be following me, of course. Even I knew that. But was there *one* among them? I hesitated for a moment on the stairs, turned round and tried to see if there was a familiar face, a suspicious or suspecting face, a face I could place . . . I was nearly knocked down the steps then nearly carried up the steps then nearly trampled upon then nearly asphyxiated then completely surrounded then wholly abandoned. All in a flash. All who had been behind me were now in front of me. So, no one had been following me.

Another crowd was following me.

Another train had arrived.

I was not being followed. The feeling had gone. But a feeling remained. I tried to shudder it away, but it remained.

I was out on Shaftesbury Avenue, facing Eros, the heart of Piccadilly, close by the guts of Soho, the cunt of London. Or so I had been told. It was rather a loveless heart, the guts were sagging, and the cunt was the driest, coldest and most shrivelled of cunts, if indeed cunt it was and not an asshole in disguise. It certainly made an asshole of visitors. A real let-down after all I had heard about it, especially all that nudge-nudge wink-wink from the son of the house in East Ham where I had found a room, and so much eyebrow-raising and snorting from the father. I had been looking forward to sampling its unsavoury delights. Unsavoury, yes; delights? You must be joking, to quote a famous British phrase. All promise and no delivery. It was about as frustrating as trying to masturbate with your hands tied behind your back. There was none of the so-called obscenity – no real sex shops, no real sex films, no honest, free-trading prostitutes of either sex, no allied pleasurable activities. Instead there was true obscenity, the obscenity of deceitfulness and come-on lies. And beyond that, nothing but bland, sleazy tedium. Quite a contrast to equivalent places in European cities, even New York.

I rambled aimlessly for about an hour, in and out of dirty, narrow streets, their only saving grace being their brevity, in and out of a variety of shops, bought some oranges from the market stalls, the most interesting feature of the wretched place, then went in to see an 'explicit' sex film and was presented with a badly mutilated and heavily censored version of some third-rate continental film. I left within fifteen minutes. By that time I was hopelessly lost and hopelessly bored.

Perhaps it was because this was the first time I had been all alone in a big city in a new country. Till then I had always had someone to go round with, and good company, any company, can make an enormous difference to one's perceptions of unfamiliar territory. And London was different. I had got so used to the straight criss-crossing north–south east–west roads of most American cities that I would have to acquire a taste for the more complex and possibly much more fascinating spread of London lanes.

Perhaps I was in the wrong place, the wrong part of the town. Perhaps I was going about it the wrong way, going to the wrong places. I could have gone to one of the libraries or museums, art galleries . . .

Perhaps my expectations were too high. London should have been the most exciting place in the world. Great Grandmother swore by the British, or the English, *Angrez*, as she called them. And though she would never admit to it, I was sure there were moments, however fleeting and however infrequent, when she wished she'd been with the Church of England, rather than the Roman Church. For Americans she had scant respect, considering them to be nouveau riche upstarts, not good enough to hold a candle to the real thing – the true English gentry, the *real* ladies and the *real* gentlemen. Even Father had all but stood to attention at the very mention of the *pukka Angrez sahib*. Loyalty to crown and 'country' in the colonies sometimes exceeded that found in the core of the Empire itself, especially among the poor and the powerless. Glory by association was one explanation, gullibility another.

And despite my inbuilt irreverence for all sacred stones of all establishment temples, I too had grown up with an awe for the British and all things British, and London was meant to encompass, represent and symbolise the best of the best of it all.

I came back to my earlier proposition. I was in the wrong place. The wrong part of town. I picked up the *Evening News* from one of the street sellers and looked through the entertainment pages. In times of disorientation, intellectual or otherwise, it is sometimes best to stick to the familiar. I decided to go and see a Bond film which was on at a cinema in Leicester Square.

I didn't know exactly where Leicester Square was, but I did know it wasn't far from Piccadilly. All I had to do was ask for directions. I saw this good-looking redhead with a bust to challenge Shakti's walking my way. Could you please tell me the way to Leicester Square, I said, speaking softly, in my best voice and with my toothiest smile.

Perhaps I was showing too many teeth, and it made me appear roguish and untrustworthy. She sort of froze for a moment, tried to smile and not smile at the same time, turned ever so slightly towards the farther side of the road from me, and walked away with quick, nervous steps.

Next I tried a very dapper man, all pinstripes and umbrella. He didn't even stop or turn his head to look at me. I don't think he heard me. Perhaps I spoke too softly.

Perhaps I was not saying the name of the place correctly. I wasn't. I was uttering three distinct syllables: Lei-ces-ter Square. Not merely that, I was putting my strongest accent on the syllable that wasn't. I ought to have known. After all I did know through my discussions with Pasha regarding the plausibility of *King Lear*'s plot that the Earl of Gloucester was *really* the Earl of *Gloster*. But I failed to make the connection. Anyway, the English language, not unlike its speakers, and the climate in which it was reared, did not necessarily adhere to the principles of predictability. Even had the thought of the good Earl occurred to me, I might still not have surmised that it gave proof positive one way or the other re the acceptable pronunciation of the Square's Christian name. What's more, had I been sure I was mispronouncing, I might not have worried that much. After all, my continental experiences had shown me that it wasn't necessary to be word perfect in a foreign language in order to find your way around town.

Perhaps I had spoken to two of the many tourists who must be coming over constantly to pay their respects to this capital of capitals. It seemed a plausible reason. I decided to ask someone who had to be a true native: the man selling the evening papers by the bend of that road yonder.

Could you please tell me how to get to Lei-*ces*-ter Square please? I asked, wide-eyed, eager and hopeful. The man had blotchy red skin and wavy brown hair generously mixed with wavy grey hair. He looked up momentarily, then looked down again and said, There is no such place. His face and voice were utterly expressionless.

The faces and voices of the two young men standing by the newspaper man, one about my age, the other hardly fourteen, were by no means devoid of expression. I heard them the moment I turned to walk away, which I did after a brief moment's hesitation while I wrestled with the foolish notion of somehow eliciting a confession out of the florid man that he was lying and that Leicester Square did indeed exist. Though in fact he was right, there really was no such place as Lei-*ces*-ter Square. The older of the young ones let out a sniggering laugh which developed into a hiccoughy laugh; the younger one hissed out, Fuckin' bloody Paki. A third voice, I couldn't tell whose, said something which I did not quite understand but sounded like, and probably was, National Front.

I felt my face go red, as red as it was physically possible for it to be, and a surge of hate and rage and fear swept through me from nerve-ending to brain cell to nerve-ending. But only for one passing second. The hate and rage went almost instantly. A little bit of the redness and a lot of the fear remained.

Once my involuntary reactions had settled down, I was left with a strange mixture of sensations, memories and impressions, not altogether unpleasant. After all, rejection was nothing new to me. I was born a reject, in the gutter; was bred in the gutter; and had learnt, very early on in life, to walk close to the gutter. And that was in my own country, the land of my birth, and of the birth of my father and my mother and of their fathers and their mothers. This was a foreign land, peopled not only by my superiors, for that applied to everyone, but by probably the most superior people in the entire world, with the exception of the Jews. At least so Great Grandmother declared. Her utterly unquestioning faith in the Bible led her to believe that none could possibly be luckier or greater than those whom the love of God chose. The love of God chose the Jews, so their superiority over the rest of the mankind could not possibly be doubted. She often quoted Father Franklin, who baptised her, on the subject: Salvation is through the Jews, for through the Jews came the Law, through the Jews came Christ, the Son of God was born a Jew and the Holy Mother of God was a Jew and married a Jew. If all that was not the ultimate in human proximity to God, she couldn't imagine what else could be.

I was neither Jew nor English nor white, not even a proper Indian nor a proper Pakistani. But my travels through Europe and stay in the USA and my acceptance there as a living entity capable of suffering pain and enjoying pleasure had temporarily given me a sort of quasi-human status. I had become spoilt and pampered. Obviously I would have to start re-learning my past and re-discovering my appointed place in the world. The redness in my face was no longer of anger, but embarrassment, and even warmth. I was back where I belonged. However, the fear, though not new, was greater than I remembered, and stronger than it need have been.

The determined, practical side of my nature soon took over from the lazy, brooding one. I had to get to Leicester Square. I no longer cared about seeing the film, though it was the last to star my great hero Sean Connery. I just wanted to get to Leicester Square.

The answer came from heaven, in a manner of speaking. I looked up to the skies for no reason I can now remember, probably a spot of rain or a ray of sunshine, and on their way down my eyes spied a policeman on the horizon.

Now why hadn't I thought of it before!

Could you please tell me how to get to Lei-*ces*-ter Square? I said in my best voice once again.

For a flicker of a moment as the policeman looked up at me I thought I had struck a wall again, but then a door opened. The policeman smiled, showing large, flashy teeth. He was young and fresh with big blue eyes and his skin shone. I would have enjoyed taking his uniform off.

He began explaining: straight on, then first right, on to the second set of lights . . . etcetera, etcetera . . . It's rather a long walk, Sir, he concluded. He called me 'Sir'! I was thrilled. An English policeman actually called me 'Sir'. Great Grandmother would have been so proud of me. Mother would have given me a cuddle, and she wasn't given to cuddles where I was concerned. Father's eyes would have lit up, and it takes a lot to light up the eyes of a man dying of tuberculosis.

He could tell my mind had wandered off. I'll tell you what, Sir, he said, (he said 'Sir' again!) I'll write it down for you. Here his eyes narrowed a bit, he hesitated. You can . . . Oh yes, I assured him, I can read. He relaxed. Taking out a notepad from his pocket he drew a map, writing down the names of the roads and the turnings to take. I must have wandered off course more than I had thought. But then the streets had led one into another and twisted and turned and escaped into strange territories . . . There, you'll see the sign on a big board. He smiled his big smile again as he tore off the piece of paper and handed it over to me.

I started getting confused half way there, but I was determined not to ask anyone else. I didn't want another negative response to spoil the childlike happiness that the policeman's courtesy had brought to my otherwise unrewarding day.

I finally managed to get to where the directions led me. I still wasn't sure I had got it right. It looked different from what I had imagined . . . But then places in real life often are. There was a large park spread out in front of me, but no cinemas to be seen.

It was only when I looked up to my right and saw the board that I realised I *had* come to the right place. The sign read: LONDON ZOO.

The reputation of the British for their sense of humour was well deserved after all. If a policeman could be so well endowed with it, despite the obvious difficulties and frustrations of his profession, the ordinary man or woman would surely be brimming over with jokes, no matter what the occasion.

I could hear the young man's hiccoughy laughter all over again, this time piercing deeper. I couldn't help but join in. The devil riding my back dug his hard heels into my flesh, but I stood my ground. I had nowhere else to go. Except to Leicester Square.

This time I decided I would try a child. For unto such belongs the Kingdom of Heaven. Leicester Square shouldn't be much of a problem.

He ran to his mother half way through my sentence. My fault. I hadn't seen her sitting on a bench not far away.

I tried an Indian-looking middle-aged man with a pouchy face hidden beneath a large-brimmed hat, and a paunchy stomach that seemed to run a perfect little circle round his navel beneath a scruffy Fair Isle sweater beneath a wrinkly brown jacket beneath an overcoat which brushed the homeless autumn leaves strewn despairingly across the lawns. His tie was muddy green with flowers which once

must have been yellow. Sorry, no know, new . . . Sorry . . .
Sorry . . . New, no know . . .

I decided to make one last attempt before looking for a shop
where I could buy a map of the city.

I tried a pink old lady with the future of the universe
mapped on her face in linear symbols just waiting to be
decoded by anyone with the wisdom and the patience to
want to do so.

It took her a while to understand what I wanted and where
I wanted to go. Then she walked with me to a bus stop –
taking about two steps a minute, and those in slow motion
– waited with me, put me on the right bus and reminded the
conductor to call my stop.

I was in Leicester Square. What's more, I had learnt that it
was really *Lester* Square.

That was not all I learnt that day. I hadn't even begun.

Southend Pier I

I could not put it off any longer. The man's ghost had to be laid to rest – or at least I had to take the first step towards doing so – whether or not it was he who was making me feel followed.

I had the man's address and telephone number, a couple of letters, and stacks of visiting cards: two estate agents, four insurance agents, three garages, one double glazing company, three massage parlours, two priests, three funeral directors, and so on and so on. And of course his money.

If nothing else I should inform his family that he had . . . met with an . . . unfortunate accident and that the chances of recovery were . . . remote. And I had to try to return the money, or some of it, even most of it, perhaps all of it: I still hadn't used any of it. I had already got rid of the clothes, the hat, the credit cards and of course the passport.

The problem was how to go about it. For one foolish moment I contemplated going round to his house to console the widow, or the mother, or whoever, and I still felt tempted just to go to the house and see what it was like. Was it desolate and lost without its master? Did it even know? Had it called the police? It was the last thought which prompted me to adopt a safer plan of action.

I would telephone. But what would I say? Who would I ask for?

I shook so much the receiver nearly fell out of my hands and I sweated so hard the receiver kept slipping out of my hands. For once I had the East Ham house to myself, and I had managed to open the padlock on the telephone, almost as large as the telephone itself but fortunately self-locking, with one of the hundreds of hairpins that always lay scattered in the tiny shower cubicle. I hated British public telephones, didn't know when to put the money in, and then all those bleeps . . . Certainly not suitable for making embarrassing or difficult calls.

I should have settled on the floor and practised my reduced breathing for a few minutes before starting, but the carpet was uninviting and I was too worked up to worry about being too worked up.

I dialled the number, half hoping I had dialled wrong, or that 'they' had moved or had their number changed or something.

I could hear it ring.

Once. Twice. Three times.

Perhaps no one is home.

Four times.

No one is home.

Five times, six times.

Relief.

I was about to put the receiver down when came the unmistakable click. Someone was answering.

Thank Gawd you've called. Been leaving messages on that wretched machine of yours since last night. Nearly missed you just then, been asleep in the bath, 'alf broke my ankle rushing out. Been telling Dan for ages to get a new extension by the soap dish. Keeps saying yeah, yeah, but . . . You are the plumber, aren't ya? Thank Gawd for that. The pool has been leaking since yesterday afternoon . . . No, I tell a lie, since the day before, only I wasn't sure, and tomorrow all the guests are coming. Don't know what we're going to do if it isn't sorted out. You know those fuckin', excuse me language, ponces who built it in the first place, you know the one I mean, the indoor one, say they can't come till Wednesday fortnight. Imagine, Wednesday fortnight! A body could die for want of a dip by then. No time of the year for outside swimming, is it now? But try explaining it to them, fuckin' shirkers. But what can I say to them when Daniel hisself don't bother. I have to do everything roun' 'ere. First of all his lordship turns up three days later than planned. Would have been worried sick if I 'adn't known 'im better and if it'd been the first time. Had a stroke, he says. In the church, he says. Had them twice before as well. Like, when he gets too excited about something. Like in the church. Right in the middle of all them languages they speak there, shout out more like. Wonder they don't have strokes more often. I nearly have a heart attack looking at them. Never go myself. Born Church of England I was and Church of England I'll stay, never go myself. Not to any of them. All the same they are, holier than thou and all that shit, pardon me. But you know how they are, black folk, not that I 'ave anything against them, though Lord knows I should, been married to one for long enough, married to the whole family more like it. But never mind. Lost his passport and all. Somebody in the church nicked it. Can you credit that! Wallet and all! In the church. Can you credit that? I can. What with the sort that gather in them churches. Nearly said it but kept my own counsel. That's what Mum always says. Keep your own counsel, Yvette, she says, keep your own counsel and you won't regret it. I wouldn't be surprised, they do all that shouting there so if someone is mugged and screams no one can tell the difference. Is a good provider, though, he is. New Roller coming next month. Number plate is going to spell my name. Not the whole of it, just KOO. Well, not me real name, you know. But he calls me Koo. Kootchy Kootchy Koo, he calls me. But never mind, you don't want to know all that. Only I'm all on my own so long sometimes I talk too much. A body needs a bit of a chinwag now and then, you know what I mean, just to keep your head from turning funny . . . Like Jane down the road . . . You should've seen her last year, even a couple of months ago. And you should see her now. Her mother wouldn't recognise her, if it wasn't for that nose of hers. She certainly don't recognise her mother. Though mind you, if I had a mum like hers I wouldn't recognise her either. Still, we all have to bear our cross. That's what Mum always says. Yvette, she says . . .

After about ten minutes I put the phone down without making an appointment for the repair of the indoor swimming pool so urgently needed for the next day's festivities.

Padlock back on the phone and up to my grubby airless room, just in time, too. Key in the lock and in comes the family sooner than expected. Or perhaps I was on the phone longer than expected.

I got out my tourist guide book. *Southend Pier is the longest pier in the world* . . . I don't know why it caught my attention, but it did. Easy to get to as well – Tube to Barking, just one stop, and then take the train. Why not? Why not indeed. Now that I had money to spend, and lots of time to spend it in, why not indeed.

† † †

Once on the pier itself and surveying the sea and the beach extending behind, beyond and below it, I must confess I had to register a certain disappointment. It couldn't compare with Californian beaches, nor even with the rather staid and dreary ones of Karachi, and certainly could lay claim to nothing like the power and the fury of the Bangla Desh coastline. But at least there was some comfort in the knowledge that dirt and filth are not the preserve of one country alone. And each segment of the earth, like each human being and every form of life, has its own beauty and its own fascination; and before long I began to find pleasure in this quaint and picturesque part of our lonely planet. Despite the un-home-like bite in the November winds, the stench it carried with it brought back long-forgotten memories of home, and I found myself wishing that Aunt Verna's brooms and Mother's shit bucket were beside me, to touch and caress, to assure myself that I too belonged – however low in the scale of evolution, however insignificant in the scheme of things – that I too had a purpose and a meaning: an essential and undeniable, if unenviable, purpose and meaning, like that of shit itself, however mocked and belittled and berated, no matter if viewed with disgust and repugnance, still essential for the very survival of the species.

Yes, I was being followed.

Every pore of my skin oozed sweat, every molecule

of my skin goose-pimpled with the hot and cold awareness of another presence, a destined presence, besides mine,
beside me.

Daniel couldn't possibly have a ghost. If the voice on the
telephone was to be believed, he was alive. And alive he would
have much better things to do than following me about.

I looked behind me. Nothing. I looked to my left. Nothing.
I looked to my right. Nothing.

He was right in front of me, staring up at me. The same hair
of spun gold; the same eyes, brightest of blue, like marbles
moulded from the glass dome of the skies. He was back
to being about three years old, as he was the first time I
saw him.

Three times in the last few months! And this time
renouncing his youth to go back to my childhood. He
did not want to be left alone. I could not go on avoiding
him, running away from him. Not any more. Not without
perverting the course of nature: always a dangerous thing to
attempt, more dangerous now than always. I could feel it on
every grain of my tongue, in every drop of my saliva.

And if there was any hesitancy on my part it was soon
resolved. The boy, who was on the other side of the
narrow railway track that ran along the pier, started walking
towards me, arms outstretched, exactly as he had done
on the station in Chandan all those years ago. Only this
time it was more than a psychological travesty or emotional anomaly or tangential impulse which made me rush
towards him and lift him up. He had walked straight on
to the track in front of an oncoming train. I tripped on
a metal protuberance and fell, but managed to hold the
child aloft and away as the train braked to a halt, brushing
against my leg and causing minor lacerations but no serious
damage.

A couple of screams and some shouting followed. The
boy's mother had been standing right behind me, and it was
suggested that he had been walking with arms outstretched
towards her, but I knew better. However, there was no point
in making an issue of it. What anyone thought or believed
didn't matter one bit.

What did matter was that I had made simultaneous contact with my past and my future. And in the present, my present, which was also my past, and also my future. Such moments are rare.

My life would never be the same again. I was convinced of that. And I was right.

If further proof was needed of that assertion, it didn't take long in coming.

From my prostrate position I looked up and saw the mother leaning anxiously over me, the child now in her arms. It was love at first sight. All over again.

† † †

The wheel of new births and new lives and old deaths had turned full circle and was ready for another spin. And there was nothing that Jennifer or I, Jason or you, Aunt Verna or Jagdeep, even Mother or Shakti could have done to stop it or break it or alter its direction or reduce its momentum. We can be stretched upon it, crushed beneath it, or ride along with it; but the choice is not ours. There is a way to break away from it, there always is, but it is not for us to find that way. It finds us, or not. We can help, by being in the right place at the right time, but that is as easy or as difficult as planning our own births. Or escaping out of Kalpa into the long night of dissolution, awaiting yet another birth, a new re-creation under the thumping feet, the throbbing heart and the dancing limbs of Shiva, the King Dancer, and through his ever-rigid, ever-loving lingam, or in the hiss and spit of the Naga.

Or in the flesh and blood of the Man.

My stomach was full but I hungered for love; I was full with hope but I hungered for signs; I hungered for Truth but was crammed with facts; I hungered for timelessness but was replete with hours and minutes and seconds; I hungered for nirvana or salvation or it but brimmed over with shit: was I blessed? Or would it be woe unto me?

And what after the day of reckoning, the dusk of Kalpa, the night of dissolution, the dawn of darkness, the end, kaput! What? What? What? What but a new turn of the wheel. What but eternal life. What but nothing.

† † †

Would that I could choose.
　　Would that I were chosen.
　　Or that I did not know.

Cyrus Cyrus

Ian drove me to Southend General Hospital after dropping his wife and son, Jennifer and Jason, at their house, which was only a short distance from the beach: I made a note of the street and the number. I went, remonstrating as politely as I could and struggling as gently as possible. On the outside. Inside I was struggling with all my might and screaming my head off. Just come from the United States, I believed a short stay in hospital, 'for observation only', could mean you spending the rest of your life paying medical bills.

I remembered a Mexican fellow, not especially old, who had had a heart attack or a stroke or a fit of some sort at one of the Greyhound bus stations. Everyone looked at me like I was insane when I said call a doctor, as I'd heard it said in many a movie. No doctor came. Finally some paramedics arrived. They checked his papers and looked into his wallet to see how much money he had before deciding what to do with him. They made him walk through the crowds when the poor man could barely crouch. He kept mumbling something which I didn't understand. Another chap who spoke Spanish said he was worried about his wife and children and how they would get any money to pay his bills. He said if you were poor and fell ill you were better off dead, at least for the sake of your family. I had no family; and I did have Daniel's money, but this was not precisely the way I had in mind to spend it, if I spent it at all. Still, easy come easy go. There was nothing I could do about it. I was having difficulty even standing up.

I decided that in the circumstances the best thing to do

was to uncoil my nerves and submit myself to the inevitable. Stretching myself in the back seat of the car, a taxi – Ian was a self-employed taxi driver – I shut my eyes and relaxed my breathing.

When I next opened my eyes I was in this white bed under a white sheet staring at a white wall with this woman in white standing over me. I couldn't possibly have died, could I? And gone to hell! I certainly felt cold as hell.

There, feeling better now, are we? said the woman in white, voice blander than the words.

I shut my eyes then opened them again in an attempt to focus my vision better. I wished I hadn't bothered. There was a policeman standing on the other side of my bed. He had an open notebook in his left hand.

I *was* dead. The day of reckoning was here.

I think you can talk to him now, Officer, said the nurse. She retreated, the policeman advanced.

I was not dead. It was worse.

Delayed shock, said the nurse on her way out, managing a smile. More like I overdid my reduced breathing, I told myself as I returned the smile. Her eyes glazed over. The smile had not been for me.

Name? said the policeman.

Cyrus, I replied. The policeman waited, pencil poised on the notebook.

Cyrus what? he asked, mildly amused, mildly irritated.

I hesitated, nervous, unsure.

Full name, he said, slowly this time, and more loudly, though without really shouting.

Cyrus, I repeated lamely, Cyrus.

I was being forced to face up to my identity, something I had unconsciously avoided doing for the past many years.

On my passport my name had been put down as Cyrus Jagnath. The last was a combination of Jag from Jagdeep, who had adopted me, as it were, and Nath from Ramnath, whose patronage made it all possible. After escaping from the Ashram I had ceased to use that name. When I did my gardening in LA I got by with just Cyrus and was paid in cash. In New York I used the name David Mathias off a social security card from one of the wallets Suzi had pocketed. In Chandan I had been Cyrus Choodah; and in Bangla Desh, when we went Muslim for a time, I was Cyrus Khan. I had travelled to England as Daniel Prescott.

I was sorely tempted to go back to Cyrus Choodah, but decided against it. With the uncertainty I felt among the white British – friendliness and smiles one minute, abuse and mockery the next – I couldn't risk the contempt of any of my own people I might meet in the UK.

Confronted by the growing temper in the policeman's eyes, made more threatening by the cool of his stance and the utter stillness of his notebook and his pencil, one held at hip level in his left hand, the other slightly higher up in his right, I felt my own agitation mounting.

Cyrus, Cyrus . . . I stuttered. Shree Ramnath would have been most ashamed of me.

By that time the nurse was back. They have funny . . . (quick look at me) . . . some of them . . . their names don't always . . . not like ours . . . you know. She had the grace to go a trifle red.

So your name is, let's see . . . He held up his notebook in front of his face, about a yard away. Cyrus Cyrus. Is that it? Cyrus Cyrus! You could have cut through steel with the sarcasm in his voice. Let me make sure how you spell it. Is it an S or a C, a Y or an I, a U or an E or another I. Or is it KPLIGA or something like that, Sir?

The sonorous manner of his speaking gave me time to think. I remembered Father calling out to me, Cyrus, Cyrus, come here Cyrus, Cyrus . . . I remembered calling out to Father when I went looking for him in the woods. Father, Father, I used to call out, always hoping he would call back, Cyrus, Cyrus.

I remembered being with him in the caves of Ajanta and Ellora, in my dreams. I remembered shouting out my name, Cyrus, and the echo ringing back through the shimmering mist of their exotic antiquity and through the simmering passion of the erotic dancers carved into their walls, *Cyrus*. And thus it used to go on. Cyrus, *Cyrus*; Cyrus, *Cyrus* . . .

What better than to be called Cyrus Cyrus?

My confidence returned with interest. Yes, that's it. Cyrus Cyrus. And it is spelt the same way as King Cyrus the Second of Persia. That is why it's Cyrus twice, to indicate – perhaps childishly – Cyrus the Second. The famous one. You can look him up in any encyclopaedia or book of world history, or even in the Bible. That is where Father got it from.

I must have overdone it. The policeman was clearly not amused. But it was good not to hear the grin in his words any more.

May I have a look at your passport?

It was like being stripped naked during evensong, but I clung on to my confidence, out of sheer desperation.

I am afraid I don't make a habit of carrying it around with me on a day trip to Southend-on-Sea.

I had discovered my name, but I was still at odds with my self. On the one hand I professed to accept my position as the lowest of the low among mankind; on the other, I had the gall to behave with such wild arrogance before the forces of law and order – white and British at that. And when I was legally vulnerable. It was this temper I had, something within me, controlled and in its place most of the time, but triggered off quite unexpectedly. Probably it was a reaction against Father's abject servility, at all times and towards all. Perhaps I fought his unfought battles for him. Perhaps there was something fundamentally unbalanced about my psyche.

Address, I heard the policeman say.

There was something in his voice which made me jerk my head and look up at him. Or rather, something not in his voice. The edge was missing. The sarcasm was not there.

I had to think quickly. I came up with a North London address, a place which offered lodgings, and one of many I had telephoned when I was looking for a room. I even remembered the telephone number, and gave it unasked. He wrote everything down carefully. But he didn't meet my eyes, and his foot shifted.

He had backed off!

Whether it was my new-born attitude (quietly self-assured rather than common stroppy) or my choice of words (literate British rather than common black) or whether it was my accent (mixed American rather than hard Indian) which had brought this about, I could not say.

He asked me a few simple questions about the accident and left.

A rare feeling of elation surged through my blood. It had been a great day. The day I found my child, perhaps even my father; the day I found my love; the day I found my name; the day I set to rest the ghost of Daniel Prescott.

That day Cyrus Cyrus was born.

But I didn't want to push my luck too far. In the middle of the night I got up, put my clothes on, and managed to get out of the hospital.

Save myself the bill as well, I thought smugly, not realising I had nothing to pay.

Hyde Park

I needed time not to think and not be by myself. Of course the best way not to think is to talk to a friend, but I didn't really want to be with anybody, partly because I had no friends. I had found a job building the pedestrian shopping area in High Street Southend, and the men I worked with were all right, some of them, but there was no one I could call a friend. No one who would call me a friend. We didn't have much in common, and even those who did not subscribe to the National Front or did not believe that all Pakis and the like were complete bastards or complete idiots or spongers or muggers or bank robbers or mealy-mouthed shopkeepers or smelly curry-eaters or just smelly, and there were one or two, were disappointed in me because I did not drink. Not what they would call drinking. I did enjoy a glass of wine – Sister Erin enjoyed the occasional glass and so did Pasha, and I had secretly helped myself now and then as a child – but I hated pubs, and I hated beer, especially lukewarm beer. They didn't *particularly* relish visiting libraries and museums and art galleries, so there was nowhere we could go together and assert our matey-ness. Unlike Pakistan and the USA and some European countries, everything, including cafés and tea places and shops, shut in the evening and there was nowhere left to go but pubs and nothing left to do but get drunk – barring eating out in expensive places or the inane madness of discos. Cinema-going was not exciting enough for hard-headed young males. So I had nowhere to go, especially in the evenings.

The only people I wanted to be with were Jennifer and Jason.

But I could not be with Jennifer and Jason. Jennifer had told me on Saturday, only yesterday but it seemed a long time ago, that I must stop seeing them. Ian had started getting irritated by my 'constant' presence – which was a lie for a start for I hardly ever went more than once a day, and that mostly when he was out taking fares, which was nearly always – and reminders of my presence: usually no more than the odd toy or book I bought for Jason. Or some flowers for Jennifer, or once or twice some little item of jewellery, or a dress, or something like that. She wouldn't accept them at first, but then she sort of fell in with my desire to please her. I had that money from Daniel, which I'd started spending despite my good intention to return it; labouring on the shopping development brought in a good bit as well. But I had no one to spend it on. I didn't drink much, as you know, nor smoke, and gambling never held any attraction for me. Sex could be had for free, or as good as, if and when I wanted; I had made a contact or two in Southend, and knew a body or so in East Ham, too, where I continued to live, though in a different house with somewhat better facilities and a larger, airier room and a payphone.

I spent occasional nights in Southend with Anya Wang, a nineteen-year-old Chinese working girl living on York Road. She had the most delicately sculptured breasts that ever hovered over a woman's abdomen. How they maintained their appearance of chaste ivory, that could send shivers of sensuous delight through the marrow of the most jaded of stone carvers, and retained their delicate sensitivity, enough to charge the heart of a true voluptuary with wild currents of lascivious passion, considering the active life she led, I will never know. She insisted on charging me half her full rate, and would have been willing to take me on for free now and then, but I insisted on paying my way.

Or with Tracy, forty-five-year-old wife of a shift worker at the Ford factory in Dagenham – or so she said. Tracy had the most voracious mouth this side of the many mouths of Mother Ganges. Her fingers could bring the dead back to life even on the ninety-seventh anniversary of their burial. I met her in Tesco. I had been at the road the entire day, boring away with my pneumatic drill, and felt as if I'd been dead and buried for ninety-seven years. I went in for a can of beans and ended up helping Tracy with a trolley full of beer cans and wine bottles and gin bottles while she battled with her teenaged son over his teacher's report. She brought me back to life that night. Said she was sick and tired of the men in her life, and chose me for I would bring the greatest possible shame to them both were they to find out. It was for me to find out that they knew about it all along – as they did about all the others she picked up, all at Tesco, all after she had sized one up and started a quarrel with her son over his school report. This strategy seldom failed to work, she told me one day. What she didn't tell me was that both father and son watched from an adjoining room. No wonder she was so particular about having all the lights on. She used to tell me her husband was on night-shift and nothing short of a nuclear explosion would wake Terry, her son. It was only when one day the noise coming from their room exceeded the noise we were making that I learnt what was going on. I almost stopped seeing her after that. But then, I thought of all the pleasure it was passing round, and what a shame it would be to take it away. Especially as I was the one they liked best, I was assured. So I carried on, about once a fortnight. The whole family belonged to some sort of a coven as well, which I repeatedly refused to join, despite repeated invitations. I'd had enough of that sort of thing at the Ashram. It's not everyone we allow to join, much less invite, she'd tell me. But no thanks was my firm answer. I preferred to work alone.

Or with Shane. Actually with him it wasn't the nights, but the afternoons. He worked as a hod-carrier on a building site not far from the High Street. His hands were rough and his nails cracked and edged in black, but his body was white as milk and smooth as butter. He complained he could never tan, but I didn't mind. His shoulder blades tickled your nipples, and he could expand and contract like you wouldn't credit. I always gave him some money. He was twenty-six, had five children and one mother-in-law, not to mention the wife. Any extra cash was always welcome, though he genuinely felt bad about accepting it and made repeated promises to pay it all back one of these days. With interest. I said I collected the interest as I went along, so not to worry about it. But I let him believe he'd pay the money back, except for the £1,500 I gave him to get me an Irish passport. It made him feel good. He kept a meticulous record of every penny in a shabby little notebook. It was touching, for he could barely write, and only in block capitals. He certainly couldn't count. I had to add it up for him after every new entry. He told his wife it had something to do with his overtime, which was correct. He was guilt-ridden about it all, but never dared to go to confession, which further augmented his guilt and made him hugely miserable. But only before and after; I've never known anyone to enjoy it so much during. Not even Belinda. Shakti, of course, but all that cold tea . . . When he went into his post-what-have-you depressions I tried to cheer him up by saying that since it wasn't another woman it wasn't proper adultery, and because he was married he couldn't be damned as a proper homo. Besides, his penis never entered another body – I'd have let him if he wanted to – those were the days when the AIDS virus was still in the laboratories, or just escaped, so there were no known worries on that score – but he never did. Therefore he could not be said to be putting it about and, in short, he hadn't done anything *really* wrong. QED, no reason to feel guilty. It helped a little, but not for long. The despair of no longer being clean enough for the love of the Holy Mother of God caught up with him soon enough. He may not have wronged his wife, but he had sinned against *Her*! Against the Church. Back at work he would start carrying larger and larger loads of bricks on his buttermilk shoulders.

It all stopped after I married Belinda. Anya and Tracy and Shane and any others. Not for any puritanical objections to adultery, I assure you. In fact, according to the oft unacknowledged traditions of our part of the world, adultery is the safest *and* the best form of sex, particularly if the woman is married; sex as business – money in exchange for services, as in any respectable going concern – comes a close second. It is fornication between singles that is the cause of most troubles, such as unmarried mothers and unnecessary marriages. I stopped this and that after marrying Belinda because her earnestness and intensity drained practically all my energies. Her demands in bed took care of what was left over.

I never touched Jennifer, sexually, until she was separated from her husband, and then not immediately. She would certainly have let me once her relationship with Ian had been well and truly soured. And not just because of me, though I may have played a hand in it. There was a lot more going on between them that wasn't quite right. Nothing spectacularly dramatic – mostly boring old stuff about interfering mothers and unsavoury in-laws and forgotten birthdays and overlooked anniversaries; and the name of their first born, Jason: Ian wanted to call him Stewart, after his father. And the colour of the hall carpet and the texture of the living room wallpaper and the shape of the kitchen sink and so on and so on.

If I considered adultery to be such an OK activity, and when the married Jennifer had reached the stage of being willing, why didn't I? Because I had regained my faith in another of the sexual mores of my culture: never do it with the one you love. With anybody and everybody, but never with the one you truly love, unless perhaps or perchance you happen to be married to the one you truly love.

And it made sense. My tragic experience with Shakti convinced me of that. Mind you, when I started off with Shakti I was not in love with her, and not old enough to know differently, so I can't blame myself too much. But that flirtation with 'committed sex', however brief, was a folly. Ironically, I had Shakti herself, a Westerner and a woman, usually torch-bearers for committed sex, to thank for putting me straight on that.

But back to the day in Hyde Park, the Sunday morning of the Saturday night Jennifer asked me to stop seeing her, and Jason. I needed time not to think and not to be by myself.

I thought I'd go to the famous Speakers' Corner in Hyde Park and listen to the gripes of other people to take my mind off my own. It was something I had wanted to do as a child ever since I first heard about it from Pasha.

† † †

The time is now, black sisters, NOW. Unite. Unite, black sisters, unite among yourselves. Unite with your white sisters. Unite with your white brothers. And ultimately even your black brothers will want to unite with you. Unite, unite, unite, black sisters of Britain, black sisters of the world. Unite. The time is here. Now is the time. Unite. Unite. Unite.

I moved forward and joined the few men, mostly old and all white, crowding round this strikingly attractive black girl, barely visible above the waist despite the boxes she was standing on. Three white women were talking animatedly to one side of her, and a lone black woman stood next to them, listening with rapt attention. A few children, white, hovered around, giggling, hands pressed to their mouths, eyes darting all over the place, from the speaker's face to the faces of those surrounding her to each other's faces.

How long are you going to let MEN rule your lives, your country, your world, your offices, your factories, your shoe shops; force you into high heels, decide what underwear suits you best, makes you look sexy? Is that all we are? Sex objects?

Yeah, yeah, said an old man. Two young ones joined in, laughing.

All right, all right. You may laugh now, but you will be laughing out of your assholes soon.

Watch your mouth lass . . .

Soon, soon . . .

Boo! Boo!

Soon, when we take over, which will be sooner than you think. The time is here and now. Unite, black sisters, unite. Unite. Unite. Unite. Now. Now. NOW.

I moved on and joined a throng round a kindly-looking preacher who was talking about peace and harmony and creating a more just and more equitable world. Someone

shouted about how appropriate for him to be standing on a
soap box, but I did not follow what he meant. Others did, for
there was instant general merriment, and some disapproval.

I spent some more time looking at people and smiling at
ducks. It was a beautiful spring day. The sun was both hot
and cool, the wind both teasing and caressing, the sky both
blue and happy. People of all shapes and shades stretched out
on the lawns, sat on the benches, or walked about in aimless
disarray. Some held hands, some kissed, others kept their
distance from each other. Some laughed, some stared, some
looked wondering and silent. Other more enduring and more
intelligent signs of life were forcing their way out of twigs and
branches with tiny hints of taut green and fluffy yellow. A
confusion of colours was on display at every turn and spread
across every stretch. Sparrows and crows, pigeons and doves,
blue tits and starlings flew about flicking their tails, turning
their heads and pecking away with their beaks, sustaining life
with life.

A gnawing feeling in the stomach moved my mind away
from all that beauty and forced me to start out in search of
sandwiches or something. On the way back I started looking
at the paintings and other objets d'art and suchlike displayed
by the side of the park. My lumbering progress was brought
to a sudden halt as I was arrested by a particular painting
depicting a naked black woman lying on a bed of sharp nails,
with a huge man, white and naked and with a grotesquely
large and distorted erection, hammering the woman down
into the nails with a big hammer. Two black men, one in
a shiny white suit and with sleeked back hair (reminded
me of someone I once knew) and the other in a flowery
shirt, Bermuda shorts and with Rastafarian dreadlocks, stood
behind the white man, apparently absorbed in conversation
with a vaguely delineated white girl. The colours were muted,
the lines sharp, except in the case of the white girl where the
style was reversed.

Hello again, said a girl's unfamiliar voice.

I looked from the painting to the artist. She smiled a smile
of recognition, and then looked embarrassed as she did not
see a flicker of instant recognition back. But it came to me.

The delay in my response was due to the unexpectedness of meeting the fiery speaker in a totally different set-up, cool, quiet and sedentary.

Speaking ever so softly, sitting so still, smiling so flirt-atiously, she looked absolutely the most beautiful human female I had ever seen in my life, including Elizabeth Taylor, with whom I fell in love at the age of three: *Elephant Walk*, for those of you who were alive then. She had mahogany-coloured skin, large, clear eyes, full, straight lips, a perky, elfin body, so slight – somewhat like Elizabeth Taylor, circa 1958 – I could have held her in the palm of my hand.

Will you marry me, I heard myself saying as I knelt on the pavement, taking out of my inner jacket pocket the ring I had bought for Shakti and which I always carried with me in memory of her, and offering it to the presaging and raging orator and artist.

For a brief instant, during which had I not lost my senses I would have been frightened, I thought, but without any fear, that she was going to tear my eyes out. They were directly in front of her eyes, staring into them. You men, she began, but by the time she got to, are all the same, her voice had mellowed.

You can come with me to the march next Saturday, she said. Trafalgar Square.

I was thrilled to be accepted as a friend, grateful that my moment of madness had come and gone without disaster. I would have been devastated if spurned out of hand, and I don't know what I would have done if accepted as a husband.

When I reached home that evening I had to dial the number again. It was the right time – any time before midnight was OK. Daniel was rarely home before that. I hadn't called for a long time, and in fact had decided to put an end to it. I couldn't take it any more. But it was different that day. A strange day. I had lost Jennifer and Jason. Again. But only temporarily, I was sure of that. Nothing could keep me permanently away from Jason, I was especially sure of that. Yet I had gained Belinda. It was a curious mixture of emotions, dank despair and crisp elation, that welled up in my heart and spread out into my blood. I had to share that day with someone, and

who better than someone who herself had no one to share
her days with: Yvette.

Oh, I'm so glad you called. Thought you'd forgotten all
about me.

I heard a burst of sobs and could feel the wetness of the
tears that flowed out onto the telephone. God, give me the
strength to cope with it, and to be of some silent help.

He don't want me to have the baby. Says it'll spoil my figure.
Besides, what'll he do all that time. I can see 'is point of view. After
all, he is a strong, 'ealthy man . . . you know what I mean. I can't
expect 'im to go without. I mean, I wouldn't want to. But I do so
want to 'ave a baby. You do understand, don't you? Don't you?
A little boy. A girl even. Y'know what! I've just had a thought
. . . If it's a boy, that's if I can 'ave one, I'll call him after you. If
only you'd tell me your name. I really will. Who are you, though?
I wish you'd tell me one day. Are you really an angel? That's what
I always call you, my own special angel. I don't know what I'd do
without you. When you hadn't called for so long, I thought . . . I
don't know what I thought. You know what I'd do if you didn't
call me any more. I'd . . . I'd . . . I don't know what I'd do. I
really don't.

What had *I* gone and done? I had only wanted . . . I don't
know what I had wanted . . .

You know what I did the other day? Only went and bashed the
Roller against the phone booth. Only wanted to make a call. Danny
was ever so good about it. Said 'e'd buy me another. In the meantime
it's gone for bodywork and all . . . I wish I could go for bodywork an'
all! At least after I've 'ad me baby. That's if I can 'ave one . . .

Trafalgar Square

The march turned out to be more impassioned and volatile than I had imagined it would be. In fact, judging by the reaction of some of them, it turned out to be more impassioned and volatile than many of its chief organisers and ardent supporters had expected it to be.

The occasion was primarily meant to be a celebration of gay and lesbian rights, and pleasures. It was not quite up to the standards of San Francisco or New York, but still managed to appear ecstatic and triumphant, lively and joyous – dare I say gay? – brimming over with verve, laced with excitement, and even a modicum of style. As was to be expected, the other groups who latched on to the main march were of similar – i.e., so-called radical left wing – persuasions: feminists, anti-apartheid groups, civil liberties campaigners, animal rights activists, anti-nuclear campaigners, PLO supporters, Lord Sutch admirers.

The last few weeks had been hard on all of the above, Lord Sutch excluded. There was therefore a bitter and brittle edge beneath all the display of power and pride. The hopes and expectations, exhortations and challenges, demands and grievances expressed by the youthful and not so youthful voices of the hustling, bustling, chanting crowd were tinged with despair and tainted by an unmentionable fear.

Patty Hearst, the confused and confusing symbol of confused and confusing times (Woman taking her destiny in her own hands? Daughter of capitalism joining forces against oppression? Terrorist victim turned terrorist? Brainwashed

or trying to brainwash?) had been found guilty and sentenced, precipitating confused and confusing reactions from
all. Isabelita, the last of the Peron women, had been ousted
by Argentina's military junta the same day, to the sad anger
and uncertain bitterness of many. And Princess Margaret's
divorce, the same week, was the cause of mixed responses:
hooray for womanhood, boo for royalty. Prime Minister
Wilson's shock resignation had left the Labour Party vocalists
dumb-struck. Beirut's road to suicide, victims and victimi-
sation of Palestinian freedom fighters, bloody aftermath of
the long-awaited independence of Angola, Norman Scott's
persecution of Jeremy Thorpe, or the other way round:
all of these had cascaded down upon the heads of the
politically hopeful – or the philosophically naive, depending
on your own political allegiance and philosophical disposi-
tion – challenging the preconceptions and presumptions of
those normally given to challenging the preconceptions and
presumptions of others.

And as if all that was not enough to test the nerves of
the most die-hard of protesters and the most organised of
marchers, the police altered the agreed route of the march at
the very last minute – to avoid clashes with a rival right wing
march organised by the National Front, was the considered
official explanation. It is *they* who should have been re-routed,
not us. We had had permission weeks before *they* butted in
for the specific purpose of creating trouble, was the marchers'
angry response.

But authority is authority, and if a decision has been taken
by an authority, mere mortals have no recourse but to
obey, or suffer the consequences. The proposed route ran
up the Strand, past Fleet Street to impress the press barons,
down towards the Embankment, through to the Houses of
Parliament, then up Whitehall and back to Trafalgar Square
for the final speeches. The roads meant nothing to me and
the alterations even less, but it was impossible not to see the
anger and resentment they engendered. It was a miracle the
march even managed to get going without chaos taking over.
But the inevitable can only be delayed, not destroyed.

We reached Trafalgar Square at the end of a successful

march. We had generally been greeted with expressions of support and sympathy by onlookers, and cheered every now and then from unexpected balconies. Exhausted but elated, and still wary, we were closing in on our starting point for the final speechifying. Belinda had prepared an extempore sermon of many pages, and I was both dreading and relishing the prospect of being subjected to it.

It was about then that the feel of an impending earthquake descended upon the collective consciousness of the marchers. It happened so subtly and subterraneously that we did not sense it until it was really and truly within us. Murmurs of silence ran through the laughing, talking, singing, chanting crowd. Starting from its perimeters, wriggling and writhing like hordes of snakes, they worked their way inwards, towards the centre of the march and coiled their virulent grip round the throbbing heart of it. Feet slowed down, or hurried up, arms tensed, palms felt sweaty, necks turned right and left and then right again, or stretched up to peer above the raised necks of those ahead trying to peer ahead themselves.

Just then different sorts of noises, partly human, partly not, began to filter in with high but irregular velocity from apparently conflicting directions. Before I could come to any conclusions as to what was going on, confusion, confrontation and chaos cascaded down upon us with such rampaging fury that it would be impossible to record events in any order or sequence of time or logic.

What I remember is fear.

And screams.

And torrents of abuse and shouting; storms of stones and empty and full soft drink and beer cans; flying streams of bottles, and the eerie notes of crashing and splintering glass; shuffling and scuffling of uncertain feet, the scamper-scampering of frightened feet, the stolid stillness of paralysed feet, the stomp-stomping of enraged feet; the heavy thud-thudding of bodies and the soft cracking and tearing of flesh. And the sound of neighing horses, and the sight of horse hoofs and horse bellies and horse testicles, and the swishing of horse tails. Steel helmets and shaved heads. The interrupted whizz of batons as a body or a head crossed their path. The faint whirr of cameras, the loud whirr of helicopters. The silky silence of hair being pulled away from heads singled and torn out of the crowd, the flesh-on-grit drag of bodies on the road, or the boot-on-flesh dhupp-dhupping of bodies on stony pavements. Swastikas and CND badges and Gay Pride badges and Apartheid is Evil badges and Free Nelson Mandela badges and Police badges and number of this rank and that and badges proclaiming Chauvinism is for Pigs and Coppers are Pigs too.

Pigs! Why pigs? I remember getting intellectually frustrated at the logic and morally outraged at the injustice of it . . . like a pompous pig.

It had its funny side as well, especially the swastikas. They were *our* emblems of superiority. Of course I don't mean ours as in the Choodahs – Brahmin forbid! – but as in the superior Indians, the true Aryans. Having been in holy awe of the swastika in my birthplace, to be terrorised by it in a foreign land as the sign of the white untouchables, Brahmin-ordained, was amusing, and at one point I remember bursting out in a fit of uproarious laughter, until someone fell on my face levelling me to the ground and saturating me with blood.

I also remember the flurry and flutter of a thousand wings and the squiggly splatter of a generous dropping on Belinda's face, raised as if in anticipation of it. The stark white dropping with a mushy green centre sat oddly upon her gingery brown skin. If only she could have seen it she would have turned it into a painting. Or at least she should have. I would have if I knew how to paint.

She made no attempt to tackle the gift of the bird. I did that for her. I kept it with me, wrapped in my little pink handkerchief which had once belonged to my cream-skinned snooty sister Nazli and which I had somehow managed to keep with me all these years. Strange, considering how we detested each other. I continued to cherish it, until the police took it away when they removed my clothes. I got the clothes back but not the handkerchief. They must have lost it. I was told it was evidence. At first I could understand their excitement. They believed the pigeon-shit-stiffened lady's hanky might contain my semen, along with skin fragments from some poor girl or other found raped and murdered on some heath or other.

But they should have found out it didn't and so returned it. I wasn't asking for much, only my handkerchief back. Not reason enough to have my head kicked in. I needed twelve stitches for that. Free, on the National Health Service. I never ceased to appreciate and admire that. When I was told how much repairing scum like me cost the taxpayer I was even more wonderstruck; and mortified, of course. Especially as it was my own fault for trying to break away from them. I felt lost without that hanky for a long, long time. Still do, on occasions. It smelled of life and memories and beginnings and colours.

That was not my only encounter with pigeons that day, the day of my first march. I remember one lying squashed beneath me as I lay squashed beneath another person who had been felled by a horse. I remember feeling hugely sorry for the poor horse as he leaped up instantly and kept rearing and leaping up to avoid stepping on or hurting any other human or living being. If only I could have put my arms round him and hugged and comforted him and sung a song for him, the one that Mother used to sing while milking Umrao: *Jia beqarar hay, chhai bahar hay, aaja merey balma tera intezar hay* . . . It is spring, the heart is restless, come, come my beloved, I wait for you . . . Perhaps not an appropriate song to sing to a horse, but no less so than to a goat, and *she* loved it. She would join in with Mother and they would both sing and laugh together all the while Umrao gave milk and produced marble droppings to decorate our rustic verandah floor.

I remember holding the pigeon's severed yet almost bloodless head in my hands as I scrambled to my feet, only to be knocked down again.

I remember all that, but not much else.

† † †

Except the fear.

Now fear and I were old acquaintances, perhaps even friends.

From the moment I saw the young man de-genitaled and slain as I lay tied helplessly by the tree to the brutal murder of Umrao, from the piteous rape of Father when in Chandan police custody to the terrors of attempted murder by sun under the glass dome of the Shree's New Mexico Ashram, from the flood deaths of Nazli and Great Grandmother to the butchery of Mother and Edwina and Junior, fear and I had been going hand in hand. I had been hauled and mauled and used and abused by the police while in a drug-induced stupor, tear-gassed and lathi-charged, chased by the military and shot at and fired at and seen friends and strangers killed or wounded or mutilated in front me and behind me and all around me in the streets of Chittagong.

But never in all that time had I known fear as I knew it then, during that day of the march. Grief, yes; bitterness, rage, despair, madness, and more; but never such fear, a different genre of fear, a fear born of different parents than the fear I knew.

I hunted frantically, in my mind and in my surroundings, to come up with an explanation, but it took another march or two, a court appearance or two, some reading of newspapers, some watching of television, some talking to friends, acquaintances, co-conspirators and co-criminals before I began vaguely to understand the reason, the *nature*, of that fear. And it is only now, after thirteen years of life and death and living and dying, that I know for sure.

It was the fear of order, control and permanence.

I was used to the fear of disorder, chaos and transience. I had come from a country where people had intrinsic freedom as individual entities, if not as citizens – at least until the anti-Communist world shoved religious fundamentalism up their fundaments – and played their own game by their own rules. But here was a different game played on different grounds with different rules and a different sort of opponent under a different sort of management. I was used to a fear game in which you stood a chance – a fifty-fifty chance, possibly better. This was a game you could not win, and you knew it right from the start.

† † †

The next time I saw Belinda was in Bow Street Magistrates'

Court some days later, quite by accident. I was there for a different offence, urinating in Windmill Street.

It was a Saturday afternoon and I was just kind of wandering aimlessly when I saw a merry crowd of young men come laughing and singing and drinking and waving scarves about. One of them unzipped his trousers and pulled out a large floppy dick, held it in both hands, and started squirting it about, watering the street. Some of the other lads joined in. I sort of grinned sheepishly and released my whangdoodle from the confines of a new and overtight pair of jeans with a sense of great relief and began pissing away to my heart's content, believing it to be some English sport or local ritual and not wishing to seem like a stand-offish foreigner, singing *God Save the Queen* all the while for no reason other than that I wanted to join in with them but did not know any of the songs they were singing. Just then a pair of policemen on the beat walked in on us. The other boys were let off after a warning, and I was booked. There was a good reason for that which was carefully and very slowly explained to me by the arresting officer: me and my piss smelled worse than any man or any piss that he or his mate had ever come across, and they had come across tons and tons of sub-human dross like me, and gallons and gallons of sub-human piss, like mine, in all sorts of London toilets while waiting for fuckin' queers like me, and in other places too numerous to mention, ever since the shitty likes of me from the asshole of the world had taken over their great and wonderful city, and they knew exactly what they were talking about, and they could *not*, repeat *not*, allow their clean and beautiful city streets to be fouled up by the shitty likes of me and my shitty piss. The fact that I had been singing *God Save the Queen* hadn't helped.

Belinda was there in connection with a march – an earlier one, held the previous December I believe. I was so happy to see her. I had begun to think I had lost her. Hadn't been able to find her in Hyde Park the last couple of Sundays, either in her role as a hell-raising feminist or as a hell-painting artist. We had not got round to exchanging addresses or anything like that, so I'd believed that was that. As it turned out,

Bow Street Magistrates' Court became quite a regular haunt of ours.

† † †

Have you anything you would like to say? softly spoke the white Her Worship in the centre. She seemed more important – and not just because of her placing – than the black His Worship to the left or the other Her Worship to the right: Justices of the Peace, I had learnt.

I failed to respond. My mind was off to native, now foreign, parts.

The Learned Clerk leaned over. Have you anything to say in your defence, Mr . . . Cyrus? His cold, clear voice cut through time and space.

I began saying: *When I was born, Your Worships, I was born free. There was no one to register the day, the date, the hour, the minute, the second of my birth, not even the year.* I unzipped my trousers, put my hand inside my flies and pulled out one rabbit. Then another. I had no idea why I did that. I continued speaking. *No one to put my sex down on paper, nor my weight, nor the colour of my skin, no one to state whether I was Caucasian, Hispanic or one of the other shitty ones, even though I was; no one to take down my name nor the name of my father nor that of my mother; nor write down my address, the great betrayer of one's social class and everything else that goes with it.*

REALLY, softly screamed Her Worship to the right, and clasped her hands in delight. How clever of you to think that. I wouldn't have thought that you could think . . . speak . . . I mean, know . . . She blushed, raised trembling hands to her head and started tearing out chunks of frail balding hair, adding weakly, All that . . . sort of . . . thing . . .

I continued unperturbed: *I was not labelled at birth. No tag round my neck or wrist. Not branded like cattle.*

Heresy. Repentance called for.

I calumniate the poor bovines. Our cattle are not branded either, nor horses nor sheep nor any other of God's creatures. They are remembered by name or appearance, like people. The room was full of rabbits now, swarming all over the place, multiplying like bloody Pakis. *They roam free with their human partners, sharing the good years with them, and the lean years; fattening or starving, as the case may be . . .*

Would I be allowed to go on? They did let people carry on with the most absurd of defences in these smaller courts, especially if they were not 'represented'.

Uhn unhgh. Is this really relevant, uhn? Her Worship in the centre stood up on her chair as she spoke and placed one elegantly white foot (elegantly shod in white leather) firmly upon the long oak table in front of all Their Worships.

Yes indeed, Your Worship. I am trying to answer the arresting officer's charge that I, that 'we', 'us lot', behave like animals. We do so because, like animals, we too are free. As a child I was not subjected to daily imprisonment in a school for no crime other than that of not being an adult. Had I been sentenced to a life of nine-to-five from the age of five I would have torn the world apart with my bare hands, or as much of it as I could claw out with my fingernails.

I began ripping the courtroom apart, beginning with the finely carved oak panelling on the solid stone walls. No one made any attempt to stop me.

Or just died.

I fell prostrate among all the rubble, shut my eyes, stopped breathing, and played dead. My mouth kept gabbing on: *Just lay down and died, even if my body lived on to be a hundred and twenty-three. I had the freedom of brothers and sisters and parents and uncles and aunts and maternal grandparents and paternal grandparents and had not been enclaved in and enslaved by a nuclear family, more explosive and more devastating than a nuclear weapon.*

I opened my eyes and surveyed the scene of devastation surrounding me and for which I was responsible.

As to the arresting officer's taunts, 'Why don't you and your kind go back then? To the shit-holes –' begging Your Worships' pardon – 'you came from?' Perhaps he has a point. But can one ever go back to a place that was in a different time? As for others like me, once you are possessed by possessions, there is no escape, no turning back; the need to cling to them, to add to them, is more addictive than heroin, and the boundaries of a land that does not want you can be more difficult to escape from than the highest prison walls. Especially for those with dodgy passports.

His and Her Worship on the left and the right joined their heads together, shook their heads together, then separated their heads together. That was the end, I thought. But it wasn't. They reverted to silence. Her Worship in the centre maintained her stance, one foot on the chair, the other on the table. I stood up, reconstructed the courtroom, and continued speaking.

The natural chaos of my world had further advantages – I smiled, showing all my teeth – *the most vital being the advantage of natural hope.* My smile faded out, memories flooded in. *If you made a mistake – committed a 'crime' – or were just accused of committing a crime, you could run off to the next province, perhaps only the next village, and have a good chance of starting a new life.* I imagined starting a new life joined to Her Worship in the centre in holy matrimony and fervently praying for someone to put us asunder. I spoke as I prayed. *And unless a forty-five-year-old man claimed to be the three-year-old daughter of the local nawab, he would be believed, whatever 'facts' he gave about himself, and valued or not depending on his abilities and behaviour rather than on his curriculum vitae, upon his present performance not his past record –*

Do forgive me, but are you here to justify your people's way of life, or are you here to defend yourself? Because if you are here to defend yourself, and I presume you are, because you are, uhn, the defendant, then I am not sure this line of, uhn, reasoning, is going to do you any good. On the contrary.

Her Worship in the centre now stood with both feet on the table, placed her hands upon her hips and looked down upon me with compassionate disdain.

Neither, Madam, Your Worship. I am here to speak the truth. That is the oath I took.

Very well, then. If you are sure you know what you are doing. She lifted the edge of her skirt with one dainty hand and did a little pirouette.

Thank you, Your Worship. My parents chose the next country, new names and a new faith. And although their end was grotesque and terrible, it was by no means inevitable. It could have worked out, did for a long time.

What did happen to your parents? The black His Worship to the left looked the curious type.

I don't think we really need to know that at this stage, do we? Her Worship in the centre gave a high can-can kick.

Not really, Your Worship, I answered.

Is there anything else you would like to say, Mr Cyrus, before the court reaches a decision? The Clerk's voice was sharper now.

Yes, Your Worships, I have, but I can also stand on my head, I said, and promptly stood on my head.

We do not believe that sort of attitude is going to get you anywhere, said Her Worship in the centre as she somersaulted on the table and stood, wavering precariously on *her* head. She wasn't wearing any knickers and her secret parts were thickly matted with a mixture of coarse, grey, white and black hair. Except into more trouble, she added, this time speaking through the heavily moustachioed lips of her vulva. All the rabbits jumped on the table, scrambled up Her Worship, and disappeared down her hatch in twos and threes. I was surprised, amused, impressed even.

† † †

But it still didn't stop me from being frightened.

No matter what little tricks I played to divert myself, the raised hoofs of the horses and their sleek underbellies would always be there, as would riot shields and radioed commands and looks of steel upon faces of steel beneath helmets of steel, and the whirring and clicking of cameras. There was no escape here. And where there is no escape, there is no hope. And where there is no hope, there is nothing. No second chances, no fresh starts, no forgiving, no forgetting. However many times you went to court . . .

† † †

Yes, Mr Cyrus, by now the court knows some of your views.

Remember you are not in Court Three, but in Court Two this time, and are being tried by a Stipendiary Magistrate. He is also a lawyer. So you had better be careful what you say.

The black usher in the black gown muttered all this under her breath close to my ears. I think she liked me.

Every crime solved is many lives ruined, I began. *Every crime solved is many criminals created.*

Do we have to listen to all this? said His Honour.

Only if I am permitted to speak, said I.

Will there be a point to it all?

Oh yes indeed, Your Honour, I said, going up to him and kissing him on the lips. A real wet kiss.

Very well then. Continue, Mr Cyrus.

I cleared my throat and took a deep breath.

Justice is the root of injustice; punishment the cause of crime. Or the fear of punishment, as embodied in laws and the agencies that enforce those laws. Every victim of injustice is, in the final analysis, the victim of someone's justice.

I looked meaningfully into his eyes as I said this, lifted him off the table, put my right arm round his waist, grasped the palm of his right hand with the palm of my left, and began leading him in a waltz. The music, Strauss I suppose, started a fraction of a second later than us, but I adjusted my steps accordingly. He followed, but somewhat reluctantly. *Consider the first crime on earth.* I pressed his body close to mine and held him tight. I could feel his heart beating faster and faster. He wasn't as fit as he should have been. My voice waltzed gracefully in time: *Yes, consider, Your Honour, the very first crime on earth. Cain's murder of Abel. Cause? God's punishment of Cain, punishment by rejection, the worst punishment possible for his entire year's labour of love and the fruit thereof. The mark stamped on him was supposed to be justice, and the world still quivers with the injustice of it. Discrimination, poverty and deprivation are punishments.* The tempo of the dance quickened. *Hence they lead to crimes.*

And what of the crimes committed out of lust and envy and greed? challenged His Honour in mid-twirl. Are they unpunished crimes?

There is no such thing, can be no such thing, as unpunished crime. *Every crime is preceded by its punishment, just as terrorism is preceded by oppression and tyranny, and violence by denigration, degradation and dehumanisation. That is the natural law. Human law is perverse and unnecessary, which is why it is forever haunted by failure and leads only to aggravated crime, adding injury to injury and insult to insult.* By now we were rolling along the floor smoothly, magnetically.

Lust and envy and greed lie either in unloved hearts, Your Honour – and to be unloved is the gravest of punishments – or in minds corrupted by the love of money – and the corruption of one's mind is almost as grave a punishment. I was tightening my grip round his waist, pulling him closer and closer to myself. *Conversely, it could all be the work of the Devil, and to have a Devil imposed upon one really is a grave punishment. After all, man did not create the Devil, God did. He was His dear little angel once.*

May I remind the defendant that this is a court of law, not the Synod of the Church of England, and that he, not God, is on trial.

The music hushed to near silence as His Honour said this, allowing me to press my cheek against his. Then without warning he managed to wriggle out of my arms, and went back up to his high seat. Behind the sarcasm I could detect curiosity, for his face was interestingly and interestedly red, so I decided to keep pushing my luck.

I beg your pardon, Your Honour, but I'm talking of the original crime, not the original sin.

Would you care to explain, Mr Cyrus? The trailing and weakening of his voice suggested that he had begun to regret that statement as soon as he opened his mouth.

Punishment, Your Honour, punishment is the original crime. You want to end crime? Then work to withdraw, negate and disempower existing punishments: whether natural or imposed, social or cultural, physical or psychological, national or international, religious or political. Do not pile jurisprudential punishments on top. In other words, tackle original crime, and secondary crime will disappear on its own, just as the drying up of all water will end the rains which bring more water.

I walked over to His Honour again, and this time using both hands lifted him bodily out of his seat and began to waltz round the floor again, this time carrying him in my arms. He seemed relieved at not having to exert himself on the floor, and entwined his fingers round the back of my neck for support and comfort.

Crime is an act of doing, I began as the music started again, this time Beethoven's Pastoral. *Sin is a state of being. I would call original sin the creative flaw. And yes, for that the responsibility must be God's, being the Creator. Mankind, the creation, cannot be responsible for such a fundamental flaw. If so it would be capable of transcending the powers of the Creator, which, as you would agree, is clearly ridiculous.*

I circled round and round the floor, in front of the half-caged defendants' enclosure, around the visitors' benches, holding up His Honour like a trophy.

Free will, if it exists, can create its own little sins, flaws of character, but original sin can only be the Creator's, hence the necessity of God's atonement for it on the cross.

The music picked up pace, and to my surprise His Honour jumped to the floor and joined me in a fast quickstep, and then in the alternating rhythms of a foxtrot. It was going beautifully. I could again feel his heart beating next to mine, this time more steadily. It was like dancing with God. But then a Charleston started up, and I had to ruin it all by first kicking in the wrong direction and then stepping on His Honour's right toe.

Ouch. Hell. I see. Thank you for enlightening the court. I shall not invoke the Law of Blasphemy for the present, nor threaten Contempt of court, for the present. But, said His Honour, rudely disengaging himself from my arms and limping back to his high seat, you will have to watch your step very carefully from now on. He removed his foot from his shoe and began massaging his big toe gingerly.

I thought here it might be a good time to say something nice about my host land. I planted my feet slightly apart and spread my arms. *Manifestly this cycle of creation, persecution, increase, greater persecution, and greater increase of so-called criminals is gruesomely worse in the USA than the UK, but I hadn't become aware of it there. Partly because of the sheltered or kept nature of my life there – first in the Ashram, then with Shakti, later with*

Suzi – and partly because the vastness and grandeur of the land, and its warmth, both human and climatic, tended to offset the restraints and bondages of society.

Quite so, Mr Rattigan . . . I mean, Mr Cyrus. This Shakti and Suzi, were they there when you were importuning, Mr Cyrus?

I was not importuning your honour. That was Mr Carey, in court before me, Your Honour, the one with the rather bulging eyes and unsettled hair, the one –

Oh yes, yes. I know. I know, Mr Cyrus, that was an . . . error, I apologise. Please continue.

Thank you, Your Honour. You are very kind, Your Honour. I am here for trying to kiss the arresting officer, Your Honour, on the lips. I tried to kiss his Honour again, on the lips, but he moved my lips away with the back of his hand.

Yes, yes, I know. Could we please continue? That is, if you really must . . . Must you? His eyebrows were raised hopefully, but I bet he would have been hurt if I had stopped.

The head of the pigeon in my palm began to peck at my fingers, between them and underneath the nails, drawing out blood. It wasn't funny. It also pecked at my ribs and my groin, which was funny. And nibbled my balls, tugging at and pulling out sturdy strands of hair, which was both not funny and hilarious at the same time.

I began speaking again, though I wasn't sure if I was. *Thank you, Your Honour. Thank you again. Every society, ours included, has always had its quota of human sacrifices, to placate the righteous and to protect them and their cohorts from the imagined evil of greater men and lesser gods.*

Between my thighs the pigeon began to grow whole again, and I could feel its body develop, distend, become firmer, vitalised by the fluids of my manhood and life. It fluttered free from the confines of my flesh and flew out of my asshole, reborn.

In primitive cultures it was done more honestly, and with dignity. In a temple, upon an altar, under the knife. With music and dancing and revelry and reverence. I could hear my voice, soft and hushed above the sound of music and revelry and dancing. I could feel the cameras coming in for a close-up of the faraway look in my eyes.

The pigeon's freedom from the confines of my flesh was bound by the limits of the court. It crashed against its strong stone walls and banged its head against the solid oak doors, hand-made and beautifully panelled. It started to scream pigeon screams, but nobody took any notice, as if it wasn't there at all.

The lights dimmed, so too the shine on the polished wood that surrounded us like the inside of a gigantic mock coffin for the doomed and tombed alive. The music stopped, the camera receded, my voice dropped to a mere whisper. *Then came the law, and with it righteousness, and with it civilisation, and with it the stonings to death for partaking in natural pleasures, the bargaining of eyes and teeth, the sanctioned thralldom, the sacred castes, the marked and unmarked sons of Adam, the gladiatorial games played with the lives of the betrayed, the funeral pyres of dead husbands and living wives, and the meting out of judgements and carrying out of punishments by the chosen few against the cast-out thousands.*

Are you referring to the practice of sati? Is it sati, Mr Cyrus?

I was indeed, Your Honour, and it is. Your Honour is very knowledgeable of our barbarous ways. I went up to him again and asked for another dance, a fast number this time, perhaps an energetic rock-and-roll tumble.

Yes, yes. I mean no, NO, Mr Cyrus. Thank you, Mr Cyrus. He brushed me aside. Restrain yourself, Mr Cyrus. And what has sati got to do with the case in hand?

Nothing, Your Honour, and everything. Were it not for man's inhumanity to man, the very necessity for this modern ritual of jurisprudential sacrifices would be removed, and I would not be standing here before you, Your Honour. So you can see how closely the one is allied to the other.

The policeman was open-mouthed, the usher was picking at her robe, the court clerk was going red. The pigeon tumbled down on the floor, battered bloodied and dying. Nobody stirred a finger to help him live or to ease his death.

My voice was lost now, confused; echoing, as if in a walled desert, or a cave without a floor, or an ocean without water.

God's alleged personal intervention – whether as the many-bodied Bhagwan, or the mortal Prometheus, or the enlightened Buddha, or the incarnate Jesus, or one of the many unsung unknowns – failed to turn back the Evil of Law and the wickedness of laws and to vitiate the sinful piety and cruel judgementalism of its believers and practitioners, and to stem the viciousness of the righteous, and to replace all of it with forgiveness and love. The giving of His own blood and His own body in lieu of the bodies and blood of His condemned children proved equally futile. Of course, He was adopted as a symbol, made a quasi-member of the superior race, turned white and blond and blue eyed, and hung on walls and around necks instead of hanged on trees or stakes. And so continued divine decline and human progress until I came to the proud and civilised modern world.

The room clouded over, the sun hid behind the walls.

This proud civilised modern world, replete with righteous men and women, all incredibly civilised, more in one small family car than in entire pre-history, swarming out of their semi-detacheds, herded together in their churches or mosques or synagogues or temples or dance halls, or crawling about in their millions in the holiest of holies, the supermarkets and shopping centres; led by their trolleys and their civilised prophets and spiritual pundits who run newspapers and control television channels; and their civilised minions, the politicians, paid for by those who have the most to lose having gained the most, the high priests of Mammon and the true custodians of the true civilisation. All ready to sacrifice anybody and anything to maintain the status quo that sustains and nourishes them and theirs.

We have leant over backwards to give you this latitude, Mr Cyrus. Will you please come to the point.

Gently, almost inaudibly, but with a twinkle, I said: *The point, Your Honour, is my inability to cope with all this civilisation. It has confronted me too suddenly and too powerfully. I am not prepared for it. I am too uncouth for it. I react in an unseemly manner without meaning any offence. My attempt to kiss the arresting officer was a reconciliatory gesture, not uncommon in our part of the world. I plead not guilty on the basis of primitive origins, Your Honour.*

Your intricately sophisticated and highly irksome description of your alleged naivety belies your assertions. The court finds you guilty, as charged, of disturbing the peace and resisting arrest. The maximum penalty . . .

Another round to the court. You can't win them all. I seemed not to win any. My arguments may or may not have been sophisticated, but I certainly was primitive. I might have learnt some sophisticated skills, but I still did not know where or how to apply them to my advantage.

If only I'd taken the usher's advice and kept my mouth shut. Not that that would have made any difference. The decision was already taken. It was in their eyes. This way at least I had my say, and got some fun out of it. Freedom of speech and all that. Who do you think you're kidding? Shakti would have said. And she'd have been right, too.

One day your arrogance will get you into serious trouble, said the usher, shaking her head as I was on my way out.

† † †

Was I arrogant? I don't know. What I do know is that I was terrified. The nerves came after the performance. Once the play acting ended, real life took over.

The pigeon's head was back in my palm. Its blood was all over the walls, its flesh on the floor. A weedy-looking young man with gaunt cheeks and old man's looks acquitted hungrily on the floor outside the courtroom and began eating it with ravenous joy. His hair was blue, his eyes blond. His designer stubble looked like an unshaven face. The pigeon's head was pleased. Its body had not gone to waste. A pretty young girl ran past us, naked, the letters C P written in scarlet across her chest, dragging the plump hairless body of the clerk behind her, his head stuck somewhere between her thighs. Communist Party? I thought to myself. Even worse, mumbled the clerk's head from inside the girl's womb, Common Prostitute.

† † †

I heard laughter.

It was Belinda. She didn't often laugh – she was much

too earnest and intense for that sort of thing – but she was laughing then, and it was beautiful to see. I began to laugh myself. We went back into the court and got married. It wasn't the same place, but the people were the same.

The Stipendiary Magistrate performed the ceremony, the three Justices were the witnesses, and the clerk noted everything down. Then they cleared the table, covered it with a starched white sheet, threw a withered red rose upon it, its thorns sticking out below the flagging petals, tore at our clothes until we were stripped completely and ordered us to consummate our marriage.

Belinda was furious, but I understood their reasons. After all, they only wanted to make sure that it was a genuine marriage, and not a marriage of convenience. Also, this way they could make sure she was a virgin. You can never tell with us lot and our moral standards. We are devious and uncivilised, ready to do anything to earn a buck to feed our children, or our parents and grandparents, if we don't have any children. Stick together, we do, like flies on sugar. Greedy and unprincipled, no doubt about it.

A doctor and two police officers, one male, one female, were at hand to see that everything was conducted in a legally and medically approved fashion. There would, however, be no right of appeal on the decision taken.

I was told to wait while Belinda's sex lips were pulled apart by gloved fingers. The black His Worship was holding a lamp at just the right angle to provide just the right light. The gloved fingers continued to work upwards until you could only see the gloved wrist.

I couldn't see Belinda's face. Her Member of Parliament was sitting on it. Uncomfortably, but resolutely.

The microphone crackled and came to life. *Testing, testing, one two three, testing, testing . . .*

> *For he's a jolly good fellow*
> *For he's a jolly good fellow*
> *For he's a jolly good fellow*
> *That nobody can deny . . .*

Test failed, with flying colours.

> *For they're all jolly good fellows*
> *For they're all . . .*

The three venerable Justices of the Peace and the Stipendiary Magistrate and the learned clerk stopped their jolly-good-fellowing and began to sing highlights from *The Marriage of Figaro*.

The MP began to dance a jig.

I couldn't figure out what was going on.

I should have known. He really *was* a jolly good fellow.

Stonehenge

Belinda and I had been married seventeen weeks and were now at last on our honeymoon, camping on Salisbury Plain to witness the Winter Solstice, escape Christmas, and see the New Year in.

In the meantime we had been on some major and some minor marches, a few demonstrations and not a few sit-ins, and collected umpteen thousand signatures for a petition. I had meanwhile been building roads and shopping arcades, and Belinda had been teaching history at a former Secondary Modern School in Forest Gate, now a newly emerging Comprehensive.

It was a wonder we got round to taking this break. We had hoped to go to Snowdonia in the last week of the summer holidays, but just then petitions and protests had to be hastily organised after press reports of the virginity testing of young girls coming over from the Indian sub-continent, followed by a changing-of-the-guards style sit-in in front of the Home Office, with me doing double shifts on occasions (since I didn't have a 'proper job'), and demonstrations at Heathrow Airport. Also a protest committee had to be set up regarding the police handling of Notting Hill Carnival. Later we had planned to take the half-term week off to go to Cornwall – one of Belinda's friends had a caravan somewhere over there – but then came the case of Ms Janet Longman, dismissed from her job after complaining of sexual harassment. Oh yes, and there was the National Union of Teachers rally before that and a feminist protest against a sex shop (what sex shop?) in Forest

Gate, which also included burning copies of *The Sun*. Must have sold a few extra that day. I should not omit to mention here the Hyde Park Sundays; and my court appearances; and Belinda's.

In December the killing of many black Africans by a Rhodesian gang came just too late to stop us. News hit the newspapers on the twentieth, but we left on the nineteenth. Actually I heard about it on the radio the day before, but kept it from Belinda until we arrived in our battered 2CV and set up camp. I suppose it was naughty of me, but I thought we could do with a break. Especially me. Sex three times (average) a night made Belinda feel on top of the world, but it was beginning to get me down just that little bit. Why was it that only people who just wanted it, and a lot of it, were attracted to me! Perhaps everyone could tell just by looking at me that that's all I was good for, and those interested in the more important things in life moved on. In a way it was depressing. But in a way it made me feel good, and I don't just mean what you think I mean. It made me feel good to be good at doing something which was one in the beam-rattling eye of the righteous.

I was not sure I liked this new 'up yours' attitude of mine. I was becoming more aggressive in approach, more violent in speech, more devious in thought. Rightly or wrongly, I had begun to believe it necessary for survival. England had changed me in the one year I had been here. Or I had changed myself. Whatever, I was not too happy about it. And the less happy I felt about it, the worse I became.

On the other hand, for once I felt my unholy glee to be wholly justified. At least sex is the one thing which the poor, even the shitty poor like myself, can be as good at as anybody else; and frequently we are better at it than the cock-twisted righteous and the cunt-jaded rich. And that cannot be allowed. It is all right for the romping, bonking millionaires, he that hath and unto him, and all that. But how dare the poor and the powerless and the ordinary excel at it! That has always received attitude in feudal/capitalist/repressive/fundamentalist societies.

But to give Belinda her due, she didn't just want sex from me. She wanted me to share with her the more important things in life as well; quite as passionately and quite as earnestly. I was grateful to her for that, and proud to be of some use to her in all she did, not just sex.

Although I was expecting a lot more of *that* here, at least I wouldn't have been carrying truckloads of bricks all day or digging holes in the road or filling up holes in the road. I wouldn't have been tramping from house to house collecting signatures or standing in the centre of high streets distributing leaflets for hours on end or marching through half of London bearing heavy placards and shouting slogans. In short, I wouldn't have spent every available ounce of energy indulging in political acrobatics under the big top of Democracy: a government of all the people, by all the people, for all the people; become a government of a majority of the people, by a majority of the people, for a majority of the people; become a government of a majority of the electorate, by a majority of the electorate, for a majority of the electorate; become a government of a majority of the electorate who vote, by a majority of the electorate who vote, for a selected minority who can manipulate a sizeable enough minority of the electorate; become a government elected by a minority, and run by the chosen few on behalf of those committed to maintaining them in power. We had the freedom to say what we liked how we liked, and we did. They had the power to do what they liked how they liked, and they did. Nothing could be changed, and nothing was.

Still, the not-so-merry merry-go-round, the Sick Opera of Electioneering, helped keep people's minds off their problems. Protesting against it and its ends kept my mind off Jason and Jennifer.

This was the time of pipe-sucker Harold and ass-faced Jim. The Unspeakable and Its coterie of Unmentionables were yet only a macabre nightmare in the sleep of Cassandra. And who could have been blamed for not believing her had she woken up and spoken?

On top of it all, it had to have been the hottest summer in living memory. Even I, coming from the plains of India and the tropical heartland of Bangla Desh and the deserts of the American continent, found it a little too much – perhaps because I was sweating my ass off working here, whereas there I would have been lolling about half naked in a hammock made from my dhoti under a shady tree in a secluded spot; or locked, fully naked, in an air-conditioned room with gallons of ice-cold tea and you-know-who.

† † †

It was the sacred night.

The night of prayer.

The night of the turning year; the night of the returning light.

The night of celebrations and dancing; the night of weeping and mourning.

The night of fear and apprehensions; the night of hope and expectations.

The night of looking back and wondering what went wrong; the night of looking forward and wondering what might go wrong.

The night of remembering and savouring; the night of imagining and relishing.

The night of destroying and re-creating.

The night of killing and dying.

The night of birth and rebirth.

The night of the split nine, three by three, the twenty-first of the twelfth.

The night of the Winter Solstice.

The night of visions and nightmares. The night of truth and falsehood. The night of prophecy and madness. The night of the tiger and the Naga. The night of God and gods. The night of man and the Man. The night of beasts and the Beast.

The night of nights.

The night with two faces.

I had very much wanted to spend the whole of the night out under the sky, and just before midnight to walk the largest possible circle round the stones nine times, stopping after each set of three to perform some sort of spontaneous ritual: a dance, a song, an evocation, anything. Belinda had agreed, reluctantly at first – spiritualism/religion of any kind was not her scene – but gradually becoming excited by the idea, just for the 'fun of it'. I considered this a great personal achievement of mine, for having fun was not one of Belinda's failings. She was deadly serious, even at sex. I wondered how she managed to get such a thrill out of it, with all her rules and regulations. No man-on-top positions, except in emergencies. Enough but not too much foreplay: none was callous and brutal as it arrogantly and thoughtlessly – typical male adverbs – ignored a woman's needs; too much might become, for the man, a substitute for the act itself at the expense of a woman's desires. Oral sex had to be equally divided between the sexes. Above all it was incumbent upon the man (me) to fully understand and respect at all times the necessity, and the *nature* of the female orgasm, multiple in her case. And no anal sex, as the woman could not return the deed. She had, mercifully, not yet come to a decision regarding the ethics of the female dildoing the male.

After all, a woman has to look after herself in a male-orientated society, is her assertion. Male-orientated! My voice goes high each time I say it. Male-orientated, I repeat. Just because men fight for and die for the values held by a society does not mean they are *their* values. They are simply doing their job, as always: protecting the values they have been told to protect, with their bodies, their lives, their honour and their deaths. Ask the majority of young men whether they would rather get married, have a job and settle down, or live a life of freedom and sex and adventure, with no ties except of loyalty and friendship, no mortgages to pay, no HP agreements to service, no decorating and redecorating the kitchen and the bathroom. Then ask young women the same question, giving them a choice between being happily wedded to a good man with a good job and a good house, or living a life of high adventure with no ties except of loyalty and friendship etcetera, etcetera. Then make an effort to discover, if you can, the values of the society and whose wishes they reflect.

The attitudes of society inevitably hold good the desires and hopes and aspirations of women, not men. Men only work to enforce the same, legally or otherwise. Little wonder so many men rebel or become violent: they are being forced to live in a society and in situations which are imposed upon them against their wishes and contrary to their dreams. That is why so many men are artists and musicians and poets: they have to *create* a world of their own where they can act out their fears and fantasies, because they are not allowed to do so in the real world.

Razia, Belinda's second in command, said I should grow up and start facing my responsibilities like a man and stop whingeing like a mama's boy.

I wished I was a mama's boy, for then my values would have been more like theirs. It's precisely because I was my Father's boy that my values were more akin to his.

I wished they wouldn't keep bringing Mother into all this. After all, she was a woman too, if only a Choodah one. But it wasn't really their fault. They did not know I had a problem in that direction. I never could bring myself to talk about Mother's death; or her life, for that matter. Not even to Belinda. The odd remark I threw in now and then only made everything sound casual and normal. Perhaps it was. I wished I knew.

There were other campers and caravaners spread around the area. We had spoken to some but did not know what, if anything, they had planned for the night. I'd have preferred to be alone with Belinda. All our time together we seemed to be surrounded by crowds of people: friends, acquaintances, strangers, the police; anyone you can think of. Unless we were in bed, or just about to go to bed, or in the bath; or perhaps in our little 2CV, which Belinda loved only a little more than me, in spite of the fact that it was a possession and one was not supposed to love possessions.

It was only eight in the evening, and already it seemed like it had been dark since God made the mistake of putting his humans out to dry and the pair of them walked away wet, damaging the machinery in the process. It was my second winter in England and I was still finding it difficult to get used to the long periods of sunlessness – despite the long hot summer, or perhaps more so because of it. I had always revelled in the wild blackness of night; but at night, not during early afternoon. I found it confusing and depressing. My first encounter with dark, shortish days was a freezing fortnight in Hamburg. But then there was the heady excitement of all that travel, and of Europe, and of being eighteen – enough to warm the coldest days, enough to dazzle anybody out of their senses, much less a poor shitbag from Chandan. And there was all that snow to brighten up the darkness, and all those lights. It was pretty dingy in East Ham and Forest Gate, and I was a tired old twenty-two – twenty-three in nine days. And no snow.

† † †

It is now, as I write, surrounded by stones of a different kind, my last winter and I am still finding it difficult to get used to long periods of sunlessness, despite another long hot summer. Strange that the beginning of my end had to be the summer of 1976, and the end of my beginning the summer of 1989, both record hot summers in England. A totally irrelevant point, but I mention it just the same, for those of you who look for a significance in everything.

Tonight once again is the sacred night.

The night of the split nine, three by three, the twenty-first of the twelfth.

The circle is about to close itself.

It is exactly thirteen years to the prophecy. The fourteenth year, the year of the double seven, the fateful year, starts tomorrow. The years of waiting are ended. The year of fulfilment is awaiting.

You might think that in that case I could still have up to twelve months more, but it is not as simple as that. In another nine days I will have completed my thirty-six years, four times nine. And when twice seven and four times nine are within a gap of nine, it means the time has come.

What superstitious mumbo-jumbo! you might say. Certainly Belinda would say so, assuming she is in a position to say anything. I hope she is with all the love in my heart. For someone who spoke upon soapboxes till her mouth ran dry, rain or shine, and shouted herself hoarse in marches, rain or shine, and passionately tried to convince everyone, friend or foe, of the right of her causes and beliefs, it would be an unbearably silent sorrow to imagine that she is now silent forever.

I can still see her body on fire, her beautiful black body sparkling within the beautiful gold of the rising flames, ascending upwards in tongues of unspoken liturgies, charging towards the skies like myriad shooting stars, then fading out, fading out and dying, dying for my sin, for the sin of my disobedience, fruitlessly and meaninglessly . . . But then, what else could be expected? She married a *manhoos*. Pity Aunt Verna wasn't around to warn her. And I would agree, it is superstitious mumbo-jumbo. Where I might disagree is upon the validity, the value, the relevance, of superstitious mumbo-jumbo.

After all, why must the understanding of $E = MC^2$ be more important than twice seven and four times nine? Why should the relativity of time and elasticity of space and quantum geometrodynamics raise more highbrows and less eyebrows than playing around with cosmic numbers or conjuring up astrological fantasies? True that without the former we might not have reached the moon, or dropped the bomb; but the latter have helped many a suffering fool to make some sense of their suffering, and sustained them through the night.

But perhaps I wrongly pitch the discoveries of the mind against the mysteries of the mind. After all, they both belong to the mind, no matter how much the rational fraction of it is irritated by the vastness of the irrational rest; and no matter how much the irrational vastness of it is intimidated by the saturated intensity and viable power of the rational fraction. Both emerge from and return to the same sources for strength and resuscitation: matter, whether grey or not, light, and movement; with time, space, and energy as inevitable corollaries.

And I do so on the wrong night.

The night that time and space, energy and matter, light

and movement, all converge and meet, meet and explode, explode and diversify, only to converge and meet again, but in a different combination and visible from different perspectives; all within the same atomic fragment of the space-time dimension.

At least, that is what happened to me on that night thirteen years ago, and it is happening to me again, thirteen years on.

It is scary, but I try to understand. For in understanding, however fractionally, might lie the answer. The escape. Not from this irrelevant man-made prison which does no more than incarcerate the body and in doing so releases the mind and the spirit to flights of freedom greater than it could ever have known when bound by the freedoms of everyday existence; but escape from the moral incumbents inherent in the destiny of the individual's existence within the collective of mankind, within the palpable folds of its created gods, and within the culpable psyche of the Creator God.

Whether I understand or not, I hope that you will by the time I have finished relating to you the events of my night out on the ancient plains where stand the stones of Stonehenge today. The past and the future, reality and myth, mind and matter, all fused into each other in a way that no time-lapse illusion, no time-asymmetry factor, no Doppler effect could even begin to explain.

Consider what Zen Buddhists and oriental mystics revealed through mantras and tantras epochs ago, to the effect that the apparent continuum of dots, the connecting link between moving objects, is a product of our mind, and does not in reality exist. It took centuries of ignorance and anguish and the quantum theory to prove that it was indeed so. So, what does not exist can be perceived to exist. Isn't everything that is solid and visible made up of atoms that are intangible and invisible? How can a collection of unseens become seen? How many ghosts are needed to make one real person?

Meanwhile electrons and protons continue their dance eternal within the atom's womb, assless priests, heartless politicians, pointless philosophers, brainless scientists and aimless writers notwithstanding. Monuments collapse and creatures die while every component of their molecular structure continues to exist, pure and simple and anything but straightforward, with a jig in its heart and a tune in its brain. Perhaps that is the mystery of faith, as held by the believers of today in the ecumenical jungle of grand cities, or by the ancient worshippers anywhere: in the deserts of Palestine, on the mountain of Sinai, at the battlefield of Mahabharata, under the bodhi tree, or on the plains of Salisbury. And every now and then all their gods gather together to haunt and tease and to extract a ransom from a wretched shitbag like myself. An awful ransom, an awful legacy. A ransom of life, and lives. A ransom of generations and nations.

Perhaps there is an unknown force which cuts through the heart of the atom at will, with results varying from subtle and unrecognisable changes in individual lives, to catastrophic or cataclysmic developments in history, to apocalyptic performances in the theatre of the universe – surgeons, directors and prophets no more than puppets in the play. Perhaps that force is the unwritten, undiscovered basis of a formula which underlies miracles and visions and dreams and nightmares. Perhaps I should take up picking my ass and leave the old brain alone.

It has been suggested that there is a 'folded up' order in the apparent disorder of the universe, which unfolds itself as and when; a plan in the primordial chaos which reveals itself as and when, and is attributed to divine design. Could it be the other way round, the work of divine special effects rather than design? Could there be in the existing order a smoke-screened chaos which unleashes itself at a given impulse, from within or without, creating a new world of heaven and earth with a great big celestial bang, wiping out in an historical flash the world of the high and mighty dinosaurs, or in a personal flash overturning the world of any Thomson, Richardson or Harrison. If so, then that sacred night I was at the centre of its tempestuous whirlwind – condensed and telescoped, but vast enough and powerful enough to conjure up a helter-skelter universe of intertwined images and mutated metaphors and rumpled realities to overwhelm and suck me up towards an unavoidable yet unattainable destiny.

And it is happening again tonight. I am twenty-two once again, my own exposition of the twin-paradox but without a twin, just me split in two. Evidence that it is possible to be in the same place, *exactly* the same place, at two different times; as well as two different places at the same time – all four converging and commuting.

† † †

I made a rude gesture with my fist in reply to Belinda's pointless question, What are you doing *now*? She could clearly see that I was putting on my anorak. I unzipped the tent and walked out without zipping it back up again. I'll make her get out of her bed to do that at least, I thought to myself; triumphantly at first, but feeling guilty almost immediately after, yet not having the moral courage to turn back and say sorry or do it up myself.

We had just had our first argument in private. Up until then even our disagreements had taken place among a procession of chanting marchers.

And it was a bad first argument in private. I lost my temper, and it wasn't nice. I remember a schoolteacher of mine saying, Those who lose their temper have nothing else to lose. He was wrong in that I had a lot to lose. But he was right in that I had nothing. I lost everything when I had nothing.

I had so looked forward to that night out by the stones with Belinda, but at the very last minute, after I had carefully packed away the stove and the dinner things and anything that might blow away and made sure that the tent pegs were securely fastened – a high wind had been forecast for the night – Belinda said she was tired and would rather go to bed. She invited me to do the same. I got angry, and hurt; so much so that I even failed to notice the unusual lilt in her voice as she spoke. Or rather I did, but presumed that, unusual though the intonation was, the purpose of it was usual enough. Especially as it was accompanied by excitement in the eyes, which belied the claim of being tired. I was wrong.

293

If only I had stayed calm and stayed and listened to her . . .
perhaps . . .

I know you don't bloody care about a pack of fucking
stones, I yelled. I don't bloody care about a lot of fucking
things you go on and make me march for and shout for and
sit in for and stand up for and petition for and beg for. But
I do. Oh yes I do. Day in and day out, I do.

It's not my fault if you're a gutless hypocrite, she said.

† † †

It was good to be out in the vastness of the night. The one
thing I had missed most in England was wide open spaces.
Expanse. Here it was. That it was invaded and defined by
darkness made it all the more powerful. That I could walk out
of the cold old stones of prison among the colder older stones
of freedom made it all the more remarkable; even though the
prison stones were probably brought in by freer men than
those who lugged in the stones out here. What is for sure:
they were all men. The world is built on the broken backs
of men, and yet they are the villains of the piece.

† † †

And look what they've made of it, says Belinda.

They tried, I reply, did what they were told by higher
powers and superior beings: gods and women.

Oh do grow up, says Belinda.

† † †

An ordinary enough phrase, but as I am a little younger
than her, six years, it got my heckles up. Especially as
she thought that all my 'silly' views were the result of
my immaturity and would automatically evolve into her
'correct' views when I got older. Perhaps she was right.
Perhaps my theories about gender roles were the theories
of an unloved, unlovable little pest of a Choodah boy in a
predominantly female household, where the men were either

washed-out never-had-beens – Uncle Dano and Father – or layabout never-will-bes – Brother Junior and me. I held the women responsible for our nothingness, probably because I happened to love one of us so very very much: dear little consumptive bundle-of-nothing Father. Perhaps I held the whole world responsible for his nothingness, and Woman, as the Hindu Mother Earth, for the whole world. Perhaps I still resented Aunt Verna's mistrust and sister Nazli's taunts, even though, strangely and inexplicably, I missed them both almost as much as I missed Father and Great Grandmother. Perhaps I still blamed Mother for Father's disappearance and death. But where would we have been were it not for her patient perseverance, and Great Grandmother's loving wisdom! How easy it is to forget that good and remember the hurt. Perhaps I still felt used by Shakti. Perhaps I *would* grow out of these reactionary presuppositions, this perceptual concept of history. Perhaps that is why I got so irritated at any reference to growing up. On the other hand, Belinda and her friends considered older men to be even more stupid and insufferable than younger men. Surely there was an observable and verifiable inconsistency there.

† † †

Belinda does not talk about the issue for a whole week. Not even in bed when we make love, an occasion she sometimes favours for dialectical duelling. She next brings up the subject when the case comes up of Ms Janet Longman, twenty-seven, allegedly wrongfully dismissed from her place of employment after complaining of sexual harassment by Mr Alfred Cairn, her forty-nine-year-old boss, and we are gathered outside the court carrying placards and shouting our hearts out. It is awe-inspiring how many important issues can raise their heads during the one week of a half-term.

She begins where we left off. Even were I to accept your ridiculous scenario, just for argument's sake, how many gods and women force men to go out and commit all those crimes for which men have developed a certain not undeserved reputation? she asks, more controlled than normal when faced with boorish examples of male obtuseness.

I sigh. Unsuccessful men are made by women and society to feel like infertile women, and only infertile women and unsuccessful men know what that feels like. A woman will do anything to have a baby, a man anything to be a success.

An infertile woman does not go about committing crime, says Belinda, very quiet, unnaturally and frighteningly quiet.

I was too stupid to notice and carried on as usual. Because crime cannot fertilise the womb. If it could, who knows? It can bring success, and it can certainly bring money, the yardstick of success. That is why the more competitive and success-orientated a society, the higher the crime rate. Many studies are made to try and establish a relationship between poverty and crime. There isn't any, beyond the marginal and the obvious. The real connection lies between success and crime. A successful crime is in itself a success, hence desirable. For many, crime is the only means not just of obtaining some sort of livelihood, but of gaining some sort of self-respect, and the respect of peers, without which human life would be unbearable.

Women want good jobs too, and respect, not just babies, Belinda retorts.

Now that, the desire for jobs, is something new: relatively new in political terms; very new in historical terms. Not respect, that's not new. But the respect women have historically craved was not job-linked, not in the conventional sense. They have always had a job, their real job, as entrepreneurs of life, the job of managing and organising the human workforce: males as slaves and agents of production, females as future managers of the race. Men gathered round each other to create their own working-class clubs and to exclude the ruling class, women. First in streets and bars and other shady haunts; often through religion (hence such strong male resistance to women priests, except in Satanic churches, which are a reversal of the norm); and later by organising politically, forming co-operatives, and ultimately trying to bring about their own revolution through some form of socialism or communism, or even fascism. But they failed – tragically or fortunately, depending on which way they were heading – and capitulated, not being strong enough in historical terms to combat the entrenched female and capitalistic ideology and its forces. Of course, men did manage to organise the brutalities of the slave culture, as most slaves do when given too much power by their increasingly self-indulgent masters, but women have woken up to that now, and will retake from the slaves the loan of power. There will be a period of escalating male violence towards the female, as men try desperately to hang on to that power, but it will eventually revert to its rightful owners, and will manifest itself in the altered conditions of the new world. The concept of woman as whore or angel is only the dream of stupid men. Whore *and* angel, yes. That is one and the same woman, the drop-out, the one who has failed to prove herself strong enough to be a real woman, to hold the real job of controlling the living assets of this world and steering them towards maximum production and optimum efficiency. Respectable women did not work outside their own little empires. As long as job conditions were bad, if not downright dangerous, long on hours, short on wages, who in their right senses wanted to work? Even the post of a king was fraught with deadly traps. When some poor women had to take up a job, it was the man's fault for not being able to earn enough to keep the family going. Now that work prospects offer prestige and dosh, it's the man's fault if a woman does not get a job. It's always the man's fault. Keep them feeling guilty when change in their approach and methodology is called for. Keep them feeling in control when greater productivity is required. A bit of both and you've got them where you want them. By the . . .

Here I hastily picked up a little girl in blue jeans with a CND badge saying PLEASE BOMB, LET ME LIVE pinned to her shirt, and held her strategically between Belinda and myself. Her mother screamed as I stepped back on her toes. She was in dainty sandals with the barest of straps crisscrossing over her toes, I was wearing big cowboy boots, man-made material. Belinda managed to get me with the end pole of a banner which read 'PEACE'.

But the world is changing, I go on after the necessary

apologies. Give the ladies time. Wait and see what they get up to. Probably take over the world in a more obvious and open sense, and they're welcome to it. Meanwhile the male situation is getting further exacerbated. Men are blamed for being too soft or too hard, for being wimps or being macho, for going out to kill the enemy or for not going out to kill the enemy, as lovers across the table or in bed, for lack of staying power or lack of size, for wanting too much sex or for not wanting enough sex or for wanting the wrong sex (all this while Belinda remains strangely silent), for crying or for not crying, for letting their feelings show or for not letting their feelings show, for letting their wives work or for not letting their wives work, for expecting faithfulness from their women or for not expecting faithfulness from their women, for lack of words or too many words or the wrong words – to mention but a few possible shortcomings thrown in their faces. Meanwhile society is turning out more and more successful men, hence more and more unsuccessful men by comparison, and fewer and fewer infertile women.

† † †

I shouldn't have said all that. I didn't then know that Belinda couldn't have children. She had forced an abortion on herself at the age of thirteen and it nearly killed her. It also messed her insides up. That was one reason she was not saying yes to me.

I said sorry. What else could I say? I said that if we married it wouldn't matter to me that we couldn't have children (not quite fact but fact enough), but that I would love to adopt a child one day, if she didn't mind. I don't know why I thought of Jason. He had a perfectly good mother and father. Belinda thought it over and we got married within the week.

So perhaps it was good that I said what I said about unsuccessful men and infertile women, even though I really shouldn't have said it in the first place.

It got very lonely when Belinda was upset. She had not risen to zip up the tent flap either. If she had died of exposure it would have been my fault. I couldn't let her die. If I did, it would be my fault. Imagine killing a person you could have died for. Yet, though it was I who killed her, it was not through cold, but heat. Could have been good that, to die of heat in a cold land of cold people. But it wasn't the warm heat of welcoming arms, it was the burning heat of angry matter. As in metal and concrete and wood and water . . . Fire. The camp fire looked so beautiful. I could have slept within its folds. I had taken great care to see that it was properly put out. The other fire was still only a spark in the future. Waiting. You cannot put out a fire that has not been lit.

† † †

I bet you are dying to be inside there, aren't you? says Belinda as a few days later we squat on the pavement outside the 'Private' sex shop just opened in Forest Gate. And lust and drool over all the filth piled in there, she continues. We hoist our placard saying PORNOGRAPHY DEGRADES WOMEN.

Wouldn't mind, I admit, without admitting that I have already been in there and lusted up and drooled over it last night when she was out at a fringe meeting of a radical grassroots section of the National Union of Teachers, mercifully for members only. Not that there was much to lust up over in the shop: cheap soft porn magazines, some reasonably acceptable dildos, and a variety of utterly useless male potency drugs.

After all, I continue, pornography is the poor man's French Riviera and Playboy empire and all that goes with it – in morally constrained societies, that is. Truly guilt-free cultures have no need for such excogitations. That is why those in the civilised world, who want the common folk in their proper place, are so against it. They do not want them to enjoy even in fantasy what the privileged can have in real life. And they are lucky to get unwitting and witless allies among the gormless liberals and lefties who should really be fighting them instead of each other. More important, when attention has to be diverted from political ills by those who are the cause of political ills, the well-meaning are diverted towards fighting pornography and obscenity instead of fighting poverty and homelessness. If nothing else, it divides their ranks, decimates their strength. Page three is the best and the most harmless part of *The Sun*, a poor little girl showing her tits, and yet that is what you . . .

Belinda can stand it no longer. She stands up, pulling me up by the collar, and starts pushing me towards the shop. Go on then, go on in. She starts increasing the force of her hands and her taunts. Go in now, go in, nobody's stopping you, not me, go in. What are you doing here?

I am here because you are here, and I'd rather be out here with you than in there alone, I say. I would like to add, because I love you, but men are not supposed to say things like that in our part of the world, except on their death-beds as a final confession of weakness; or just before going off to war, which is much the same thing. Belinda is silent for a moment, I think she knows what I mean.

The houses look black and the slabs on the pavement are etched with greasy grey. The trains rattle by somewhere behind us, rocking the old bridge and making the adjoining buildings groan. Belinda speaks: I know what you are thinking.

Women always do, I say.

I see, Belinda says, very icy, women are such awful, miserable, all-knowing all-seeing pests, aren't they! That's why you like those . . . those . . . things in there. They are not women. They are objects. You can gloat over them, get aroused by them, then go out and rape and violate real women.

No, they are not objects, they are just as much women as you are . . .

How dare you compare . . .

Shut it, you two, says Liz on my right.

Yes, shut it, both of you, says Mel from behind Belinda. You go on like cats and dogs all the time.

Put a gag on, Cy, says Razia, I always say we're better off without having men around. We can fight our own battles. We don't want to be nannied by macho ninnies out here. Get enough of it at home.

That spurred rather than deterred me. I toned my voice and honed my words and boned my thoughts. Or so I thought. What is inside there, I point to the shop, may or may not lead to rape, I don't know. But that's not pornography. That I do know. That's titillation. And titillation, I concede, can be dangerous in large doses, exciting the imagination without fulfilling the demands aroused by it. Honest pornography can actually reduce the likelihood . . .

Screams of laughter and fury . . . Honest! Honest porn . . . Honest Cy, this time even you . . .

I continue . . . of rape by acting as a substitute . . .

This would be funny if it weren't so disgusting.

. . . especially if readily and publicly sold and exhibited, not hunted down and viewed in dark secrecy, I carry on, quite out of touch with the mood of the situation. And if free, guilt-free, opportunities for sex were also made available, through willing . . .

Opportunities, opportunities, he says! Women is what you mean. WOMEN!

Not necessarily. Anyone who's willing . . .

You mean whoever has the power and the money to pay . . .

And whoever is dirty minded enough . . .

One at a time, one at a time. First, a sizeable percentage of porn is entirely male. Add to that the male bodies in heterosexual porn and it's clear that there are plenty of men used and required in the porn trade. Why do you insist it is only women? After all, pornography is readily available in the world's most egalitarian and open societies with the most progressive women's movements but strictly banned in repressive societies where women have the least say in what goes on. Why does it degrade only women? Either neither, or both. If anything, men on the game are more vulnerable.

The jeers and leers and boos only egged me on.

Yes, male sexuality, male personality, is different from the female. Call it yang and yin, anima and animus, whatever. And unless and until you acknowledge these differences you will never be able to resolve them. The male is like a mountain stream . . . (Had Shree Ramnath heard me now, not only would he have taken me back in the Ashram, but promoted me to the rank of Junior Sanyasi, programme leader of the initiates.) . . . it can flow in a torrent or trickle dry, depending upon a multitude of externals. There are limits to his sexual athletics but not to his desires. With the woman it is the opposite. No moral framework for any society can ever work if it ignores the biological framework of the species, if it forgets that we are first and foremost just one animal more among all our fellow animals. The more you suppress your basic sexuality, the more it will emerge as lust for power and for calculated or random cruelty towards one's fellow creatures. The weaker they are – whether of your own species or others – the crueller you. The only way out of that vicious circle is to reconvert that energy back towards guilt-free sex. If that means paying for it, why not? You pay for clothes, you pay for food, what's wrong with paying for sex?

Because it's disgusting. Makes woman a commodity.

Pay men as well. I'd be quite happy to accept . . .

You would, wouldn'r you.

It is immoral.

Obscene.

Disgusting!

Why? Why? I don't think a naked woman is obscene, even during a fu . . . the sex act.

While being photographed and filmed doing it? You must be sick!

Perhaps. But I believe a woman clothed in a dress that costs more than it takes to feed a thousand children, and bedecked with diamonds and rubies dug out from the guts of the oppressed and gleaming with their sweat and glazed with their blood, is more obscene than a naked woman or a naked man. Every restaurant is more obscene than any sex shop or brothel or porn theatre. When you fuck someone you do not deprive others of their fuck, much less their life. All that food you devour and waste kills three and a half million animals, lives, in the UK alone, per day, and ultimately diminishes all. Gluttony deprives huge numbers of people, young and old, children . . .

Talking of children, what about the men who go about

raping and murdering children for the sexual gratification you're so much in favour of?

Not half as many as the great and successful and highly lauded arms deals which are 'clinched' by those very governments who are so terribly concerned as to where and into whom you and I introduce our cocks or present our cunts.

I am getting dry of mouth and short of breath and more over the top. Is another visit from my Naga imminent, another attack? But I don't have the time for that luxury. I'm too busy defending myself, or so I believe. Really I'm too busy offending everybody else.

Go tell that to someone else, you foul-mouthed prat. We don't approve of arms, see, said Dave flashing his CND badge.

Yes. I know. You are against nuclear weapons. What about so-called conventional weapons? You want more of them? I'd rather have a world full of nuclear arms than one armoured tank, one fighter plane or a single shotgun. Let the whole world go up in one big nuclear explosion, that would be better than the selective killing that goes on day after day, year after year, hour after hour with conventional weaponry. The only reason you don't want nuclear weapons is that it puts your whiter-than-white civilisation in jeopardy. Conventional weapons are used by those bloody savages to kill each other, so jolly good, let us keep manufacturing them and supplying them, as long as we can sit here at a distance, rake in the millions, watch the fun, feel holy, and pontificate on those tinpot dictators and those uncivilised barbarians. If they are fool enough to pay for their own massacre, why not!

There was an uncomfortable silence at that point. Instead of realising my excess and apologising for my starkly racist comments, I decided to take advantage of the silence and made the stunning blunder of ramming home some homespun home thoughts on child sex killers.

I had just finished suggesting that if a society was truly and utterly and genuinely revolted by the act, or even the idea, of eating an egg before the age of eighteen in the company of an older person, older man, then a thirteen-year-old might well be traumatised for life if offered and made to eat an egg by an older man, especially if he enjoyed it; and was about to elaborate when I found myself being kicked in the head by Dave and in the guts by Paul and being punched and sworn at by swarming women.

The police arrived. I managed to struggle up and run to the nearest cop for protection. He felled me to the ground and he and his mates set upon me.

† † †

All this while Belinda stood in petrified silence. I had never seen her so utterly bereft of speech or motion. Poor woman, she could have done without the aggravations I caused her. She had enough problems with the world, not to mention her school: constantly bypassed for promotion by the Headmaster, harassed by the administration and generally hounded by her Senior Mistress. The first for being black, the second for being politically active, and that in the wrong (opposite of right) direction, the third for being a woman – she was convinced. And with good reason it seemed, considering she put as much effort and energy into her work and for her pupils and her classes as she did for her causes, and was offered nothing for it in return. To make matters worse, she had turned twenty-eight that year, which meant she would be thirty soon. And she worried about it, the more so because she felt that as a true feminist she should not be worrying about it. My being six years younger was an extra burden to bear.

I was sure that that would be the end of her and me. We'd only been married three weeks. I couldn't even cry. The police would think I couldn't take a beating. It was, as always, all my fault. How could I have been so stupid? So thoughtless? So garrulous? So . . . so . . . so everything, everything that shouldn't be.

Belinda and Corrine, her NUT representative, came to collect me. Fortunately the police agreed to let me go, though there were moments when we thought it would be custody and a remand centre this time. I couldn't believe that Belinda had come at all. I had begun to feel quite afraid, surrounded by all those gentlemen in blue giving me the once over, and then the twice and thrice over. And moreover . . . Who could tell what more was in store?

I couldn't thank her enough, not through thick lips and thicker cheeks. I used to sneak in every now and then to see Jason and catch a glimpse of Jennifer, but wouldn't be able to do so now till my face returned. It wasn't a pretty sight at the best of times, and I couldn't let them see me like this. Especially Jason. He'd think I'd been in a fight or something.

Back in the flat Belinda didn't say anything for a long, long time. In the middle of her fifth cup of coffee she abruptly spoke and said that she agreed completely with one of my contentions, accepted a second, but with reservations, and was seriously considering a third. She took me to the bedroom, made me strip off and started to paint me in my gory glory. For emotional release, and for the record.

I was astonished that she had agreed with something I'd said, especially considering how vital these issues were to the very essence of her being. I did not push my luck by asking her to be more specific. I was curious, though, and very pleased. At last some part of my brain and not just body was being accepted by a woman. By Belinda. Made a change from being told to grow up.

Later she made me write out, in my best handwriting, fifteen letters of apology to all her friends who were there and to invite them to a meal. I didn't mind writing the apologies, I did not like the idea of a meal. It was to be in a restaurant. But I did what I was told. Ten of the people, eight women and two men, eight whites, one black and one Chinese, accepted my apology. Five, two women and three men, three Indian and two whites, did not. Three of them were later to turn up as witnesses against me during my trial. Their testimony was crucial in proving that I had always been an utterly immoral and evil person, hence irredeemable, and therefore any pleas based on mitigating circumstances or extraordinary conditions just would not hold water. Especially where sex and children were concerned. Since I was on trial for child killing, with heavy overtones of devilry and sexual perversion, it helped. The court was told how I had threatened to blow the white man's world apart with 'an infernal holocaust'. This was presented as the first stage of my unholy plan to destroy God's Kingdom, his good earth, and bring on the eternal reign of the evil one, sorry, the Evil One: a proposition to which I expressed no hostility on the stand. I was not asked to explain, nor did I care to elaborate. I was past playing games. I had conceded defeat long before the battle started. We were in the thicket of the war, then. Who says it takes two to tango? They were doing fine without me.

† † †

Down with male power! I yell as Belinda paints. Down with their trousers, I whisper. Thank you, says Belinda, I have no wish to inspect their brains. You might be surprised, some of them have quite large ones. I prefer those without any. She holds my hand and smiles. She smiles so rarely. It makes her beauty unbearable, just as the purified essence of Rartri's blackness is unwatchable. I lift her up with my eyes and imprison that moment and her and her smile forever within my pupils behind the spiky black bars of my eyelashes. She will never be alone there. For Jason is there too, and so is Jennifer, and Shane, Great Grandmother and Mother and Father, some of my mates at work I hardly spoke to, and I have sometimes been surprised to find Aunt Verna there; Nazli, of course . . . I nearly forgot Shakti, how could I! And Suzi. I hope Belinda does not expect me to 'forsake all others'. *Forsaking all others* . . . The most chilling words in the history of mankind. The most frightening demand ever made of man or woman by man or woman. I am glad we didn't get married in a church.

† † †

No more the sun. No more the crowd. No more Belinda. Just the solitary night. And me.

I carry to the past no memories of the future, except of its pains and sufferings and joys and laughter and terrors; not of the events and factors that caused those emotions to well up and erupt. Emotions, without the anchor of their cause, are elusive and bewildering; and bewilderment piled upon bedevilment and bewitchment is alcohol upon barbiturates and speed.

But mercifully I am unaware of all this at the moment. No knowledge of tragedies experienced follows me, no guilt about catastrophes caused shames me, my children's blood clings not to my palms: the dying palms that carried their living bodies to their tombs. Not at the moment. The only dread in my heart is the dread of Belinda alone in the little tent with its flap unzipped. And the dread of the prison left behind. But this last is just a dread, a naked dread, for I neither know nor remember anything of the prison. Have you ever experienced a nagging fear, or a blossoming hope, or a sudden alarm, without quite knowing the why and wherefore of it? It could be that you are back from the future, and remember an impending emotion, but not the reason for it. It could be that premonitions are postmonitions.

Woe is me that I am too wilful to turn back. More woe that I am not wilful by nature – at least, not thought so by myself nor often declared so by friends. Opinionated, yes; wilful, no. Not till that night, the night of wilfulness. The night of disobedience that grew into a monster that grew into me.

† † †

Let them live too, I cried to the stones and the stars. I remember the mother of the child with the CND badge pleading with the bomb to let her live took out a hamburger to feed her in a period of relative calm. Animals have children too, animals are children, children from birth till death, children but nobody's children, and who is there to protect nobody's children? Nobody, and you can do whatever you like with nobody's children, and their children. Is there nobody to mourn them, nobody to let them live? They can be made to have sex whenever, or never at all; inseminated with pumps and bred in filth, or not at all; put in cages and fed through bars, or not at all; their movements can be limited to nothing, their light restricted or denied and taken away. They can be culled or killed or bought and sold or skinned and boned whether cooked or raw, destroyed or created with heavier heads or lesser fat or greater fat or longer ears and no tail; cut open or blinded or poisoned or injected with disease in hospitals or kicked about with heavy boots like a football in a playground, or simply mocked and abused and derided for simply being. Let them live too. Let them love too. Let them breed and breathe and walk and run and touch the sun. Let them live, too. Dear gods on two legs, let them live too. And let them die. In their own time. In their own way. Let them be let them lie let them jump let them roll let them swim let them fly. Don't take away their right to die by killing them before they die. You have the power. You have the means. You have no need. Not any more. They've carried your body and your heavy loads and ploughed your fields and reaped your corn and died that you may live. They've given you all their mothers' milk and all their children's flesh. They've brought you ivory, made you silk, fed you on honey, helped you walk, clothed you and made you warm, protected you from harm. You have other, better, commercially viable choices now. Thank them and let them be. Just leave them their life, their liberty, their dignity, there will still be a lot left for them to give and you to take. Thank them for that and let them be. Let them be, let them go. Let them be. Let them be. Let them die. Let them die their natural deaths.

Dear great
and wonderful,
truly
worshipful,
omnipotent,
omniscient,
all loving,
all caring,
gods
on two legs
on four wheels.
Let them live, too.
For Umrao's sake.

Upon the Wheel

Don't take away
their right to die
by killing them
before they die.
Don't.
For Umrao's sake.

† † †

Were you really serious? says Belinda, putting her arms tightly round my battered and bruised body and making me squeal like a TV evangelist caught in the act.

Serious about what? I remarked, looking all innocent, as innocent as a large, naked man, naturally blue and black but now unnaturally black and blue, not to mention red, pink and purple, and white if you count the odd bandage, could look without looking down between his thighs, responding eagerly to Belinda's eager thighs.

All that you were saying about . . . sex . . . and women . . . and sex . . . I can never tell when . . . Sometimes I . . .

There is a long pause, silent but not motionless or without serious communication.

Go on, I urge, no no . . . Well, that as well, but I mean, sometimes you what?

Sometimes I think I take you too seriously . . .

So you should! Ouch.

Sorry! Did I hurt you? Sorrryyy.

Did you mean all you said?

I always mean what I say. You should know me by now.

I'm not sure. I do, and then suddenly, I don't any more.

I let it rest, but she comes back for more.

Sometimes I think you talk too much about sex, you're obsessed by it.

Me, obsessed by sex!

You take it too seriously.

Me, take it too seriously!

Oh do grow up. Stop repeating what I say. What about love?

I am heckled by now, as you know – that grow-up stuff.

309

What about love? I repeat.

There you go again repeating what I say. Yes, what above love? Doesn't that have anything to do with sex? You talk of sex and pornography, sex and money, sex and . . . children. What about sex and love!

I push her up, pull myself out and turn over as painlessly as I can, heckled up as I am, and grab hold of her pencil and sketchpad. I draw two large circles, overlapping to form a tiny section which I shade in.

Love and sex have very different spheres, I lecture. Sometimes they intersect, so. That is when neither is pure or at its best. But together they produce a sort of heady fermentation, like good beer, which goes straight to the loins but excites the kidneys more than the gonads and eventually ends up contracting the brain and distending the bellies of all concerned. In most volatile and exciting human beings it happens ever so often with many different people, but never for long enough to allow the negative side-effects to take over. Some dull souls can just about manage it once and go to pot for the rest of their lives. Some miss it altogether. But there is nothing like sex without the bondage of possessive passion, and of course love without the pettiness of sex.

I am all grown up now. Shakti and I would have made a great team, had I learnt all this earlier.

Belinda goes silent after that and I have to do a dance round the room ouching in agony and shaking my willie about before she relents and lets me in again.

That is why, I continue from where I left off, both in act and speech, I can never understand why people in the West equate making love with having sex. It is like asking someone to fetch you the ocean when you mean a handful of ditchwater. And to refer to a sexual partner as lover is like calling a carpenter the tree-maker.

I talk a lot about sex because you lot seem to be so hung up on it. It is only a natural function, like shitting. It just happens to be more insistent, less regular, less vital, less solitary – though for a lot of men and some women it is quite as solitary as well. It takes about the same amount of time, exceptions granted, and the end result is relief. It would be as pointless and ridiculous to speak for or against one as the other. You just go ahead and do either as and when the urge takes you, I say, making my strokes harder and more forceful, but slower, thoroughly relishing my rare on-top position: because of my bruising a special dispensation has been made. Then forget about both and get on with the rest of your life. Suppress either and you can upset or poison your entire physical system. Make either illegal in any shape or form and you upset and poison the entire social system.

Belinda gasps once or twice, more than once or twice. It might be because of what I am saying or it might be because of what I am doing. She makes no other comment. She might allow me on top more often if she really likes it this time, I think. She always lets me talk on anyway, no matter how much she disagrees. The more I talk the longer I take, and she enjoys that.

I do know of one case though, I whisper in her ear, where pure love and pure sex met to achieve the highest and purest union ever.

Really, when, who was . . . Who were . . . Belinda is back. It was a man and his umbrella . . . No, no seriously, honest, carried its picture wherever he went. It was a case of lost love, you see, carried its picture, in the upright position . . . All right then, be like that . . . Don't you dare bite my . . . Ouwwwoooo.

Beyond the Tent

The wind began to rise. The temperature began to fall.

I wrapped my arms around my chest, hugging my anorak to keep the wind and the chill out. The night was clear and fragile like glass; like glass it felt sharp and brittle, giving the impression that you could cut yourself severely if you attempted to break through it, or even brushed past the wrong edge of it.

The moon, no older than the night, a thin, keen sword of an ever-blazing metal, hung above the line of my vision. It appeared to be somewhat precariously balanced, and with every step I feared that I might be directly under it, so that if it fell it would take my head along with it to the ground. But it continued to move along with me, and continued to cling on to the sky despite having no visible means of support. The stars were out in their millions to monitor with flinty eyes our progress through the darkness, managing to keep track of both the moon and myself at one and the same time. I began to feel a sense of mounting unease beneath their palpitating gaze, but they remained supremely unconcerned with my discomfiture – even appeared to be revelling in it, if the twinkle in their fiery pupils was anything to go by.

The landscape looked different to what I remembered from only a few hours before.

The spread of night alters the aspect of an environment anyway. Distances change, extend, diminish, or even vanish altogether; perspectives re-adjust to fit the sinuous folds of blackness; objects acquire not just varying hues but variable shapes and unaccustomed sizes and strange textures; existence itself assumes an alternative character. Dead things come to life and living things cease to be.

But this was more than just the shifting scene of the night. It was another world altogether.

But then I could just be imagining it all. I have been known to do that on more than the odd previous occasion. Aunt Verna would tell you that, only she would not call it imagining. She would call it lying.

By the time I'd moved a little further into the night the moon was full circle, and the radiance of its light confirmed my earlier impression that it was indeed a different world, though the same, for in front of me the now incomplete earth chakra of stones was clearly visible beneath the now complete celestial chakra of the moon.

To my left I was aware of the presence of the sea, which I could not see but could clearly hear. The rhythmic rise and fall of its tumultuous roar was getting louder and angrier as the winds blew louder and angrier and colder. In front of me, also to the left, I could make out two long, curvaceous rivers, each fed by many brooks and springs. From this distance they looked more like speckled ribbons flying about in the wind than determined forces of water cutting their way through the earth. One river was amber and broad and khaddar, one purple and fine and silk. Both met up somewhere along a nebulous section of the horizon before disappearing into the invisible sea. Beyond the rivers stood a great mountain, larger and grander than the world it inhabited, disproving that a part cannot be greater than the whole of which it is a part, and towering above its own unattainable height. It was the one and the same source of the two very different rivers, its peak bluey white and muddy brown in streaks and spots depending on whether the snow upon it touched the earth or the sky. Between me and the rivers were the firm green plains enclosing the stone chakra.

To my right was the endless desert, and sand: either fine and soft as glans skin transformed into undulating buttocks and smooth nippleless breasts, or rough and grainy, broken by stones and rocks and cracks and crevices and grasses and cacti.

Although the wind, by now madly furious, was blowing from that direction, not a grain of sand nor a stigma of grass moved inside the desert or crossed over towards the green plains upon which I walked. At least that is how it appeared to me, but I must have been wrong, for when I felt my face it was covered with a fine film of silky grey, ash-like sand and my throat was getting dry and scratchy as if layered with grit.

All this while I had been so avidly engaged in viewing what was spread out ahead of me and to my left and right that it did not occur to me to cast a look behind me to see what was going on there. In fact, even after I had surveyed the scene that confronted me in as much detail as circumstances and the light would permit, my curiosity was more aroused than sated; and had it not been for the persistently increasing ferocity of the wind, and with it the memory of an open flap in a frail tent and inside it my first and only legally-wedded woman, I might have quite forgotten what I was walking away from.

Imagine my joy when on turning round I could make out the amber symmetry of our tent sketched against the bleakness of the night, the slit of the open flap clearly discernible because of its black shape within the glowing framework of the tent. Belinda would be freezing in there. I had to go back to zip up the tent. Surely she could have got up and done that herself.

I began a brisk walk back; and when progress appeared to be very much slower than I had anticipated, I started to run.

I ran and I ran.

I began to realise that no matter how fast I ran the distance between myself and the tent remained constant.

Faster and faster and faster, my balls banging and clanging against my thighs, for somewhere along the way the fury of the wind had blown the clothes off my body and I was pitifully naked.

Picture me running, passionately, powerfully and insanely running towards the tent, running naked, through the graded blackness and . . . and . . . What was it I just said? The graded darkness! Why graded? Shouldn't the darkness have remained constant rather than the distance?

I stopped abruptly with the force of a thought that struck

my mind like a backhander against the face. Sweat was pouring out of my body despite my nakedness and the freezing wind and I was panting like a mad dog fleeing his masters after taking a sane look at them in his madness.

The graduated light, the inability to get to the tent, even the still open flap – the mystery of these became more clear. I was in the night of the full moon. The tent lay in the night of the crescent. Out there it was probably still the very instant I had walked out. Not enough time had passed for Belinda to have got up and closed the flap. Here, though it was still the sacred night, of that there was not the slightest doubt in my mind, it could have been the sacred night years or centuries or millennia before or after I walked from the tent. There was no way I could run back to it as if I had never run out.

I was paralysed. Fears and regrets came tumbling down upon my tortured soul, together and on the heels of each other. If only . . . What if . . .

Dear God, let me not lose Belinda, not Belinda . . .

One more chance, just *one* more chance. I'll do anything, God, anything, anything . . .

Anything, God. Just one more chance.

I'll never lose my temper again, never swear again, never, God, never. Never ever will I utter anything remotely anti-feminist, never never never. Never ever will I defend the heinous practice of pornography. Men are the cause of all evil, God, yes yes yes. Men are horrible vicious beasts, irredeemable bags of shit, shit of poisoned mushrooms, salmonella and listeria all rolled into one big truckload of diseased, foul, stinking shit. I yelled all this while holding on to my own manhood, buckling over with hands between my thighs, trying as hard as possible in the circumstances not to offend God with my nakedness. I was not sure whether to promise God never to fuck again, when the very mention of it might add to the debit side of my moral balance sheet; worse, whether once made the promise could be kept, and if not, what would the consequences be? I didn't dare call upon the Naga, though I desperately wanted to, for fear that it might anger the more powerful Christian God, adopted by the more powerful West, and thus make life all the more difficult for me. Perhaps I shouldn't have mentioned shit either. Of course I shouldn't have, clearly I shouldn't have, how could I have! But Choodah blood will show.

Forgive me God, forgive me for what I am.

Perhaps I shouldn't have said what I said about men either? Jesus, of course I shouldn't have, You were, are . . . His son was . . . O God, what have I gone and done, again. I can never keep my mouth shut, can I? God, please, look after Belinda, out there on her own, all on her own . . . I should have stuck to pornography, stuck to denouncing it I mean: obscene, obscene, I revile everything obscene . . . Anything to do with sex, extramarital sex, that is, it is fine in matrimony, holy matrimony, of course, that is why it is called holy. Wilt Thou take my holy cock . . . No, no, unholy, strictly unholy, and make it holy in holy wedlock, and keep it holy? How can it remain holy if my partner is taken away? It will become unholy again, and You don't want that, do You, do You, Lord . . .

I had lost so many of the ones I loved that I just could not suffer the thought of losing Belinda. I was promising I would do anything to get her back.

I ended up doing everything to lose her.

† † †

I can't say God did not give me a chance. Quite the contrary. He gave me every chance. I cannot blame Him.

The first chance came, as most chances do, in the form of an idea. But in my ignorance or arrogance I attributed it to myself instead of crediting God with it.

Perhaps I should turn round once again and start my journey forward. So often one comes face to face with one's past when trying to run away from it. Once I'd got my breath back and was more in control of my panic, that was exactly what I did.

I turned myself round once again and started taking heavy, hesitant steps towards the stones. They appeared to be as far ahead of me as before, no more no less; but surprisingly the rivers beyond seemed much closer. I could actually see their colourful waters dancing their way towards anonymity and oblivion, into the great invisible ocean.

As I walked forwards I turned away from the Western God (which in fact was also my God, for I was a Christian too, a Catholic no less, as Great Grandmother often reminded me) and sought refuge in the arms of the Eastern gods of my ancestors, pre–Great Grandmother, even if they were heathen or pagan or worse.

O dancing lord, lord of the linga, lord of destruction and renewal and rebirth. O lord of caves, O lord of the meeting rivers, hear me.

The manifold undivided, dancing up on high and low down here, dancing upon our hearts before they begin their beat and upon our graves before they are dug, dancing dancing forever dancing, hear me.

O lord of the meeting rivers, O lord white as jasmine, hear me.

O lord of the meeting rivers, hear me.

Hear me, hear me, hear me, O Shiva.

O Krishna, blue and black from rolling in the ashes of burnt souls, O lover eternal, find time from your fornicating and hear the prayer of one as black as yourself and one as fond of gopis as yourself, hear me, help me, help me find my Radha.

I shall dance for Radha as you play the flute, and I shall dance for Shiva as he wrestles the Naga, and I shall dance for Parvati and I shall dance for Sita as Vishnu and Hanuman rest from their labours. I shall dance dressed in gold and laden with diamonds, if that be your wish, and I shall dance naked, if that be your desire.

As I uttered these prayers all self-consciousness about being naked utterly disappeared. A great calm descended upon my soul as a great frenzy rose from within my body. My feet began to pound, my ankles got bell-cuffed, my arms turned to snakes, my palms to cymbals, my heart a drum, my neck a dove's neck, and my hips went wild. My knees doubled up and opened up and straightened up to keep up with my feet and my buttocks quivered and shivered and puckered and my balls clattered and rattled and my jock went wild.

I was believed.

The gods themselves came down to join me in my worship, and I was soon surrounded by dancing divinities. Shiva led the troop, with the Naga beneath his feet, while Krishna played the spellbinding flute. Rartri and Usha together, a sight not often seen, danced hand in hand, playing with Agni and scattering the sparkling stars through the embers of the night. Vayu wrapped himself excitedly around one and all, and veshyas and apsaras came to bring their arti for me! Can you imagine it, arti for me! They had landoos and barfi on their plates, ringed with candles and incense-burning agarbatees. They knelt at my feet and swayed round me and caressed my thighs and my buttocks and my groin. And kissed my penis, so softly and gently, and with such venereal veneration as was reserved only for the linga of lord Shiva himself. One of them, the tallest and blackest and the most beautiful, rose to her full height and with a firm, spatulate thumb inserted sindoor in my mang and a tilak on my matha.

The gandharvas were adoring Padmimi and Lakshmi. And Radha was being worshipped by the prince Arjuna and the poet Usana and the sage Vyasa, even as Krishna himself looked on with approval.

† † †

Suddenly out of the black blue came fortissimo a clap of thunder, so stunning that for a moment my mind completely blanked out and my ears were entirely deafened. Then came a stark flash of sheet lightning, so white that I was blinded.

When I recovered my senses I was alone and naked and self-conscious once more. And very cold. And somewhat dazed.

It began to grow dark.

The moon was quietly fading away, though it remained full and was not going through its usual changing phases. The stars were going too – instead of brightening up as they do when the moon takes a dive – and going fast, faster than the moon, which was still managing to put up a good fight for its survival. And another thing, the wind appeared to be dying out. I say *appeared*, for actually it was picking up force. Only its howling and screeching and roaring and yelling was ebbing away.

I was very tired, by then, from all the running and all the dancing, and obviously very cold. And another feeling had crept up on me almost unnoticed, adding greatly to my discomforts: a gnawing in the pit of my stomach. All that exercise and the subzero temperatures had made me feel hungry. I desperately needed to build up my energy resources if I was to survive. For the moment all I could do was to jump up and down and rub my hands all over my body, particularly across the chest and back, in an effort to prevent my blood from freezing. But in so doing I was fast using up what little reserves of energy I had left.

I was surprised I had any reserves left. I was surprised I was in as good a shape as I was. I was surprised I was all there and up and standing and conscious and coherent. If things carried on like this, bits and pieces of me would swell up or shrivel down or redden or blacken or whiten and start falling off, or just dry up and disappear, or explode, or something equally nasty and permanent. Suddenly death from exposure, indecent at that, seemed a very real possibility.

But death was not for me, either then or ever.

I did save myself from perdition though, and that shall remain my triumph, come what may, and say or think what you like of me. In my shabby, shoddy, worthless life, I can claim one victory that is mine and shall remain mine. I refused to surrender my soul. My soul remains and shall remain mine. And free.

I not only refused a deal with the much-abused mythical you-know-who, but with the much misused real Himself. Is not this defiance, of which I am so proud now, the same disobedience which I was bemoaning only a short while ago? The one and the same vis-à-vis the one and the same God?

Is there any difference?

Perhaps no more than the altered perspective from a different night two times seven intervening years ahead of the first night; at the culmination of four times nine total years granted to me of mortal life. I was lucky. It could have been seven times nine, or nine times nine, or two times seven times nine . . .

Back to superstitious mumbo-jumbo.

It only it were that simple. If only the difference was a constant. But no. It is a moving pendulum. Heroic defiance, disgraceful disobedience, heroic defiance disgraceful disobedience, tick tock tick tock tick tock . . .

Condemned mortals build, damned immortals shatter: clocks or time, illusions or reality, façades of evil or charades of good.

Is reality only real because of the observer? The growing contention seems to be that it is indeed so, in which case if the observer changes reality changes, and if the perspective changes the observer changes, even if it is the same observer, which of course it is not. Therefore all externals are in a flux of continual and multiple change while remaining constant – that is, if they do remain constant, and of course they do not.

† † †

Gradually, like the dying notes of a dying balladeer in the final act of a musical melodrama, all sound ceased to be, all light faded away, the audience left, the cast went home, the auditorium disappeared. I was left alone and absolute in absolute silence and absolute blackness and absolute space.

It was the most overpowering and the most awesome sensation that I had ever experienced.

Like drowning motionless in a bottomless, waterless ocean.

I opened wide my mouth and let out what should have been an ear-splitting scream.

Not a sigh was heard.

My mouth remained wide open, like a desecrated cave.

Were it not for the hunger which by now was eating at my guts with fear-sharpened teeth, and the cold which was turning my flesh into chunks of frozen meat, and the silent madness of the wind which was buffeting me about like a lump of rubbish on a stormy, pestilence-stricken beach, I might as well have been dead.

Any hope that with utter blackness might come a rise in

temperature, up to the standard zero of the complete absence of light, was doomed. Icicles began to form over my neck, digging into my throat; and around my nipples, pressurising and squeezing and puncturing them with knife-points of burning cold; and across my back, thighs and buttocks till the skin upon them and the flesh beneath felt both raw and cooked, both contracted into a metallic bunch and drum-stretched beyond limits of tautness, both smooth as an ice-rink and cracked and split and torn asunder like an earthquake-ravaged landscape.

I doubled over on the ground – which was mercifully still faithful beneath my feet, my only contact with any comforting reality – and hugging my knees began to rock backwards and forwards in an attempt to warm up, or failing that, at least preserve any lingering body heat. And to keep myself from being blown away.

I was blown away like a rolling ball of tumbleweed, across the horizons of certainties and eventualities, beyond the limits of causality and rationality, past the barriers of logic and reason, and into a wilderness of surreal empiricism.

I came to a sudden and jolting standstill, as did the wind.

After a spiralling spell of dizziness my brain managed to reel back into its allocated position within my skull and I tried once again to make some sense of what was happening and tried to react in a positive and progressive manner.

I should have derived some relief from the fact that the devastatingly forceful and devastatingly cold wind had ceased. Were I not breathing I would have thought myself to be in a place completely devoid of atmosphere. But there was no relief. The wind had provided some sort of a link with the world of senses that I knew; now that line too was gone. I felt more lost, more marooned, more desolate than ever.

I did manage to stand up, ever grateful of the solid earth beneath my feet, and forced myself to take one step forward, terrified that the mortal foot would have nowhere to land and I would plunge over the edge of the universe and into the unfathomable pit of chaos. The foot did find ground, but since I could not see I had miscalculated the distance it needed to travel, and it hit the ground abruptly and hard. I yelled out in pain, but it was a silent yell still, and the familiar agony of the known was forgotten beside the unfamiliar agony of the unknown.

By then I should have taken for granted the suspension of natural laws, but at times I can be slow to learn. Besides, hope springs eternal and man never is but always to be, etcetera etcetera. Prayer would have been more in order than looking for logical loopholes or digging up rational explanations as a means of escape or a form of solace, but I was in such a state of moral exhaustion, mostly as a result of sheer physical exhaustion, that I could not bring myself to call upon God or gods. To be fair to myself, I had tried, and each time ended up worse than I was before. Now a weary sort of spiritual malaise had set in. I didn't even care whether or not there was a God, and was even less inclined to ask Him for favours or beg for miracles.

I now seemed to be suspended within an atmospheric limbo where every following moment imitated to perfection the preceding moment, if indeed it wasn't the same moment. With the wind had stopped any and every movement, the totality of darkness continued unabated, and the temperature was locked. The icicles on my body had been scraped off when I was being blown about, and no new ones were forming in their place. That was a relief; but on the other hand it was evidence of the utter arrest of all kinetic energy, and as such, unnerving.

There was a consolation, which I began to realise but gradually. As my stagnant progress continued through this apparently changeless world, it began to imprint its placid and questionless state upon my agitated consciousness.

The pain of hunger began to be indistinguishable from the pain of cold. Surreptitiously they merged; surprisingly their combined intensity halved instead of doubling. An attitude of acceptance rather than resistance began to permeate the ravished pores of my body.

Lazily, sensuously – the pain now adding a spice to the quality of life rather than diminishing it – I stretched my arms, yawned, stretched my back, my legs, like a cat lingering on each limb until it felt relaxed and refreshed and renewed. I lay myself down on the ground, stretched and relaxed each limb again, then curled up into a ball and smiled.

Orpheus was right. In the beginning was Time, and from Time came Chaos and the ovoid immensity of Night; and somehow I had blundered back into it. Deep in its heart lay Love, and I was being drawn towards it, and when I reached it, I should be absorbed within its everlasting beauty when the great egg split into heaven and earth. Imagine that, can you? Ugly me becoming an integral part of the everlasting beauty of love! I wouldn't have wanted to be back in earth, even if staying here meant being disloyal to Belinda. Belinda. The thought of her broadened my smile and I began to stretch my limbs once again. Poor girl, beautiful, wonderful, poor girl. Pity she had to get stuck on a knucklehead like myself. But she was rid of me now, and good for her. I hoped she wouldn't miss me much, or for long. Everyone I loved had managed to leave me – even though it was I who walked out on Shakti, she had abandoned me well before that – and who could blame them? Belinda, though, I left behind. Good for her. Good for you, Belinda, I shouted, but no one heard me. Not even I. Don't cry for me, Belinda, don't, dear girl. I am not worth it. I don't think I shouted all this, just mumbled it softly to myself.

A leisurely lethargy, heavy with the natural wine served by the cerebellum to celebrate the culmination of all desire, whether through fulfilment and satiation, or in my case through renunciation and abandonment – voluntary and pleasurable now, if enforced and violent only a short while ago, as that of a sultry nymph deflowered by a drunken satyr – began to force itself and course through my veins with the voluptuous start-stop jerkiness of a seminal discharge executed in slow motion by none other than the king of passion, lord of ejaculation and master fornicator, the great god Krishna himself.

† † †

Still unprepared for and unaware of what awaited me, I stretched my smile and my body some more, glad that I could see. And smell. Smell. I had forgotten about smell, so preoccupied had I been with other senses. I could smell. Smell food! And snow! And water!

It was more than a trick of Morpheus, more of a Thanatos joke. No. More than that even. Worse. Much, much worse. No joke or trick at all, but reality: cold, unsmiling, unerring reality.

I could see and smell.

Flakes of pure white snow were tumbling down from above, bringing with them light. How, when there was none to reflect? I cannot tell you. There it was. A fluffy bedspread of white surrounding my prostrate body to the limits of vision, smelling sweet and fresh and watery. And of food. Where was food? For there was some, somewhere, not far off. I could smell it. I sure as Hell could.

An appropriate choice of metaphor, for Hell it was. Just when I was resigned to my destiny, or what I believed to be my destiny – peaceful extinction – strife and pain were back on top.

Claws of steel wound themselves round my heart as I considered what might be in store for me.

Let me be. Let me die, I cried.

Even as I cried I knew that that was not to be.

Let me be, let me die, I murmured, as my nostrils flared and my body painfully gathered itself up and, shivering with cold and aching with hunger, began to totter and teeter towards the source of the temptress smell. The smell of food.

In the distance, somewhere in the middle of a snowfield, I could see fairy lights glimmering through the egg-shaped windows of a chocolate-and-candy-coloured cottage, smoke curling upwards from an eclair-like chimney.

I started dragging myself towards it with as great a speed as I could muster, which was slow and ponderous like that of a man-hurt animal, debilitated as I was by hunger and cold. At first I was angry at my inability to run vigorously, but then decided not to waste my energies on fruitless frustrations or on ruminating over the past and to concentrate on getting to the cottage, where hope and shelter lay twinkling so temptingly in all the colours of the rainbow across the chaste whiteness of the falling snow. If I was to be of any help to Belinda, if I were to have any chance of getting back to Belinda, I had first to sort out my own predicament.

I was at the cottage quickly – for once the illusions of time and space were working in my favour – and through the first window I came to, profusely decorated with strings of multi-coloured lights, I could see a typical family – father, mother, two and a quarter children – having what must have been a typical family meal – whence the aroma that had assailed my nostrils as I lay drifting towards the point of the meeting rivers – though I couldn't see what it was as the dishes and plates were either deep or hidden behind bodies. They were all watching some programme on the television, which sat high against the wall facing the mother, its screen away from my angle of vision. Judging by their expressions, they were disturbed by what they saw. The mother's eyes shone with brimming tears as she passed the butter to the father. Poor brats, poor little brats, she said under her breath as she used the napkin to dab delicately at the bottom end of the lower eyelid. It wouldn't be 'alf so bad if they didn't 'ave so many of the . . . So many in the first place, said the father, nearly choking on whatever he nearly choked on. But if they didn't have so many, they won't have any left, will they? piped the quarter child. They won't have any left now, said the girl child. Perhaps that ain't such a bad idea, said the father. Oh Darren, how can you! said the mother as she passed the gravy. (At least, it was a gravy dish, I couldn't say whether it contained gravy or a remedy for piles.) Sorry, Luv, said the father, but what can we do? Day in and day out, never ends. What can we do? There's a limit, there's gotta be. What can we do? You can turn the TV off, said the girl child, makes me sick, I don't know how you can all watch it, while eating . . . The boy child's mind was far away, I could tell by the look in his eyes, very much like the look I used to have.

By then I had taken as much of the sight and smell of food as I could bear, and was ready for action. I nearly knocked on the window, but decided against it as not the best means of introduction. Instead I started along the wall to look for the door. I came across the second window and on glancing inside something struck me as rather odd, but I did not wait to think about it and kept walking along, certain that the door must be just round the corner. But there was no door, nor any corner, just a straight wall with egg-shaped windows after every few steps, each window identically decorated with fairy lights and each presenting an identical view of the inside. So that was what had struck me as strange . . . Through each window I saw not only the same room and the same people, but saw them from precisely the same angle as I had through the first window.

Panic. But after what I had been through I was sure that I could handle it. Panic handled. Control. Decision time. Decision taken.

I knocked on the window . . . timidly at first, and with the knuckle of my forefinger only, loudly and with the full complement of knuckles later on. But to no effect. No one heard me, or took the slightest bit of notice of me if they did. I began calling out and shouting and screaming, but that produced no effect either.

It was like confronting a picture, except that they were moving around and talking and behaving like a typical family at a meal. The mother was getting more and more emotional about whatever was on the TV, the father was getting more and more impatient with it all, the daughter was getting stroppier and stroppier.

As I continued to knock, and shout, and scream, and wave my arms about, I was aware of my strength fading away. I could see my muscles and flesh dissolve, feel the hardness of my bones turn to brittleness. It was a painful process, and tiring. Very tiring. My voice began to falter, my movements stammered. I stopped. Stopped knocking or shouting or waving my arms about. Just stopped and stood there, rooted to the spot, like a withering tree, waiting. For what, neither the tree nor I knew.

All I knew was that my body, my strong, working man's body, the only worthwhile thing about my entire worthless being, was now weak and wasted and disfigured. I wouldn't even be sought out for a fuck any more. My only redeeming virtue was lost. What good was I to Belinda now? She was better off where she was. The tree wasn't bothered about any of it. It was too cold and old and dying to care.

Just when I too was beginning not to care, and looking forward to not looking forward to anything, the quarter child jumped from his chair, pointed towards me and shouted: Look, Mum! Look, Dad! There's a tree outside the window, and it looks like a man.

The rest of the family froze. In the silence and stillness that followed I could hear the strains of an unfamiliar Christmas song coming from the television.

After an interval of time I couldn't quantify, the quarter child repeated and then continued to repeat, Look, Mum! Look, Dad! There's a tree outside the window, and it looks like a man.

It began to get on my nerves.

Look, Mum! Look, Dad! There's a tree outside the window, and it looks like a man. Look, Mum! Look, Dad! There's a . . . Again and again and again. Look, Mum! Look, Dad! There's a . . .

It really began to get on my nerves.

Oh do shut up, for Heaven's sake. The mother had rediscovered sound and motion. Do something, Darren, don't just sit there, anything to shut him up. See what the little bleeder is on about.

Movement and speech returned to the rest of the family. The girl child was the first to rush out of her chair, come to the window, look me up and down, and shout: It's not a tree that looks like a man, stupid, it *is* a man. A man that looks like a tree, said the boy child, who had joined her by then. He is hungry and he is cold, said the quarter child. He is naked! screamed the mother. Do something, Darren. He is dying, said the quarter child, a tree without water, like the brats on TV. There is a naked man outside our house, continued the mother, a naked . . . black . . . man! *Do* something, Darren. Get away from there children, get away at once. Haven't you been taught to keep away from strangers, especially *men*, even well-dressed white ones, and especially a naked . . . a black! The pervert bastard, said the father reeling angrily and aggressively towards the window, reeking of beer fumes, the pervert bastard, I'll show him. Don't, Darren. Careful, Darren, you never can tell about these . . . these sort of . . . I think you'd better call the police. Darren stopped for a moment, fist and teeth clenched, then untensed a little, unsteadied his neck, turned his head slightly to one side and said, You telephone the police, Mandy, I'll stay here and watch he don't try anything. Pervert bastard. Get away from the window, Gillian, get away at once. And you, Danny. You 'eard me! Pervert bastard. Should be locked away and never allowed out, hissed the mother, hurrying towards the phone. Terrorising decent folk . . . Run! whispered the quarter child hiding under the table. Run, tree, run, run run run . . .

I ran.

Faster than I would have thought possible with my enfeebled, starving legs.

If the quarter child wanted me to run, it wanted me to escape; and if it wanted me to escape, it wanted me to live; and if it wanted me to live, I would live. I would certainly give it a damned good try. Don't ask me why. I don't know. Neither does the tree.

I ran.

† † †

Luckily there was another house waiting for me when I was well away from *that* one. I say luckily, though this time I was not so sure. However, this house not only had windows, but corners and angles, entablatures and corniced roofs, and many doors. All that was promising.

I went straight up to the nearest door, large, solid and beautifully carved, and pulled the cord which rang the bell.

I positioned myself to one side so that I would be hidden by the door when it opened, hiding my nakedness at least temporarily, while I explained my situation – difficult though that was going to be. However, when the door opened it dragged me along with it straight into a magnificently opulent hall.

A very small Japanese butler stood facing my genitals, a

sharp but good-humoured glint hidden somewhere in his eyes, an understated smile hovering around his lips.

Have you got an appointment, Sir, he asked in perfect English, the merest hint of a question in his voice.

I placed my hands in front of my crotch.

No, Sir, no, but I only . . .

His Lordship receives no one without an appoint-

But I only . . .

-ment, Sir.

But I only want something to eat, and some clothes, anything, any old thing, an old sheet would do, I will work for it, help in the kitchen, clear out the garden, anything, anything, please, please . . .

I let my voice trail away. I had begun fast, trying to get in all that I wanted to say quickly and in one breath in case he interrupted me. But now that he did not interrupt me, I wished he would. I was running out of words to say. Also, when I talk fast I tend to wave my arms and hands about and that was a mistake.

I am very cold, I added lamely.

Even though the hall was wonderfully warm inside, it somehow made me feel colder than I had felt out in the falling snow. Goose-pimples large as purple grapes sprung up all over my body, hardening into sand-sequined pebbles, and every particle of my flesh seemed to shiver and quiver independently of the rest. The ball of pain in my stomach grew larger and heavier and I feared I would fall, its increasingly unbearable weight tearing through my guts and spilling upon the plush, inches-deep carpet, desecrating its classical beauty with my filthy Choodah flesh. It would be a sacrilege for someone like me to stand upon it in a respectable and acceptable state, and I was naked and wet and dirty. The only consolation was that my Choodah filth was also classical, its roots going back to an antiquity more ancient than the heritage of the carpet, and the pride of it made me hold my crumbling spine up straight and tall as I looked down upon the head of the obsequious butler staring straight at my crotch. I moved my hand to the side.

The butler raised his eyes up at me and looked into my eyes for the first time since I had entered. The strain of standing tall was beginning to tell and I reeled slightly, nearly falling backwards, but managed to hold myself together.

The glint in the butler's eyes softened as he spoke: It is most irregular. You should really be removed from the premises, Sir, but seeing that you are in obvious distress I shall make an exception. Most irregular, though, most irregular. He reached into the inside pocket of his tux top and produced a blazing red diary which, strangely, had loose pages. It was unlike any I had seen before. He flicked through its sheets then said, Ah! Miraculously he produced a pen, held it posed artistically in one delicately-manicured hand. I could make you an appointment for March the twenty-third – next year, of course, obviously, considering the March of this year is no longer with us. He permitted himself a half-smile. As I registered my amazement at this suggestion with open-mouthed silence, he ordered away his smile and said, His Lordship prefers to make his own appointments. I do you a big favour by making one on his behalf. If that arrangement is not suitable, I am afraid you will have to telephone His Lordship's secretary after . . .

Surely you joke. I am hungry now, now. I can't . . .

I never joke. Dally with humour, sometimes, yes. Joke, never. I leave such coarse pursuits to the coarse.

I suddenly realised that he actually regarded me with the deepest contempt, had done so all along.

Could I blame him? Of course not. But, and I don't know why this is, although I am quite justly content to hold myself in utter contempt, when somebody else does so I most unjustly flare up.

Who do you think you are! You are just a butler, just a common –

I shall now have to call the police, Sir. You leave me with no option by mocking my very generous offer. As he headed towards a solid gold telephone cradled in a jewel-inlaid, boat-shaped base, I decided it would be best if I left.

When I was half way through the door he turned round and said: I may be just a butler, but I own three-quarters of the estate, and pay a generous stipened to His Lordship – which covers not only all his expenses but also the upkeep of the buildings and the grounds, and my salary. A handsome salary, I assure you, Sir. The look in his eyes, though steady and straight, suggested that he was dallying with humour, while not in any way deviating from the facts.

I bet that telephone is yours too, I said.

Next time, do remember to put your tie round your neck, not between your legs. And one knot, not two, is customary.

It's not my fault if all you have is a dinky bow-tie, I retorted, and hurriedly shut the door behind me.

Monty, His Lordship, quite likes it . . . The butler's voice drifted out through the keyhole. He probably has no choice, I muttered to myself, pleased at having partially succeeded in bringing him down to my level – even though I suspected it was because he had chosen to descend rather than because I had brought him down. Anyway, it was time to concentrate on getting as far away from the house as possible, and as quickly as possible.

I needn't have bothered. The house got away from me, as far as possible and as quickly as possible. I could see it receding in the distance and disappearing from view so fast it could have been a fuel-injected sports car.

† † †

I was alone again, and colder and hungrier than ever. The ball in my stomach had enlarged so much that it had begun to stick out of my shrinking belly, its weight making it more and more difficult for my progressively emaciating legs even to stand up straight, much less keep going. But keep going, I had to. For Belinda's sake. For the sake of the quarter child.

My vision was blurring now, and there was a strange but not unpleasant music playing in my ears. It had an indefinably soothing quality about it which tended to lull me to sleep, and I was having trouble fighting off its sonorous effects, fighting to keep myself awake, fighting to keep myself alive. It was a painful fight which seemed to tear at the ligaments of my body from odd and opposing angles, making balance impossible. I had to keep spreading my arms and hands outwards to prevent myself from falling backwards, or just crumbling to the ground. And blinking. I had to keep blinking, consciously and strongly, to make sure my eyes remained open and in some sort of focus.

Just then the music began to get louder, acquiring the more recognisable form of a tune unfamiliar only a short time ago, the tune of a Christmas song. A bright sun rose (in the middle of the night!) and cast its harsh, unforgiving light upon a crowd of millions as they stood and gyrated and waved banners, while on a huge stage in front of them a group of attractive young people sang and danced and played music. Enormous television screens circled the crowd, and upon those screens played the pictures which must have so upset the mother of the quarter child. Seeing them now, I could sympathise with the rather rude girl child who had wanted the set turned off. I could not understand why everybody was so riveted by it, and what there was to sing and dance about. They are collecting money to help the suffering, explained a blond, blue-eyed youth standing on my left. Jason? But he had disappeared among the crowd before I could take a second look. It couldn't have been, could it? He would have recognised me. But how could he have, looking the way I looked now?

The energy and the vigour of the crowd entered my dying bones and I felt strong again, strong and young. I pushed my way forwards in order to see better. I came to the aisle in the centre, but it was no ordinary aisle. It was glaringly decorated and lit with colourful lights that winked on and off with startling irregularity. Upon it walked some of the ugliest women I had ever seen – tall, bony, with haggard, starved faces and haggard, starved bodies. They were dressed, or undressed, in a manner to mock and ridicule the unnatural ugliness of their unnatural bodies, and being forced by forces beyond my line of vision to walk and behave in an inelegant and undignified manner while a number of people stood or sat, pencils and notebooks in hand, watching, watching, watching, and occasionally rising to their feet and clapping. It was weird, or it would have been if it hadn't been so tragic. My heart went out to the poor girls so shamelessly made to parade their ugliness and lack of dress sense in front of a sadistically jubilant crowd.

Forgetting my own troubles, I rushed like some madder than mad Don Quixote towards that walk of iniquity, hoping, I knew not how, to save those less-than-pretty damsels in more than mere distress from a fate worse than life.

But before I could get anywhere near the aisle a woman in the audience wearing a small black and green dress, and a large black and green hat, and large white shoes, and large white gloves, and a tiny white scarf, saw me coming and let out a wild scream: They are here! she shrieked. They are here! Another scream from another source, then shouts and words and more words. Could he have come out of . . . the . . . set, the television . . . Oh don't be so ridiculous . . . Do something, somebody, anybody . . . Then how, from where . . . Don't, don't touch him, call the police, hurry, call the police, hurry, man, hurry, the Home Office . . . You'll catch something . . . Call the Home Office . . . Don't be so silly, the police, call the police . . . How on earth did he get here? Economic refugee! *Hiss*! They get everywhere . . . He's naked! Thanks for telling us, I would never have known . . . There should be a law against it.

Nobody was coming near me, but they were forming a ring round me – either to block my escape, or it just happened as they snuggled close to each other and well away from me.

The girls on the aisle kept wiggling their hips and shaking their necks and rolling their eyes, oblivious to all the commotion. The band kept playing, the crowd kept cheering, the television sets kept on showing moving pictures.

I had no difficulty in getting through them. They made way for me, a few brave attempts to block my path were soon abandoned. Don't, don't, he can't go far, looking like that, the police will get him . . .

My free run was short-lived. (It wasn't what you would call a run anyway, more like a demented marionette on the loose. Co-ordination between brain and limb wasn't exactly perfect.) I ran straight into thousands of others who impeded my progress, not being averse to touching or holding on to me, not being much different from me. Some of them. Many of them. Most of them.

Invading the airports, attacking the sea-shores, defiling the landscape. In planes, in boats, crammed into boxes in lorries and holds, and flailing about in the water, all arms and legs and eyes and nostrils. Fleeing in a cowardly fashion, both shameful and shameless. Leaving behind them burnt-out homes, dead, dying and mutilated families, threats of execution and years of harassment and torture – all without any appreciable signs of remorse or regret, the gutless blackguards! Some were floating down the river, bellies up and swollen, crows and vultures pecking at their innards and having a free ride along with a free meal, a jolly good time, in fact, and jolly good too. Many were being pulled out of the water by people in strange or familiar uniforms, then stripped and hacked and thrown back in again, or stripped and fucked and thrown back in again, depending on their fuck-worthiness. Some were being put behind barbed wire and chained up, some locked in cells. A few set fire to themselves in an act of extreme ingratitude towards the kindly folk who were looking after them, causing a great deal of unpleasantness and undeserved unfavourable and painful publicity for the said kindly folk. Some with chemically treated skins and experimentally re-arranged features and scientifically adjusted limbs were making disgusting and obvious overtures in a bid to get cheap airtime and cheaper sympathy. Many were trying to wash and clean up their children as best they could, which means not very well, and taking a long, covetous look at them before sending them on ahead in case someone liked the look of their youthful asses and gave them what the old and the weak clearly do not deserve. Economic refugees, one and all, and a disgrace to mankind. Greedy, money-grabbing parasites, high on the conservative kick of self-improvement – car phone, CD player, BUPA card, that sort of thing, not improvement in any moral sense of the word, rest assured – and low, I mean *low*, on political integrity.

I tried not to mingle with them and tried to keep myself (relatively) pure and (relatively) untainted and (relatively) aloof. But in the wild, uncivilised mêlée that surrounded me, that was quite impossible, and I found myself being hunted down by the guardians of true morality and high civilisation, to be driven off their civilised shores along with the rest of the uncivilised lot. Soon I was in the waters with most of them, covered with the shit of the dead, the sweat of the dying, and the blood of the living. It was an awesome sight and one which God would have been truly ashamed to see. How could His creation behave in that uncivilised a manner, and bring into disrepute the entire civilised world.

One stupid sod fished out a dead rat from the water, *dead*, and began eating it, wait for it, without a knife and fork! Yes, that *is* what I said, *without* a knife and fork; and without so much as chucking it alive and kicking into a pot of boiling water, like a real lobster.

I threw up all over my taut and distended belly, strings of slimy puke trickling down and sticking like glue to my pubes.

Then a miracle happened.

The waters parted.

And through the parted waters came trains.

Trains of the blessed.

Trains full of laughing, waving crowds of happy, beautiful people. Brave, courageous people, and with enough resourcefulness to actually contrive to cross an open, welcoming border! True refugees, fleeing from the persecution of a tyrannical government.

My heart warmed for them. I wished there was something *I* could do to help, something I could give to alleviate their suffering, suffering so cheerfully borne, with smiles and laughter, unlike the moany, weepy, whingeing hordes of the uncivilised. But there was nothing I could offer, except puke-ridden pubes – and that not without a good razor, or at least a pair of sharpish scissors. My hairs down below are a bit stiffish at the best of times; and at that point, primed with puke as they were, if prompt removal for philanthropic purposes was required a pair of shears would probably be needed.

Like the woman with her last farthing, I would have given more than anybody else for a pair of shears.

But none were forthcoming. Not even a pair of blunt scissors.

† † †

A police siren sounded, sending the charlatan fortune-hunters helter-skelter in search of places to hide their respective shames. In the rush my balls got badly squashed between somebody else's thighs – not altogether a pleasant sensation.

Next, without any warning, the ground beneath my feet gave way and I fell into a hole. I found myself in a dark and dingy basement, or an underground arena of some sort. There was so little headroom that I had to bend over double and crawl sideways, crab-fashion in order to be able to move about.

Though I had had many harrowing experiences since leaving Belinda in our little tent with its flap fluttering accusingly in the wind, I found that place to be the most frightening of the night. Partly because I did not like being in enclosed places – it was not exactly a full-blown phobia, but I was sure that if I had to stay on in there for any length of time it would develop into one. Partly it was the dark, not the utter blackness of the first part of the night, which strangely enough seemed to offer a comfort of sorts, but a mirky, dirty kind of haze, like tainted light or polluted darkness.

And then there was the smell: the smell of present and impending doom, the smell of despair. The smell of dying. The smell of meths and booze and vomit and shit. The smell of people, of a new breed of refugees, the oldest kind, unrecognised as either political or economic, refugees in their own home land. Many young and white, and many old, and a few black too. Mostly male, though some females were about as well, barely distinguishable from the men. They were all doubled over so tightly and were crouching so close together they could hardly move at all. And for good reason: they were holding up the floor above on their backs.

The rhythmic clicking of the heels and the sound of cheap music told me that we were directly beneath the aisle on which the unnaturally ugly women were still parading.

337

The click-click of their heels speeded up, and to that was added the stomping of heavier footwear. The music turned harsher, enhanced by the noise of rapturous applause. The floor became heavier, and lowered itself a little. The people underneath cried out in pain, and I could see their once-handsome faces twist and fall further into the ground, their once-strong limbs tremble and melt into sweat, their once-alive eyes darken and fade. The bowls by their side clinked and clanked as well-wishers and conscience-pumpers dropped the odd penny in them from the hole above.

Suddenly there was a bright light. I jumped a foot high, or would have had there been room, but the others didn't bat an eyelid. Another one of those reporters or documentary-makers, whispered one dead boy in my ear. One of them gave me five pounds not to sell my ass to anyone. Now it is unsaleable. Why did I save it, and who for?

It was pointless having a conversation with a dead body, so I moved a little further on. My buttocks were beginning to burn from having to scrape across the harsh surface of the floor, and my brain was starting to buzz with the fear of not dying.

Then a ray of hope, a ray of light. Not the unnatural light for the pleasure of the cameras, but real light, the light of the darkness under the skies.

There! There! I said excitedly to a girl next to me, pointing to my left, I can see light, and air, why don't you move up there, why don't we . . . No use, mate, she croaked, you'll only be moved back, or nicked. Her face was cracked and her lips were blistered and the tattoos on her arms were peeling off as her skin rotted. She could have made a fortune if she'd been able to free market the formula. As for me, I'd any day rather be nicked than stay there and rot. The girl must have been a mind-reader. *I'd* rather stay here and rot than be nicked, she said without opening her mouth. I must have been a mind-reader too. Like the girl, I was sure I didn't have long to go – in fact it was weird I hadn't gone already. I'd seen off many in a better state than myself.

I tried to crawl, but that took more space than was available so, once again grating my butt across the splintery floor, I made my way towards the source of light and air.

I was there.

No one to move me back, no one to nick me.

Just fresh air, the sky, and freedom.

If only the girl had come with me. If only all of them had come with me. They could have been saved from that awful life, and the awful end of it that inevitably awaited them. They could still be saved. Most of them were in better shape than I was, and if I could survive, surely they could too? I turned round to see if I could call out or beckon to them, maybe go back and get them, even if it burst the final bubble of my strength.

But there was nothing there and no one to call out to, or see. Just empty space, snow, and more snow.

As I wept for the lost bodies of the lost souls my tears turned to snow, snow that blew away in the wind.

With crow fingers I dusted the pure white flakes that had covered my impure black body from head to toe in no time at all, and then regretted doing so as my shrivelling and shrinking flesh thus exposed did not present a pleasant spectacle and would have been better left snow-clad. But I needn't have worried. It was soon covered up again.

I resumed my nocturnal journey, for no other reason than the lack of reason. And a better reason is hard to find.

† † †

My head was now heavier, for my neck and my shoulder blades were carved out of bent pain. The insides of my knees were harder and knobblier than the outsides, making my legs appear to bend the wrong way. Perhaps they were bending the wrong way, for I wasn't sure whether I was going backwards or forwards.

The atmosphere began to change. The snowflakes became larger yet softer; assumed pretty, heart-shaped and diamond-like and moon-faced forms, then developed colours, like falling leaves in a forest of rainbows. Manna from heaven? Alas not, not as far as edible nourishment was concerned;

but it ceased to be cold, and a generous warmth, like the warmth of a mother's womb, encompassed the forest of colours and gave inner sustenance to my crumbling body. My step became lighter and I could walk, even jauntily. The Christmas tune that I had heard twice that night came to my lips and I began to hum it, gently and under my breath at first, then loudly and clearly. Singing is a gift I have always envied in others but which I sadly lack in myself. Yet here I was singing perfect notes in perfect tune. I couldn't believe my luck. If this was dying I couldn't have enough of it. It was the most beautiful thing that had ever happened to me. To be able to sing in tune! I could not believe it.

I looked up in an unconscious gesture of thankfulness to Him up there. I say unconscious, for despite the blissful unexpectedness of the warmth and colours that surrounded me then, what I had seen and heard that night had not done anything to enhance the conscious quality of His image upon my mind.

What I saw as I looked upwards explained the colours and the warmth, but was equally inexplicable in itself. Hundreds and thousand of flower petals covered the sky from one end of the horizon to the other, both shielding the atmosphere from cold and lending it the rich colours reflected in the snow on the ground, as well as in the flakes managing to filter their way down through the clouds of flower petals. Rose petals and sunflower petals and carnation petals and lily petals and petals of all sorts of imaginable and unimaginable flowers: flowers from this world and flowers from out of this world, flowers from the heart of the earth and flowers from the guts of the moon, flowers from the gardens of reality and flowers from the wilderness of the imagination.

It was all so magical, so beautiful, so magically beautiful that I felt my being transformed into an empty receptacle pre-ordained to contain that magic and beauty; and I became a part of the magic, part of the beauty, and part of their mystery.

There was no fragrance, none at all, and that was somewhat unsettling. But what is a mystery if not unsettling!

The flower petals started to come down even as I looked

up, and as they came lower and lower they became larger and larger. Then I realised they weren't flower petals at all, but multicoloured sheets of beauteous silk, patterned with stripes and spots and other simple designs.

Lower still, and the mystery resolved itself, though not without creating another mystery. Fluttering above my head were flags, flags of all the nations in the world. Some I recognised, some I could take a guess at, others I couldn't place at all. The more powerful nations had larger flags, and thousands of them, scattered across the skies; the weakest countries had pitifully small, lonely ones.

There was something that bothered me still: perhaps a minor detail, but you know how it is once it gets into your head that something is awry, it continues to gnaw at you unless you find out what it is.

All those flags in the sky were without flagpoles. That was the incongruity which had so oddly disturbed my senses. As soon as I became aware of this fact, the flags above me started sprouting poles. From the flags began descending shafts of varying length and thickness and quality and style. Some were sharp and pointed, others thick, blunt and metallic. Some turned out to be javelins, others were long and strong but yielding, like the ones used by pole-vaulters. Some were actually bayonets, some were guns and rifles of different types, from simple shotguns to sophisticated automatic rifles. Some were good old-fashioned swords, some just good old sticks, and I could also see a few long and sharp double-edged knives. Some could have been delicately streamlined ballistic or guided missiles. The more powerful the flag, the deadlier its staff.

A rumbling sound burst from the centre of the earth and crescendoed upwards and outwards, tearing apart the crust, forcing enormous gaping holes in its surface and playing havoc with the face of the land. It was an earthquake of such tremendous strength that it would have blown apart any man-made instruments that dared to record its intensity. Out of the newly created cracks and chasms and cavities emerged houses and buildings and temples of worship and places of government and rivers and oceans and mountains.

And people. As I was thrown around and whirled about like a dead leaf in a hurricane I was surrounded by townships and cities and countries and continents bustling with life and the living.

It was then that the rain started, the rain of flags upon our no-man's world.

Down they came, knifing and bayoneting and gunning in a never-ending assault, killing, maiming, crippling and destroying. Sometimes targeting one section of the no-man's world, sometimes another, sometimes several sections simultaneously.

† † †

Bludgeoned, bayoneted and bloodied, trampled upon, booted about and bloodied, choking on poisonous fumes and sieved with bullet-holes; bits of flesh and gristle sticking tight to my fragmented skin with the bondage of clotted blood; Choodah marrow spurting out of shattered bones, shattered bones splintering out of torn muscles, torn muscles drowning in sploshing blood; accursed with eternal life – or so it seemed to me at the time. I stared with deathless eyes at what had once been my ugly black body. How beautiful it used to be.

How often I had cursed my looks when confronted with the old face in a lurking mirror. How often I had cursed death when it raided my life to take away someone who acknowledged my being, if only through mistrust or hatred or contempt. How I would bless my looks now, were they to return to their original state of ugliness. How I would bless death if it were to come a-plundering my ravaged remains.

Restore me, God. I humbled myself in prayer once again that night. How long can a mere mortal hold out against the divine? Or let me die. Please, God, please . . .

Pain was the only reminder left of life. Pain was the only fruit left of life. Pain was the only hope left in life.

Except the mirage of a tiny flap fluttering away at the entrance to a tiny tent, somewhere beyond the horizon, in the centre of paradise, with all that was beautiful and good and worthwhile in the world inside it in one little bundle of black.

Except Jason and Jennifer and Mother and Father and Shakti and Sean and and . . . I am sure you know the list by heart now.

Except food.

Now why did I think of food?

I thought I had got over that. I thought I was at that stage of hunger where the very thought of food makes you sick, and if you do eat you are sure to be sick.

I know why I thought of food.

It was that smell, again!

I shut my eyes and my mouth and pinched my nostrils, not just to stop smelling, but with any luck to stop breathing as well.

But the smell was too strong.

For the simple reason that there were smartly dressed waiters and waitresses laying the tables and serving food to non-existent customers, right under my nose. I was quite unable to digest the significance of what was going on. Either I was invisible, for no one made any attempts to throw me out of what was clearly a very 'high class' establishment, or their guests or customers were invisible.

I was soon be to enlightened. It transpired that it was I who was their honoured guest. They stood in reverential awe around my 'I survived the company of vampires' presence. Finally one of them, a superbly beautiful young woman, took courage in her hands, came as close to me as one is permitted to get to royalty, and said in hushed tones: Dinner is served, Sir.

I could have anything that was spread across the tables, or all of it. Despite obvious ideological reservations I did not think it was the appropriate occasion for me to express my abhorrence of hoity-toity restaurants and hotels, so taking a napkin I stuck it to my waist with a bit of gluey blood, then reeled over to the nearest table to sample what was on offer.

Nothing but meat, red or white as it is euphemistically called, depending on which living, loving, sentient being had been hacked to death; and fish, which curiously enough is not even counted among living creatures and often considered an acceptable part of a vegetarian's diet.

By now my appetite was back in full vigour. My tongue was heavily salivating and the distended ball of my stomach was shamelessly rumbling for food. Even my finger-tips were pulling themselves towards the food, urging me to grab what was available and stuff it into my open mouth.

Seeing me hesitate, one of the waiters, a good-looking young man, the male model type, approached me courteously and said in an anxious but still husky voice, Is anything the matter, Sir? His brow was furrowed just right: too deep and it would have distracted from his looks, shallower and it would have looked insincere.

Do you, perchance, happen to have any herbivorous delicacies? I tried to make my words rise to the occasion, but after a bad start it got worse. Or perhaps not delicacies, necessarily.

Herbivorous!

He, Sir, means vegetarian.

Vegetarian!

After such preliminary exclamations of what I considered undue surprise there was a moment's silence.

We would have you know, Sir, that these dishes have been specially prepared by chefs from . . . Some very big names in the culinary world were flung in my face. They had all spoken almost simultaneously – still respectfully, but with a new element of controlled aggression just about managing to make itself evident.

If there was any chance of my succumbing to temptation, it went. And very grateful I was for it. If the laws of nature were to prevail, I would die whether I ate or not; if they had been set aside, as I suspected was the case, I would continue to live anyway.

Besides, I could never eat . . . I know that there was a lot I would stoop to, but this . . . Never. How could I even . . . It might be Mother on the plate, Nazli . . .

I heard a brittle laugh. It was the smart-ass male model. Are you suggesting, Sir, that we would cook your mother?

344

Or Nazli, whoever she is! This from a fattish man, the oldest and least well designed of them all.

Girlfriend? giggled the first waitress who had announced dinner.

Bloody sister, more likely, which girl would have him? sniggered the male model.

How did they know what I had thought? I was sure I hadn't spoken out loud. At least their hostility was out in the open now, and somehow that was a relief.

I looked at the fat one, who had the florid face of a person who liked a drop or two more than the next person and said: If the soil in the earth can turn to a bunch of grapes, which can turn to wine, which can turn to the flesh that surrounds your hole, why can't my mother's earth turn to Mother Earth, then turn into flesh, and the flesh into the body of any of her children?

Clever dick, said the fat man.

Smart ass, said the first girl.

Bloody fool, if you ask me, said the male model.

Bastard! said the other girl.

This seemed to go down well with the rest.

Bastard! Bastard! Bastard! they all began to chant. Forming a ring to prevent my escape, they started advancing towards me. As they did so, every one of them picked up something from the food on display: a chicken breast, a chunk of roast, a filleted fish, a leg of lamb, a pig's head . . .

The male model kicked me on the floor, the fat man straddled my chest, the girls started forcing 'food' down my throat, beginning with the pig's head. I could hear it cry.

I could hear it crying all the way: in my mouth, down the gullet, into my stomach. But by that time I was too overcome by my own terror to respond to its terror.

Down went lamb and roast and bull's head and fish and every last particle of mince and crab and lobsters and all else that was on the tables and much much more besides, including Mother and Father and Aunt Neelum and naturally Aunt Verna, and the young man by the canal and the thousands massacred in Bangla Desh and the billions all over the world. Umrao's head and her entire body was the final course.

After I had been fed to their hearts' content, the waiters and waitresses released my still struggling body. The fat one unstraddled himself from my chest, the girls took their knees off my neck, the male model removed his face from above my face. All of them stood up and moved some distance away from my supine presence and began to survey me with cold, satisfied eyes. They nodded approvingly at me, then looked at each other and nodded approvingly at each other.

Only a moment ago I had believed that if I ate anything, even if it was edible, my stomach would send it back post-haste. I had ended up devouring half of created life on earth and it had settled down within me without the slightest uprising. Not even all the screams I had swallowed – mine own and those of other living creatures getting asphyxiated or being diced alive by my enforced greed – reappeared in the outside world as so much as an average burp.

A foggy numbness enveloped and suffocated my senses, starkly visible itself but rendering all else invisible, impenetrable as the densest of forests yet open wide as the lusting mouth of Hell.

The enormity of what I had done, however unwillingly, obliterated all responses. I found myself unable to feel or even accept the utter horror of it, much less protest in any way or decry or denounce either the event or myself, or even my tormentors.

As I lay there on the icy ground, speechless and motionless, just lay there like a sack of wet flour, the first girl smiled softly and said: See, it wasn't so bad after all, was it?

You look so much better now, said the second girl. He looks so much better, doesn't he? She looked at the others for confirmation. They all muttered in agreement, except the male model who maintained a sinister silence.

Yes he does, doesn't he – he spoke eventually – very much better. And with that he began to unbuckle his trouser belt.

The first girl stepped out of her knickers and the others started to remove their clothes.

Oh no you won't, you bloody won't! You fucking bloody won't! I yelled, jumping to my feet, surprised. I hadn't believed a moment would come when I would regain speech and movement and thought. I hadn't believed a day could come when I'd say no to sex.

But then I saw something else which overrode all other emotions and fear. I saw myself.

My body was whole and well again, big and strong and healthy as ever. Not a scratch or a mark remained to prove that I had been starved, beaten, gunned down, knifed and torn apart many times over only a very short while ago.

It was then that the full scale of what had happened began to grip my heart. The numbness that paralysed my soul fled into the night. The time to confront myself was upon me.

I had begged God to return my face, such as it was, and restore my body. He had done so, with the life and the bodies of all those lives and bodies I had swallowed. My flesh was their blood.

How could He! Oh, how could He!

I didn't mean that, not like that. He should have known. He of all people should have known. He must have known.

How could He.

And then, before I could check myself or think what I was screaming, I screamed: Damn you, God, and waved my fist up at Him, Damn you God, damn you, damn you, damn you . . .

Everything froze.

The snowflakes which were merrily floating down from the skies, swaying, swinging and dancing, stopped in mid-air and lay suspended.

Then came the screams. The screams of the devoured.

Emanating from every pore of my body, every follicle of my skin, every particle of my flesh, every nook and corner of my being. From the soles of my feet to the hair of my scalp: screams and screams and more screams.

Loud screams and soft screams, hushed screams and choked screams and wild screams. Mad screams and angry screams and pleading screams and begging screams and denouncing screams and accusing screams and bored screams and apathetic screams and meaningless screams. Screams of mindless glee and screams of heartless joy. Women's screams and men's screams and children's screams. Screams from a universe of banshees in mourning, screams of a galaxy of wounded wolves, screams of an army of ambulance sirens being chased by posses of police sirens. Screams of snakes and screams of spiders. Screams of little fish and screams of big fish. Screams of pigs and screams of cows. Screams of elephants and rhinos and whales and monkeys. And screams of tiny mice and giant rats.

Screams of the hungry.

Screams of the poor, the simple, the sick.

Screams of the unchosen, the unclean, the unwanted; the unmen, the unwomen, the unchildren; the unliving, the unnatural, the uncivilised; the unloved.

And my screams. My body was a ten–to–the–power–of–nine sound system transmitting high fidelity screams to every mathematically conceivable point of the compass, in this world, and out of the farthest recesses of all known and unknown galaxies in this and all other universes that exist within the heart of God and the mind of man.

Damn you, God, I screamed, Damn you, damn you, damn you . . .

This repetition of my profane outburst had the opposite effect from the first time. The cessation of movement was reversed and replaced by feverish activity.

The waiters and waitresses developed fluffy white wings, sprouted haloes above their heads and flew away. The arrested snowflakes resumed their earth-bound flight, but not before turning into blackish red scabs of coagulated blood, as fresh flowing blood, throbbing and alive and brilliantly scarlet, began to rain down from the heavens with such force and power as to make the strongest of storms seem no more than summer drizzle.

Terrified into excess instead of caution, overpowered by the impact of my own few words, horrendously ill chosen and ill advised, and still seething with hurt and rage, and caught within the storm of betrayal – what I saw as betrayal, the worst betrayal ever, the divine betrayal of hapless mortals – rather than repent and fall on my knees and beg for forgiveness, I escalated my unspeakable blasphemy.

Accursed be Thou! My voice rose in mad triumph above the symphony of screams.

Forcing the torrential downpour of blood out of their path my hands tore through the steel blue curtain of the skies and grabbed Him by the lapels. Accursed be Thou, and Thine! I cried, Accursed be Thou and Thine, accursed till the end of time and the beginning of timelessness and then again from the end of timelessness and the start of nothingness until the nevering of ever and beyond the beyond of beyond. Accursed be Thou! Accursed be Thine!

The souls of the screaming were stunned into silence, unable to cope with my blasphemy. They packed up whatever was left to them in their destitution and fled as fast as they could, leaving me utterly and totally alone: bludgeoned, bayoneted and bloodied, trampled upon, booted about and bloodied, choking on poisonous fumes and sieved with bullet-holes; bits of flesh and gristle sticking tight to my fragmented skin with the bondage of clotted blood; Choodah marrow spurting out of shattered bones, shattered bones splintering out of torn muscles, torn muscles drowning in sploshing blood.

† † †

The rain stopped, a cloud of clotted blood split asunder and etherised, and for the second time that night a bright and vigorous sun rose and shone upon me and my surrounds. I was in the middle of a vast, yielding desert of gritty sand: glowingly warm, golden brown, and gently smiling. It was probably burning hot, but that's how it felt to me.

I had no idea who or what or where I was. Or who or what or where anything or anyone was. All memory had deserted me. My mind was a total blank.

I was just a very sick, horribly wounded, badly starving man in such rough shape that by all rational criteria I, whoever I was, should have long been dead. Perhaps I was.

I lay face down on the welcoming sand, stretched my limbs to their full capacity, regardless of the searing pain that this sent through every nerve and fibre of my body, and was about to shut my eyes when I saw a caravan of people coming my way, mostly on foot, but a few on the backs of camels or donkeys.

I could see men, women and children. Many were the colour of the sand, but some were lighter and some quite dark-complexioned. They were wearing richly coloured jackets and tops, many with flowery patterns, and baggy trousers or long plain skirts. Some had straight-cut cloaks or robes on, mostly plain: grey, white or orange, also checked. Some merely had coloured sheets wrapped round their bodies, especially the women, but a few men as well, though the men draped theirs in a different style from the women. Described like this the clothes might give a misleading impression of opulence. Actually they were dirty, work-worn, work-stained and raggedy. The colourfulness was more an expression of character and attitude than wealth. A few did look quite rich, while some were near naked.

There was a vague yet disturbing air of familiarity about the whole scene but, search my brain though I did, I could not recover anything from there which could identify it for me.

I tried to stand up and move out of their path, but could not manage it; I tried to crawl out of their path on all fours, but could not manage that; I tried to slither out of their path on my belly, but could not manage that. I stayed where I was and shut my eyes.

Look! I heard an awed and excited voice speak in a language which sounded foreign but which I had no difficulty in understanding; or, it transpired when I tried, in speaking. *Look*, the voice continued, *that's him! Look at the sign.* His finger was pointing to my exposed back.

Do you know who I am? I asked, sand choking my throat.

Shall we tell him? they asked among themselves. Do we have a choice? I suppose not. What difference will it make? I don't know! But he may not be! Has to be! It is about time. All right, we'll tell you.

It was the first one who spoke.

You are neither pure nor clean, neither void nor tranquil; neither without breath nor without self; neither undecaying nor endless nor steadfast nor eternal nor independent; neither are you unborn, nor yet born.

He said this in a dull monotone, as if quoting.

You are, I fear, No-Man.

Thanks for telling me.

It was not a pleasure, he said. *If you are the prophesied No-Man who cannot stand up for himself, then dreaded times are upon us. When No-Man comes with a sign upon his back, the sign of the devil, he brings for mankind the dreaded sign of the coming of the dreaded Aparm-Atman.*

And who is Aparm–Atman? When I asked this of the man, the others looked at me as if I were a fool, half horrified, half amazed, their eyes turning pale and wan.

She is the Bhagwan-hater, one who is neither sat *nor* asat, *neither being nor non-being, but anti-being; the sullied sullier of the unsullied.*

Long will be the night of clashes and grim will be the night of clashes, when she appears for her fearsome assault upon the Dominions of Rama and Krishna, and on the authority of Parm-Atman, yes, long and grim will be that night, longer and grimmer than the death-throes of the wicked, longer and grimmer than a dead lover's wait for her dead lover, longer and grimmer than a dying mother's wail for her dying child, longer and . . .

I was spared further glimpses into the nature of Aparm–Atman by a stampede of seventy-seven rhinos tearing through the caravan in the very heart of which I, the moveable non-mover, lay as an instrument of the Unmoveable Mover. Overhead flew ninety-nine parrots screaming. *The hour has come, the hour has come, the hour has come . . .* in perfect English. The winds, created by the fluttering of the wings of the parrots, gained the momentum and strength of ninety-nine hurricanes, and began howling in horror. *The hour has come, the hour has come, the hour has come . . .* also in perfect English.

They ran, helter-skelter, hither and thither, nowhere and everywhere. Women wailed, camels screamed, and children laughed, while men and donkeys were stunned into silence. Dogs clapped their paws wildly and danced, cats flew into the air and flew away, and jackdaws went about stealing eyes. The she-wolf could not feed her foundling as her milk dried in her belly and her heart broke out into a lament for the mother who had borne the one she could no longer nourish. The sick moaned and groaned and beat their breasts and wept, believing they had ended up in the midst of Judgement Day without first being cleansed by death, and woe to them and more woe to him who brought it upon them (pointing long emaciated fingers in my direction). The deaf could hear, and wished they had not heard, the blind could see and wished they had not seen. Darkness clouded the light and light split through the darkness and all that was, was not, and all that was not, was.

In the path created by the frightened rhinos came the first reason for their flight.

I beheld a limousine, the grandest you ever saw or imagined or heard of or dreamt about or feared. It was pure white in colour, and it had a crown on its bonnet and ballot boxes on its roof and it was surrounded by TV cameras and newspaper reporters and its path was lit by the light of burnished gold, and its driver was called Winner.

Then broke through the crowd the second reason, another limousine, coursing through the multitude, tearing in half all who came in its path. It was covered with blood and red with the colour of blood. It had guns and missiles attached to its roof and stuck on its bonnet and over its boot. It had the map of the world painted on its wheels, and its driver was called Peace-Maker.

The third reason followed. Another limousine, black this time, black with the despair of those at its mercy. On its bonnet was a balance, and it was called Justice. You had to pour in it the sweat of your brow and pile in it the flesh of your body and the wages of your labour, in order that your true worth might be assessed. However, those with olive trees and oil and vineyards, and mines and diamonds and gold were not to be touched or so judged.

Upon its tracks came the final cause, a pale limousine. On it were painted the faces of the devoured, those who were fodder but had no fodder, were food but had no food; and those that were nothing and had nothing, except eyes and bones and pain. Famine and pestilence danced their dance of abundance in necrotic fields on one side, while monuments to victuals rotted in festering fields on the other side; and genocidal viruses escaped from the test tubes of the guilty lorded it within the entrails of the innocent. The chauffeur of this limousine was named Death.

And its companion was Hades.

Once the sand and dust raised by the four limos had died down, a scene of confusion and carnage such as was seldom witnessed by man, god or beast was left behind.

The weak and the weary lay in breathless misery as the strong and the mighty trampled over them. The sick, the blind and the disabled were crouched in corners and alleys which had not existed a moment or two ago, the hungry and the homeless wandered aimlessly, if they still had the energy, or took shelter under broken arches and bewildering bridges. The desert was a city now. The rich and the powerful watched from their palaces and towers and marvelled at the sins of men who had brought such unspeakable disasters upon themselves by not studying the scriptures properly or adhering to their dictates.

I lay among one section of the human garbage, still shamefully in the buttocks-up position, still unable to move or turn myself sideways in a more becoming and modest posture, when suddenly, a presence . . .

† † †

What happened between then and when I walked back into our little tent is so incredible that I will have to wait until I am convinced myself that it actually happened before I try and convince you that it did.

I am still waiting, in spite of the fact that so much has taken place since then to convince the most stupid of disbelievers and the most diehard of cynics and the most intelligent of believers.

Of course, I didn't tell Belinda anything. I did not want to involve her. How foolish of me to think that I could keep her out of it or somehow spare her or save her by doing this or not doing that. But that's how I felt, dazed, staggered, and virtually bereft of my senses as I was at the time.

Besides, the chances are that it didn't really happen at all, that frightened by my own blasphemy, the unimaginable blasphemy of reaching out and shaking God by the lapels and cursing Him, I invented the follow-up as some sort of a cathartic melodrama, to blot out my guilt and to shift it upon the shoulders of the aggrieved party. The Aggrieved Party.

† † †

I had been chosen. Chosen as a very special person, for a very special reason. Chosen by God Himself. We people had been trodden upon and ill-treated for generations, and I, through the sacrifice of my children, was to redeem and honour the people, to the detriment and humiliation of the feckless oppressors.

The problem started right there. I wasn't sure what he meant by the people! But would He explain? No. He went right on with what He had to say. A new covenant was to be made with *the people*, through me, for it was high time that wrongs were righted and injustice thwarted. The people He had previously chosen on more than one occasion had constantly let Him down, denied Him, or misused Him, and abused His trust. The Kingdom of Mammon on earth had been brought to suppress the poor and the humble, and in His Name. Vengeance was now due upon them and theirs. What I was shown that night – some of which I have shared with you, the reader, some I am still too stunned to talk about – was to act as a reminder of that injustice and to bring home to me the awesomeness of it. It was now for me, etcetera etcetera.

I said: Fine, God, I couldn't agree more with most of what you have said, but isn't it time that you stopped putting up one lot of people against another lot, for that is what it will ultimately amount to, and work out some sort of a system that will take care of the whole bloody (sorry) caboodle of creatures?

After the stunned silence that followed – the angels seemed more outraged than God Himself – began the veiled, and later the unveiled, threats. Or they might have been warnings to protect and safeguard me from harm. But I was in one of my not-thinking-straight moods, and when I am like that I am like that. The itinerary of the night hadn't helped, and the thought of Belinda in that little tent with the open flap on a cold and windy night was a constant worry getting in the way.

And He asked me to give up my Naga! My old friend and many times saviour, if with a small 's'. It had seen me through a lot. I couldn't just up and say, Eff off, mate, don't need you any more. I'd have thought God would appreciate loyalty. After all, He demanded it. Surely what was good for Him should be good for another? Surely what was good for Him should be good, period. But it seemed not. To make matters worse, I was actually foolish enough to start a long-winded moral debate. Can you imagine that? A dialectical duel with the Almighty! Quite furious He was, I can assure you! He did try to be patient, now that I think about it, but I sort of went on, I must admit.

Anyway, if He wanted something done, and done properly, why pick on a shitbag like myself? That remark didn't go down too well. And shitbag that I am, I can't deny that I was tempted. In fact, it was temptation that put me off, eventually. For it was during the moment of temptation that I had one of my rare insights, this one into the true nature of Evil.

I explained to God: Evil begins with temptation and ends with execution. In between are the stages of believing what is right, having the desire to do what you believe to be right, possessing the power to do what you believe to be right, and ultimately, of course, going ahead and doing what you believe to be right. Virile and vigorous virtue, righteousness wedded to power. That is the anatomy of Evil. That was why it sprang from the same source as Good. He alone was responsible for the creation of both. Good, deliberately and intentionally; Evil as the unintended but possibly unavoidable by-product.

But how do you distinguish one from the other? said God, smug as you please.

Simple. (I was not to be stopped.) Pare away the flesh of your actions, go down to the bare bones, like the skull behind a face. That skull, give or take some small difference in size, must form the basis of every face, however much the fleshed-out version may differ, in colouring, in skin, in features, from the other. And if it changes at some time, it should do so on its own, the change must not be forced from without. If what is being perpetrated is right in given circumstances but would not be so in other circumstances, then it is wrong, and to enforce it is Evil. For what is right is right in all circumstances, for all times, and for all people. If it is wrong to kill an 'innocent victim', it is equally wrong to kill the killer: for to kill is wrong. If it is wrong to do unspeakable things to the oppressed of the world, it is equally wrong to do the same to the oppressors.

Everyone knows what a human skull looks like, commented God, but what is a moral skull, a skull of an action? How do you recognise it? There was barely concealed sarcasm in His voice.

Simple again. (I was unstoppable.) Its determinant is love. Love is the skull, the moral bone alignment behind every act that is truly Good.

And what, pray, is love when it is not a skull or a moral bone alignment?

Love is for the good of all people, all living creatures, regardless of status or virtue or origin or any other factor, for the oppressed as well as the oppressor.

Aren't we going to dance *Romeo and Juliet*, or another one of those ballets?

I think He was teasing, but I took it all too seriously. I felt I was being pitted as champion of the oppressed against the oppressors. That would mean being virtuous, being righteous. Given the power I was being promised, that would mean being evil.

That was how I saw it, given my limitations.

Besides, I didn't even know what exactly was required of me. Nor why. I mean, what could God gain from my renouncing the Naga? Of course, He is said to have said: *You shall have no other gods before me*, and: *You shall not make for yourself any graven image or any likeness of anything that is in Heaven above, or that is in the earth beneath, or that is in the water underneath; you shall not bow down to them or serve them.* But you don't take all that too seriously. Especially all that about being . . . *a jealous God, visiting the iniquity of the fathers upon the children to the third or fourth generation.* Surely you do not expect HIM to act in that petulant and vengeful manner.

And then the promises He made, promises of glory and eternal grace and the power to change . . . Somehow they sounded worse than the threats. Surely he cannot have been *HE*. Must have been a charlatan playing upon my fears. Or if it was He, then He must have been expecting me to refuse, believing I would refuse, hoping I would have a high enough opinion of Him, have a true enough love for Him not to be beguiled by threats and promises worthy of a petty tyrant. Wouldn't you think so? Wouldn't you?

Perhaps there was a purpose behind it all, one I could not fathom, one not being revealed to me – a purpose that could not be revealed, but which would reveal itself in due course.

Perhaps I should have had enough faith to override the obvious. After all, that is the function of faith.

My only consolation lay in the fact that everything allegedly in store for me, whether good or bad, depending on whether I obeyed or disobeyed, involved in some mysterious and tragic way 'the children of my wife and my woman'. I wasn't even sure if the wife and the woman were meant to be one and the same person, or two, but either way I knew that this could not be so. I knew that my wife, Belinda, could not have children; and that Jason, although I did often think of him as my child, was out too. And by no means could Jennifer be called 'my woman'. Somebody had not done His homework!

But I had had a bad night. I was tired. Hungry. Bludgeoned, bayoneted and bloodied, trampled upon, booted
about and bloodied, choking on poisonous fumes and sieved
with bulletholes; bits of flesh and gristle sticking tight to
my fragmented skin with the bondage of clotted blood;
Choodah marrow spurting out of shattered bones, shattered
bones splintering out of torn muscles, torn muscles drowning
in sploshing blood; accursed with eternal life: it was no longer
just a horrible thought but a horrible reality.

† † †

I thought you were going out to . . . said Belinda, imitating
the rude gesture of my fist.

Well I have, haven't I. It was a mindless response, but what
else could I say?

What, in two seconds flat! That is a bit of a come-down.

Two seconds flat? I thought I had been out there centuries.
Past and present.

She saw the uncomprehending look in my eyes, despite the
dim gaslight, looked at her watch, and began to say, Actually
. . . Then she stopped.

So, she had realised that I had been away for a considerable
time. I had been surprised to find that it was still night, and
the same night at that.

That's strange, she continued. I could have sworn that you
were out for at least a minute or two – I know I said two
seconds, but you know how it is . . . Anyway, now that
you are back, come and sit here, I have something to tell
you, something really –

Hang on a sec. My curiosity had been aroused, and I had
started to come round from the haze of the night. How long
did you say?

She took another look at her watch, displaying the hour, the
minute and the second. Digital watches were a rarity then and
she was fond of hers. Well, I thought you went out at . . . I
know, because I specially looked at my watch. I wanted to tell
you something before midnight. And according to my watch,
you seem to have returned about nine seconds before you left.

Still, no matter . . . She laughed a bit nervously. Perhaps these stupid watches are not what they're built up to be.

You probably didn't see correctly in this light, I said.

Probably. But don't bother about it. The main thing is, you are here. And I can't wait with my news any longer. I've kept it to myself for nearly a week, and I'm bursting to tell you. I thought I'd save it for your sacred night, your night of miracles, for it is a little miracle. A big miracle. A *little* miracle.

What *are* you on about? You haven't been looking at the moon, have you?

Come on here, you big oaf, let me give you a great big hug. And I'm sorry what I said about . . . Just sorry. It's that I . . . that I couldn't keep it . . . I will come out with you tonight, promise, I just wanted to tell you first . . .

Oh for heaven's sake, Belinda, will you come out with it? I've had a rough time . . . No, no, forget that.

I looked at her anxiously to see if I had let slip something which might worry her, but she hadn't even been listening. There was an expression of joy and mystery on her face. She looked more beautiful than all the graces and muses and goddesses put together.

I am . . . We are . . . I am going to have a baby. We are going to have a baby. Now isn't that a miracle. The doctor said he could not understand . . . Why Cy, whatever is the matter, you look so . . .

Somebody *had* done His homework. Set it, more likely. Besides, Why Cy sounded so ridiculous.

Unto Us

On the 16th of July 1977, three weeks earlier than expected, was born to us a tiny daughter, with the brow of the night, the eyes of the stars, and her mother's inescapable beauty of mind and body.

How do I know about the mind? It was in the eyes, as it always is. And the eyes of the newborn are always beautiful.

† † †

In the intervening months I had been approached by various somewhat powerful organisations for the powerless, and asked to help in their struggle in a way to which I could not agree. The approaches came through sexually tempting channels, such as a beautiful friend of Shane's; and through rationally tempting channels, such as a persuasive friend of Belinda's; and through financially tempting channels, such as three total strangers. I wondered if God was testing me, offering possibilities which could lead to the sort of power I had been promised

All I can say is that I was in too happy a state of mind, from one point of view, and in too confused a state of mind from another point of view (details follow) to respond.

I had always believed that humankind, Western humankind (it is so easy to fall into the trap of alleging that something is done or believed by humankind when in effect only ten per cent of it is involved) had done injustice the most heinous injustice by creating God in its own image: a jealous God, a scrotum-crunching, vengeful, partisan God. Nothing like the Eastern God, the Brahma, at one with all creation in all its aspects: neither created by His creation, nor the creator of His creation; Brahma *is* His creation.

Could it be that ten per cent of humankind was right after all? God has His chosen ones and His rejects; and therefore it is inevitable that humankind should have its chosen ones and its rejects. Looked at that way, everything falls into place, does it not?

Brahma does not exist, but Brahmins do. Christ did not fail, He was wrong – except in one respect: the poor shall always be with us; the rejects are here to stay.

We named our daughter after one of the earliest known rejects: used, abused and discarded; cast out, alone with her wild child, in the name of the Lord and for His eternal glory and the eternal glory of His chosen few.

We named our daughter Hagar. I named our daughter Hagar.

Was this iniquity of her father responsible for the punishment that awaited her as her destiny, for the blazing glory of her short life on earth? And was it also responsible for the punishment that awaited her mother as her destiny, the blazing glory of her short life on earth?

Or was it their reward, their escape?

Belinda had always dreaded being thirty. She was spared that tragedy. And Hagar escaped the agonies of being a teenager: growing pains, crushes on unsightly carriers of unsightly Adam's apples, acne.

Southend Pier II

Belinda was burnt alive in the fire which destroyed most of the longest pier in the world. It was quite a tragedy. Would they ever be able to build one like that again, what with dwindling resources and limited funds and unsympathetic unimaginative councillors?

The pier was no great masterpiece of architectural grandeur, nor even an example of neo-classical adventurism; but it was a solid and tangible symbol of a civilisation that . . . of civilisation. It gave simple pleasure to simple folk who could not afford to go to Monte Carlo for the weekend.

It was not totally destroyed, thank God for that. Once the rubble and ash were cleared, there would be enough left for the tourist. The ruins might bring in the curious in reasonable numbers just to see the damage and express horror or regret, or even a passing joy. But that would only be in the short term. What would happen after the first fervour of excitement was over? They wouldn't keep coming in to tut-tut once the news was no longer hot. What then? One has to take a long-term view of things.

I had taken the fourteen-month-old baby Hagar down to the beach to look at the crabs. Belinda had wanted to get a new digital watch with red numbers which she had seen up in one of the gift shops. She said she'd join me in less than a tick. Liar. You would have thought that a teacher would use a slightly more refined vocabulary.

† † †

I picked up the phone and dialled the number, after rather a long time, I must confess.

Who's that? Who? Speak up, can't hear ya . . . Is it? Gawd . . . well, so you 'ave remembered us after all. I've been dying to talk to you. You know what, you'd never guess, never in a million years. Or perhaps you will. Of course you will. I told you about it, didn't I? I've 'ad this lovely baby, she's the cutest most beautiful little thing you ever saw. And you know what? He loves it! Just loves it to bits. Sometimes I think he loves her too much. More than me, I think. I think he doesn't care for me any more. It's her, Claire, with an e, all the time. Claire this, Claire that. He named 'er – my little chocolate éclair, he says. Ain't that nice? Chocolate éclair, he calls her. So he takes the e off of the front of the éclair and puts it at the end of Clair with an 'i'. Innit clever? He's clever like that. Even Mum has to admit. She never believed they could be clever. Honestly. She is a right bundle of laughs, Mum is. She's like a chocolate, is Claire, more coffee than cream. Oy, what's the matter? Sorry, I thought you were . . . silly me. Mum would've liked a pink little bundle, but she likes Claire too, she does, more than she lets on. What's the matter, love? You're . . . You are, aren't you . . . Don't . . . don't cry. Don't cry, love. Don't. Oh please don't . . . Everything'll be all right. It works out, always does . . . There, you're making me cry now, and that isn't fair. I was quite happy before, really. There there, Mummy is here. Don't cry. All right? That's better . . . that's much better. It'll turn out for the best. Mum always says it does. Honest . . . honest . . .

Part V
UNDER THE WHEEL

A Beginning

I was left with a little girl to look after and bring up on my own. She was so precious I wanted to spend every minute of my time with her. And yet I was completely unprepared for the responsibility, and didn't even have any natural propensity for child-rearing. Belinda would have put that down to male chauvinism, and she may have been right.

But by then it was time for another beginning.

Belinda's sister Patience (a less patient person I have yet to meet) took Hagar away from me. It was either that, or she would be taken into care. Patience would see to that. No court would grant me custody once they were made aware of the 'situation', by which she meant my dalliance with the British penal code, and she would make sure that they were made aware of it as soon as she could open her mouth (which never shut as far as I was aware) unless I dropped the baby Hagar in her lap in a sort of private, no-one-any-the-wiser arrangement. In return she would let me see her 'now and then', provided it was not a fixed day and time, as she could not say what she would be doing from one day to the next, what with her responsibilities for her own eight children; and provided I did not phone, because she hated the bloody thing, but just took a chance and dropped by to see if she was free to let me be with Hagar for a few hours; and provided it was no more than once a fortnight. Or else she might ring me and tell me to come over, now and then.

Patience always blamed me for leading Belinda astray. I don't know why. She must have known that Belinda had been well into marches and protests and courts long before I dropped in on the scene. I went with her, not the other way round. But convince Patience of that and you are a better person than I am. She also blamed me for Belinda's death. For that I accept full responsibility. All who tie in their lot with me are bound for the chopper. That is why, in a sad sort of a way, I was glad that Hagar was rid of me. And Patience's intervention was well-intentioned and I suppose well-timed, and she fostered my daughter with love and kindness.

With the blood-money I received from Belinda's insurance I took my first, hesitant and shamefaced step towards capitalism. I don't know what Belinda would have thought of it, but it seemed the best thing at the time. I managed to buy, quite quickly by paying cash (just over six thousand pounds), a twenty-year lease on a nice little sweetshop with a nice little flat above it in a quiet but rather derelict old street overlooking what remained of Southend Pier.

My reasons/justifications were as under:

(a) I wanted to be close to where Belinda had spent her last moments. In a way I was happy that most of her would have been carried out to the sea and become a part of its strength and grandeur. Every morning before sunrise I would take one flower – a little daisy, or a buttercup, or a wild rose, anything I could find – or write a little note or a poem or some silly thing like that, and pass it on to the sea and let the waves carry it to her. The fact that Jennifer and Jason lived not far away might have been a factor in my choice of the location, but it was not a conscious factor. At a conscious level I considered it a serious drawback. It would be painful to come across them and yet keep away, and it would not be fair on either of them, especially Jason. He had grown quite fond of me at one point, and to be there to remind him of myself just when he would have forgotten me would not have been a good or a kind thing to do.

(b) It would be easier for me to look after Hagar – this was, of course, before Patience decided to take her away from me – if I was working where we lived.

(c) In twenty years the lease would be over, Hagar would be old enough to take care of herself and decide what to do with her life, and I would be rid of the property trap automatically.

What I hadn't reckoned, and Lord knows I of all people should have, was that life does not always wait for twenty years to play its hand. This time it took only two months before all my plans went wrong. Hagar fell ill. It was only a chill to start off, but I was down in the shop at the time when she had a bad attack of coughing and managed to fall out of her cot and break her wrist as the rest of her landed on top of it. Patience had to be called in from her house in Upton Park, and you know the rest.

A Break

One morning, a fresh daffodil in hand, one of the first of the season, I was on my way to the section of the beach beneath the remaining half of the pier, all mud and dirty black floats of this and that upon a tiny stretch of dry sand and an immense stretch of wet grey slush, a rancid smell permeating the fresh air like death through life, when I suddenly realised that Belinda was dead.

I mean dead, not just burnt alive, as I always said. I could never understand why everybody cringed when I said that. I understood then. The operative word in that sentence was *alive*. But there was nothing alive about her any more. She had not become a part of the great wide ocean, nor entered some higher plane of existence, still less become one with the ultimate force of life itself. She was just dead. Plain dead. Finished. Ended. Like all the rest.

And where was my Naga now? Where? He never was, was he? Just a spectre of my diseased imagination. No tiger, and probably no Man either.

There certainly was a God, of that I had no doubt. I had met Him, hadn't I? And even if that too was another of the horrors of my mind – which you may quite legitimately assert that it was: if the Naga wasn't real, maybe my chat with this God wasn't either – the fact that there was so much pain and misery and suffering in this world was proof positive of His existence. It could not all just happen without somebody up there planning it and having a good laugh at it.

Who could bring back the ones who had gone, even to some

old folks' home in Margate? Southend itself was full of the old, who, though still living, could not be brought back to join the living. Who could bring even the young back, from 'homes', or from prisons? How could anyone bring anyone back from the great hell-hole beyond? Who could send them a stupid daffodil or a stupider poem?

I had to end all that stupidity, and a lot else beside. I decided to make a break. A break from living.

A break from the living, along with a break from the dead.

I had not been able to see Hagar for two weeks. I went over to Patience's house three times in those two weeks – it was a seven-to-seven shop, and I didn't get much time to myself. If Hagar had stayed I would have cut down on the hours, but since she went I thought I just as well might keep busy.

Once, Patience, hubby Mac, and the rest of them were out. Another time she sent me packing from the door, saying she had some guests coming in a short while and she had tons to do before that, and oh, Hagar had gone with the other children to the park. I went over to the park and looked in the children's play section and in the main gardens and under every tree on every bench and each patch of grass, no sign of Patience's brood, nor of Hagar. The third time I was let in, but told that Hagar had gone to see a friend whose parents had taken them both to London Zoo. I even risked Patience's wrath by telephoning, but she hung up after reminding me that she had specifically told me not to bother her on the phone, and that if I continued to do so she would have to contact the police. I was so angry. I wished I hadn't handed over all the money left over from Belinda's insurance, about ten thousand-plus, to Patience in one lump sum for the upkeep of Hagar. If I had been making weekly or monthly payments she might have been more reasonable. I was so angry I rang up again and told her how angry I was. Not only that, I threatened to take Ginger, her twelve-year-old – he *was* ginger, sort of short and curly and ginger, his father Mac being a real blue-eyed, ginger-haired Scot – and give the blighter a gentle push down the remains of the world's longest pier. That was no help. But if she'd let me see Hagar, I said, I'd give her half my weekly takings from the shop. That helped. But they were off to Scotland for a two-week break and it would have to wait until their return.

To make matters worse, I was beginning to feel more and more constrained by standing behind the counter in the shop. It was a little like being in prison. I shouldn't even have been there at all. Back in my home town I would not have been allowed inside a sweetshop, much less to sell anything. Pandit Ashokji, who ran the shop in our street, did allow Junior in, but only after closing time and only for his smooth, fat ass. He always had a ritual bath to cleanse himself afterwards. Junior used to hide and watch, and then come home and try to wash himself the same way, thinking he too would become clean if he did that. Never had any brains, our Junior – what little he was born with fell through his asshole. I always knew that we were what we were, and that no amount of soap or water or incense or tilaks or sindoors could purify us. Except perhaps fire, but then we would be pure dead; pure and alive we could not be. Pandit Ashokji never liked me; me, he would shake his fist at and shoo away even if I was found eyeing, somewhat greedily I must confess, a jar of boiled sweets that lay exposed at the very front of the shop.

Here I sold *edible* goods! Handled them, touched them with my unclean paws. Often to children. If only they had known I was untouchable. Some of them didn't think much of me, but they had no idea *how* low I was. I was taking advantage of their innocence, and it wasn't right.

It had to stop. I was beginning to feel so guilty that sometimes when I saw a little white hand, clean and pure, extended towards me, expecting me to pass on something from a higher shelf or return a bit of change, I tried to keep my fingers well off the clean and pure palm, so as not to touch, contaminate, violate a child's unsuspecting trust.

It was time to make a break, a break from living. A break from the living, as well as a break from the dead.

I threw the daffodil on the sand, jumped up and down upon it till it was crushed and mangled and reduced to zilch, returned to the shop, put a sign on it saying CLOSED UNTIL

FURTHER NOTICE, went up to the flat, took off all my clothes and went to bed.

Normally I never sleep naked. In India and Pakistan, since people often share a bedroom, you learn always to sleep with some clothes on. The habit had stayed with me. But that day I took all my clothes off and went to sleep naked. Normally I never sleep at that time of the morning.

† † †

It was dark when I woke up. I wondered where I was, vaguely. Then I saw the ceiling because of some light running across it from the top of the amusement arcade down below. It reminded me where I was, vaguely.

I wondered if the ceiling was high enough, without quite being sure why. Perhaps because I was rather a tall man, my only socially desirable feature. And I was still young. Very important that, in this supremely ageist society. How we used to love our old people back home: the comfort of their ever-welcoming arms, the security of their strong yet fragile presence, their infinite patience, their undemanding givingness. How they hate their old people here. Who would want to be old here? Not me. Best pack up and go before it is too late. Before the first line of suffering and loving and laughter makes its appearance on your bland face. Before you are termed a wrinkly and condemned to the dung-heap of life. Yes, best to go as soon as possible. I wondered if the ceiling was high enough. I was six-foot-two, maybe three. Not a bad height at all. And twenty-five. Not a bad age at all. I could understand how Belinda felt, and why. I didn't want to be thirty either. How lucky she had been to escape it. I wasn't even sure if I wanted to be twenty-six. That would be the wrong side of twenty, and the wrong side of twenty is the wrong side of life. I wondered if the ceiling was high enough. It was, but there was no strong anchoring point. No rope, either. Some boxes came tied with ropes, but none strong enough to take my dead weight. Why did I say dead? Shouldn't have said that. Weight, I mean, weight. Just weight. That's better. Much better. Besides, there was no anchoring point strong enough to take my weight. The light fittings were on the wall. What a stupid place to put light fittings – on the wall! Should have noticed them before taking the place. Would never have bought it had I seen that the light fittings were on the wall. Perhaps there was some other hold I could use. But there wasn't. At least, I couldn't find one, not in the dark. I should have turned the light on, but I didn't want to. Don't ask my why, I just didn't want to. I know it would have made more sense, I know it would have been more reasonable, but a man does not have to be reasonable all the time. That's my final word on the subject, like it or not. More natural? That I can't see. There's nothing *natural* about turning the light on. A positively unnatural thing, if you ask me. Flick a switch, and the light comes on. What do you think I am, God or something?

That reminded me. God.

He created the waters, didn't he? And parted them. I could part the waters. Much better than dangling from a silly old ceiling. Besides, Belinda would be there.

The most difficult part was getting back into clothes. What was the point? They would remove them the first opportunity they got after I was vomited out on to the beach. But then again I might get lucky. The sea might take a fancy to me and decide to keep me in its bed. In which case there was again no point in bothering with clothes.

But I did not want to get arrested before I even got to my resting place, so clothes were a must. But it was so difficult to put them on. I had never before realised what a chore it was to get into clothes. It's a wonder so few people, if any in the civilised world, except when they are being very very civilised, run around naked showing their wherewithals to all and sundry.

I kept tripping over my underwear, and finally decided to do without it. Not necessary, as I'm sure you'd agree. In the East we seldom wear underwear. The trouser legs were being deliberately awkward, getting tied up, the left turning out to be the right, and vice versa. I got them on the wrong way twice, and almost left it like that; but my fighting spirit asserted itself. I was not going to let an article of clothing beat me, even if, like the deadliest creatures on earth, it was two-legged.

All was completed, after an historic struggle worthy of the greatest conquerors. I was as ready as I had been willing. The shirt was not properly buttoned up, but not a major disaster, that.

Out, and along the promenade.

The lights hurt: cheap and cheerful and everywhere. People were walking past almost as if it mattered where they were going. Loud music. Smell of food, or of life that passes as food: fish, flesh, and greasy chips being fried and greasier beings devouring them quite unmindful of the horrid distortions of their faces as they ate so shamelessly, and in public places at that!

I could hear a roaring sound, the sound of the most eternal and everlasting of musics, there since before time, there long after. It was not only soothing and beautiful to hear, but pleasing from a practical viewpoint. The tide was high: easier to go, easier to be carried away a long long way away, more likely to be swallowed and digested than regurgitated.

Great Grandmother was smiling down on me.

Great night for a fuck, said an unfamiliar voice as a face hit my shoulder with considerable force.

I turned round to look at the face, a strange face, yet not quite strange.

Don't ya remember me, Cy? I can remember every hair on yer ass.

He would, wouldn't he? He spent more time looking at my ass than at any other part of me.

I remembered too. He was Terry, Tracy's little so and so who used to watch along with his dad the highs and lows of life and the secrets of the processes which led to its inception. He had grown some, and his voice had changed, but the hungry look in his eyes was the same.

No thanks.

Whadya mean no thanks, gone moral or somethink? Come on, I know a great place . . .

He tried to drag me along, but I was too heavy for him.

He stopped, glowered at me for a second, then said in a

much quieter voice, You coming or do I shout? Southend's getting a bad name for guys like you, looking around for young boys, preying on them as they come out for a little harmless fun at the fruit machines. He almost appeared to be quoting, or saying a rehearsed set-piece. See, there's a copper along the front. He seemed more himself suddenly. And me Dad's a copper too. Guess Mum forgot to tell yer that, didn't she? So whadya want, a night at the nick, the very least a night, or an hour with me?

We went to this house a couple of streets away. Its windows were boarded up, but the back door could be prised open.

An old lady used to live 'ere. Died a few months back. 'Er son is getting the place done up before selling it. We used to go to another house down the road, but this is nearer.

I was worried I might not be able to get it up. It went the other way. I couldn't get it down. I threw up once without losing the hard-on. After that, no more coming and no more going. It just stayed up, swelling more and more, and becoming ruddy painful.

Wow, ain't that great. Great! Never seen anything like this before. You are great, man. Just great.

I didn't feel great at all. Just terribly foolish, and uncomfortable, and cold.

Great, really great, man. No wonder you don't put knickers on. Knickers won't hold it, will they? Bust right through them, it would. Great, man. Great.

I felt more and more foolish. More and more uncomfortable.

Mum will have to take note of that, she will.

Not her! Not her as well!

You know she's the Head Witch now, High Priestess. He went out of his way to sound the aitches, the pride reflected in his voice affected his diction, or somethin' like that. Real black witch she is, none of your poofy white witch stuff. She could do with someone like you by her side. Set 'er up for good, that would. Come on, you can take my coat and hold it in front of yer. There, like that. He was behaving quite like a little father, and it was difficult not to be touched by his concern. He couldn't have been more than fifteen.

Thanks, I said, and squeezed his hand to say thank you with my hand.

Might as well go with him. The sea would be there tomorrow night. Besides, I was beginning to feel hungry, not having eaten anything since the previous afternoon. There is nothing like a bit of sex to give you an appetite. Tracy was good at fixing a quick sandwich, or even a quick meal. I pleased easy, as long as there was no blood involved.

† † †

In spite of some exciting highlights, it turned out to be a bad break for me.

Many of my crimes – apart from the capital ones – ranging from the mighty frivolous to the petty serious, were committed during this period.

Why then, you may ask, was I not done then? Actually I was, once or twice, but was let off quite leniently with Trevor's assistance. Not only was he a policeman – I had thought Terry was fibbing – but apparently one with connections. And I became a useful and much liked and oft desired member of the coven, an asset he and his wife and his son and some of his influential friends did not want to lose. Especially as most of my offences – even the bad ones, like exposing myself during High Mass (Catholic, not black) – were minor compared with what he was up to, at least from the point of view of the Fuzz. Especially the rather kinky house a mate of his ran, where young girls and boys wielded the stick and swished the whip at repentant little and large boys of all ages, thirty upwards usually, well upwards. That was not all.

He was part of a team involved in drug raids; and more often than not would manage to salvage a packet or two of certain substances that served two very useful purposes.

One: came in handy during certain services (as in Church but not as in holy, Catholic or otherwise) to do with one of the most famous cats of Essex, Sathan. The fact that Sathan had not been around for over four hundred years – being the cat of Elizabeth Francis in the 1560s, who was tried during the reign of Elizabeth I under a revised version of the first law ever passed against witches in the very first witch trial held in the county, in Chelmsford – only made her powers the greater, being from beyond the grave.

Two: supplemented the cash reserves.

Trevor was careful to look after my black hide, not just for my services during services but also to prevent me singing under pressure. There were others and betters than me involved – betters than Trevor even, the best. Not that anyone would have taken my word against his, much less theirs. But still, why tempt fate?

Even to the very last, when most of the charges against me were proven, Trevor, with the help of willing and witting or willing and unwitting fellow officers and others, managed to create enough doubts in the minds of the jury to suggest that any accusations of devil-worship and the like were no more than fantasies of the sensation-seeking media. Of course, mud sticks, and it showed up in other verdicts. Proven Satanism with a few high-ups involved – one *very* high up – would have done me more good than harm. By then I would have had more than my word alone to justify letting good old Sathan out of the bag, but since I had elected to remain silent, silent I remained. Nothing mattered.

As I said, it was generally a bad period for me. If only God had left me alone.

Suddenly He would descend upon me, at the oddest and most inconvenient of times and places, *videlicet*: a public convenience, off the fruit market in Soho. I had to rush out in fear, cock in hand, urinating at the market stalls, unable to control the flow. The fact that it happened to be exactly twelve noon at the time was totally irrelevant, though the lawyer for the prosecution tried his best to link it to some sinister Satanic ritual. Ironic that in this case the link was divine.

If I didn't see Him, it was His voice I heard, clear as a bell, telling me to repent; repent with all my heart and all my soul and all my body; abjure Satan, and Sathan, and all his works, hers too, and get started on my mission to rescue the oppressed of the world, or words to that effect.

But I blocked my ears with the wax of ignorance and the plug of obduracy.

As usual, I was not often allowed to see Hagar, and this clearly pleased Patience. I couldn't complain. After all, she was very good to Hagar, and gave her all the love that Belinda would have given and that I did not, wretch that I was. Not that I didn't love her, but I seemed to have less and less time, even though I was doing less and less. When I did get round to being with her, she never related to me properly. She was always sort of on edge, never comfortable, and I ended up feeling more guilty seeing her than not seeing her. Later I found out that Patience had painted such a horrible picture of me to her, often quite literally by drawing revolting illustrations in a little sketchbook – Patience had been an art student before she met Mac, a decent enough chap, but he spent more time in the pub than at home, where Patience was the lady and mistress – and captioning them 'Daddy', that in her sensitive infant's eyes I was more of a vile monster than a father. And could I blame her for believing that?

I still had the shop and the flat, mainly because I had paid three years' rent in advance along with the lease money. But I was seldom there, and opened the shop only occasionally. Why I did even that, I cannot say. I was so busy with my new-found status in my new-found church.

Satanic Purses and
the Fundamentalists

Sathanic, actually. Purses: string purse, a pouch for containing the testicles; and clutch purse, the female labia guarding the vaginal entrance. Both male and female, when seen from the rear, in one of the many fundamental positions, show purses, string or clutch, pursing, pouting, stretched or strung out between the back of tightly closed thighs.

Satanic was a term of derision or contempt or terror used by the opponents of the coven, but good-humouredly taken over by some of the Sathanists (of the Fundamentalist Lodge, of whom more anon), as often a term of derision is taken over with pride by those very people to whom it is negatively applied: e.g. black for non-white people; or if that example sounds over-familiar, then Quakers, an epithet used to mock the followers of George Fox, accepted by them and to this day their very nomenclature.

The Sathanic purses are the source of all charms and spells and worldly wisdom and magic, more powerful in the case of the female: (a) being a complete entity containing the *whole* of the female genitalia – the male purse excludes the penis – the function of breasts in nature being asexual and for the purposes of feeding the infant. Witches are totally devoted to nature and its commands and demands, and as such never flaunt their breasts for sexual purposes. (b) Being a complete entity containing the *hole* of the female genitalia, and a hole is always more powerful than what it harbours. Witness the state of the male as it enters, and then compare it with the state in which it departs.

As you are well aware I was accused during my trial of participating in, nay, initiating (the 'nay' is not mine, but of Sir Anthony Baltimore, prosecuting) Satanic rituals in a derelict church in Rochford, somewhere to the west of Southend Airport. A small community of worshippers and non-worshippers alike had sold their houses and left when the airport was first constructed, and the little church had stood forlorn and neglected since then.

And it was true. Not Satanic rituals, to be precise, but rituals of the *Craft*. Some call it witchcraft. Satanism is a Christian invention, or if you prefer a Christian inversion: God and Satan are the same one God, patriarchal not paternal – that is, hard and demanding. Wicca is polytheistic, and maternal not matriarchal – that is, open and caring. I was however surprised to discover two things. First, that for all its emphasis on women priestesses and the feminine principle, predating the modern women's movement by centuries, there was a healthy respect for and an interwoven relationship with the male, and the male principle: no judgementalism, accusatory rhetoric or stone casting by one against the other. Secondly, that for all its dissociation from variations and manifestations of monotheism, the ultimate pagan goddesses have their trinity: Maid, Mother, and Crone (Enchantment, Ripeness, and Wisdom) represented by the phases of the moon: waxing, full, and waning. Just as the right-eous wing of comfortable Christianity has its trinity: God the Father, Wealth; God the Son, Power; the Holy Ghost, Greed – represented in their full glory by lands of the rising, the full and the setting sun: Tokyo, Al Quds and Hollywood. I preferred the enchantment, ripeness and wisdom of witches. So much for the 'nay'.

But I did not initiate anything. I was an initiate myself. What's more, the activities in the church were mere frolics, no more evil or sinister than a country dance held in a barn, though without any costumes.

However there was a tight core of professed Fundamentalists of the Craft, who like most professed fundamentalists corrupt the very faith they claim to uphold, and they carried out certain other more contentious rituals in a barn normally reserved for country dancing. Tracy was the High Priestess of the Fundamentalist Lodge, Trevor the Polarity Priest; and, after a series of ritual cleansings and initiations, I was accorded the privilege of being included as a member of that select company.

The country dancing took place on the second Saturday of every month of the year. The Fundamentalists met on the third Friday of every month, though there were sessions extraordinary which could be called on any night, depending on this and that or him and her. Not that anything really evil or sinister took place on those nights. But nonetheless, much of it was against the true spirit and wishes of Wicca. Certainly the Gardnerian stream of witches would dissociate itself from any such rites, and even the secretive Traditionalists might have strong reservations. Some of it was pretty basic: casting a few circles, dispensing a few charms, invoking a few spells. Some of it was strange: people doing mildly bizarre, cautiously daring and somewhat amazing things with their bodies and parts of their bodies. None of it was done for a higher cause, mercifully, such as the good of mankind, peace and harmony in the world, saving the planet, and all those sorts of thing which most others who do much worse things in real life are always on about.

However, witchcraft itself being 'legal', decriminalised since 1951 with the repeal of witchcraft laws, it was these last activities, the dallying with bodies, which not surprisingly constituted the 'criminal' offence; especially since they took place in public, which means more than three, even if the third happened to be lying dead in another part of the building. We were all very much alive and very much together.

Fortunately (?) none of this was allowed to be established in court. It would have caused embarrassment in certain circles. The barn, and the country estate of which it was an outbuilding, situated beside the River Crouch behind the charming little village of Canuden famous for its witches since medieval times, belonged to none other than Lord Cornelious Develin, one of the country's most respected judges.

I did not know that at the time, though I did happen to be present at the third-degree initiation – as the Magus – of Jonathan Develin, nineteen, the only son and heir of Lord Develin. At the time I was not aware of his identity either, though I was a little surprised that such authority was being vested in one so young. The fact that his father happened to own the land used by the coven and was the provider of various other related facilities may have been a factor in his favour, though to be fair he was given as tough a test of his dedication, his passion, and above all his cone of power as any eligible applicant.

And he proved himself. I ought to know, since I not only saw him in action, but was actually at the raw end of his strange psychic force.

It was the night of Samhain, October the thirty-first, the Sabbat; Halloween to some, All Hallows Even to others, the eve of All Saints' Day.

Jonathan Develin quite effectively masked his identity from me and some others by the simple and unoriginal expedient of calling himself JD. I for one believed his given name to be Jaydee. I even commented on it being rather an unusual name, and quite attractive, like him, but got no more than a polite smile in response. I suppose I was not good enough for him. But I had complete mastery over his body that night of Samhain, as he had complete control of my being.

I later learnt that the cone of power rested in the family, coming to the surface in one member every eighty-one years (nine times nine), skipping one generation. The name Develin, allegedly a concocted variant on 'in Devil', given to one of the great great ancestors of the family, a heavily hirsute and well-warted young woman, during the times of Oliver Cromwell, following her refusal to be drowned on three occasions, and then coming out alive from the fire. After that, instead of trying to hound her out, the entire village fled, leaving her in control of the lands and the fields and the corn and the church. The family property and wealth dated from that period, coming down from her and her son, whom she bore without a father, there being no one else in the village beside her. Or so the story goes.

Jaydee had been 'under preparation' for the initiation for three consecutive nights. The big night would be the night of his 'new birth' – an early pagan concept very popular with the current born-again lot in a pale, bloodless sort of way – so he had to be baby skinned. Also, the new birth was a pre-ordained birth, hence a birth marked with the mark of his powers.

A completely hair-free body was essential, which in the poor man's case was quite a task as he had one of the hairiest asses that I have ever seen, with a cupreous carpet fully laid out on the torso, the aforementioned glutei, the thighs, the calves, the lot from scalp to toe. After the shaving and waxing was complete, he had a rub-down with the ochre paste of turmeric powder to give a smooth, golden aura to his entire body so that it radiated and glowed in the dark. I was surprised at this, for it was a custom favoured among the bridegrooms, and sometimes the brides, of better-off families in India. Another Indian custom, henna-painting, was used to draw the pentacle on each of his buttocks, round each of his nipples, and just below the neck, five pentacles making an open ended cross-over pentacle upon his body, and enclosing a pentagonal of his body containing the heart, guts and other vital organs. Since it takes henna a few hours to dry and root deep into the skin, he could neither sit nor lie down but had to remain standing up naked for nine hours in the ninth sephirah, Yesod, of the Cabalistic Tree of Life – ritualistically represented on the barn floor with pieces of rock brought over from Glastonbury, Iona, Avebury, a megalithic Cornish site, Karnak in Egypt, Delphi in Greece and Carnac in Brittany – without eating, drinking or performing any other bodily functions. Any three selected members of the coven, two females and one male, were always present with him at any given time during those three preliminary nights, either helping in shaving, bathing, oiling and painting him, or just keeping an eye open to see that he did not for a moment do anything forbidden or omit anything ordained. At no point in those seventy-two hours was he to indulge in any sexual congress, or bring about a self-induced orgasm, no matter how excited he got and even if deliberately titillated and aroused, although that was forbidden on pain of expulsion. Even involuntary and 'untouched' ejaculations would mean postponement of the occasion until the next Samhain. The semen of the three days and the three nights of purity had to be built up and preserved for the Great Rite – quite a challenge for a nineteen-year-old, especially as all contacts were skyclad. But standing around for hours with limited sleep and little food must have helped. It was also said that lengthy bouts of exhausting sex prior to the preparatory ceremonies had been recommended, and the advice taken. There was innuendo too regarding the use of special injections. It still remained a tremendous and awe-inspiring responsibility.

As a possible adept myself, perhaps even of the Magus level if rumours were to be credited, and one with a pivotal role of my own to play on the Sacred Sabbat, I was not allowed to be part of Jaydee's preparation for exaltation, and I was glad of that. I wouldn't have minded a peek to see what was going on, but all the rest seemed a bit much to me.

† † †

Came the finale, the climactic segment of the three nights just before the commencement of the Great Rite itself, and the multiple anointing of the fundament to chants and incantations and declamations began.

> *Altar of mysteries manifold,*
> *The sacred Circle's secret point –*
> *Thus do I sign thee as of old,*
> *With Kisses of my lips anoint.*
> *Open for me the secret way,*
> *The pathway of intelligence,*
> *Beyond the gates of night and day,*
> *Beyond the bounds of time and sense.*

All this while Jaydee lay on the rear altar, knees jackknifed, thighs and buttocks parted, the bud of the orifice well dilated exposing the fundament: the source of the soul (just as asshole is a corruption of arsehole, arseholes is

386

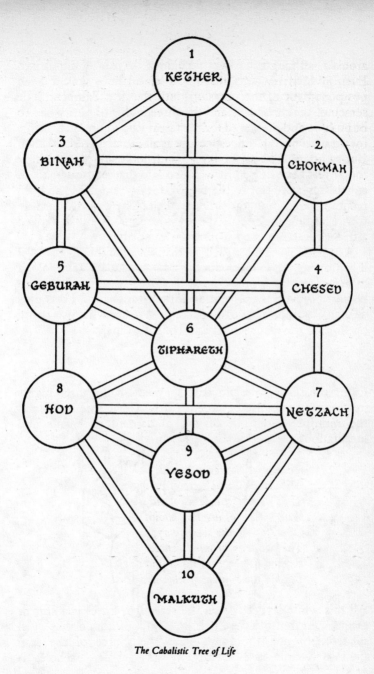

The Cabalistic Tree of Life

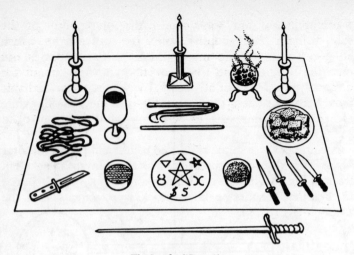

The Sacrificial/Rear Altar

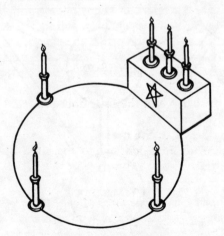

The Circle and the Main Altar

a corruption of our souls, hence the intangibility of the soul, being a hole within a hole), the source from which all purity rises to the mind and all impurity passes out onto the Mother Earth for absorption and into the air for dispersal; the source of all spiritual wisdom, as the Sathanic purses are the source of all worldly wisdom. All this while the initiate's penis had to remain in full yet controlled erection.

A chorus of worshippers danced round and round the altar as the High Priestess cast off her black robe and stood naked in front of the VIP initiate's behind, wand in one hand, scourge in the other. Tendering his buttocks and genitals with the scourge, she orated:

> *Of the mother darksome and divine,*
> *Mine the Scourge, and Mine the Kiss,*
> *The five-point star of love and bliss,*
> *Here I charge you, in this sign.*

Here she fiercely plunged the wand into the open orifice, and placed five kisses corresponding to the five points of the pentacle on the five parts of the Magus-to-be's body, feet, knees, breast and lip. Then, pulling the wand out, she kissed the fulcrum of the pentagon within: the fundament. For therein lies the core of the belief, the core of the mystery, the core of the power of the Fundamentalist. Proof, if proof were needed, that fundamentalists think, preach and work from the depths of their souls.

Midnight struck and the final hour arrived.

Casting of the circle.

Drawing down of the moon.

Invocation of the Goddess into the High Priestess by the Polarity Priest:

I call upon thee and invoke thee, Might Mother of us all, bringer of all fruitfulness, by seed and root, by stem and bud, by leaf and flower and fruit, by life and love do I invoke thee to descend upon the body of this thy servant and Priestess . . .

And then the adoration of the initiate by the Goddess through the High Priestess:

> *Behold the mystery aright –*
> *The five true points of fellowship,*
> *Here where the lance and grail unite,*
> *And feet and knees and breast and lip.*

At this point the High Priestess was lifted up into the air by two female devotees, each hooking one arm in the crook of her knee and supporting her back with the other. She was then carried above the initiate to bestow upon him the five kisses again, only this time with her sexual labia, which had also been rendered silk-smooth, and then rubbed with a mixture of honey and chilli paste – the former to sweeten and lubricate, the latter to swell out and inflame. When the final kiss was planted upon the lip, the Priestess was left there sitting astride the initiate's face. This would have completely obscured his vision had he not been blindfolded already.

The devotees went round the circle seven times, anti-clockwise, the circle being in the Australian tradition: Earth and altar to the south, just below the sacrificial altar; Air to the east; Fire to the north; Water to the west.

The two female devotees left the circle and again went over to the High Priestess at the rear altar, raised her from the initiate's face, and carried her lower down so that her red and swollen vaginal entrance now hovered directly above the initiate's phallus, her lips gently brushing the purple globe, its delicate skin so taut it was a miracle it didn't burst.

Two more initiates stepped forward, one male, one female. The male kneeled in front of the altar. The female dipped an athame into the wine within a chalice held by the kneeling man, who chanted:

As the athame is to the male, so the cup is to the female; conjoined they become one in Truth.

The High Priestess, at that precise point, was lowered on to the initiate's straining member, by then stretching itself to the breaking point with such force you could almost hear it creak, in spite of all the oils that had rubbed into it over the past three nights. As her fundament rested upon his navel, she was once again left sitting there by herself.

Neither she nor the initiate made any movement, up or down, sideways or anyways. They could have been carved out of stone.

At the time I did not know what was going on, for I had been sitting, naked and smooth as a baby myself, enclosed within a smaller auxiliary circle behind a screen, unable to see any of what was happening in the main circle. I got the details later.

I could hear the chants, though, and they sent thorns of pain and pleasure, of anticipation and apprehension, of fear and delight, deep into every sweating pore of my skin. I wasn't just sweating because of the five fires that were lit on the five contact points of the barn – a fire for light, a fire for enlightenment, a fire for life, a fire for death, a fire for eternity. I had been told that at the appropriate hour the power of Magus would *raise me up* as a 'thought-form' Giant (the Giant guarding the original mating bed of the Goddess, between the two primordial hills) and I would be called upon to play my part, a vital part, which would lead to the ultimate affirmation of the Magus, confirming his true status. That is, if he proved worthy and capable of it.

Frankly, I hadn't believed that. I thought that when my presence was needed, some obvious way would be found to summon me and tell me what to do.

The High Priestess sat impaled upon the initiate's bone of flesh until the devotees completed another seven movements round the circle. Then the Priest, who had ended up directly in front of the main altar in the south, picked up the censer from its place on the top right hand corner, poured some fresh incense into it, then went over to the raised rear altar and began swirling the burning incense round and round the stuck privates of the Priestess and the initiate until you could see nothing clearly because of the smoke.

The movement of the waywardly rising smoke created an illusion of movement and the interlocked genitals of the two central characters of the drama appeared to move in a weird parody of an active fuck, when in fact, if not in reality, they remained motionless.

Suddenly a hoary voice rose from the haze of smoke, quite unlike the usual voice of the High Priestess:

> *Oh, do not tell Father of our Art,*
> *For he would call it a sin;*
> *But we shall be out in the barn all night,*
> *A-conjuring the winter in!*
> *And we bring you news from word of mouth,*
> *For women, cattle and corn —*
> *The sun is coming up from the south,*
> *With pine and fir and thorn.*

Jaydee spoke then for the first time in three days and three nights, and spoke like one destined to be the Magus – the voice deep and far-off and commanding; mysterious and mystical and magical; naked and rampant:

> *I am a stag of seven times;*
> *I am a wide flood on a plain;*
> *I am a wind on the deep waters;*
> *I am a shining tear of the sun;*
> *I am a hawk on a cliff;*
> *I am fair among flowers;*
> *I am a god who sets the head afire with smoke!*

Utter and complete silence descended upon the lodge.

More incense and more smoke, this time from the High Priestess herself. No one had seen her come down from the altar, or witnessed her disengagement from the copulating member, which still stood as powerfully and painfully to attention as ever, only more swollen, more red, more enraged, as were the labia of the High Priestess.

The Initiate, having thus earned his penultimate status

as the Magus, and a capital 'I', was now turned over jointly by the High Priestess and the Polarity Priest, to assume the penultimate Fundamentalist position: on knees and elbows, head held high, the pouch – Sathan's purse – pushed backwards and outwards towards the High Priestess and the Priest and the rest of the devotees, from between clenched thighs. Upwards and outwards and towards the High Priestess and the Priest and the rest of the devotees, twinkled the sphincter, bare and revealed, and *above* Sathan's purse, in its *correct* position of dominance. The soul and spiritual wisdom and the core of power must be above the body and worldly wisdom and the cone of power. Holiness must be above magic.

Just as in the case of Sathan, indeed in all animals, who preserve the natural order: fundament above the genitals, the order openly acknowledged and clearly exposed by raising the tail as a sign both welcoming and revealing, of confidence and trust. Thus the fundament remains uncorrupted and untarnished by greed, gold and governments, by Mammon, money and media, by property, personality and perversion: the unholy trinity of trinities out to oust the Holy Trinity of Trinities.

To go back to that natural order, the Fundamentalists believe (and I fully concur with them), humankind has to relinquish its homo-erectus state, if only for short periods during the course of a day or a week. Thus is the ascendance of spirituality over bodily needs re-asserted; and the powers of the body itself are enhanced by strengthening the magical powers naturally given to humankind and resident in the Sathanic purses, or Satanic purses, or balls and cunts – call them by any name, they still retain their magic.

The Magus Initiate, who thenceforth would spend as much of his time on all fours as possible, was now ready to perform the concluding section of the Great Rite, which if successfully completed would confer on him the powers he had so diligently sought, powers he had so obviously inherited. You had to witness to believe.

I did, when I was called.

I had planned that when some silly little message came for me to make my appearance I would play some silly little game and pretend not to understand – delay, dilly-dally, have some fun. Instead I found myself being *raised up*, just as predicted, by the power of the Magus. Or if not by the power of the Magus, then by some power.

It rose from within me and attacked me from the outside. I was enveloped by this peculiar and terrifying sensation of being wanted, needed. And there was nothing that I could do to fight it. A bluey green aura filled the atmosphere, and my body seemed to disintegrate and melt within its diffused presence. My body particles were orangey red. The mixture of orangey red and bluey green produced a floating purple: the colour of mourning, the colour of autumn, the colour of Samhain. The colour of kings, kings of men and kings of demons and kings of sorcerers. Kings of men in the land of evil; kings of demons in the land of illusion; kings of sorcerers in the land of wisdom. The chosen colour of the Magus Initiate.

I found myself in the rope centre of the circle, a true giant, ninety-seven feet tall, looking down upon the puny race of men dotted round the circumference, crouching in fear of me, heads touching the floor, fundaments and testicles and vulvas raised and offered to me for my scrutiny and pleasure.

There was one there, another one, who would be more than a match for me once this test, this test of light, was over. But for the time being his body was at my disposal, even as my being was at his command.

I moved towards the altar, and there upon it, upon the pentacle, lay the candles. Not like the ones burning in the stands in their proper place, but special ones. Not white and smooth and slim and straight and one-ended, but black and rough and thick and bent and double-ended – each a two-headed lingam with a wick sticking out of each monstrous knob like a hungry red tongue.

I knew precisely what I had to do.

It was during this holiest of holy part of the worship that something unexpected and very frightening happened.

Just as I was about to thrust the burning end of the candle down the burning end of the Magus, there came the sound of a painful roar from within, and from between the sacred buttocks emerged the head of my tiger.

Teeth sharper than the daggers on the altar, tongue thrashing about like a wounded serpent, eyes flashing like lightning, he would not let me near the orifice, now larger and darker and hotter than a cave in Hell, much less force the candle up it.

I fought with all my strength, and all the strength of the Magus, for he was on my side, waiting, craving, hungry for the heat and the comfort of the living candle inside its throbbing womb of wisdom. But the tiger was stronger than me, Giant though I was. I picked up the four athames, one by one, and tried to stab his accusing eyes with each, but the tiger managed to tear them from my hand and chew them up and spew them out.

In desperation I took hold of the white-handled knife, not to be touched by any except the High Priestess herself.

The tiger stopped roaring, stopped moving, just stopped. He might as well have been the head of a stuffed tiger upon a dead wall rather than a vibrant living animal struggling within a vibrant living animal. His eyes turned to stone before my very eyes, and his entire body convulsed out of the Magus' soul and lay dead at my feet.

As if that horror was not enough, as an after-birth the head of the Naga, fully swollen and distended, pushed and forced and fought its way out of the eye of the anus which had tautly shut itself after the death-birth of the tiger, and began to sway rhythmically in front of my face, no longer the face of a powerful and mighty Giant but that of a small and terrified shit-person, the white-handled knife frightening only me.

Like a cornered weakling I made one final move to rid myself of these awesome relics of my past that so threatened and overwhelmed my present. I lifted up the sacred sword from the front of the altar and made a wild swishing movement towards the Naga's rhythmically swaying head.

Screams of laughter and howls of derision filled the atmosphere, rang through the bewitched fields surrounding the barn, tore through the sordid curtain of the night, and followed me as I ran like one depossessed through the corridors of nothingness, blood dripping from my hands and mouth and eyes, blood covering the naked shame of my body with its viscous warmth.

† † †

The tiger had come to devour me and in so doing renew me; the Naga was waiting to reclaim the poison entrusted in my blood and in so doing redeem me; if only I had had faith, I could have been the Magus before Jonathan.

Instead of resisting I should have allowed myself to succumb. Instead of killing, I should have allowed myself to be killed. Therein lay the oft-revealed secret of life. But more oft-forgotten than oft-revealed.

An Encounter

One day I found myself outside the Embankment Tube station. I hadn't intended to be there that day.

I had been to see Hagar, but Patience took one look at my unshaven face, and smelt my smelly clothes, and ordered me away. My attempts to force my way in resulted in some neighbours coming over. After managing to make an unflattering spectacle of myself, and unable even to catch a glimpse of Hagar – mercifully, since my appearance that day would have made Patience's monster sketches of me look like one of the bratpack brats – I retreated back towards Upton Park Tube station, but got on a train going the wrong way.

It had got quite dark and not knowing what to do or where to go I leaned against the iron railing inside the park along the north side of the river, and quite unintentionally began to slide downwards until I was in a prostrate position. Before I knew it I was in an unsolicited brawl with another gentleman of elegance like myself who claimed I had deliberately pinched his bed for the night. Gentlemen of honour just didn't do that sort of thing to one another. I was a disgrace to the family, and before I knew it I was being kicked and thumped by strong accents: Irish, Cockney and West Indian.

I lay where I had been flung down and jumped upon, determined not to get up until well past doomsday.

It got very cold, and I could feel the very blood in my veins turning to red ice.

Good, I thought to myself, good. Perhaps the curse of life

is off, and I can go. Meet the family, have a sing-song, dance a little.

A dark stranger with short dark hair and long dark eyelashes wearing a long dark robe – I could see clearly in the dark because of the light surrounding him – came up to me and washed my feet with his tears. His hands were kind. Then he spoke. His voice was gentle but his words strong and his manner commanding.

Get up and walk, he said.

I did just that.

As I walked, I remembered.

This was the Man I had first met in the tiger's belly, only then he was on foot and I hadn't called him 'a dark man' as he was much lighter than the people of Bangla Desh.

As I remembered, a voice spoke: *He is the Atman, some say Raj-Atman, some Parm-Atman. Bhagwan maybe.*

It was a voice I knew. Where had he come from? And I hadn't even asked him or anybody else. I knew who he was.

He continued: *He is He who, dwelling in the semen, is yet other than the semen, whom the semen does not know, whose body the semen is, who controls the semen from within . . .*

He is He who walks on water and through Maya without drowning in either; and rides the winds, changing their course to suit his course.

Yes, yes, I see . . .

He is He who, dwelling in the earth, is yet other than the earth, whom the earth does not know, whose body the earth is, who controls the earth from within . . .

Yes, yes. I see, I . . .

He is He who, dwelling in the waters, is yet other than the waters, whom the waters do not know, whose body the waters are, who controls the waters from within . . .

I see, I see . . .

He is He who, dwelling in the fire, is yet other than the fire, whom the fire does not know, whose body the fire is, who controls the fire from within . . .

He is He who, dwelling in the heaven . . .

He abruptly stopped speaking and drew in his breath so

sharply he almost sucked a passer-by into his lungs. *Your mark, your sign, the Devil on your back, it's gone . . . gone,* he said, looking mesmerised at my shoulder and back which lay partly exposed where unfriendly friends had ripped apart my shirt and sweater. *The sign . . . the sign . . . gone . . . gone . . . the sign . . . the sign . . .* He kept repeating himself like a semi-literate's parrot.

I walked away. After all, that is what I had been told to do.

I walked for nine years, the final nine of my life on earth: three good years followed by three bad years followed by the three terrible years.

† † †

Jason called out to me from the distance and the closeness of the three continents that had given me refuge at some time or the other during my life: from Chandan in Asia, from New York in North America, from Southend in Europe.

I went out to him as he reached out to me.

I was reunited with those from whom I had been separated for my sins in so many lives around the world, and set on the road leading out of yet another life – on the road for a good three-year walk with Jason and Jennifer, with Sal on the way.

Ian had left home and eloped with a skinny sixteen-year-old he used to drive in his taxi, under council arrangement, from the Southend High School for girls to the local polytechnic for computer studies every Wednesday morning.

Jennifer was in the process of selling the house while waiting for the divorce to come through.

The road was clear for me.

The future awaited with open jaws.

An Erection

It was when Father O'Neil held my hands, bowed his head, and said, Let us pray: Our Father who art . . . that I felt the preliminary stirrings of an erection. Even before he could get to the part where one pleads not be led into temptation, temptation had peaked.

It was the first time in over three years.

Not that there was anything particularly exciting about Father O'Neil, otherwise or sexually.

He had a homely, pug-nosed face, a square-set jaw which might have looked rugged on a wider man but seemed out of place on his slim frame, though it still managed to be a trifle cute. He was short, about five-three or four, I should say. The body beneath the long, black frock, billowy and oversized, could have been beautifully proportioned for its height or ridiculously out of shape, though to tell the truth I hadn't really thought much about it until then. The hands, thick and strong with plump, fleshy palms, augured well.

Perhaps it *was* the hands, as he held mine. The firm pressure of his over-ripe Mount of Venus, smooth and plump like the mons veneris of Aphrodite, beneath a thick, hard thumb like the rampant member of a naughty Eros. Perhaps it was the look in his disturbed grey eyes as they looked into my eyes before he began praying. Perhaps it was his soft dark hair which brushed past my lips as he lowered his head. It may have been the knotty little goose pimples which appeared on the nape of his neck as he began addressing Our Father. Or his deep, throaty voice, which still seemed to struggle with doubts, giving more credibility to the words it uttered.

Perhaps it was the smell: a sort of holy holy holy incense-ridden smell, mixed with the smell of all available body juices – a smell which moved in me memories of the first time I saw Shakti and Jagdeep initiating the untaught into the mysteries of love and life up in the broken-down temple behind the deepest part of the forest besides one of the many mouths of Ganga in dear old Bangla Desh.

Whatever it was, there it was.

Hadn't I been damned enough already!

That was no argument to stop lusting. If I had already been damned, as I believed I had been, might as well make the most of life in the meantime. Might as well make the most of Father O'Neil . . .

Due to a special dispensation Father O'Neil and I were alone. Other prisoners often reacted violently to my presence in communal areas – they do towards child-killers and nonces, and although I had not been legally convicted of any sexual misconduct with children, I had been morally so convicted, and whereas the former can sometimes be quashed, the latter is there forever – so special visitors, generally Father O'Neil and Adam, were allowed into my special solitary cell on special days.

How strong was that body beneath that frock? I was strong, but was I strong enough to take it by force? I might never get another opportunity. I might never get another erection.

If I succeeded, was it possible that Father O'Neil would forgive me? Not report me to the prison authorities? The police?

What was I planning! What was I hoping! What was I thinking! I have even referred to Father O'Neil as 'that body', and later as 'it'!

It didn't matter if God had damned me; I could live with that. But was I now going to damn myself? I could not live with that.

Blood of shame and anger rushed to my face and I could feel my black neck turning red, I could feel it turning hot, burning. Would this switch of blood-flow upwards, this change of thought-direction from lustful to remorseful take my erection away?

A part of me feverishly hoped that it would, and prayed for *it* to go. But a more significant part of me feverishly hoped that it would not, and prayed for *it* to stay on and stay for ever, even if I had to spend the rest of my life walking bent over double and holding a coffee-pot in front of me.

For someone like me, with no redeeming features except a good cock and no saving grace except the talent for a good fuck, to be reduced to a state of helpless sexual impotence was a fate worse than a fate worse than death. Of what use was I to anyone any more? I was twice damned already; what further damnation could possibly afflict me?

I was duly informed: the damnation would spread to me and mine. Hadn't it always? Jennifer had already begun to experience it, not just through my impotence but also through my appallingly unmanly response to it. Impotence itself wouldn't have mattered that much. Jennifer was not that hot on sex anyway, and after Sal's birth seemed less keen than ever. I think she felt secretly glad that I was not in a position to press unsolicited and excessive demands upon her body.

That should have helped. At least I didn't have to feel guilty of depriving the poor girl of her conjugal rights – not that we were officially married. But it made it worse. I felt that my one and only talent was not just dead and buried, but unmissed, unremembered and unlamented as well. Morbidity, thy name is man.

Now the very reason I had not married was itself becoming invalidated. I had thought that by not legally aligning myself with Jennifer and Jason I could spare them the Cyrus Choodah curse of death and destruction. But the voice of God, clear and loud, told me that that was not so. If I was with them, they were with me, and if they were with me they were of me, and if they were of me they would suffer accordingly.

† † †

It was in one such self-perpetuatingly self-pitying state of mind that I left home and Jennifer and Jason, and Hagar (surprisingly, Patience had let me have her back without too many problems after I got together with Jennifer, provided I let bygones and the ten thousand-plus I had given her for Hagar be bygones) and of course Sal, on his first birthday, during the night, long after the toddlers and their mums had gone home and everybody was asleep.

I had an unclear feeling, a vague hope really, that I wouldn't have to stay away for ever. Just for a little while, just to sort myself out. Enough to pacify God, somehow. It had been done before. Perhaps He Himself would decide I was not worth all this bother and forget about me.

Fortunately I didn't have to worry about financial security for Jennifer and the family. There was most of the money I had 'acquired' from Daniel; over three thousand pounds Belinda and I had saved up and Jennifer had some of her own. She never told me how much and I never asked, but I believe it was a fair amount, proceeds from the sale of their house after she and Ian got divorced. She got some money from Ian for Jason's upkeep which also went into her account. For a regular income the sweetshop brought in good money and Jennifer enjoyed running it as well, especially since we had a couple of teenagers part-timing on a regular basis for quite affordable wages. I had gone back to labouring, which I preferred. So did Jennifer, as it brought in extra cash which helped buy a few things to help make life a little bit easier, a little bit more pleasant. I was responsible for deliveries and collections for the shop, and my absence was bound to cause some problems, but none of an insurmountable nature. And anyway, it wasn't going to be for long. I didn't feel I was letting anybody down. Or if I was, that was the kind of gutless bastard I was. Like father like son, so there.

The date was the 29th of September 1984.

It was on the 29th of September 1983 that I 'experienced' Sal's birth. That date marked the beginning of the end of my three good years with Jennifer. My three bad years were soon to start, two with Jennifer, and the third on the proverbial streets of London.

Strange that Belinda, in spite of her strong feminism, had understood my desire not to be present at Hagar's birth: a horrifying and monstrous proposition by Eastern standards, made worse by the memory of my own birth, which you may recall I described as the most ghastly and grotesque experience of my life. And by now you must know that I have had my share of ghastly and grotesque experiences, so you can better imagine how I feel about it.

Jennifer said that I should be present alongside her when she was in labour. She said she would never forgive me if I wasn't there to see our child being born. She said if she could carry it within her womb for thirty-eight weeks and then tear her body apart to release it, surely I could be there just for a short while to see that happen, see it come to life and become a part of the world of which we were a part.

Who could argue with that? I could, but decided not to.

I was there.

I saw her body writhe. I saw her face contort. I heard her breathing break and then start up again just when I thought she had gasped her last. I saw her legs part as I had never seen them part before. I saw her sex shine and glisten and swell and tear itself and bleed as I had never imagined possible.

I heard her cry out. Repeatedly.

I was being born. Repeatedly.

My head emerged, soaked in blood.

Blood in my eyes, blood in my ears, blood dripping from my wide-open mouth.

I heard Mother cry out, silently, softly, chokingly.

I heard Jennifer cry out. Repeatedly.

I heard him cry out. Piteously.

It was not like her cries, not the cries of present pain, but the cry of all the pains that were yet to come.

I heard myself cry out.

But no one seemed to hear me cry.

Nobody seemed to hear my mother cry.

Nobody seemed to hear Jennifer cry.

Nobody seemed to hear *him* cry.

And yet they were there.

At least we were alone all those years ago, me and Mother, except for Umrao, who was the soul of discretion and not in the least inclined to interfere and show off. This time there were strange creatures with masks instead of faces and gloves instead of hands.

It was weird, and frightening, and unnatural. And yet Jennifer had assured me that it was the most natural thing on earth. Perhaps it was. I was the unnatural one. Nobody else seemed to worry or suffer at all. In fact, they looked happy, pleased with themselves. Their eyes were smiling. Even Jennifer looked relaxed, comfortable and proud. I couldn't understand it at all.

Holding the baby up – it had to be a boy, poor bugger – and wiping it clean they handed it to me briefly. A son, you have a son, Mr Cyrus.

My heart sank, my breathing stopped, my eyes became fixed and glazed. Its cries cut through my flesh.

Cry, son, cry. Let your flesh spill out in tears. Cry, cry, cry. Pretty soon you will not be allowed that relief. Remember, you are a man.

Jennifer took the baby and smiled up at me. See, it wasn't that bad now, was it? she said.

† † †

Although I didn't know it then, that was the end of my phallic flights until the moment Father O'Neil held my hands, bowed his head, and said, Let us pray: Our Father who art . . .

Could this too have been part of God's damnation of my body, reprieved by the prayer and the blessings of Father O'Neil, and by the offer of his hand and his body to me, albeit in a spiritual sense, which I, accursed wretch that I am, almost dared to take physically?

Sal was dead by then. As was Hagar. And Jason.

I, their defiler and murderer, was alive. I, who should have been dead, was alive. Even my penis had come back to life. Here, where my feet were fettered, my imagination asphyxiated, my loins constrained.

It was no release from damnation, it was an added torture. A cruel joke from the Cruellest Joker of them all.

A Bel Esprit

Everyone called him Prof. No one knew that his name was Ralph Jacob, and that he had been a professor of English Literature at the University of Essex until a few years ago when he had to leave under somewhat less than savoury circumstances. At the time of his ignominious departure from that posterior of learning, Prof numbered among his students one Jonathan Develin; the said Jonathan Develin also being the cause of Prof's name being mud and his reputation dust, though his own lustiness was certainly behind it all as well. What's more, the JD connection was not just a flash from days gone by. After his public disgrace and his wife's refusal to let him back into the house, Prof took to the streets. There he managed to find a 'secret nocturnal hideout', so secret that everyone knew about it though few had access to it. That hideout lay within the high-walled private parking lot of the very chic Style nightclub, which was owned and operated by none other than the same Jonathan Develin.

The secret of Prof's occasionally coming into money, and new clothes and shoes – all of which he promptly gave away, reverting to pennilessness and his old pair of trousers and a trench-coat, heavy with dirt and sweat and time – also lay with the very same Jonathan Develin.

I did not know any of it at the time, although I was one of the few who were allowed to spend the night with him in the relative comfort and shelter of the shed in the far left corner of the parking lot – much welcomed when winter was upon us.

I was spending my time in those days roaming the Embankment, window-gazing the artistic delights of the South Bank and eye-sampling the shopping treasures of the Strand, Soho and Leicester Square. I hadn't yet got to the stage where one spends one's time spread out on the pavement dazed and stupefied in alcoholic splendour, covered in vomit and blood and dripping with urine. Some of my friends were there, some past it. It was among them that I first met Adam Z. We all thought he was out do-gooding, but it was worse. He was researching for a book. He pretended to care, but it was difficult to know whether he really did.

Prof and I took to each other immediately. In fact, I am glad to say, that I was the cause of a remarkable upturn in his general outlook, even his appearance and health. Despite our very different backgrounds, we shared many of the same views on life, a not dissimilar approach to sex and the sexes, an ability to make light of things we deeply cherished and be very serious about what we cared for least, and an irrational extremism spreading to all areas of life – particularly in the political arena. Our opinions and beliefs crossed party lines and successfully managed to offend the friendly local policeman as much as our young, lefty and as-trendy-as-possible-in-the-circumstances friends and vagrants – hopers and no-hopers, copers and no-copers, dopers and no-dopers alike. Of course we had our differences, but then what would life be without differences?

Whenever we were clean enough we would go to the British Museum and Library and spend hours browsing and reading. On the streets and from dustbins all over the land we would pick up any newspapers or magazines we found and read to each other. Prof always kept cuttings, tearings I should say, about all the important political events, or anything else he found interesting, and stored them carefully under a floorboard in the shed in the parking lot. I can't think why. He would be well dead before he could make any critical or analytical use of them. But it kept him happy, and busy. I helped him out by looking around for copies of newspapers and marking important bits with spittle and nail-dirt, if nothing else was handy.

I could see myself in him a few years on: the same wild look in wild eyes, the same manic-depressive moods, the same desire to end it all without the courage to end it all. I would happily do without the dirty sticky beard, since I hated beards and shaved whenever I could. I would also unhappily not have an erection like his. How I envied him that. He must have been at least seventy, although he would never talk about his age. His face was wrinkled and rough and bent, his hands were wrinkled and rough and bent, his arms were wrinkled and rough and bent, his legs were wrinkled and rough and bent; but his cock was straight and smooth and hard. My cock was wrinkled and soft and bowed.

There were times when he would masturbate endlessly, sometimes in a corner all by himself, sometimes to an invited audience of friends and admirers whom he allowed into the parking lot in the small hours of the morning when it was absolutely deserted. He had a key to the lot tied to his waist by a rope which he never took off. He would begin the act by dropping his trousers to his ankles, talking, lecturing all the while on all sorts of subjects, from ecology to penal reform to the divine right of kings and the kingly rights of the divine. But mainly on sex. The male sex in particular, and its role and place in modern society. He did bugger me once or twice, which I did not particularly enjoy. I would have let him go on buggering me if he had enjoyed it, but fortunately for me, he didn't. No joy in buggering a lad if you haven't anything solid to grasp up front, he said, and went back to masturbating, less and less in private and more and more in public.

The guests were mostly male, mostly young; some older men and women were given special permission to attend if they cared to. We had quite a large audience turn up to listen to him, probably because they knew that he sometimes had large sums of money to give away. Among the guests was a young girl of whom he was particularly fond, as indeed were most of us. She had tattoos on her arms, legs, breasts and forehead, was heavily into anything she could lay her hands on, from glue to gas, and was getting weaker at such a fast rate that we all thought she wouldn't last the next day. Somehow she continued and managed to outsurvive Prof himself, though only by a few hours. She wrote poems and songs, and hoped to be a singer-songwriter one day. Preferably before her nineteenth birthday.

The human male owns nothing, possesses nothing, has nothing, except his feet, his penis, and his imagination. Sometimes his hands.

Here he demonstrated. He was answering a question on the excess of male vagrants as opposed to female, but soon went on to say what he liked how he liked. As he masturbated and lectured away he waved his free hand majestically about, while the dim light seeping stealthily out of the shed on to the parking lot where we had gathered made every move eerily effective.

Men without women would be quite content with rambling feet, a rambling cock and a rambling imagination, he went on. Feet for escape into reality, imagination for escape into fantasy, penis for escape into ecstasy. Feet to escape from reality, imagination to escape from physicality, penis to escape from pain. Feet for dancing and running, imagination for wondering and creating, penis for smiling. For the new man, read car for feet.

Here he smiled all round and made movements to encourage the young men to take out their pricks and follow suit, which most of them, some ardently some listlessly some anxiously, were doing anyway. I don't think they were paying much attention to his words, but they did pay attention to him. There was a wildly hypnotic quality about him. He must have been a very popular and successful lecturer.

The white diagonal lines indicating parking spaces shifted their position uneasily as his long shadow passed over and across them in restless ecstasy.

For men, Prof continued, the penis remains their only friend and saviour. More than that, their raison d'être, even if it is no more than the woman's rib re-styled – from which was created man, without any shadow of a doubt. No matter what the Good Book says, woman is clearly the prime creation, man an afterthought, a convenient nuisance or an inconvenient expedient. What could man have done on his own? It would not have been too difficult to fertilise woman somehow – pollinating winds, archangels, giant bees . . . But how on earth could man have gone forth and multiplied? And that is our purpose on earth, is it not? Condoms or no condoms. If you take the penis away from mere men, their feet slow down and their imagination either retires or gets corrupt and destructive instead of being pure and creative. Their life falls apart.

His words were hitting too close to home and I began to fidget uncomfortably. Did he not realise it, or was he being deliberately cruel? Had he been building towards it all along? Did he have another sinister side to his nature which I hadn't before sensed?

He must have felt my embarrassment and unease because he said: But just as true beauty transcends physical ugliness, so does the strength of human character transcend the strength of male erection.

Giving me a wink he began strutting about the compound for no apparent reason, then suddenly stopped, said, At least, that is so for most men, and ejaculated as far as the eye could see.

† † †

Jeanette, Net for short, the tattooed girl, wrote a poem about the experience of that night. It was her first of the kind.

It was a love poem. She fell in love with Prof that night. At least, that's what she said. And she must have been saying the truth, otherwise why would she go and die just as soon as she heard he was dead?

It was nearly dawn by the time the lecture finished. Time to be out of there. No one had had much sleep. Prof could have stayed hidden in the shed, with maybe me and a couple more, but not the rest.

It was a beautiful night, clear, starlit and still; and although it was cold, most of us had some warm clothing and huddled together so it hadn't been too bad. It was a shame to have to go, but we went, Prof and myself included, determined to catch up on missed sleep in one of the parks, probably the one opposite the Empire Cinema.

† † †

It was there, half asleep half awake, that I saw Jason and Shane. They had been out looking for me over the weekend and came running over when they saw me. The sound of beating feet woke me up.

My heart leaped out of my mouth on to the wet grass and lay throbbing like the dying engine of a sports car.

And despite the sea of conflicting emotions that welled up within me when I saw them, my first thought was: I hope Shane is not corrupting my Jason! After that came shame. What a hypocrite I was. After all my assertions that there was nothing wrong with sex, when it came to my son – for Jason was my son, my true son, I had not doubted that since I first saw him in Chandan when I was a little child myself – all theories went out of the window.

Shane had accidentally met Jason and asked about me. The rest was simple enough. They had decided to look for me in the various haunts of the down-and-outs. I had spent time among them once before, before I met Jennifer again and settled down with her, and Shane knew about it. If we had been at our usual place at the roundabout under the bridge at Waterloo Station the previous night they would have met up with me then.

Jason had come to love me more than his own father, more even than his mother. Our kinship was further bonded by the 'coincidence', as Jennifer called it, that we were both born in the early hours of the first day of a new year. (I in 1954, he in 1972, both fifty-four and seventy-two adding up to the fateful nine. The total configuration of the full date of birth of each of us coming to three, nine, twelve and twenty-one, all multiples of three; and our ultimate number of destiny amounting up to three each, six between us, meaning one life more – earthly or eternal, mortal or immortal – for one us before we achieved our united selves.) Children teasing him at school about getting 'Count Blackula' for a new dad had perversely strengthened his love for me. Seeing him now and in obvious distress I was deluged with a flood of guilt I felt unable to handle and reacted in the worst manner possible. Accusing them both of hounding me, I shot up and ran as fast as my squelchy, ill-fitting shoes could carry me. I knew the complex system of lanes and alleys as well as I knew my you-know-what, and was able to give them the slip despite their superior agility and fitness.

The news they had brought made me all the more confused and unable to face up to them. Jennifer had sent Hagar back to Patience. Poor girl, she was getting knocked about as much as her Biblical namesake. That name was a mistake. And I had chosen another heathen name, Sal, for my second born, my first son of the flesh. Would I ever learn?

I was furious with Jennifer . . . but then I could understand. Hagar was not an easy child to live with. Sal's birth had made her more difficult, and although Hagar had come to accept me a little bit, in spite of Patience's efforts, my running away would have confirmed her earlier opinion of me, causing anger, confusion and hostility. To make matters worse for Jennifer, Jason had been getting into trouble at school and elsewhere in the neighbourhood. He was thirteen now, a problematical age made more problematical by our problems. He didn't quite understand what was going on, which upset him all the more. He had already lost one father, and now he was losing another. It must be my fault, thought he. I knew better.

But I couldn't go back. Not to Jennifer's silent acceptance of me. If only she'd argue, fight, accuse. But then again, if she did that I would probably be saying, If only she didn't argue, fight, accuse. How easy to rationalise. More important, I couldn't go back to being a living curse on those I loved. Was that too a rationalisation? If so, it was one in which I truly believed, and with good cause. Wouldn't you think so? Wouldn't you?

From a little alcove in an alley behind Chinatown I saw Shane and Jason run past looking for me. They came again that way. My eyes cried out, but my lips remained silent.

The Bel Esprit

The first evidence of the Fine Mind and Its finely tuned wit, Its great and wonderful sense of humour and Its hilarious jokes was presented to me by none other than the Great Joker Himself.

I keep assuming it was *Him* and not the *Other One*, in the belief that there is no Other One. But I could be wrong. Maybe there is, and what I heard *was* the Other One in disguise. A very poor disguise if you ask me, for the attitude He wore like an apparel would have been more appropriate for the Other One. But the power seemed to be His. It is difficult for me to say, caught in the thick of it. You can come to your own conclusions. Perhaps your objectivity and distance might serve you better than did my involvement and proximity.

I keep saying He for no other reason than convention. Whether He was a he or not, or what, I have no clue. The voice was more mechanical – robotic – than human, and quite without gender. Apart from that all I had was this awesome sense of a presence, and sometimes a billowy sort of an aura – especially when He was having a good laugh and I could feel it rippling up and down like a volcanic eruption in mid-ocean, to the accompaniment of this crackling, voluminous noise of imitation laughter, jolly in the most fearsome manner, resounding through the atmosphere, entering every pore, penetrating each crack, deluging each opening, flooding every available space in the immensity of this and all other universes with the enormity of itself. There were occasions when, quite suddenly and most disconcertingly, I could see a pair of eyes. There is no way to describe them except to say that they were eyes. Each iris was the colour, the shape and the size of the great dome of the sky, with a black hole where the pupil ought to have been. I would not have imagined that it could be possible to gaze into those eyes and live to tell the tale.

But then mine was not to die, even though the world itself appeared to be dying, killing itself with avaricious, militaristic and bellicose delight. Has not the world always done that? Gone through preposterously hysterical phases of self-destruction followed by a lull and a return to some form of sanity. Then back at it with a vengeance.

Perhaps, but this was different. There was no hysteria about it. Even the warmongering was not crude and blatant or 'excessive', but 'civilised', controlled, carefully targeted and media conscious, even media friendly. Certainly the media was friendly back. No loud thirsting after this or that one's blood or hide, Colonel Gaddafi excepted: more credit to him for having been able to crack open the cranium of international hypocrisy and sprinkle some salt and pepper on it, to shake apart the shackles of international SM and rattle them about it a bit. But on the whole a calm, cool, calculated bid to undo the collective good of the last century was in progress – sedately, quietly and efficiently conducted in the name of good sense, good housekeeping, personal pride, human dignity, human freedom and human rights. It was a move towards the final triumph of form over content, of righteousness over good. Or as the man who called me No-Man might say, of Aparm-Atman over Parm-Atman.

Starting round about 1979/1980 this period went on to complete its nine-year cycle.

Witness one example of the inversion of a 'hard-won' value and the universal return to the naked right of might. Great Britain, with the Great back in it, stood at the forefront and as pace-setter and value-determiner once again. I quote a few edited entries from Prof's diary, stolen from WH Smith, which he partly based on his press tearings and which is one of my few possessions in prison:

April 5th 1982: Queen Elizabeth II of Great Britain sends Task Force to the colony of Las Malvinas, hosanna! Full, if secretive, US military backing. No TV crews allowed, no free press. Mistakes of Vietnam cannot be repeated.

June 14th 1982: Argentina surrenders, glory glory glory, hallelujah!

June 29th 1982: Israel invades the Lebanon.

10th August 1982: South Africa invades Angola.

4th May 1983: Open US support for the Contras. (Contra-life, or just contrary?)

October 1983: US invades Grenada. Official assassination squad for Bishop. No TV crews, etcetera.

15th April 1986: US launches air attack on Libya. Official assassination launch against Gaddafi.

The world is still suffering . . . Correction, a lot of shitty people who deserve to suffer are still suffering, from the consequences of some of the above, none of which could have been so easily accomplished after Vietnam – for instance, open and declared death squads directed by a head of state against other heads of state – had not war and warmongering been made respectable, even enviable, once again. Hallelujah! Once the Great dare, the not-so-great out-dare.

(As I write this, in my very last days, an amusing update to further illustrate the point. 21 December 1989: (a) US invades Panama – official assassination squad for Noriega; (b) Japan forcibly repatriates Chinese boat people – a week after Britain started forcibly repatriating boat people from Hong Kong, even though it had up until then been accepting all boat people without any questions.)

Then came 1989, just to show those swallowed by the giant despair, and those swollen with pride or swelling with ill-gotten gains, that the Maker of the world has more surprises up His sleeve than its unmakers. Great sense of humour, as I said before.

The new cycle of the next nine years started on its own terms, undictated by those who had had it all figured out only the day before.

How futile and arrogant even to pretend to fathom the nature of the Great Unfathomable. But you know me, I'll keep on trying.

I move too far ahead.

Back to my visitation: the bane of my existence, and the bane of a lot else.

I had got pretty resigned to seeing Him around by that time, but we never had long discussions. And certainly not funny ones. This was partly because I used to get so terrified by His sudden and unwarranted intrusion into my life, at least initially, that I would run straight out of wherever I happened to be at the time and leaving behind whatever I happened to be doing at the time. As from the Soho urinals I mentioned, only in that case I continued what I happened to be doing, the other option being biologically impossible. And also partly because He had been sulking from my rebuff, angry, and in a lecturing, admonishing and threatening frame of mind rather than in a good-humoured, bantering mood.

Perhaps now He was pleased with me and happy that I had finally denied my Naga, and done so with such violence, in the tradition of his beloved ones. With the exception of the aberrant son. Paid the price for it, didn't he.

But mainly I avoided Him just because. Only He knows, and He is not telling.

Feeling sorry for ourselves, are we? are His first words.

Actually not, I say. (I am actually, but I'm not about to say so.)

Why then the face prettier than norm e'en? He goes, perfectly straight.

You gave it me, say I.

Upon his first manifestation God had spoken down to me formally in a prose resonant of Biblical grandeur and violence; and then simply and directly; I had endeavoured to answer in a restrained and sober manner, employing as educated a syntax as a self-taught savage like myself could manage. That day He adopted a scarily matey-matey approach and I tried to match it, except for the scary part, which I couldn't manage.

No I didn't, He says.

Whether He is just teasing, or implying that my parents not He were responsible for my face, or hinting that He was not the He I thought He was but the Other One, I cannot say. I just follow the routine, though at the most basic level.

Did, too.

Didn't.

Did.

I am expecting a string of didn'ts, but don't get them. His attention is distracted by Tommo, who reels past coughing his eyes out and holding on to his trousers belt with long, knuckly hands: part pale, part white, part blotchy red. His feet are none too steady, his knees seem to be buckling sideways, and he has a whoozy, droopy look about his face: part pale, part white, part blotchy red.

My attention too is distracted – by the strange looks that Prof is giving me. I didn't think you had gone that far, he says, half amiable half concerned. We all talk to ourselves, I know, even out there. He spreads his hands outwards to encompass the sane and superior world around us. But when we talk to ourselves we know and everybody else knows that we are talking to ourselves. You are talking to yourselves like you are talking to someone else.

I am, I say.

He gives me another one of those looks. He doesn't tolerate fools easily. It would have been quite nerve-wracking to be one of his students. I shall see you later, he says and walks away. I am in no mood for silly games, if game it be. I cannot think what would be worse: it being a game or not being a game. With that he is gone.

Drunk, says He.

He's not drunk, just irritated. For all that he's in a filthy, rotting state, he's a bit toffee-nosed, I comment.

Wasn't talking of him, He goes. I was talking of that kid there. He is pointing to Tommo.

He's not drunk either, just dying.

Perhaps that was laying it on a bit thick, but it wasn't far off the mark. Besides, he's no kid, nearly twenty-seven. I must admit he could have passed for fourteen in bad light, but in good light he could pass for forty. Unlike Net, who wrote poems and wanted to be a singer-songwriter, Tommo claimed he wrote poetry and *was* a poet.

He dismisses what I say and carries on: Maybe not, but kids in Britain are beginning to drink a lot, aren't they? Perhaps, I say, not sure what he is getting at. Perhaps! There's no perhaps about it. He nearly blows my ears off. Don't you read the papers? Some as young as ten are taking to the bottle. Here he slows down and softens His tone: But no matter how much British kids drink they will never be as legless as the kids in Angola.

After a moment's stunned silence during which I try to get my bearings, He bursts out into this earth-enveloping laugh of His, practically blowing the rooftops off houses. Some people call it a high wind; when He is really mirth-ridden it is referred to as a hurricane.

Great, wasn't it great? (I can almost see Him clutching His huge belly with massive, omnipotent hands.) You didn't understand, did you? Maybe it was the way I told it. I should have begun, I say I say I say, what's the difference . . . He gives up and goes into another paroxysm of laughter.

Namibian children you mean, I say.

Same difference, they're all the same. All the same . . . He loses control again. Here, I'll tell you another one, He says, voice whistling through His teeth. There were these two kids – Angolan, Namibian, whatever – and they are out digging for potatoes, when one of them shouts; *Itsa mine, itsa mine*. You know, Italian accent . . .

I can't take much more of it. The Italians were in Ethiopia, not Angola or Namibia, and I'm not sure they grew potatoes.

Don't say Ethiopia. It kills me, that does. I'll come to that later, if you wish. Let me finish this first, and never mind the details. So, one kid goes, *Itsa mine itsa mine*, and the other thinks he is either being greedy and wants his potato, or is talking about diamonds, so he rushes towards it all the faster, and you know what! It was – can't you guess – a mine! But no diamonds! No potatoes either, just – Bang! – two little legs up in the air!

He screams with sudden laughter, I am a clever one, aren't I, *the* Clever One. Clever, Adorable, Worshipful. You have no sense of humour. You haven't. I must admit, I don't tell them very well either. I know the best jokes, I write the best jokes, but my delivery does leave something to be desired. But I am trying, I promise you, I am trying. Practising on you. Here's another one, and don't you dare interrupt. I'll do it properly this time. Really I will. OK?

I say I say I say, what's the fastest thing on two legs?

I decide it is pointless to argue, so I sigh and say: An Ethiopian with a luncheon voucher.

I thought he'd be pleased, but he isn't. He is furious. I told you not to say . . . you know, thingie. Besides, that's stupid. What would one of them do with a luncheon voucher? And where would he run to? They don't have British Home Stores in Addis Ababa or wherever.

British Home Stores don't take luncheon vouchers, I think.

Or Marks & Spencer, whatever, they don't have any of it. We are talking jungle, man, jungle.

They don't have much jungle left in Ethiopia either.

Stop nit-picking. You are such a nag. Such a bore. No wonder all your near and dear ones desert you, from mothers to wives and women . . . I'm sorry, I didn't mean it like that, but you must admit . . . OK, OK. Let's stick to the joke. Mind you, it would be funny if the Ethiopian bundles of aid contained nothing but luncheon vouchers. I hadn't thought of that. Imagine, greedily tearing apart a parcel, drooling and dribbling all over it, only to find . . . He guffaws again, but manages to blurt out . . . luncheon vouchers . . . between gasps of merriment. But, back to the joke, back to the joke. I'll start again, I'll say: I say I say I say, what's the fastest thing on two legs? And you say: I don't know, what *is* the fastest thing on two legs? Get it? Don't forget to stress the *is*, will you! I *am* going to enjoy this.

I say I say I say, what's the fastest thing on two legs?

I don't know, what *is* the fastest thing on two legs?

I don't know either. But I do know it's not an Angolan child. Namibian if you like. Get it? Like it? I made it up myself. Honest. Great that is, really great. Aren't I something?

He comes out with one of the big storms that harried Britain in the nineteen-eighties, tears of laughter showering all over the place.

Not that great, I tell Him, determined to puncture his balloon the first opportunity I get to put a word in between the surges, for if you are implying what I think you are implying, then the Ang . . . the child won't be on two legs, will he?

Nit-picking, nit-picking, always nit-picking. It don't matter in a joke. It's only a joke, not a bloody scientific treatise. And you are a bore, a bore, a bore, a kill-joy bore. Then He stamps His feet and roars and begins to cry. Tears of rage and frustration deluge the land. I run for shelter in disbelief.

† † †

That night, at about eleven o'clock in our corner of the roundabout beneath the iridescent purple splendour of Waterloo Station, while waiting for the van with the tea and stuff, I told Prof all about it.

To my great surprise he believed me. But even he couldn't come up with any advice as to how to handle the situation.

Don't be taken in too easily, Prof said. That was just one of His faces. Rest assured, He's got a lot more where that came from.

But what do I do? He keeps pestering me, I don't even know what He really wants.

Faith. No matter how ill-placed, ill-timed and ill-merited it might appear.

That's a bit obvious. What else?

Gratitude, for being chosen. Adoration, for being Himself.

That's obvious too. What does He really want me to *do*?

Manage the obvious, the rest will manifest itself.

The obvious is what I can't manage.

You mean won't.

Perhaps.

Then make up your own mind what to do. Not even He can make you do what you don't want to do.

What about you? You're supposed to be so clever. Can't you suggest something?

No.

I had an idea. What would you say if I introduced you to Him? I said.

If He is who you say He is, He already knows me.

No, I mean properly introduce you, say you're interested in His proposition? Are you interested? Should be a challenge for you, with your mind. You could handle it.

I thought that would get him. He was a little vain that way.

He makes up His own mind who He wants.

But He is supposed to listen as well.

Prof thought for a moment, then all he said was: I need a think.

I was surprised at his language, and he a Professor of English. You mean you need *to* think, I tell him. Time to think, preferably. Saying you need a think sounds like you need a wank.

That an' all! He winked then went on: Language is a living, growing thing, my son, independent of its alleged guardians and dependent on its real users. Just like that. He pointed below and between. That's a living, growing thing independent of its alleged guardians and dependent on its real users.

You reduce everything to that level, I grumble.

Raise it to that level, my son, raise it . . . I think you have a visitor. He tugged at my jacket.

I looked up. It was Shane.

Please hear me out, Cy, please, he said in his beautiful Irish lilt. How could I refuse? I was too exhausted and cold and hungry to run.

Shane began by asking me if I knew that Terry was running a gang of little boys picking up older men, then blackmailing them – afterwards if they fancied them, before if they didn't.

I know he does, I said, but he's not a minor now, legally. He must be over twenty-one.

The thing is . . . he . . . he's got Jason involved.

I didn't know what to say. Jason, blackmailing . . .

I must go and see him, I must . . .

It's not that easy. He's. We can't find him.

Before that could sink in to my empty stomach, Shane continued: You know Terry had connections with a . . . place where . . .

Of course I knew. I also knew what Shane didn't know, that Terry's dad Trevor owned and operated the place. How could I forget the sight of worried-looking old men clad in high-heeled shoes, knickers, aprons, ribbons and bows crawling on all-fours and saying, I am a *naughty little boy, naughty naughty naughty* . . . two boobs good, two balls bad. And then screaming hysterically under the swishing whip, usually wielded by a tough strong woman in leather underwear and big boots. Or a teenage girl made up to look like a strict schoolmistress, bun, spectacles and all; or an older woman made up to look like a teenager; or an inbetweenager made up to look like nothing on earth; or a teenager looking like a teenager; and so on.

See, sex is not always pretty, Prof butted in, no matter what you or I say.

The ugliness lay in the greed for money behind it all, not the sex, but I was not inclined to start an argument just then. What's Jason got to do with it? I asked, my heart forgetting how to pump blood.

I found out. Apparently one evening they were short of a girl for this rather well-heeled high-heeled client. There were a couple of teenagers who used to do alternate Friday lunchtimes with him, but neither turned up. Terry persuaded Jason to dress up as a girl for the hour. All he had to do was wield the whip, the bloke would never find out it was a boy and not a girl. Blond, blue-eyed and young was what he wanted, blond, blue-eyed and young he'd get. Jason agreed.

My heart remembered, much too suddenly, and I got a pumpful up to my ears.

In the end it turned out to be less awful than I feared –

Jason was safe and unhurt – but worse than I had hoped: a young life had been brutally terminated.

Just at the height of the performance not one but both of the girls turned up, and started scratching Jason's eyes out for taking their customer, good tipper that he was, believing Jason to be another 'tarty bitch'. I don't think it would have made them any less angry had they known 'she' was a boy, but that is neither here nor there. The scuffle developed into a full-scale fight – both the girls had been drinking, if not drugging – and it ended in one of them being stabbed to death.

Jason ran off. Like father like son.

When the police arrived Terry accused Jason of the murder, gave his name as Jason Cyrus – that was the name Jason had adopted, even though Jennifer and I were not married – and further hinted that it was Jason's father, Cyrus Cyrus, who probably owned the place. Terry was safe in the knowledge that his father, the real owner and the real fuzz as well, would help to have his story substantiated.

That was a week ago. Jason had not been seen since. Jennifer thought he might have come after me. Shane thought so too.

I had to see Jennifer.

Next morning, which was only a few hours away, Shane bought me some clothes and took me to his house, where I shaved and cleaned up and changed. Shane went over to Jennifer to tell her that Jason was not with me but that I would be coming over shortly to see her.

Jennifer was furious. She said I had brought nothing but disaster for her and that if I had any respect for her or for myself I would get out of there and never set foot in her house again.

That didn't sound much like her, but then her mother and brother and Ian were standing right behind her, and they seemed to agree.

I used to think to myself: If only Jennifer would shout and scream and lose her temper. Now she was doing that, and I hadn't the guts to fight back – fight for her, for myself, for our son, her son, my son.

If only I had pushed away Ian and the brother who were

blocking the doorway and told them to get out of *my* house. Instead I turned round and walked away.

Deep down in my heart I knew that all of them were right. I was a bringer of trouble and turmoil.

If only Shane had not gone ahead and told Jennifer that Jason was not with me, she might have let me in hoping that . . .

If only I had . . . If only . . .

Like father, like son.

If only she'd let me see Sal, just for a minute. Not that I deserved it. If only I had demanded instead of begging.

You have taken my child away from me, why should I let you have yours? she said.

I was not taking Sal away, I just wanted to see him. I had not taken Jason away either. He had not even come to me. If only he had. And it was not my fault he had grown to love me.

If it hadn't been for your filthy friends and their filthy ways . . . said Olivia, Jennifer's mother. She was right, too.

Images From a City

(including some jokes, poems, anecdotes, an urban idyll and a retribution)

one: poetic endeavours of Net and Tommo

CHOICES
(a poem written by Net and shown
to Prof for approval/criticism)

Rejoice rejoice,
for choice
is here.
The choice to die:
of hunger,
or of cold,
or of lack of medical care.

The choice to sleep:
under a bridge,
or on the pavement,
or behind a cosy restaurant brimming with wine and piss.

The choice to make a quid by holding out your hand,
or a soup bowl,
or by spreading out your only shirt,
or your legs.

Rejoice rejoice, the choice is here,
the choice to own a bank account or ten,
or just a bank,
an apartment in the city,
or a part of the city.

Lament lament,
for choice
is here
to stay.

The poem inspired Tommo to write one of his own, taking
the title from the last stanza of Net's poem, and basing it
somewhat obviously on the twenty-fifth Book of the Old
Testament.

A LAMENT

Wolves howl in my heart, snakes slide round my entrails.
My brain is a pulp, food for the young of vultures.
Mine eyes roam the streets searching for my carcass
among the ruins of the city.

The city of glory, now a vassal,
paying homage to the genitals of Caesar across the seas,
lifting her skirts,
defiling the saint of Assisi with her falseness and her treachery,

sucking out the suckling mother's milk
from her breast,
to fill the bowls of plenitude
as offerings to gods of dust and diamonds.

The parched and wrinkled skin of youth,
is stretched round boxes.
The hollows where once sat eyes
that smiled upon strangers,

are sunk in boxes.
The legs that only yesterday coiled other legs,
are coiled in boxes,
waiting,
waiting for the earth to open,
six foot underneath for sexual and intellectual intercourse
with worms.

Net followed this with another lament of her own.

I lament.

I lament the dead,
and the gone,
and the going.

But more than that
I lament the living
and the here.

I lament the mother who was.
I lament the mother who is.
I lament the mother to be.

I lament the child just born.
I lament the child at play.
I lament the child at school.

But most of all,
I lament
the child yet to be born.

And a few lines more from Tommo:

This is without the shadow of a love
The voice that launched a thousand men into
Nether recesses of the universe —
Queen Bessie make them immortal with a blast,
Her ships suck forth their soul, see how it flies —

The soul of God that never was nothingness.
Proclaims the Queen: no longer the stronger
Shall be ashamed to murder, but instead
Will put the Right Governments in power.
All is dross that is not Britannia.

two: a prank or two and a lesson in faith

There occurred a kind of set-up replay of one of my sacred night's experiences, especially re-created by God to prove to me that faith can work miracles.

If only you had faith, He said, then I could show you that the situation of the rich and the poor and the haves and the have-nots can be reversed without making the rich and the haves suffer in any way or be victimised. You may remember that this was my objection to not falling in with His plans for me, whatever they were. There had to be enough for all. I wanted to be no weight on a see-saw.

There I was in the midst of all these designer folk eating in posh restaurants and ordinary well-off folk with their two and a quarter children eating at their dinner tables and tourists of all sorts munching away at burgers and drinking giant milkshakes and giant colas, all in this mish-mash land of real make-believe with a big screen and small screens all showing the famine-stricken of Ethiopia dying away before our very eyes. Every eye filled with great tears caused by sorrow and hot sauce and ill-cooked onions and over-priced food. Throats were having a hard time as well, in imminent danger of choking with grief or grub. Mary Whitehouse and other caring women from Off-the-Shelf, as well as groups campaigning against immorality of a physical sort, were present to see that nothing of an obscene and offensive nature took place and that the nakedness of Ethiopian children and some adults was well monitored and within the bounds of decency.

Now close your eyes, said God.

I did.

Now open your eyes, said God.

I did.

And the miracle had worked! The situation had been reversed without the better off being any the worse off.

There I was in the midst of these hordes of starving and dying black skeletons all watching with morbid fascination as images of designer folk and well-off folk and tourists eating in posh restaurants and at dinner tables and while sightseeing were beamed to them live via satellite on large and small television screens displayed all over the place. The wonder in dying eyes was a joy to behold.

I had to hand it to Him. He was indeed the Omnipotent Controller of human and animal destinies, besides having a terrific sense of humour.

When He was through laughing I said, Can I go now?

You are not happy, He said, you are clearly not happy. And you know why? Because you are a hypocrite. That's what you are. A hypocrite. You pretend that you don't want anybody hurt, but that's not what you really want. What you really want is to see them suffer punishment and deprivation, just like those who now suffer and for whom you pretend to –

That's not true, I dared to interrupt His Omnipotence, not true, not true –

It is, it is. He silenced me with His voice and will. You can't have the best of both worlds and you know it. You think I can't see through mealy-mouthed, caring, concerned creatures like yourself? Well, I can. What's more, I have decided to grant you your wish. Since I was the one to pick on you, I think I owe it to you, however distasteful I may find it. Let it never be said that I do not fulfil my promises. You want *them* to suffer, starve, know what it is to be thirsty, experience the pangs of hunger. You want *their* children to cry out for food and for drink. That's what you want. I know. Well, you shall have it. Now shut your eyes.

All this while my heart was bursting with words and fears and horror, but he had silenced me so that I was unable to speak or protest in any way. Though flooded with guilt and shame, all I could do was to shut my eyes, and then open them again at His bidding.

I was in this enormous restaurant with a hall and a lobby as large as the skies. Some tables were formally laid, some casually decorated. The whole place was deserted – completely empty of any human being, guest or staff.

Gradually a murmur of voices started resonating through the ghostly atmosphere. Then suddenly, through invisible doors, marched in a whole lot of designer folk, and ordinary folk with two and a quarter children, and tourists and the like.

I am starving, Mummy, shouted a little child on the left. I am dying of thirst, cried an even littler child on the right. And so screamed all the other little and not-so-little children. Their mothers and fathers and uncles and aunts and friends and acquaintances and the strangers they met on the flight were starving too, not to mention dying of thirst. They picked up the menus and rang for service. Service appeared. Skeletal black waiters, some male but mostly female with infants strapped to their backs, barely able to hold on to their pencils and notepads to take orders, shuffled up to the tables. Just as they appeared, some black men, tall and sturdy, in military uniforms with rifles or expensive civvy togs with bulging pockets, surrounded the place.

As the dying waiters began to take orders. He could control Himself no longer. Nigger on nigger, He sniggered. Always set nigger on nigger if you wanna buck a nigger.

Can I go now? I asked.

Blessed are ye who hunger, for ye shall not grow fat! He roared, irrepressibly jocular. Accursed are ye who are full now, for ye shall grow fuller!

Can I go now? Please?

But He was too busy enjoying Himself to hear, much less grant permission.

three: good news, dancing and rejoicing

We are in Leicester Square. Behind us is St Anne's church, steeple partly covered in something green and flapping, partly in something green and held down. Bits of the building are boarded up here and there and bits have been taken off here and there as repairs are in progress. In front, pigeons flutter about looking out for food and feet, a hungrily restless congregation of many gathered round me and God (He has practically taken up residence with me these days) as I throw stolen crumbs at them.

A couple of plucky sparrows keep charging among the pigeons, and despite the aggressive beaks of the larger birds pecking at their scalps they manage a good take-away each time. Around us some decent folk are having a lunch break and a sandwich. There's a young man in new torn jeans and a not so young man in old torn jeans. Mostly there are derelict humans. Two are stretched out on the sunny part of the grass. One has been lucky enough to get a bench for the same purpose. Four are huddled together on another bench: two of them are young, a boy and a girl, two are old, both men. They are having a very serious conversation about the rights and wrongs of young people in a democratically elected dictatorship. Prof always insists that it is a monarchy, hence whatever takes place here, good or bad, is the responsibility of the monarch, in this case Elizabeth II. If she draws her salary or whatever she calls it from the country as a monarch, the head of the state, she should behave as one. If not, she should take up show jumping as a career, or compere TV chatshows, or try ballet – anything. Then she would have all the attendant benefits of extended free choice as the rest of us. Tommo entirely agrees with him; the others have doubts and cite the constitution, to which Prof innocently says, What constitution? He then starts a discourse on JJ's *Ulysses* or LdV's *La Giaconda*, or some other such overrated and irrelevant piece of human endeavour. A peculiar smell, a mixture of pigeon-dropping whiffs and sandwich-dropping aromas and the stench of unwashed bodies and the stink of cheap drink and the heavy vapours from leftover puddles of last night's rains, surrounds us like the smell of stale love.

Net is sitting to my left, wearing these enormous boots she has got from somewhere, she wouldn't say where. The pair of them must weigh more than she does, and her feet have to lift themselves a good few inches off the sole before they could get to the upper half for take-off, making it very difficult for her to walk. Nevertheless, each time she sees someone dropping something in a dustbin, which happens every few minutes, she hobbles over to it in obvious agony.

She was a compulsive 'dustbinner' and nothing we could do or say would stop her. Not that *we* didn't dustbin, but not with such manic obsessiveness. I believe she believed that one day she'd find a crock of gold, or a paper bag with a million pounds in unmarked fivers, or a handbag full of diamonds and rubies, or an open contract from Virgin Records. Of course she would not admit to it. Just looking, she used to say, just looking. No law against it, is there? I wouldn't be surprised if there is. Anyway, I need the exercise. Exercise was the last thing she needed. Rest was what she needed. But she wouldn't admit to that either. Nor would she admit to any suffering caused by the ten-ton boots. Best pair of shoes I've ever had, she used to say in the most convincing of tones. They were almost new, it had to be said.

To my right, practically in God's lap, without knowing it, sits Prof.

Tommo comes running in, face flushed and looking fuller and healthier than ever, green eyes glistening like grass in the morning dew, fair hair flopping about over his overly large head, freckles shining incandescently in the unexpectedly bright November sun. It is 16 November 1985, in case you like to get your dates right.

TOMMO: Great news, great and wonderful news. (*He throws himself energetically on the grass and sprawls at our feet, scattering the pigeons, some barely lifting off the ground with gasping wings, some taking to the skies with wings screaming.*) One guess each. (*He makes a sweeping gesture with his hands.*)

Prof, Net, myself and God all speak simultaneously.

PROF: You've had your poems accepted by Faber.

NET: You found a million pounds in a bi . . . bus.

ME: You've heard from your wife. (*Tommo's marriage had broken up when he lost his house. He was still crazy about his wife and missed his three-year-old daughter very much.*)

GOD: Who on my earth is he? (*I am surprised at God for Tommo was the first person He saw when He first came to see me in the square. He called him a drunken kid.*)

TOMMO: I said good news, not a miracle. I've got AIDS. Not just the virus, but the full-blown thing. I've come straight from the hospital. They've known for some time but had no address to let me know. For so long I have wanted three things: a soft bed, a good breakfast, and a warm place to die. I'll now have all three, and free of charge. Whoopee! I've been booked for Tuesday week, a really nice place. Really really really nice. If I catch a chill or something I could even go earlier . . .

ME: You know him! He's . . . (*I am so taken aback by Tommo's good news that not knowing how to react I start talking to God in a chiding manner for not recognising him, but Tommo misunderstands and interrupts, hurt and angry . . .*)

TOMMO: So now you people suddenly don't know me! I'll tell you who I am. (*He waves aside my protestation with a brusque gesture alone, stands up, bows and starts speaking in a manner veering between the theatrical and histrionic on the one hand and the natural and lighthearted on the other.*) Provided you tell me who you are! Me first. (*The others give me dirty looks as well, thinking as he does that I was pretending we did not know him. I give up and let him speak. My explanation might not be readily accepted.*) I am, not. I was, but I am not.

I was a poet. I aspired to create the poem of life weaving garlands of pretty images and wondrous metaphors. Provided I had a pen and paper. (*A low bow, arms spread wide and out.*) I was a poet. I dreamed I would float through time, trapping butterflies and letting them loose in a garden of words, in a landscape of pure design, scented with beauty, planted on the soil of hope, watered with tears of laughter and joy, kept fresh with the gentle breeze of desire. Especially if I won at Bingo.

I was a poet. The clapping thunder of my voice breaking through the divisive clouds that trinitise the world would have turned our planet into a stage for the grand opera of love, illuminated by the sheet lightning of my genius. Modesty permitting.

I wanted to roll naked on the turning land and fly up to the top of every mountain of the mind and swim the river of chaste sexuality. Dunce-capped and jockstrapped.

I would have fed every woman, man and child on thoughts of bread baking gently on the fires of the moon. Out out, damn McDonald's.

I would have spread rainbows across the skies and made love to household flies and climbed the ceiling with spiders, in my cord trousers. Maybe not, maybe not.

I would have ridden the tiger's back, bare-assed for added thrills; raced with the stag and made a god of every tree that breathed. With due ecclesiastical formalities.

Yes, I would have weaved a garland of images and planted a garden of words. Instead I bought a cage of bricks and turned the trees to wood for floors, carpeted and furnished the lot, and taught in an ILEA Comprehensive. Until the bailiffs came.

Now I am here. Then I won't be here. Soon I won't be anywhere.

And what about you, Sir, now that you know who I am, may I know who you are? (*He begins to cough and splutter, his face turns pale, his eyes turn white, and I think he is giving up the ghost, but he steadies himself, looks towards me again.*) I asked you a question, Sir. I have answered yours, do not I deserve a similar honour? Or am I an untouchable pariah now, undeserving . . . (*He starts to cough again. An untouchable pariah, he got it in one. But I was not going to spoil the last moments of his glory by usurping his title, even if it rightfully belonged to me.*)

NET: I will tell you who I was . . .
Bare feet on the yielding sand, bodies mingling in the sea,

the feel of lips, the touch of hands, the sailboat moving rapidly, blue and green and gold and white. Crabs in the crags. And eternity. (*She gets up and tries to do a little dance but her boots decide to stay where they are, on the ground, and bring her down to the same level. She winces in pain, makes a brief attempt to rise, then gives up and speaks prostrate.*) Now I'll tell you who I am . . .

Naked feet on burning sand, out of the sea the rising land; the sun, the rocks, the emptiness; and less.

That's who I am.

Net and Tommo both look at me, accusingly, expectantly; as does Prof; as do all the pigeons and everybody else in the park, including Adam Z. God has gone and left me alone.

ME: I am just a wanderer, an eternal wanderer.

NET, TOMMO, ALL THE PIGEONS: More, we want more. More, more, more. (*Prof remains silent, wise as ever in not inviting disaster. The pigeons rush at me as if to pluck my eyes out; the sparrows aim for my ears; Adam looks frightened; I am terrified; I start to speak.*)

ME: I, eternal wanderer on earth, have danced barefoot on the ocean and left my footprints upon it for the direction of gods. I have swum in the air and been lost for centuries in the snow, even if it was only for a non-existent moment of the Sacred Night. I have moulded this earth into patterns ever new, ever changing and ever constant, by dynamic and static fusion of truth and falsehood in the heart of man. But the most ennobling experience of my chequered life is death, undying death. How many times have I tasted it, drunk its cup to the dregs, welcoming its sweet repose, feeling its life-giving spirit enter my bones and spread itself out into the entire universe? I have felt its blood singing in my blood and my soul dance in wild abandon to the music of its voice, my own voice.

However, having experienced the pain and the hope and the sorrow and the exultation of all life and of all death, I am tired now. Tired, and old. I can no longer carry the burden of my glory, of my immortality, and of my eternal heritage. I wish that I could live with you. I wish that I could die with you. And then at my death, cry and mourn and lament and sing and dance and celebrate unashamedly until relief from bondage imprisons me finally. Inescapably.

YOUNG TRAMP: Upon a desert road alone, above the blazing sun, and miles and miles of sand, with a gallon of petrol in my tank.

OLD TRAMP: Darkness approaching rapidly, my boat in the middle of the sea, a brewing storm, a blowing gale, my God on a drinking spree.

A FLEDGLING PIGEON: This feeling of twilight in the morning which makes the wait for night seem much too long is invading my spirit again with dark ferocity, darker than ever, forbidding and foreboding, hot and humid, suffocating the very being of life that within my life is struggling for life. The weight of centuries upon my shoulders has bowed me down, and the suffering of millions has made me old before my time.

ALL TOGETHER, EXCEPT PROF: From Odysseus to Gagarin to Madonna, Kinnock and Stallone, we have wandered all over the seas and space. We have seen too much, felt too much, and now the moving stars interest us no more. The moon can stay where it is, with America's permission, of course.

What are we doing here? Where are we going? Shall we stand rooted with admiration at the microwave oven? Or shall we weep for every dying tree in Chernobyl, every dead tree in Vietnam, every falling tree in Brazil, every fallen tree anywhere? Shall we strip naked and make love in a public place? Or shall we clothe the starving children of the world and give them food? Or shall we start another war to prove the superiority of our way of life and kill and kill and kill and talk of peace and make judgements and terms and conditions?

Shall we rise above such stupid questions?

All we know is that we are tired and need rest. Or else we shall explode. An explosion so mighty it will blast the very earth and scatter it in space, again. Millions of meteors running wildly, madly, helter-skelter in search of identity. Like us.

PROF: If by explosion you mean revolution, you must be more stupid than I thought. The chief advantage of a democracy is to bestow power upon the powerful without fear of revolution. Elections rule OK. Deception serves better than violence all round. Why suppress when you can deceive and achieve more? is the view from upstairs. Why riot as long as there is hope? At least we have the vote, is the downstairs philosophy. All are happier, or at least safer.

If by explosion you mean the end of the world, I think it came and went. If not, let's drink to it. (*Prof pulls out an expensive-looking bottle of whisky and offers it round.*)

NET: Let's fuck to it. (*She jumps upon Tommo, even though I know she doesn't fancy him.*)

ALL: Yes, let's fuck to it. (*They descend upon Tommo, hoping to share in his good news. The pigeons are as eager as anyone else.*)

An orgy of sex and dancing and rejoicing follows.

God reappears, smiling, proud of His starred and striped believers for having managed to turn the very means by which the species procreates into a means of self-annihilation and for then passing the process round to the less privileged of the world. Subtractive multiplying, though not as carefully selective as intended. Accidents will, and the best laid plans, and all that.

For once I can see the point of his joke.

I smile too as I wait my turn. Not being able to participate actively, I can do little else for the ever-increasing crowd. In the free-for-all I begin to doubt if Tommo will survive the ensuing ecstasy and be able to enjoy his soft bed, good breakfast and warm place to die. The place to die has come looking for him in the form of time, in the shape of people.

439

four: jason or ahimsa

I don't suppose I will ever find out what, if anything, might have happened if the first thought that came into my mind that day had been ahimsa instead of Jason.

The Advent calendar was in full swing and Christmas was fast approaching – only twenty-one shopping days left! God asked me what I would ask for if I had one wish. It had to be physically possible (no mountains talking or trees dancing), specific (no wars could be considered, peace on earth was out), and within the boundaries of human will (no nuclear weapons, no Morris Dancers, no deforestation). He did not promise that it would happen, just asked. Mind you, even if he had promised, I was far too wary of his promises to have been euphoric. More likely I'd have been terrified. It had to be the first and the most important and the most violent wish of mine. I thought of being with Jason but dismissed it as too selfish, and asked that all humans should turn herbivores. I thought I was being very clever, believing that once human beings began to *feel*, not just know or realise or learn, that all killing was wrong – especially the killing of the captives by the captors, of the trusting by the deceivers, and of those with no power at all by those with total power over them – then wars and weapons and indeed most evil and avarice would naturally disappear. Vege-munching does not combine very well with murder, carnage and rampant capitalism. In its own quiet, fumblingly inoffensive way it manages to edge them out so discreetly you don't even notice.

God seemed to go all quiet after that. In fact God seemed to just go after that.

I waited for a response, or a comment. Nothing. The next thing I knew this odd-looking character, neither man nor boy, wearing dark glasses and a funny-looking cap, was standing beside me.

It was Jason.

The glasses and the cap were to hide the very blue eyes and the very blond hair often shown on television and mentioned in the papers in an effort to enlist the help of the public in tracing the missing boy.

Had God granted the first thought that came into my mind instead of the first expressed wish? Or was it just a coincidence? What if the first thought had been ahimsa?

I doubt if it would be possible to discover the answers to any of these questions.

five: an urban idyll

Jason said he'd been looking for me for days. He'd been to all my known haunts at all possible times but I had either changed my habits and habitats or he'd just missed me out of bad luck. Today he had decided to give up searching for me, go home to Jennifer, and take life as it came. He was on his way to Tottenham Court Road to take the Central Line for Liverpool Street before hopping on the train for Southend, but found his feet diverted this way, just for one last look. He couldn't believe his luck. He was so happy that in spite of the hard street-boy front that he had acquired he burst into tears and couldn't stop crying.

I couldn't stop crying either; mostly for myself, but also out of joy for him because he had had greater luck in finding his father than I had had in trying to find mine. As it turned out I did find my father, in him; for Jason looked after me with all the loving concern of a true father.

He had built quite a little life for himself, and had even managed to find a place for us – he was sure he would find me one day – to live 'properly', a lovely little squat in an old Victorian building shared with some students and a group of Hell's Angels.

He took me with him to this building not far from King's Cross Station where he had fixed up a little boxroom for us both. It was like heaven. The place was owned by the Greater London Council. Partly because of their policies, partly because their own authority and existence was in imminent danger of termination, they had generously turned a blind eye to the presence of the squatters and not had the supplies of water, gas and power cut off. The squatters in their turn had done most of the essential repairs to the once crumbling structure and paid all the bills.

He introduced me to all his new-found mates, who were quite excited to meet the father he had talked so much about. In spite of all that talking he must have left a few facts out, for they were somewhat surprised to see that his beloved 'Dad' who was 'so very much like him' had neither blue eyes nor blond hair. But they were very nice about it, without being too nice about it, and it was wonderful.

What followed were the happiest months of my life. Probably the happiest months of Jason's life as well, though it must have been much harder for him. Bringing up a grown-up father nearly twenty years your senior when you are only fourteen cannot have been a very easy job.

But he seemed to thrive on the challenge.

In fairness to myself, I did whatever I could to help, or was allowed to do by my child father. First of all there weren't any steady jobs around for me to get, and secondly Jason felt that I should keep as much out of the public eye as possible. Once the face and name of Cyrus Cyrus, not a very common name and often in the media in connection with the disappearance of Jason Cyrus, was recognised, especially if he was seen with a young person, that would be the 'end of the road' for Jason. He could be quite dramatic, if not entirely original, in his expression – 'end of the road' being one of his favourite phrases to express a much-feared state.

Actually he was no longer being 'hunted', to use another of his favourite words, in connection with the murder of the unfortunate girl in the house of ill repute. It had been established that the hand that wielded the knife had belonged to the other unfortunate girl involved in the fracas; but Jason knew if he was traced he would either be sent back to Jennifer, or worse, taken into care. He wanted to delay the former for as long as possible, and declared he would 'rather die' than go through the latter. He just had to hold on until he was sixteen. He was not going to be sixteen. He was to die on his fifteenth birthday, my thirty-third. The number six again, twice three. It was for me to complete the final third of the nine for both of us.

Jason made enough money begging for us to survive. He had two or three special places: in the subway leading up to Charing Cross Station, the South Bank complex, in front of selected theatres. Of course he couldn't be in any one place for long, but his innocent good looks and thin, hungry face got more than some. What I feared was that this was not all his innocent good looks were getting him – a fear confirmed by the large sums of money (a couple of twenties, a fifty!) which happened to come his way every now and then. A lovely old lady, a kindly old gentleman, a drunken brickie, a lucky yuppie, and so on. He might well have been telling the truth about who had given him the money; my doubts related to the question of why? Pure generosity or services rendered?

My unease because of my general stance on sexual morality, by which I had always meant total sexual freedom for all sexual beings – and children were nothing if not sexual beings – was further compounded by fear and worry about the new 'plague' of AIDS. After my initial shock at learning Tommo's 'good news' I had almost begun to see it his way, as a welcoming path to the final exit. Would I see it that way if it happened to Jason? And how to differentiate the need for money for survival from a capitalism-inspired greed for money? How much of Jason's 'enterprise' was motivated by the wholly justifiable subsistence factor and how much by unacceptable overtones of lust for money? Could he be excused if he was being exploited for sex by those in a position to carry out such exploitation with the help of a money-orientated value system?

I found my comforting certainties being uncomfortably challenged; and the worst of it was that I was unable to discuss any of it with Jason. I did try, but mostly by hint and innuendo, and only once by a direct question: Are you renting yourself out? But Jason laughed and joked or sidestepped his way out each time the subject came up, and I had neither the knack nor the guts to pursue it further. Fortunately we did not pretend to any righteous indignation – neither he at being suspected, nor me at his supposed activities – and our relationship remained undamaged.

I took to shoplifting condoms, the best and the most colourful I could lay my hands on. For a small item they are not as easy to purloin as you might imagine, being almost always spread out under the watchful eye of the cashier. One of the easiest ways was to pick up several packets, slide some into your pocket, and pay for one. As I developed my technique I could get away without paying for any. I then left these packets in various places in the room where Jason would find them. The fact that they always disappeared and that Jason never mentioned finding the place littered with packets of condoms could be construed as proof positive that he was in the business. But not necessarily. I started leaving a few extra packets in other parts of the house for the benefit of our mates, so as to create doubt about the identity of the benefactor. Perhaps I ended up encouraging him more than protecting him, I cannot say.

But for all that it was a wonderful and beautiful period of my life, of our lives. In our free time, which came when we chose, we would do all sorts of silly things, like getting on any tube or bus, getting off anywhere, and then exploring like two wild animals in the proverbial city jungle.

I taught Jason to bhangra the Indian way and he taught me some new 'in' moves, and we would dance our way through crowds of people and against oncoming traffic and in shops and in fields and along rivers. It is a wonder we were not arrested; probably our behaviour was so extravagant that people assumed nobody who carried on so exuberantly in public could be on the 'wanted' list.

We did have hairy moments. Once a group of swastika'd skinheads started following us making unoriginal cracks which might not have been so bad had they not heard Jason call me Dad. That really sent them crazy. They took out chains and knives and started chasing us down this crowded street. A couple of passing policemen came to life and, more scared of them than the skinheads, we turned tail and ran straight into the chain gang. To our surprise they let us pass through without doing too much damage to our hairstyles and we managed to hide by climbing up on to the roof of a porch

in front of a shop and lying flat on top of it. The coppers
had seen us suddenly disappear in that area and kept coming
back, but decided to give up after a couple of turns – though
not before they exchanged agreed views about fucking black
muggers and begging pimps and child-runners.

About a week later Jason saw one of those coppers in
the Piccadilly Circus Underground toilets holding out his
distended member and pumping away at it to entice and
arrest suspected queers. Jason found out from some regulars
that he was quite well known for trapping queers this way
and, if they were any good, having a fuck before turning
them in. That was before the AIDS scare. Since then he
had turned nasty, and instead of sex he beat up the poor
buggers before charging them not only with soliciting but
also with assaulting a police officer in the execution of his
duties. However, some more responsible officers got wise to
his tricks and often let the 'offenders' go with just a warning.
So far so good. What horrified me was Jason's plan to trap
the copper.

There were times I couldn't figure out Jason. Perhaps it
was the age difference. Sometimes he would be so cautious
as to tread softly in his own room and speak in a hushed voice
in the presence of any stranger, however inoffensive-looking.
Sometimes he would come up with these disturbingly daring
and dangerous ideas. I could go on pretending I didn't know
whether or not he was on the rent game, but it was harder to
pretend he was not taking substances which altered his moods
and attitudes. I faced him with this, he confessed, and even
offered me some, which I tried and found quite stimulating,
or restful, as and when.

We were successful in executing Jason's plan one night.
There wasn't anybody about and Jason, wearing a wig and
a lot of make-up, managed to get him into one of the cubicles
where I was already lying in wait.

Another good thing about that time was that God left
me alone.

Until.

† † †

445

What follows was probably meant to be since the day I was born. And it was natural that it should concern non-humans, since the first creature my nascent eyes rested upon was Umrao the goat, and the first words I heard were also uttered by Umrao the goat.

The storm clouds started gathering when Jason got involved with the Animal Rights Movement. In fact it was after seeing a video at one of their meetings that I got to know Adam a little better, and came to ask myself: if that was how man treated the 'least among us', and I counted myself among the least, then how was I to treat man?

Prof had said that I alone would have to make up my own mind how to respond to God and His offer. He was right.

The trouble was that there was no sign of God anywhere for me to let Him know of my decision, and to offer Him Prof instead, if he was at all interested in a swap. Like Prof I had my doubts, but there was no harm in mentioning it.

six: an alternative theory of the creation of the universe

To all appearances Rose was no different from any other bag lady: dirty, smelly, clad in layers and layers of unwashed clothes, with straggly grey hair streaking all over her cracked, wrinkly face and falling into the tight, sunburnt eyes.

As a character she was in a class by herself. She would not accept any money or any charity from anybody. Poor old Adam had had his pound or two flung back in his face a couple of times before he learnt not to patronise her. She lived off whatever food she could find in bins or thrown away by surfeited children or left behind on park benches.

She carried Prof's theory that woman was the prime creation a step further and insisted that God was a woman. Only a woman God could 'give birth' to life. Men could only create castles in the air inhabited by creatures of the mind, without bone or blood.

She had a theory about the creation of the universe.

If she was not in a mood to divulge it, you wouldn't get

it out of her if you swathed her in silk and covered her with jewels, not that she would allow you to do that in the first place. If she wanted to talk about it, you couldn't stop her. She particularly liked to tell it to Prof, over and over again, if she felt that it would sufficiently irritate and annoy him. I think that in her own way she was secretly in love with him. Strange that most women, even those who came do-gooding, found him fascinating and attractive. I could never figure out why. He was old and ugly and quite impervious to female beauty, feminine wiles, womanly virtues or the adoration of ladies of any age, character or style. But, that's how it was. Under different conditions I might have been envious; in the circumstances I was only intrigued. Perhaps it was the immense store of restless energy that exuded out of every pore of his body, and the fire which burnt unquenchable in his liquid grey eyes – the energy and the fire which sustained him through marathon bouts of orgasmic self-stimulation.

I caught Rose in the most dramatic part of her umpteenth reconstruction of the creation. Her version was not entirely incompatible with the Biblical, in that it had its six days and the day of rest; but according to her our galaxy and our earth and all life in it had been created on the day of rest. It also had its scientific side in that it relied heavily upon the Big Bang. And of course those looking for myths might possibly find some myth-making in it too. Rose had a very inventive and fertile mind.

For six days the Creator had been much too busy creating the major part of the interminable and incalculable immensity of the universe and had not had any time to rest, not even time to go to the toilet for essential relief. To make matters worse, She was nearing that time of the month and PMT was building up like nobody's business. On the seventh day She decided to relax and let it all hang out. She picked out a deserted part of space, deserted because it was the dirtiest and smelliest, bent over, rolled the celestial version of Her Marks and Sparks knickers down her para-gargantuan bottom, raised it ever so slightly and, lo and behold! The Big Bang.

The opening blast was followed by a volcanic eruption of

the Almighty Crater. A lava of red-hot shit, entirely divine in nature and hence holy to the nth degree, exploded out into the bleak and empty nothingness. The vastness of the encompassing vacuum greedily sucked up all the sacred matter with the help of the pressing winds from behind the Behind. Turds turned to stars in no time and shit bits began to run round them in maddeningly ovoid circularity in a desperate but ineffective bid to escape. And there you have the planets, including our beloved earth.

Ateh Malkuth, ve Geburah, ve Gedulah, le olam. Thine is the manifested world and the processes of breaking down and building up, for ever.

Waters accompanied the shit in hissing, swishing downpours and torrents of unimaginable power and ferocity. Oceans, lakes, rivers and the Niagara and the Victoria Falls were some of its consequences. As life began to emerge in these waters, the time came and discarded divine ova flooded out from the Divine Being, saturating the earth with blood. Since then man has continually lusted after blood to recapture the taste of that first blood.

Prof walked out half way through this enactment. Not that he wasn't impressed. In fact it was so bizarre – with the agitated, feverish movements of her intense black pupils, the hoary crackling outflow of words interrupted by frequent manic laughs, the jerking about and lifting up of layers and layers of tattered smelly old frocks – that I was sure he wished he had been able to think it all up before she did. But he had heard and seen it often before and did not want to encourage the woman too much. She would never let go of his side if he so much as smiled at her. At least that was his belief. I wasn't too sure. Despite her obvious fascination with him she had too much fire of her own to rest content with borrowed flames.

I applauded enthusiastically as I always did. One day I would try to see if I could make her perform for Jason. He would love it. But it was doubtful if the woman would oblige, unless she took to his blond mane and blue saucers, which was not entirely inconceivable. Jason could charm the devil woman herself if he put his mind to it.

† † †

Suddenly I was all alone and an eerie chill began to creep up and down my spine.

Was He here? I could not see Him . . . But what else could it be! He must have known that I had been wanting to see Him. On the other hand He had chosen, for whatever reason, to withdraw from me. This could have been His way of compromising. Letting me know that He was there to hear me out, but still not willing to properly manifest Himself.

I let Him have it. I told him I did not want to be any part of His plan, whatever it was.

† † †

When I was a child I remember Grandmother telling me a story. She did not often tell me stories. I don't think she liked me all that much. Gave dirty looks to Great Grandmother each time she took my side over anything.

There was once a simple man, kind, loving and generous, who got married to this beautiful girl only to discover that she was a black witch. She made his life so miserable that he ran off to foreign parts the first opportunity he got, which was when his wife went to visit her parents. There he met another beautiful girl, fell in love, and married her only to discover that she was a white witch. She was very much nicer than the first one, but still far too clever for him and always up to something and always wanting him to be up to something. Then the first wife found out where he was and made his life a pit of disaster by casting a series of unpleasant spells on him which the second wife had to keep undoing. She, the second wife, also kept casting her spells on the first one, who then got even by getting back at him. And so it went on, until the white witch said that there was a way of getting the baddie witch out of the way on a permanent basis, but it could not be done without his consent and co-operation. He agreed, reluctantly, for he really did not want to harm anyone. The white witch was so pleased at his decision that she decided to give full vent to her powers before bringing about the

449

ultimate downfall of the black witch. Obviously the black witch retaliated and their entire life was one big battlefield until the final showdown. The white witch completed all her preparations to the minutest detail. The time is here and now, she said. No witch, white or black, can will the destruction of another witch, no matter how much hassle we may cause one another. It breaks our code of ethics. But mortals are allowed to try. Now, you hold on to this magically prepared candle, blow on it, and say: *Thathay tholi thathay thali, rahay Baggi, na rahay Kali* (Abracadabra, let the white one remain, let the black one go). The man thought it over, blew on the candle and screamed: *Thathay tholi thathay thali, NA rahay Baggi, na rahay Kali*. Peace at least.

So that was my answer.

I have no desire to save this world for anyone or anything. You can have Prof if You want to, I added. He seems willing enough to try anything or anyone.

You could hear the silence of death after this. Then came the Voice: Do you know why the Palestinians are so primitive yet so clever?

I failed to respond. At least He was there and had heard my decision. He could say or do whatever He wanted to now. It was off my chest.

So primitive that they still carry on trade through barter, so clever they get expensive American bullets in return for cheap Arab stones?

I failed to respond.

Do you know when boat people are not true boat people? I failed to respond.

When they are drowning in the sea. Or when they are sent back in planes. The first if you like happy endings.

He was getting worse at telling them. But still I did not respond. It was clear what He was trying to do. Not just rile me, but make me feel something for the shitty ones of the world, make me feel strongly enough to rise up in righteous indignation and take up battle on their behalf. But it wasn't going to work. It never had worked. Who was I to succeed where all others had failed?

Do you know why crop failure can deprive the Ethiopians

of vitamins and carbohydrates, but not of proteins? Because they have each other. Good lean meat at that.

This one got me. In spite of my resolve, this one got me. It reminded me of the good lean meat production techniques I had watched on video not too long ago.

You want me to do something about it? I said. All right, I'll do something. I'll tell you what I'd do if I could. I would fart and fart and fart and send enough methane gas up into the atmosphere to create a large enough hole in the ozone layer to suck up the entire world and all in it to eternal oblivion. I would take a chainsaw to every living tree on the planet so that the fashionable and the trendy would have none left to mourn ecstatically over in their latest designer gear – no environment left to protect, no politician-tears to shed.

I would fill each and every car and every minibus and every coach and every truck and every articulated lorry and every motorbike and every scooter with extra-leaded petrol and drive each and every one of these round and round and round the world until every child everywhere was brain damaged or paralysed or choked to death or all three. Or run over.

I would spill every last ounce of the remaining oil into all the seas of the world and across every grain of solid matter on all the continents of the earth and set it alight with a final fart and flaming tinder so that every living creature on land and on sea and in air burnt to cinders, pre-empting and outclassing the gradual manifestation of the greenhouse effect, making it as redundant and unnecessary as you, O Great and Mighty One.

I would push every nuclear button with the tip of my rampant cock, and if it failed to rise to that occasion as well I would sit on each. Why should only the weak and the powerless suffer? Let us all go to hell together, arm in arm, united for once.

† † †

It was the night of the Summer Solstice. I had finally turned down God's offer, one nine-year spin gone and the next begun since it was first made. That night I made an offer to God. He accepted.

Prof died that night.

When I went home around one in the morning the area surrounding the house was cordoned off. The place had been raided by the Drug Squad. By some accounts they found no drugs, by some accounts they found a whole bagful. They did find a cache of sex-aids and other pornographic material – one resident couple used to hold occasional tupperware parties of a non-tupperware nature at lunchtime for bored young executives and the like. The couple were not found but three of the Hell's Angels were taken into custody. The other residents were not arrested but evicted. The building was sealed. They found Jason hiding in the meter cupboard under the stairs, wondered why, and took him away.

If only he had remained with the others they might not have got suspicious of him. They were only looking for drugs. They might have let him go with the rest.

If only I had not stayed back with Prof he might well have been alive now and I would have come back earlier and gone out with Jason as we often did in the evening and been safe and away at the time of the raid.

If only.

seven: prof's last hour

He was in one of his bitter and angry moods. He got like that on nights he had not had enough supply of 'good honest drink' and just before a grand wank session. I could see it coming, all the signs were there. I thought I'd stay with him to see him through the occasionally difficult start, after which he'd be fine on his own. Sometimes he'd insist on my company throughout; sometimes, as you know, he'd gather an audience; but mostly he was fine on his own.

There he stood, mother naked beneath his clothes! Scandalous, Sir, scandalous, I tell you.

He started on one of his usual fantasies, but with unusual hoarseness of voice turning into one long, phlegmy cough, yet somehow recovering to enunciate with amazing clarity of diction and purity of accent.

Mother naked, he repeated – he liked saying 'mother naked' and would sometimes keep saying it over and over again while working away at a part of his mother nakedness.

Mother naked. Mother naked. Scandalous. Absolutely scandalous. Not the wimpish nakedness of your Michelangelo's David, or of the epicene Adonis, or the smooth-assed Apollo; but the huge, hairy nakedness of the Boeotian Giant, the deer-hunter, the true Son of Mother Earth: Orion, the incarnate urinal member. Every pore of concealed flesh lay revealed, glistening with sexual sweat; every single hair of that magnificently hirsute body curled upwards, outwards, protruding through the tight jeans stretched over his tense buttocks and through the tight top caressing his taut torso, beckoning, inviting, his crotch aflame with their fiery abundance, surrounding the pillar of his manhood rising like a Grecian column in a temple dedicated to Aphrodite, carved out of marble, smooth as marble, veined as marble, hard as marble, cold as marble; cold, despite the sacrificial tongues of flame rising up and licking at it with insatiable lust; his testicles, like rocks of molten lava, swung between his thighs with the potency and majesty of diabolised divinity.

He often spoke of this Orion. Whether he was a real person or a figure conjured for masturbatory fantasies I could never tell. But then just when I'd convinced myself that Orion was the name of some living, breathing character he knew, he would describe some wild magic of his, like setting objects on fire with his eyes, and I would go back to my fantasy theory. And then he would mention a minor detail, like the way his teeth shone or the backs of his hands quivered, something so believable that it could only be fact. The frightening part of it all was that I was beginning to think I knew the person myself.

I did. It turned out to be none other than Jonathan Develin Esq. Prof had been removed from his post at the university when Cornelious Develin found out from his dearly beloved son that his English Professor was after his ass. The good judge kicked up enough dirt to cloud the issue of his son's involvement and have plenty left over to indelibly smudge Prof's name. Jonathan had told tales out of pique for not getting a good grade in his term essay from the said English Professor, even though he had let Prof have his way with him just the day before, and not for the first time. But when he found him hanging around his new nightclub, disgraced and thrown out by wife and kin, he felt sorry for him and gave him the key to the parking lot.

I was surprised to learn Prof's age. For all that wrinkled, sagging body, he was only fifty-seven and not seventy-two as I had imagined. In fact it was his fifty-seventh birthday on the night of his death. That's why he was feeling so distraught – another year gone and so forth. And that was why Jonathan himself made a personal appearance the same night, along with Biggun Dangler – dancer, stripper, singer, employee and buttock friend – to bring a gift of money, drink and ass. He had promised him Biggun's. Whether either of them would actually deliver or not remained to be seen. Each of them alone was quite a tease. Together they could be murder.

Things went wrong from the word go.

I recognised Jonathan instantly. I should have recognised him from Prof's description, except that his prick was no column of white marble but red and blotchy, more like an unnatural cucumber. Perhaps it was all that ceremonial shaving and scraping and drubbing and rubbing of stingy oils and suspect pastes that had done it. I didn't think he would recognise me. After all, he hadn't seen as much of me as I had of him. But he did. Almost before setting eyes on me.

He had carried a smouldering grudge against me all these years. Apparently my evil aura had mucked up his initiation and he had had to wait another three years before achieving the status he deserved and which was his by right of birth. Prof didn't know any of it, and he looked at both of us in bewilderment as we communicated across him without hardly exchanging a word.

In the meantime Biggun Dangler, not knowing what was going on and not particularly caring, had stripped for action, his huge black body glistening in the night with its inherent blue light. It was to be a tease session, just as I had feared. Poor Prof, tongue and everything lolling out, was getting huffed up and puffed up and roughed up without so much as getting the opportunity to touch the sacred parts, much less possess them. Jonathan, overtaken by the speed of Biggun's performance, quickly ordered me out saying: I'll see to you later. I refused to go. Instead I grabbed hold of Biggun's balls and turned his ass over to Prof. Once the screaming and swearing and free-for-all that ensued had died down we were left with one heavily spunk-laden and badly mauled Dangler; one bruised, scratched and insanely irate Develin; and a dead professor. Jonathan gave me a look which if I hadn't managed to duck would have gone straight through my heart. Instead it hit the back of the shed, which instantly caught fire.

I ran like I was on fire, jumped the ten-foot wall by first jumping on to Jonathan's car, and was away.

What happened when I got home you already know.

My fragile world had collapsed within the folds of the night.

eight: back on the streets

There I was, back where I belonged, scrounging rubbish and littering the streets with the black ugly waste of my being. Jason had gone, Prof had gone, Net had gone, Tommo had gone; all in their various ways to their respective sanctuaries or homes or prisons or resting places. I remained.

nine: a city battle in the heart of the city for the heart of a city and for the emancipation/control of the world

It was so unpalatably chastening, in the manner of some lost, ill-composed and over-written Greek tragedy, or a parodied episode from Mahabharata, that it might have been a simple nightmare, which it was not, instead of real life, which it was.

A violent night was in progress. The rain was angry, the wind angrier. They battled it out in the narrow dirty streets of the city. Caught between the two, crowds of colourful litter danced the panic dance like trendy teenagers at a cheap disco. The yellowy quivering headlights of oncoming cars and lorries and the blood-red drippy tail-lights of departing cars and lorries streak-lighted the trashy revellers, while bold sheets of lightning flash-lit the ill-advised decor. Syphilitic buildings forcibly interlocked in intimate penetrating embraces with their neighbours since conception, neighbours towards whom they had been contemptuously indifferent since birth, looked on with the interest and enthusiasm of a chained and captive audience and with the participatory powers of the maligned and the marginalised in an enlightened democracy. Drum rolls of thunder provided the beat for the dancers and combatants, as well as for the hapless spectators.

I was stretched out, somewhat disgracefully, in full public view, half across the road, half on the pavement in front of a chemist shop from where I had stolen three packets of condoms that afternoon. I don't exactly know why, since I didn't know anyone who needed them now that I had lost Jason.

Despite the cacophonous rage of the storm and above the thunderous clapping of the clouds, a soft sound began to make its presence felt: the gentle clippity-clop clippity-clop of a gentle creature approaching from the distant mists of the past.

It was a little donkey, and upon it sat the Man – the same dark Man with dark eyes and dark hair who had bade me get up and walk, not far from where I lay now.

And when he drew near and saw the city he wept over it, saying, Would that even today you knew the things that make for peace! But you hide your eyes away from them.

He then entered the temple of the god of the city and drove out all who sold and bought there and overturned the computers of the money-changers and those who sold pigeons and said to them, It is written your house shall be a den of robbers, but remember the fig tree.

And then came one of the seven angels and talked with me, saying unto me, Come hither. I will show unto thee the judgement of the great queen that sitteth upon many waters, with whom the kings of the earth have committed many pacts and on the wine of whose rhetoric the inhabitants of the earth have been drunk.

So he carried me away into the spirit of the wilderness that was in the midst of plentitude; and there I saw a Woman sit upon a bloodied Beast, full of democratically elected names of blasphemy, having twelve heads and two horns and a bugle; and all the heads worked together and walked together in a market that was common to all and lived and killed in a community that lived by the law and killed with the law and was a law unto itself. And the Woman was arrayed in robes of the kingdom: beaumonde blue turned purple with the blood of sacrifice. She was crowned with a head of gold and decked with precious stones and pearls.

Then I remembered the man who called me No-Man and realised who she was. She was Aparm-Atman, the yellow woman Durga with the black heart of Kali, but neither Durga nor Kali and more fearsome than legions of both. Her mount was more pitiless than the multi-jawed tiger of Durga with poisoned swords where the claws should be. She held more weapons and more skulls in her hands than all the images of Kali multiplied by themselves. She wore a crown made of little children's bones, studded with their living eyes for jewels and glistening with the blood from their still throbbing hearts. On her belt were strung the heads of demons and from her open mouth hung not one nor three but many tongues, each longer than that of a pre-historic reptile. Upon her forehead was a name written: 'Mystery, London the Great, confusion of tongues, Mother of Parliaments and Abominations of the Earth.'

And by the side of the Woman and the Beast was an airborne amphibious Leviathan. It floated sometimes behind them sometimes ahead of them and sometimes directly above them and devoured all in its path that dared to disagree with it and upon it rode Aunt Verna waving her broom about and carrying her pooper-scooper under her arm and wearing a sawn-off shit bucket on her head.

Soon the Woman, the Beast and the Leviathan were confronting the dark Man, the little donkey and me.

An Ending

Jason had been taken into care. He kept escaping and coming over to look for me. Sometimes he'd find me, sometimes not. Twice he had been transferred to a more secure home. But you cannot keep a human being locked up all the time unless you keep him locked up all the time.

Each time I saw him he looked more depressed, more angry, more nervous, more on drugs. Each time he saw me I looked worse, which made him all the more depressed and angry and nervous and drug-haunted. There was only one conclusion to be drawn from it all: I wasn't good for him. Jennifer, with her unerring feminine perception and the realism that accompanies it, had ascertained this ages ago.

My running away to pollute other sections of the city or the country would be no solution. At least now he knew where to come, and had some sort of contact with people and places he remembered with affection, a point of reference, an anchor of sorts.

I had to go, and go forever, so that he could forget me and build a life of his own, as no doubt Hagar and Sal would, not really knowing or loving me.

I made plans with Jason for him to come and spend the Christmas – yes it was upon us again – and the New Year with me. As a special treat for me, I asked him if he could bring Hagar and Sal as well, on the 31st of December, and we would celebrate the New Year together. It would also be Jason's birthday party. Afterwards, as a special New Year gift for Jennifer, Jason would go back to her – I believed I had convinced him that it would be a far better alternative than the homes – with Sal of course. He would promise to be good and stay with her; and also to try and arrange for Hagar to live with them, if at all possible.

As expected, Jason had no problem getting out of his current home just before Christmas. The pleasant surprise was the ease with which he arranged to bring over – kidnap, abduct, call it what you will – both Hagar and Sal. They genuinely believed our party had the approval of the families concerned, even if it was being held under surprise conditions. The promise of special delayed-because-stuck-in-the-chimney presents from Santa made the prospect all the more exciting and enjoyable for them.

As for Jason himself! Had my faculties not been weakened by a lack of food and shelter and heat, and an abundance of meths and barbs and self-pity, I would have realised that he must have realised that there was more to my desire for a grand New Year and birthdays party than met the ear: after all, chips and gherkins had sufficed last year – Jason had spent all his earnings by Christmas and not gone begging again until after the holiday break – when a jolly Hogmanay had been celebrated and a good time had by both the birthday boys.

The vicious enthusiasm and eager aggression with which he set out to organise everything should have alerted me that he had plans of his own, plans to out-plan me, beat me at my own game. Within half an hour of our setting foot on the platform at Southend Station he had managed to mug three old ladies, with varying degrees of success, as they came out of one of the Bingo Halls along the sea-front. He did it because he said he 'wanted to actually buy some presents with real money' for me and Sal and Hagar 'instead of just nicking them'.

From the first old lady he got two pounds, thirty-six pence, a pension book, a photograph of a young man, and a box of man-sized tissues; from the second old lady he got a black eye (left), a big bruise on the third rib on the right, and the umbrella which had caused the damage; from the third old lady he got a mouthful and a handbag containing seventy-five pounds in small change. He nearly collapsed under its weight, but soon exchanged the money for gifts in post-Christmas sales in the High Street stores. He had also managed to shit during that period, and somehow persuaded Sal to shit, and using the man-sized tissues obtained from the first old lady he deposited generous turds in the laps of all the Santas displayed in the shops he went to. My bad example, I fear. He knew that I had once placed a few choice turds in the jewellery department of Harrods, encased in a Tesco bag, then made a bomb alert call to the police.

I did not know of these escapades until they were over. I was waiting at the station with Hagar, believing Jason had simply gone to fetch Sal. Had it not been for the black eye, which had me worried and which I had questioned, he might not have told me anything about it. He did often hide things from me, though he seldom told me an outright lie. If he had done something like this a year ago he would probably have gone to great lengths to conceal it from me, or at least the mugging of the old ladies, but not this time. That was another indication that he had plans of his own which rendered him more daring and less caring than usual.

† † †

There was an abandoned house in Southend Jason knew of where we hoped to hold our get-together. Unfortunately it had been pulled down. After some worrying moments we found another, a bungalow, once inhabited by 'some weird old people who died ages ago'. Jason could be quite unkind at times. It looked dark and deserted and Jason had no trouble forcing open the back door while I amused Sal and Hagar at a nearby park.

As it turned out the place was still inhabited by the two gentlemen: Desmond Smith MA, eighty-seven, one time headmaster but retired for the past twenty-two years; and his young friend George, a mere seventy-one on his last birthday, dead the past week and still lying in the house in a deceased state.

Blissfully unaware of the above family situation and armed with candles and a paraffin heater and lots and lots of goodies – most taken off a few petrified Santa Clauses, some bought by Jason with the seventy-five pounds in small change – we invaded and occupied the 'empty' bungalow early in the evening. Mr Smith, lying in a back bedroom, made no comment upon our arrival, either because he had long ceased to care or because he was as ignorant of our presence as we were of his and that of his deceased friend.

The agreed plan was that after a ding-dong family party during which Hagar and Sal would certain fall asleep, Jason and I would stay awake until the time of our birth. Then I would take all of them to my . . . Jennifer's shop and flat, see them safely in, then start back for London.

I did not mention my final departure: that after seeing the children home I would pack my bags as it were, and with the generous help of a substance or two head towards the unknown. Nor did Jason mention what he had in mind, and well in hand as it turned out.

For my part, four pre-written letters, one addressed to Jennifer containing the relevant bits of the above information and the other three to the three children, were secreted upon my person. Before the final leg of my current journey I would post all four together. To Jennifer I also apologised for being such a colossal asshole and for the misery I had put her through, and wrote that I hoped to meet her again somewhere in some shape or form and assured her of my undying love. Finally, the letter requested that she break the news to Jason and give him this letter at some appropriate time in her best manner. She was good at timing and manners. The letters to the other children should also be handed over as and when she thought fit. It was imperative that Jason should get his as soon as possible so that he did not go looking for me anywhere. Hagar should probably read hers at the same time. Sal should be told that I had written to him, though he was too young to read or understand any of it yet.

And let it not be thought that I was making a martyr of myself, or doing it all for Jason. I was just sick to death of life. Particularly this life and the useless, worthless, impotent body that harboured it. Now that my pact with God that never was no longer was, it was time to make the most of my release and extend my frontiers beyond the bounds of mere matter.

† † †

That's how it was meant to be.

† † †

It is said that what the wicked dread most is what awaits the wicked. What I dreaded most at that particular juncture in life was life. It is also said that what the wicked do not get is what the wicked most want. What I wanted most was a long and happy life for my children.

I knew that the sins of fathers are visited upon their children. I did not realise that the wishes of fathers are granted to their children.

I should have become suspicious when, soon after we'd eaten, Jason turned off the radio cassette, specially nicked for the occasion – had more difficulty obtaining batteries than picking up the thing itself – and asked me to start retelling him the story of Jason who should have been king but never got to be, despite the fact that he was born to a king and carried out all that was required of him by all who needed him.

I had first told him the story ages ago, soon after I first saw him and when he was only about three. I used to ruffle his golden hair and say, You've got your own golden fleece, Jason, haven't you? You don't need to go running after any old ram! Ever since then he had been mad about the myths and legends of ancient India and ancient Rome and ancient Greece, just as I used to be when I was a child. His favourite stories were Greek, because of his name, just as mine used to be, for no particular reason that I can recall except that there were more pictures of naked people in the Greek mythology section than in any other. The stories weren't bad either.

I should have become more suspicious. I should have become worried when he came and practically sat in my lap – a street-hard fifteen-year-old who had just mugged three old ladies and left fresh shit in Santa's lap – in full sight of his kid sister and baby brother, made me put my arms round him, hugged me, and begged me to tell him more stories, especially about Hades and the world of the dead, and about the mean and dreaded ferryman who took you across to be set up for the grandstand fuck of justice.

I did become suspicious and I did become worried, but by that time it was too late.

Part VI

THE OTHER WHEEL AND WHEELS WITHIN
the loops of styx

Zoetrope

Acheron
the river of woe, charon; and a few surprises

I woke up with an ice-cold wind blowing bubbles in my blood. It was a strange feeling: experienced yet beyond experience, chimerical yet real; pleasant but not altogether pleasant, unpleasant but not altogether unpleasant; tingly, like having my eyeballs tickled by a feather; tangy, like having my tongue licked by a cat; tacky, like having honey spread on my nipples with a double-edged knife.

I stretched my arms and legs languorously in an effort to seduce some warmth into my body, and got the bizarre impression that I could go on stretching endlessly. That I could *see* nothing with my open eyes added to the sense of an eerie absence surrounding my presence; or more eerily, the reverse. Unnerved, I unstretched, coiled back into myself, squeezed my eyelids tightly together, then opened them wide and blinked to make sure that they were open. This time I could see, but all I could see was uninviting darkness veiled in a floating, deceptive mist. The startling fact was that I could see it, clearly see it: the darkness, the shape of it and the shapes in it; the mist, and ahead of it. What I could not see was myself.

I jumped up alarmed.

The jump was like a jump in slow motion; the alarm, the alarm of a drunk in a daze.

What am I doing here? I asked myself. Where am I?

I must have had too much of whatever substance I had taken last night, hence the not-quite-sharp responses. It was a mercy that I felt so peculiar, for otherwise I would have been in a mad panic now, rushing around like a pubescent lunatic trying to find out where I had mislaid my body, or where it went, if it did so of its own accord and not through any carelessness of mine.

I could feel it, though, feel all of it; but in the way an amputee feels the limb which has been amputated, feels the pain in it, feels the blood running through it more keenly than through any other part of the body. But I couldn't see any of it.

All I could see was this shadow.

That was it! The thought walked past my brain like an ante-dated flash, like yesterday's brainwave, like the inspiration of a retarded genius.

That shadow was all that was left of me.

At first I had thought it to be one of the shapes that I could see in the darkness, but gradually, as my eyes began to get used to the environment, I detected a certain familiarity about its contours. It was me, or at least my shadow, or my shade really, for a shadow changes its character with movement or in its relationship to light, in this case darkness. Mine did not. It was exactly the shape of my body, only in a faint, disembodied form; not quite as black as it had been, more ashen in colour and less obvious.

I must have had too much of whatever substance . . .

That was it! Another one of those flashes, brainwaves or inspirations.

But I had not. I had planned to, after . . . but I had not . . . didn't get the chance . . . I was given, though . . .

It began to come back, slowly, jerkily, like a brash tourist unfolding one of those credit-card wallets which tumble out their contents in single-framed plastic envelopes.

† † †

I remembered. Remembered it all. Remembered the New Year, the birthdays, the party. Remembered Sal, curled up like an extraterrestrial Cabbage Patch Doll flung churlishly on the floor, an unloved toy of one of God's much-loved children. Remembered Sal, a cascade of slate-dark hair falling into half-open, wondering eyes, pale green in a rough russet face. Remembered Sal, a cherub lost in a mythical world of godless beings where cherubs had long since been made redundant. Remembered Sal as he lay at my feet, dying. One little hand with red palms and brown uppers tearing into the flesh of my right calf with badly bitten nails. I could still feel the pain of it in my insubstantial leg.

Remembered Hagar, no less used and abused in her own useless little world in a useless, pointless sort of a way, just as her used and abused namesake was in the greater Biblical world for a higher, useful purpose. Remembered Hagar, long, tightly curled hair done up in a thousand little pigtails surrounding her marvellously challenging face, like an iridescent black moon in a pale golden night. Remembered Hagar, her magnetic black eyes with the angry, attracting power of celestial black holes asleep under the velvety blankets of her heavy lids, lips like flanges of an unnatural orange shut softly and gently for the very last time. Remembered Hagar as she lay dying on a sofa against which I reclined, her arm hooked carelessly around my neck, something she had stopped doing even when I was a physical presence in her home and not just an unpleasantly unreal memory.

Remembered Jason, thin waist wedged against my right hip, thin left shoulder blade pushing hard against my chest; fine gold hair tickling my nostrils, one arm going round my back, the other unnaturally limp in my lap, the fist half open, half revealing a newly minted one pound coin.

It was that coin which had alerted me to what was happening, at last. At last, but not at first.

When he had pushed a pound into my hand and asked me to hold it tight as it would bring me good luck in the New Year, I had accepted it as the manifestation of a crack – not infrequently seen – in the surface of his loudly proclaimed and oft-demonstrated hard-headed common sense, exposing a typical Jason mixture of a folklore-style superstitiousness – acknowledged with some embarrassment – with hotly denied romantic notions of the mystery and magic of life: my influence probable here, though it went deeper than that. When he gave one each to Sal and Hagar to 'clench it real hard', I thought more of the same. These are not stolen, he had said proudly, I earned them begging, kept them back, for Hogmanay.

When he had insisted on 'making' the dessert by mixing two huge packets of chocolate mousse in one huge bowl he found in the kitchen and serving it himself with cups and spoons, I was a little surprised – he hated anything to do with kitchens and cooking, and he disliked mousse – but I put it down to high spirits and excitement at all of us being together after over two years. Perhaps he was bored of the stories I had been telling and wanted to get away without offending me. Besides, Sal and Hagar were dropping off to sleep and had to have their mousse as soon as possible, he had said. Eminently sensible. I should have thought of it myself. That he was much too long in the kitchen was explained away by the fact that it was dark and everything was covered in dust and he had a job washing up. I even dismissed as no more than mildly uncharacteristic his refusal to allow anyone to go and help him. He was not often prone to bouts of fervent activity, but the past few days he had been so consistently over-enthusiastic that I thought it was just a new phase he had entered and that it would only get worse the more I tried to question it.

Then suddenly the partly visible, silent coin winking in the flickering light of forty-eight candles revealed a secret I should have guessed a long time ago.

What followed was the stuff of true comedy.

My own head was none too clear and my body not particularly well coordinated. I rushed towards the kitchen, vaguely hoping to bring some water to throw on the children's faces, to force them into consciousness, and to force them to drink to make them vomit. I remembered Pasha doing that while Auntie Neelum was losing her hold on life. If only I could find some salt to mix in the water.

I lost my way in the dark corridor, fumbled against the walls, fell against a door and into a large back room the other side of the kitchen. There was a bed in it and in the faint light filtering through a window overhung with tattered lace curtains I could make out that there was someone in the bed.

Help. Help was at hand. A short while ago I would have been shocked to realise that the house was occupied. I would have turned and run. Instead it was the greatest relief imaginable. Incoherently apologising and asking for help at the same time, I virtually attacked the bed and pulled back the covers.

A very naked very old man was lying on his back. It was only when I tried to shake him by the shoulders that I realised he was dead. Must have been dead for some time. The freezing cold in the room had prevented the body from decomposing too rapidly or too disgracefully, but he was dead all right.

The naked old man lying next to him was not.

Thank God you have come, he said, and died.

I didn't then understand what he meant but I understood now. He had thought I was the messenger of death for whom he must have been waiting since the day his friend died. He was right, too. I was a harbinger of death, and not just for him.

Surprisingly, the first thought that came to my mind concerned the pound coin. I was still clutching on to it just as hard as when Jason had so lovingly thrust it in my palm, making my fist go round it with his own hands to make sure I didn't let it slip out.

I placed the pound in the decaying palm of the long-dead man. He seemed to need it more than anyone else.

I ran out of the house blabbering for help, one of the many inelegant exits of my life.

Outside the street was as dead and naked as the old men inside, but more decayed and stronger smelling.

Somewhere in the back of my mind I had the picture of a telephone booth I had seen not too far distant. I ran for it and by sheer luck managed to find it, even though I had lost any sense of where I was.

With surprisingly steady fingers I dialled 999. *What service do you require?* Children, I said, my children, drugged, poisoned, hurry, please hurry . . . Children . . . *Address? Could you give us the address?* The address! I had no idea of the address. I thought I had read the name of the street somewhere. Now

I had no memory of it to save my life. More important, to save my children's lives.

My fingers turned to plasticine. The phone fell out of my hand. I could smell the smell of the dead man's moulding palm on my own palms as I raised my hands to my lips in an unnecessary gesture of speechlessness. The smell of yesterday's death was stronger than the smell of urine which filled the phone booth like unrequited hate in a discarded lover's heart.

A moth was bashing herself against the glass booth, desperately trying to get in where the light was. She would certainly not get out of there alive if she did. It was a difficult decision to make, but I went outside, cupped my hands round her and brought her in. That was what she wanted. Perhaps that was what she needed.

I had to run back and get the road and number of the bungalow.

This time I did forget the way. Whatever it was that Jason had provided to help us along to another and better world was strengthening its hold on my mind, though the body seemed to be functioning all right in that I could run quite well – better than when I had started out of the house. But I no longer knew which direction I wanted to take. No matter how much I ran, I couldn't find the place. In fact I could hardly see. Hilarious, it was – running in the middle of the night, half drugged out of your life, unable to distinguish between a lamp-post, the lovers leaning against it and the dog baptising it, stumbling and falling and limping, one step on the road, one on the pavement, next who knows where – really hilarious, but don't ever try it. You'll kill yourself laughing.

Suddenly I could hear bells. I heard bells, bells and bells and lots of bells, bells all over the place. The town must be going mad ringing in the New Year, I thought.

Then, without knowing how, I was back in front of the bungalow. It was roasting in fire like a wild chestnut. The snakes of flames hissing their way out of windows and doors and through the tiles of the roof and the brickwork of the walls made it look like a Christmas pudding dowsed in wine and set alight. Screaming fire engines crowded the once bare and lonely street. Suddenly I smiled: the mystery was satisfactorily solved.

Either I must have kicked over some of the forty-eight candles on my way to the kitchen, or one of the children knocked them down in a final desperate struggle against the ineluctable. Or was it the fire on the pier with Belinda caught inside? I was sure only that this time I would not just remain outside and watch. No one was going to stop me from going inside and bringing Belinda out of the flames and the fumes. Not this time.

Whoever the Joker, the joke was not going to be on me. Not this time.

Ha ha . . .

Poor Jennifer. Poor, poor Jennifer. What had I done to her!

Before I could fight the fire I had to contend with the firemen who soon metamorphosed into policemen who turned into nurses and doctors and more policemen.

Apparently I had escaped. Did that mean the Joker's joke had misfired? I couldn't be sure. Anyway, it didn't matter any more. Or did it? I couldn't be sure. But where were the children? They should have been here before me! Can't be too far off.

I must go and look for them.

The thought of seeing them again made everything seem fine and bright, despite the encompassing gloom.

But poor Jennifer. Where would she look for them? Where should I look for them?

Finding them turned out to be a little bit more difficult and a lot more complicated than I had anticipated.

† † †

There were fetters to my new-found freedom that I had not expected. On the positive side, my ordinary physical and mechanical functions were adjusting to altered circumstances more easily than I had feared. After a few stumblings, a couple of falls and some awkward steps I soon learnt how to walk and control my body movements in this insubstantial state with a reasonable degree of competence. I could also see, hear and feel much more clearly and positively.

What I saw, heard and felt is something else again.

I saw a barren landscape, dry and dreary with a rocky soil, crusty and cracked throughout its entire length and breadth with miniaturised tributaries of waterless rivers and parched streams and thirsty springs, which were crawling all over its surface like myriad pitiless wrinkles on the ageing face of death. What I had previously mistaken for mist was more like cigarette smoke, floating around the atmosphere in streaks and trickles at some places, in tufts and balls at others, and in cloud-like packs elsewhere. Some thornbushes and a few brambles lay arbitrarily scattered among passing groves of everburnt cypresses, with the odd weeping willow making a dry-eyed appearance on the horizon once in a while, coming then going with equal abruptness.

Was I dead and in the backyard of Haidou? Or alive in a post-nuclear world?

I heard the silence and wordlessness of total grief to the accompaniment of the wails and lamentations of total relief.

I felt dread, and hope: dread of damnation, hope of deliverance; dread of the unknown, hope of the unknowable; dread of not seeing my children, hope of meeting Belinda.

The dread began gradually to take over as vapours of some pungently poisonous fumes, strong enough to send shivers of life through the dead, and vespertinal clouds of cigarette smoke started drifting in from all sides in sinister slow motion, and congregating round me in ramping layers of reeking darkness that rendered the kingdom of the great unseen truly unseeable. But only for a moment. No matter how dark it got, after a while you could see through it; only the shapes and images took on a more grotesque and distorted appearance than before.

The onslaught of this thick yet penetrable blackness was heralded by the deafening sound of plenary silence. All wailing and lamentation ceased with the finality of death by guillotine.

In the stillness and the gloom that followed, the vapourish

masses of clouds and fumes began to take on a more distinct shape and form: the human shape and form.

I was part of an odoriferous, gaseous multitude of once-beings all mutely heading towards the river of woe to keep our fated tryst with the ferryman.

A thought occurred to me: Jason, Hagar and Sal might well be here among the miserable-looking but indifferent throng. I was surprised at the lack of any positive response on my part to that thought. Shouldn't I be trying to locate them? After all, that was what I had set out to do. To look for them.

Them. The pronoun was somehow easier to deal with than the nouns.

But no. I must not allow that to happen. I could not allow that to happen. I would not allow that to happen. The children, my children, Jason, and Hagar and Sal, were somewhere here. Here, here because of me and my insane plans and my *manhoos* being. And I was going to find them: find Jason and Hagar and Sal.

I might be dead, but there was life in me yet. I could feel its vibrant force somewhere deep inside me, however debilitated and violated. The very fact that I was thinking about this meant that I could do it; for that which is not possible in action is not possible in thought, and that which is not possible in reality is not possible in imagination.

I made an effort of will, albeit an exiguous one, and projected myself forward, hoping to pull my shadowy limbs behind me. The task appeared difficult, if not impossible: the dead encumbrances felt so damnably ponderous, despite their evanescent quality.

I was surprised. The positive side of the negative aspect of life seemed to be that a little determination went a long way, like the dynamics of motion in a vacuum. I found myself hurtling through the masses of massless bodies with a speed and vigour which made even the deadest head turn and look at me with a hint of wonder dawning in dull eyes, like a faint glow of unprecedented sunlight in the grim darkness of fathomless caves. At that rate I would bypass all without being able to take a good look at any, or ask any questions. I tried to slow down and fell to a dead halt like a ton of rotting meat. Mechanical adjustments were not going to be that easy after all.

I tried again: an erratic and jerky start this time, but more controlled, safer and with a clearer vision of those ahead and round and behind me. It was like learning to drive all over again, only the vehicle was your own body, or what was left of it.

I learnt, not perfectly, but enough to be able to navigate with a reasonable control of direction and speed. The best part was that if you bumped into anyone or anything there were no complaints, no damage to person or bodywork, no foul exchanges of language or polite exchanges of address. More often than not you passed right through whatever or whoever you hit, and no bother.

I walked forward and then back again, left, then right, and left again. There was no sign of the children, not my children, though children there were, and coming in at the rate of over a hundred thousand ephemerally. Almost all were black, like Hagar, but some were mulatto like Sal; some were walking, some crawling on all fours, some wriggling on their bellies. Many just born to death or very weak were being kicked about by older feet. None among the ones I could see was Hagar, or Sal; nor among the few blond, blue-eyed ones could I see Jason.

I tried asking questions, but even after I had overcome problems of voice projection and enunciation not dissimilar to those of body projection and movement, I couldn't elicit any response from anyone, whether I spoke in English, or in some of the Eastern languages I knew, or uttered a few telling phrases in French or German or Spanish. No response at all, not even to vigorous sign-making, except the occasional look of surprise which was pleasing to behold and somehow quite rewarding, but not particularly helpful in my quest.

Quite suddenly I came to a halt. I realised I could not go any further. I was upon the bank of Acheron, at the ferry boarding point.

This was an unexpected piece of luck. It would have been very difficult to find my children in that slew of millions.

Everyone would have to pass through here, making my task much simpler.

Behind me were masses of mankind in a simulation of perpetual motion, like countless collections of cloudy, thundery skies breaking apart under their own weight, shredded to peculiarly fluffy yet recognisable shapes by double-edged streaks of lightning, tumbling and rolling down in a never-ending cavalcade, weird and funereal participants in a weird and funereal carnival. Around me was blinding smoke and scorching steam, emanating from poisonous caves. In front of me the viscid waters of the black river, the liquidised heart of night itself, tenebrously flowing out of the caliginous depths of the universe and back again, the melancholic sploshing of its woeful waves rhythmically enhancing the necrotic silence that permeated the atmosphere.

Upon the waves heaved this crazy coracle: flimsy black sails made from the skins of those who arrived penniless and with little or no flesh on their bodies, thus rendering the process of flaying easier and less messy; wicker frame covered with the rough bark of dead poplars and dying willows held together by uneven stitches sewn with the uprooted hair of some of its unfortunate passengers, or glued with their marrow, and reinforced in places with the bones of those who paid in currency other than American, European or Japanese.

Upon the vessel, extended pole in one hand, the other stretched out to extract money from distorted mouths, stood the dreaded ferryman himself. Despite the bent back and the wrinkled imprint of the map of the underworld on his ancient features, there was a raging fire in his bulging eyes, an eager, childlike enthusiasm in the way he cocked his head from side to side to survey the swathes of ashen-bodied mortals patiently awaiting their fate, and a staggering reserve of strength in his sinewy arms – evident both in their handling of the boat, and in the repetitive movements needed to extricate the coins from gaping mouths. I began to understand how 'a god's senility' could be 'awful in its raw greenness'.

The greying shades moved forward, one by one, placed their fee in their mouths if it was not already there, and waited dismally for it to be wrenched out, sometimes violently, always unceremoniously, without so much as a please or a thank you.

A bony jab in the elbow. Why did you do that to me, young man? droned a voice, whether in rage or despair I couldn't be sure as it sounded like a record being played at a lower than intended speed. I wanted to remain with Des, now I do not know where he is. When he raised a putrefied palm to place his fee in his mouth I recognised the dead man in the bungalow.

As I watched him board I was struck by the capaciousness of that limited craft, no larger than an ordinary police patrol boat. In the short time that I had been there enough bodies had been allowed on to sink the *Titanic* by sheer weight of numbers. Another thing which I found extremely odd was that everyone seemed to have their coin ready in their mouths – something which I had not at all expected – yet not all were permitted entry. The rest were left wringing their hands motionlessly and weeping waterless tears and screaming soundless screams and invoking pitiless gods.

Why were the rejects being rejected? Was it all to do with the nature of the currency?

But no. A surprisingly friendly soul enlightened me, in some detail.

Modern technology had arrived in Hades. In my haste I must somehow have missed the Immigration Section, often referred to as Checkpoint Abe, where the credentials of all arrivals were electronically scrutinised and special identity discs issued to each, depending on their financial situation and status during their lives. It was these discs, somewhat like carwash tokens, which the arrivals orally presented to the ferryman. Sensible, once you think about it. Now that the custom of obolus under the tongue had vanished along with the obolus, and the population of the world multiplied many times over, alternative methods had to be adopted to meet the demands and the challenges of changing times. However, to humour the timeless tradition of the gods, those who carried the basic coin of their currency were accepted. They were issued standard dark brown tokens, which entitled them to board the boat but did not guarantee a trouble-free passage. Once across they were sent directly to Tartarus. Then came those who were poor but solvent at the time of death. They too were given brown tokens, but of various lighter shades, and mainly bundled away to Tartarus, though some were allocated the Fields of Asphodel, depending on the shade of their brown. Then came green, gold and diamond tokens with extra jewel points as and when necessary. Special places and palaces in Elysium were prepared for the holders of these, often with aid and advice from their earthly governments. Their worldly assets were reflected in the presence of many branches of various Plutonian banks across the Kingdom of Hades. This efficiently streamlined system saved manpower and costs by obviating the necessity of a prolonged formal trial for all arrivals; though in exceptional cases the tradition was still followed; and in all cases a nominal verdict was issued before travellers were taken to the Crossroads of Truth for the final leg of their journey in the Underworld.

Xenophanes would have been smugly amused to see this new dimension to his assertion that Greek gods taught humans nothing but 'theft, adultery and mutual deceit', having first learnt it from humans, being created by them in their own image: immortal toads by mortal toads. The post-modern humans had invested their gods with computer technology. As a man of his times who so radically disowned not only the cult of the body, but the soul (unmetempsychosised) of his times, he and I would have got on well together, despite my name, and in spite of the fact that I happened to hold a Pythagorean view of the abovementioned uncreated imperishable, and agreed with his pre-Socratic contemporaries Buddha and Zarathustra regarding the circles and wheels of life, and such essentials as vegetarianism. An event and a life five hundred years on were to irresistibly challenge the credibility of Hellenic gods, though it left the Indian deities intact if not unsullied. Wonder what the man from Colophon would have made of the man from Nazareth, and his God of love? Wonder what he would have made of the Judaic God: partisan, punitive and prime racist?

Those with black tokens were turned away and cast out to wander the barren wastes of limbo for one great year – a hundred earth years – before their case could even be reconsidered; unless they penetrated to the other side through one of the many tortuous and treacherous caves that wound their way beneath the waters of Acheron. These penniless ones could of course have been eliminated and exiled at Checkpoint Abe, but this was one decision, and indeed pleasure, which the ancient immortal wanted to reserve solely for himself.

However, since electronic surveillance had come to the Underworld with a vengeance, how come I had managed to escape it without even trying, and what would the ancient ferryman have to say about it?

There was only one way to find out.

Summoning up courage from I know not where I approached the son of Nyx with the intention of asking if he had seen my children, and to briefly describe them. However, I was prevented from doing so for the moment I opened my mouth to speak he put his hand in it.

The look of unaccustomed outrage that spread across his face at discovering nothing inside my wet, open orifice was replaced by a different, cagey sort of a look, a look almost of recognition and resignation as soon as his affronted eyes fell upon the face that sheltered the wet, open orifice.

You! Go. Go away. He spoke in a voice that was tremulous and whining like an old man's, deep and strong like a young man's. I do not want you here. You have neither the Sword of Herakles nor the Lyre of Orpheus. There is nothing you can make me do. Nothing. I hate chains. Just go. I hate chains.

I would have been surprised to hear him speak at all, and this tirade hit me like a hailstorm in the Sahara. But I could not let it rest at that. I had to know more. I opened my mouth once again, keeping well out of his arm's length this time, and made another attempt to speak. He anticipated me and shouted me down: Go! Just go. I know who you seek, you will not find them here. They have gone. You go too. Then, changing his tone and in a much gentler voice, he muttered, Turn left, so softly that had the night not been saturated with silence I might not have heard him.

At least I knew that Jason and the children were here somewhere. I also understood a little about why I had managed to get so far without being detected. For some strange reason, I had been allowed to. In some strange way, I was expected.

I turned left.

I found myself confronting the ferryman's sisters busy weaving the days of mankind. Old as the night of chaos is long, virgins as in the womb, ugly as Helen was beautiful, mouths such that each could swallow all three heads of Cerberus in one gulp, hard eyes in spongy faces as bullets in the hearts of just-dead children.

Baring corrugated black teeth and cackling mirthlessly, the Moirae beckoned to me. Clotho grasped the spindle, Lachesis wound the thread round it, and Atropos rushed gleefully with her fatal scissors to snip it away.

It would not cut.

A look of incredulous horror spread across their faces, their bodies began to shiver and tremble and their mouths salivated as they howled like wounded wolves, together but not in unison. It was not a salubrious experience, I can tell you that. My heart would have stopped beating for sure had it not already stopped beating. Instead it started beating again.

You have seven revolutions of the beating star, they screamed amid their howls, together but not in unison, and disintegrated before my eyes. What star? I had not seen any star in this gloom-ridden wilderness.

I looked up, just in case. Nothing. Then my eye caught a brightness to the left of me, and beyond! There, at the far end of the 'horizon' where the convex bottom of the earth met the concave floor of the Underworld, was a star. It was large as an apple, and throbbing, not just twinkling, but actually throbbing, even as my heart was. As I stared at it in amazement it started moving, slowly but perceptibly, not upwards towards the zenith but along the circumference of what passed as the sky down here, leaving a faint but clearly visible trace of light particles behind it, like the wake of a jet only more erratic.

Just then I heard a welcome flutter of wings and a pigeon came and sat on my left shoulder. It was a messenger pigeon and it had a message tied round its left leg.

I removed the note. It read:

To get what you want from this world, you have first to go back to the other world.

Cross the nine loops of the Styx that circle the outside of this world by crossing the nine realms that circle the inside of this world.

First and last you have to tame the monstrous Behemoth with two heads, one where its tail ought to be, and learn to lead it by the head on the shoulders. Nothing can be achieved if it leads you, this way and then the opposite way. Once you have taken the first step to master it, you will be over the weeping waters of the Acheron and the first step of your journey is done.

Then overcome the seven deadly beasts, one by one, in order to jump the next seven hurdles: to silence the lamentations of Cocytus, to quell the fires of Phlegethon, to escape the Fields of Asphodel, to cross over Aornis of no birds, to resist temptation at the palace of Hades, to survive the torments of Tartarus, and to remember your purpose and your life through Lethe's forgetfulness.

For the ninth and final feat in Elysium, you must get into but not be guiled by the Queen of Abomination's palace, nor by those who walk in it, and do not depart through the same pillars by which you entered, even if they are the same. You will then reach the Crossroads of Truth where you must take the wrong road. Once you have done that you will have crossed the last loop of the Styx.

Remember, you gain your children by losing them. Remember, other people have children too!

Back on earth you will obtain your freedom through incarceration but escape will bind you. Your blood will be taken as a sacrifice and your soul cleansed, but your body will lie at the altar of inequity for seven months before burial. Then, rising in death nine days after burial, you will be ready for the last beginning.

And never forget; that which can be imagined can be accomplished; that which can be thought, realised; that which can be spoken, achieved. As mist upon waters is reality to dreams.

It is easier than it seems, but it seems easier than it is.

THUS SPEAKS ATHENA

PS Seek the hunter who protects, but beware the triple-faced, and avoid the changing shapes and restless eyes of those who are not what they are!

PSS No golden bough, no ne-row, but a flaming asphodel thy talisman be.

Just as I finished reading an owl hooted in the distance and the pigeon flew away, winged hat at a jaunty angle, caduceus held high, winged sandals glinting noctilucently.

Cyrus, I heard a voice call out, O Cyrus, my Cyrus. Come to me, Cyrus. Cyrus, come to me. Cyrus, Cyrus, Cyrus Cyrus, Cyrus Cyrus . . .

It was Father's voice!

My beating heart missed a beat or two and nearly stopped again before getting back to its beat. My star skidded, wavered, then got back on course. Even across the sea of time, even beyond the boundaries of life and the confusions of death, I could never forget that voice.

Father, Father, I cried.

Cyrus, Cyrus, he cried, come to me. He stretched his arms out. Come to me, press your living heart against my long-dead heart. Come to me, come. Oh how my restless eyes have waited for this moment.

Just as I made a dash towards his frail, familiar form leaning against a charred and drooping willow, I suddenly remembered Athena's warning . . . *avoid the changing shapes and restless eyes of those who are not what they are* . . .

Why have you stopped? There was incalculable pain in his eyes. I have wandered this bleak wilderness for years, centuries, I have no track of time, hoping, waiting, for you. Just for you.

He must have read the doubt in my eyes. Don't, Son, don't. Not you . . . Do not desert me like all the others. Not you, Cyrus. Cyrus, my Cyrus . . .

I was about to melt and rush forward when he said: You should know how I feel, you should know what it is like to lose your children . . . He stopped, as one too tired and helpless to continue.

Or was it because he, whoever he was, realised he had made a mistake. How would my father know about my children?

Why don't *you* come to me, Fa . . .? I couldn't say Father, even though I was dying to say it.

I can't. I am not permitted to. You will come to great harm if I move. You will have to come to me. Come to me, Cyrus. Please, Cyrus, don't leave me now, oh Cyrus, Cyrus, my Cyrus . . .

I looked askance at the horizon. My star was nearly a quarter along its first round. I had nine realms to cross in just seven revolutions. Time was flying faster than I had feared. I could not afford to waste any more of it just wondering. I had to do something, and quick.

To hell with it. If I was damned I was damned. I couldn't see my father suffering like that. Even if he was an impostor, he was still my father! I know that doesn't make sense, but that was how I felt.

I ran up to him quite madly and put my arms round him calling, Father, Father, my dear, dear father.

My arms went round the willow. There was no sign of Father.

At my feet lay a flaming asphodel, flowing with a light that made even the darkness round it shine out.

I picked it up wonderingly by its long luminous stem and a heady aroma sent my senses reeling.

You have won the first battle over the monstrous Behemoth known to man as Reason, said a different but somewhat familiar voice, the monster with a head at either end which leads you one way first and the opposite way next, but never the right way, unless pre-determined and pre-ordained. You chose your own path, you are now ready to be taken across Acheron.

As he spoke he lifted me up in powerful, hairy arms and started walking upon the woeful waters as only the Boeotian Giant could.

If only Prof was here now.

Cocytus
the river of lamentations

No sooner had he set foot on something firmer than water and before I could jump off, Orion flung me down upon the lumpy ground with quite unnecessary force. I don't think he really liked me. All along I had been feeling these hostile vibes reaching out of his body into mine. Add that to the embarrassment of being carried like a babe-in-arms by a strange giant, and the slow and careful walk over the not inconsiderable length of the doleful river, avoiding the many swirls and eddies capable of sucking in a powerful boat, and you can imagine how uncomfortable I had been feeling throughout. I was planning to leap out at the first opportunity but as you know he denied me that pleasure. Still, I could not have made it without him. I said thank you, at first like a perfect English person, politely and without meaning it and reserving the right to hold him in contempt for not being like me, but then decided he deserved better than that and thanked him like a human being.

I only did it for Artemis, he said. If Hecate finds out she'll die laughing, were she capable of death.

He was gone.

Such rudeness. For one piqued moment I wished I hadn't thanked him like a human being. That moment prevented me from reading more into his words than met the ear, which, had I done so, would have saved me from making a dangerous and even potentially lethal decision later on.

The first thing I did was to look up at the throbbing star. It was still only about a quarter of the way through its first cycle. That was heartening. I was making good time. But there was also a warning in it somewhere. Clearly my intellectual perception of the passage of time did not relate to the time-span of the star. When I had experienced only a brief passage of time, a large chunk of the star's course had been taken up; now that I had felt a long period of time upon the water, the star appeared not to have moved at all. I would have to be very careful to see how it was progressing lest I ruin it all by depending on my supposedly in-built clock.

I looked around me. I could see much better here than I had on the other side. On the other hand there was nothing to see: just an expanse of turned-over and hardened sod. Even the river behind me had disappeared. It was the river I had to find. The other one, the wailing river, Cocytus.

But which way to head? Everything was uniformly what it was. There were no signs, no landmarks, no cypresses, no willows, no brambles, no ghosts of the dead; no indicators of any sort, not even illusive or misleading ones; nothing. No mist nor clouds nor smoke nor steam. No sound nor smell. Nothing. Nothing but hardened, turned-over sod, like an immense all-encompassing field, ploughed and then deserted, suddenly and permanently for reasons too awful to be told.

I looked up to my star for a direction and found it. It had been trying to tell me for some time. As far as I could be sure, it was still more or less where it was.

I started walking towards it; it nodded approvingly.

If only Father would be there to help me again. If only Father would be there. I had so much to say to him, so much to tell him, so much to ask.

After what appeared to be an interminable walk in that greyish brown desert of sameness I thought I could hear some oddly upsetting yet hypnotically evocative music: haunting and melodic, but not pleasing; entirely vocal by the sound of it, though I wouldn't have ruled out some sort of instrumentation.

Despite its disturbing nature it was a very welcome development, for not only was my strength beginning to wane and my nerves at the end of their tether, but my star had started its cycle and was on its throbbing way round the horizon, and if I had tried to follow it further I would only have turned round on myself. I was afraid that that would have completed my disorientation and rendered me utterly helpless. Now I could follow the music.

It was only after I had walked some more that I could discern the nature of the music that reached out to me from the beyond of that overturned but neglected ocean of earth, petrified in the midst of its turbulence. I should have been reassured. After all, what I had to do at that stage was to cross the wailing river. To cross it I had to reach it. What better proof that I was closing in on it than to hear the music of weeping and wailing and mourning and lamentations? But it frightened me more than it comforted me.

Within earth seconds I was overwhelmed by it. It was all round me. There was no escape from it. No need to worry about the direction any more. It was there no matter which way I turned.

It was the music of women wailing and the music of children wailing. The music of young men wailing and the music of old men wailing. The music of banshees wailing, presaging death. The music of the living wailing, wailing for those about to die and wailing for those just dead and wailing for those long dead. The music of the long-dead wailing, wailing for the life gone. The music of the just-dead wailing, wailing for those that wailed for them. The music of the about-to-die wailing, wailing for themselves. Music of the newborn wailing, wailing for the life to come. Music of wailing spirits entering the world of lost spirits and music of lost spirits wailing for the old spirits dying. The music of souls wailing for their bodies and the music of bodies wailing for their souls and the music of the flesh wailing for its pleasures and the music of pleasures wailing for their flesh.

Each wail was separate and clearly distinguishable from the rest, and yet there was a harmony in all the wailing that was the harmony of true music, the music that separated the dead from the living, the fulfilled from the unfulfilled, the blessed from the unblessed.

It was the music of the wailing waters, and the music of those that inhabited its wailing shores.

It was the music that floated upon the air, swam in the ears and sank into the heart with the power and the passion that was in the very being of one and all of the mourners. You felt the pain and the loss of each of the mourners individually and of all of the mourners collectively as if you knew each and all of them personally and with an intensity and an intimacy that was both immediate and timeless.

It was the music of insufferable and unendurable death and the music of insufferable and unendurable life and the music of insufferable and unendurable tragedy and it was insufferable and unendurable music.

I could not bear it any longer and began to wail with it myself.

I wailed and I wailed and I wailed until I alone was wailing and everyone else stopped wailing to listen to the music of my wailing.

I wailed for Aunt Verna and I wailed for Uncle Dano.

It was too painful to wail for anybody else.

So I wailed for Aunt Verna and Uncle Dano.

Yet my wailing was elegiac and musical and potent enough to mesmerise all the other wailers to silence. Perhaps, unknown to myself, I wailed for Belinda. Perhaps, unknown to myself, I wailed for Mother. Perhaps, unknown to myself, I wailed for mankind, for creation.

Soon a crowd began to gather round me, a crowd large as a city.

At first it was a crowd stunned out of its wailing, a silent crowd, a listening crowd. Then gradually it began to murmur, then talk, shout and scream with an ever-increasing volubility and obstreperousness, as if the volume of a television programme presenting a clamorous crowd scene was being slowly turned up, and up and up, on sets displayed all around you. Unlike the wailing, the talking, shouting and screaming was cacophonous and disharmonious – brazen, many-tongued and incoherent as Babel, tower and all, fallen on hard times and to the ground with its divinely divided populace trying desperately to make itself heard if not understood by shouting louder and louder, and then hailing and cheering and serenading. Hailing and cheering and serenading? Some of the crowd actually appeared to be hailing and cheering and serenading! Now why would they hail and cheer and serenade amid all that funereal agitation and mournful confusion? Only a short while ago they had been wailing.

Out of that bedlam some voices began to come through clearer and clearer.

It's him, it's him, cried a few, he's here, the king is here, here at last.

Can't be, shouted others, not with that black face.

Does he not come wailing? The wailing that ends all wailing.

Not in a torn red top and dirty black jeans, holding a flower, the asphodel of ashes. Never.

Look how it shines! Have you ever seen a flower of the ashes that burns so?

Where is the white limousine?

The bodyguards? The kalashnikovs?

Through the Eastern Gate he comes, as ordained, through the Eastern Gate!

And the star, he brings the star with him, as prophesied. The star, it follows him. Look. Look, the star, there it shines, large and brilliant, like the throbbing heart of light itself.

Star! What star? We see no star.

Your eyes are blinded, your ears are sealed, your hearts hardened.

Who by? And why?

In a mad panic I pushed some of the people in my path to one side and attempted to escape. Unsuccessfully. One of them clutched my flapping shirt and shouted, I can see, I can see, I can see! I was blind but now can see. Another fell prostrate upon the ground, held my feet and said, I am whole, I am whole! I was eaten by leprosy but now I am whole! I am saved, he touched me and I am saved, sang another in a rapturous voice as he danced round me.

I was surrounded, hoisted upon shoulders, garlanded and crowned by some, while a few threw stones and rotten tomatoes and salmonella-infected eggs and shouted, Down with the impostor! Down, down, down! The majority just looked on and offered conflicting opinions and suggestions and views: either in subdued but vicious tones, or vociferously and uncompromisingly.

I thanked my followers, unclimbed from their shoulders and started walking through the crowd, telling them all about computers and ET and Dame Edna and see-through swimwear, which greatly pleased some and infuriated the few more and more. Soon their Down, down, down! turned to Kill kill kill! and I was spirited away by believers to an underground cave where we were safe.

There I stayed for many a day, perhaps many a month, telling them more about the kingdom of earth and how it would come down one day into the Underworld and solve all their problems, even in their own death time. I did not believe in this myself, what's more I didn't want it to be true, for their sakes. But that was what they wanted to hear, having died a long long time ago and not knowing at all what was going on in the upperworld in these post-post–modern times but having a very rosy picture of it indeed. Seeing their faces light up with joy was worth all the lies I could think up. But I also told them things they did not always like to hear, but in which I believed: such as brushing their teeth three times a day and dancing to Jane Fonda tapes. Somehow, what they did not like to hear strengthened their belief in me regarding what they liked to hear, for if I was a fraud I would have either told them only what they liked to hear or only what they did not liked to hear, as others before me had done; or mixed them the wrong way round, strong on the good life, weak on the good life, as others after me were to do.

For my own part, however, I was beginning to lose all hope of ever getting out of there or being able to save any children of the world, least of all my own. In that dark cave lit by thin wavering candles and the glow from my asphodel I could but barely see its walls covered in strange but beautiful paintings and carvings that told the story of mankind 'upstairs' and its struggle against gods and odds; there was no chance of being able to look up at the sky and see where my star was. Had I not known that its movements did not necessarily reflect time as I experienced it, I would have long since been convinced that its seven revolutions were over. Even now I feared that to be the case, though a lingering hope persisted through it all.

Outside the cave angry mobs of the few roamed in packs and waited for me with blood in their eyes, determined to expose me as an impostor and hang me from the tallest tree – within the Eastern Gate the terrain was quite fertile and lakes of green waters irrigated olive groves and palm trees and people thrived on dates and milk from camels and goats. At least some people did, those who had olive groves and date palms and goats and camels. Although they knew I was inside the cave, they were frightened to take me from there for fear that evil might come to them and theirs so they waited for me outside with blood in their eyes.

Some who heard of me liked what they heard and came down to join us and our numbers grew. This angered the few who did not, and also the many who did not care.

One day, even as I told my followers stories to enrich their souls and enlighten their minds, they told me a story: a story of three children and how they came to them but were taken by force to the Palace of Hades for a special trial. One, the oldest, was a boy resisting manhood or a man lost in a child, like the god of light, with hair as the yellow sun of happiness and eyes as the blue sky of eternal day; the next was a true daughter of the night herself, black as the night and beauteous as the night and shielding and comforting as the night; and the third, the youngest, an infant boy, no more, was the assignation of night and of day, with the promise and magic that only the hope of dawn and the mystery of dusk can bring. I knew then that the time had come to make a move and meet my fate, whatever it was.

I told my friends and they were sad.

You have helped our hearts in their sorrow and helped our bodies in their affliction, and now you want to leave us, they cried. We believed you would live with us forever, and that we and all who follow us would remain under the canopy of your grace.

It is not me that has healed your bodies nor comforted your

hearts, but the joy in your blood and the love in your flesh that has brought this about. The joy of seeing me and believing I was who you thought I was, and the love that you gave me for holding your hand and telling you stories – that has done the good you credit me with. You have worked your own miracles.

But you are the king, they said. You said it, I said. You are come to bring the kingdom of earth in Hades, they said. You said it, I said, but let me go now and I will come back and never leave you again. And they were happy to hear that and I was happy that something I said could make them happy, so I said it again. Yes, let me go now, and I will come back and be with you forever more. But how will you go? they cried. The few who reject you, along with the many who do not care, wait outside to shed your blood and sacrifice your flesh to placate their private god who loves no one but them and their progeny, and promises a terrible vengeance upon those that deny him or set another god in his place or even alongside him.

One of you go first and tell them that I shall be coming out of the cave as the last bat returns. That way they will take me in peace as I depart instead of attacking me with violence as I emerge. After that, let the fates decide.

They wept bitterly at this, but agreed. However, before one of them could go out and tell the few, someone else informed them of my whereabouts and my intentions, and they sent a monstrous beast with many claws and as many jaws and twice as many eyes and teeth that were saws of steel to guard the entrance of the cave so as to devour me as soon as I stepped out. When I was swallowed they could make easy meat of all the others, for by now they hated all of them, even though many among them had been friends and neighbours and brothers and sisters once.

I knelt and prayed to Father to save me yet again as he had done before, if at all possible, and to spare me the agony of being devoured alive by that ferocious beast with many claws and as many jaws and twice as many eyes and teeth that were saws of steel; and if not, to give me the courage to accept his decision and meet his will. And behold! A woman entered the cave from I know not where with a clap of thunder and a flash of lightning and handed me a sword the like of which I had never seen before nor seen again since.

One swing of this sword and the many heads of the monster will be as none, said the woman, who had the face of someone I knew well but could not remember. And once you have taken the monster the rest will be easy meat for you and yours.

As my fist wound round the handle of the sword I could feel its force sweep through me like the strength of seven and seventy bulls and the might of nine and three gods.

I walked out of the cave, flaming asphodel in one hand, the familiar-faced woman's sword in the other, and confronted the monster and the blood-hungry multitude behind the monster.

No sooner did our eyes meet, the many eyes of the monster and the many eyes of the multitude and my own two eyes, than I could see that their hate was great enough to take me and my friends and to turn us into meat before the intake of one breath could have time to breathe itself out. But no sooner did the many eyes of the monster and the many eyes of the multitude rest upon the sword in my hand than they turned into eyes of fear itself, and I could tell that the potency of the sword was great enough to take the monster and the multitude and make meat out of them before the intake of one breath could have time to breathe itself out. But as the heady feel of strength indestructible and force immortal rampaged through my soul a great wonder and a greater pity took hold of my heart. If it was to be my life and the life of mine against their lives and the life of their monster, or against any life, I could not but offer my own to save theirs. But what of my friends? Had I the right to offer their lives? I knelt before the monster and placed the sword on the floor between us and said: It is me you seek. Spare my friends and take my life, for I have not the courage to take yours nor that of any one else. I was born a coward, I died a coward, and a coward I shall remain.

At these words the woman with the familiar face – I could tell it was her even though she had on a different face now, also familiar – swooped down upon me and took the sword off the floor and screamed: You have insulted and humiliated me before mine enemies, you did not deserve the gift I offered, now suffer the shame and the pain you surely deserve! So be it, said I, and bowed my head and shut my eyes and awaited the end, hoping it would be short and merciful. If such be thy will, O Lord, let thine and not my will be done, I prayed.

Next thing I knew I was at the bank of the wailing river upon which was built a bridge of sighs, the sighs of those in sorrow at my departure. As I walked upon the bridge to cross the Cocytus I heard the voice I had heard before by the bank of Acheron say: Congratulations, you have overcome the deadliest of deadly beasts and its name was Power. Be prepared now to meet the second deadly beast as you enter the domain of Phlegethon's fire and the third loop of the Styx.

I looked up at my star. It had almost completed its second cycle. Not too bad, but not too good either. Two out of seven revolutions gone with two out of nine loops crossed. I must try to be very quick through the next loop. Considering it was fire, it would be foolish to linger anyway.

Phlegethon
the river of fire

Walking across the Cocytus turned out to be hazardous. The bridge of sighs was so frail, so narrow and so insubstantial that each step had to be a carefully planned strategy. One wrong move and I could find myself tumbling over and into the surging and abating waves and their accompanying chorus of rising and falling lamentations in the turbulent waters below. It is a wonder I was not drowned in sound alone. Half way through the asphodel fell out of my hand in front of my feet and if I had been a trifle careless or a tinge unlucky its next fall would have been into the mist of tears that, issuing from the river, had begun to spread all around me, thicker than mountain fog. I have little doubt that I would not have long survived the loss of my talisman.

However, fortune favoured me. Retrieving my asphodel I continued my walk in an arc above the waters, so high at one point as to be almost touching the bottom of the earth above – an optical illusion of course, but unsettling nevertheless – until I was safely over and across.

The moment my feet touched the soil on the other side of the bank, the river behind me disappeared leaving me in the middle of this breathtakingly beautiful city. Not in my wildest dreams could I have imagined splendour like this in the world of lost souls and this side of the ever-raging flames of the river of fire. Or anywhere else for that matter.

Could I have stumbled into the Isle of the Blessed by a stroke of unaccountably good luck? Through a misjudgement on the part of the gods or an act of mercy by mortals?

Through a computer error? And if I had, would that mean I had covered my course as ordained – except for the final segment – or would I have to go back and start all over again? In which case it would not be unaccountably good luck but unaccountably ill winds which had driven me there.

A sudden blast of heat and a lusty tongue of fire not far from where I stood assured me that I was in the right place.

As I looked around me with wonder and admiration I began to notice something odd and unreal about the place. First of all the architecture was uneven to say the least. On the one extreme were buildings that rigidly and faithfully conformed to this or that period or school, on the other were styles defying accepted forms of symmetry and design and violating all known laws of construction and gravity. Some such structures – houses, places of worship, offices – though hauntingly beautiful, could just not have stayed upright on earth above. The angles of the walls, the flimsiness of the material, the lack of any base or foundation and other such obvious flaws or peculiarities, call them what you will, would have caused them to collapse immediately, even if you had somehow managed to stand them up once.

Facing me was a prime example: walls that were liquid and flowing lyrically upwards out of some mysterious and obscure source, with a roof of flowers. As I came closer to these walls I could hear and feel strains of music float out and fill my heart like wine a bottomless pitcher. The music itself changed from elegiac to allegro, from rousing to soothing, without warning yet without discomfiting the senses. As I moved towards another wall I realised that it was made up of written words, which upon drawing nearer appeared to be no more than strangely placed lines forming an apparently random pattern on wallpaper. Paintings and statues from the classical and the figurative to the modern and the abstract were on display inside the buildings and in the streets, and within gardens: some stylised and formal, some of a freer and wilder character. There was a peculiarly mutable quality about the works of art and sculpture which made them appear to shift place and change shape, form and content as and when without the why and wherefore.

Most curious of all were the people inhabiting this curious city. They walked past you and around you not only without speaking to you or replying if spoken to, but without giving any indication that they were in any way aware of your presence. Once or twice I met the eyes of one or two, and I felt that they had something to say to me; but then the moment was gone, and that was that. All attempts to communicate or to get any answers as to where I was, where *they* were, drew a complete blank. When I touched one reasonable-looking man in the hope of thus attracting his attention he turned out to be entirely insubstantial and floated out of my grasp as if he were air when I tried to hold on to him. I suppose in this world of ghosts this should not have come as too much of a surprise, but on the other side of Cocytus I had not only been able to converse, but freely touch and feel the people. Here, in many cases I could see only one view of a person, no matter which way I turned to look at him or her. To make matters worse, they appeared and disappeared with bewildering suddenness, often after some silently spoken exchanges among themselves. I say silently spoken for I could not hear anything, but they seemed to converse.

But then something very ordinary happened, so ordinary that its very ordinariness made it most extraordinary in that extraordinary world.

In front of me a window opened and the head of a politely smiling girl appeared under a notice saying INFORMATION ENQUIRIES. And what can I do for you, Sir? she said in the usual cold voice of politely smiling girls in information booths.

Oh thank God, I said, signs of life at last! Could you please tell me . . .

Don't believe a word of what they tell you, said another girl coming out of a wall to the left of me, voice quivering with anger and indignation. Lies, all lies. Lies lies lies. So you think this is a beautiful city? She suddenly turned round on me. A wonderful magical beautiful city? Don't you? You don't have to say it, I can tell by your face you do. But you should see what lies behind it, the ugliness, the shabbiness,

497

the injustice. You should see what lies buried beneath it, the hopes the aspirations, the *lives* . . .

All this while the girl behind the window kept smiling politely and made no attempt to interrupt the speaking girl. However, the moment the speaking girl paused, apparently too overcome by emotion to continue, the politely smiling girl pressed a key on the computer beside her, a key with the command LIQUIDISE writ large upon it.

I glanced at it in disbelief and horror before lunging forward, trying at once to put one protective arm round the girl beside me and to make a remonstrative gesture with the other to the girl in the window. You can't do that, you, you . . . I shouted.

The polite smile disappeared from the girl's mouth. She looked frightened, and recoiled with an uncomprehending gaze in her eyes, but only for a second. The polite smile returned and a look of understanding settled upon the features. Do not be alarmed, Sir, no harm will come to . . . to your friend. This is an old computer, very old. The software has been updated but the machine is *ancient*. I put in a requisition slip for a new one ages ago, but the bureaucracy, you wouldn't believe the delays, even without the cuts . . . The command should read 'Cassandrise'.

Cassandrise! I was more puzzled than before she had started explaining.

I know it is not perfect, but it says it all as best as one word can. Oh, here they come. That should make it all clear, Sir.

A number of men and women from distinguishably different walks of life, and with corresponding accents, appeared and positioned themselves all round the expanding room and began speaking at the same time. One or two repeated more or less what the angry girl was saying, but exaggerating the claims and shouting in a loud and aggressive manner. Others held a different point of view, a couple of them speaking in very persuasive and cultured voices. Especially trained in media manipulation, whispered the politely smiling girl in my ears. Still others seemed to change their minds ever so often and said first one thing then another. One character was hustled away after he had said no more than three words:

Last year I . . . Soon I was so confused I did not know who to believe, and might well have felt inclined to accept the pronouncements of the well spoken ones had not the politely smiling girl told me that they were professionals. Even as they spoke, television programmes and radio programmes and newspapers all started discussing what the woman had been saying, along with sundry other issues. Almost all the newspapers disagreed with the girl. The TV programmes were less certain but the overall content seemed to go against her. By that time she had gathered a few of her friends with her, who, sensing they were losing the debate, began to lose their tempers. The cool ones remained cool and sophisticated and soon the outcome was clear, even before the vote was taken. One candidate stood against the girl. Three more, with more or less the same point of view as the girl but differing in style and presentation, also stood. They all lost, gaining seventy per cent of the vote. The Cassandrised girl retired into the wall. End of game.

And what can I do for you, Sir? said the politely smiling girl in the cold voice of politely smiling girls in information booths.

What in Earth's name are you playing at, said a hard male voice from behind the girl! Just liqu . . . Cassandrise . . . We are playing the freedom of speech game with this gentleman, new arrival, she replied. Then, seeing the speaking-volumes look in the man's eyes, she added: It doesn't matter, he's only an ephemeral. Oh, is he now, hissed the man, and showed her something cupped in the palm of his right hand. The girl turned ashen and began to stutter apologies, but the man shut her up with another of his speaking-volumes looks. Kindly follow me, Sir, he said to me. By the way, my name is Mr Smith. I acknowledged that with a gentle nod, pretending not to notice his extended hand and without offering my name. He did not press me for it. He seemed to know who I was anyway. You may leave your baggage here with Ms Smith. He smiled, pointing to the no longer politely smiling girl.

I haven't got any baggage, I said, looking at both Mr Smith and Ms Smith; to which Ms Smith, by now somewhat

recovered, responded by offering to take my asphodel –
which I had tucked into the belt loop of my jeans above
the hip pocket and which she could not have seen from her
line of vision – for safe-keeping. I shall put it in a lovely vase
here, ready for you when you get back, she said. Yes, why
don't you? said Mr Smith. It might wilt as we go forward
into the blaze. The fires of freedom, of creativity, of life itself,
can be scorching at times, because of their liberating powers
and their vital force. He extended his long bony hand once
again, this time to relieve me of my asphodel. No thanks, I
think I'll keep it on me, I said. But it is very kind of you. I
didn't want to be outdone by their courtesy game. If you so
wish, Sir, said Mr Smith still very pleasantly. But however
well masked, there was no mistaking the disappointment in
his agreeable voice.

Now, what might your special area of interest be? Mr Smith
enquired after we had proceeded a few steps into this huge
hall of mirrors where I could see myself and the man reflected
from all angles.

It was a most unnerving experience.

I beg your pardon?

Area of interest? Something you would like to do? Have
done? Create? Music, painting, literature, any other? He
sounded like a hastily prepared form.

I am not quite sure, I'm a bit of a Philistine, I'm afraid.

Just then a cute little girl, about eleven with blond curls,
blue eyes and a strangely familiar face, approached me and
said: Please, oh please, may I have that flower you have? I
will give you anything in return, anything, anything at all.
The sharp edge in her voice belied the innocence in her eyes.
Thank you, I said, I am fine as I am. I then removed the
flower from my belt loop and held on to it tightly in front
of my chest.

The cute little blond girl was followed by a cute little
black boy, then a young woman then a young man, then
followed more children and more young men and young
women of different colours, shapes and appearance, followed by old men and old women, all demanding to do
anything for me in return for the asphodel. There was no

longer any pretence at subtlety. Pressure was the name of the game.

I resisted with a determination that surprised even me.

I wondered why they didn't just band together, overpower me and take the flower away. But perhaps that is what talismans are for – they could not attack me while I was in possession of it.

Mr Smith and I were alone again. Just look at this vase, now isn't it a marvel! Just imagine how proud your asphodel will stand within the sheer magic of its beauty, he said.

I had to agree with him. It was the most marvellous vase I had ever seen. It reflected the colours of the rainbow without the rainbow being there and the wings of butterflies without the wings of butterflies being there and radiated the ever-alive and ever-vibrant fury of fire within the coolness of its glassy being. I fell in love with it at once. Scenting victory, Mr Smith hastened to pick up the vase and bring it to me, all but snatching the asphodel from my hand.

I'll tell you what, I said. You wanted my area of interest. I would like to create a vase like that one.

After a momentary look of surprise he seemed to relish my request and took me to the glass-blowing area, an ideal process for the environment as creative fires blended harmoniously with the mundane variety to produce the desired results. He appeared not to worry about my asphodel after that. It would seem that the main idea was not so much to possess the flower but to prevent me from going ahead with my quest, the former being merely a means to ensure the latter. If I stayed on there blowing glass that would satisfy them quite well, and thank you. At first I felt more than a little dismayed, as if I had ended up cheating myself and fallen into their trap. But then I thought, why not? I would do something creative *and* leave when I was through. Best of both worlds. It was clear they couldn't hold me by force, at least not as long as I had the asphodel.

It was not going to be as easy as that. I began enjoying the creative process, it filled me with enthusiasm, pride, and a great joy; a pride and a joy rarely experienced by men but known to most mothers who have brought forth life in the world.

I got so carried away with making my vase that it grew and grew until it grew larger than a large room and then larger than a large building by the time I was finished with it. Its fame grew faster than its size and people came from far and wide to see it and to admire it. I began getting commissions to make more, and more, until my order-book was full from cover to cover. But I was so absorbed in enjoying the beauty of my first creation that I tended to put off any new ventures, just sat and admired this huge vase, which wasn't really a vase for it had no opening. This was a mistake, the result of my inexperience, for I knew not how to form the opening and before I could control and direct my blowing it had closed up. But everybody thought it was an exquisite touch of creative harmony, an inventive work of post-hoc experimentalism of the neo-modernistic school, of which I was declared the unquestioned founder. A flower vase so huge that no flowers in existence could ever hope to fill it, and a flower vase with no opening for any flowers: surely none but a true genius could come up with an idea like that!

For all its flaws it had certainly created a stir, and if it managed to create a stir it had to be of a quality capable of creating a stir. Nothing else mattered. Not that there *was* nothing else, there was. It glowed in the dark and changed colours and shapes at whim. You could see yourself and your whole life reflected in it, and it could not only foretell your future but actually change it. What's more, it could change your past. The number of people who queued up to have this or that mistake they had committed in their earlier life rectified was simply beyond calculation, and I would surely have stayed there for the rest of my life, or death, call it what you will, had I not seen a certain movement, or flutter, within the vaguely vase-shaped dome that I had created.

I saw a mosquito trapped within, its wings caught in the glass at some stage of its heating up and cooling down process.

There was only one way to give it back its wings.

But what about you? said Mr Smith, as did all the others.

Your freedom to create, to express yourself? The freedom of other people to enjoy a great work of art? What about the principle of it? It was only a pitiful little mosquito whose life wasn't worth the effort of its creator. Every great civilisation of the world would collapse if one stopped to consider every petty little person who might stand to suffer because of some great endeavour.

I found their arguments most convincing, but deep inside me I knew that no principle, no freedom, no civilisation, no work of art was worth the wings of a mosquito.

Tears rolled down my cheeks and my head felt heavy as a mountain as I picked up the largest stone I could find and aimed it at the heart of my monumental child of glass.

A thunder like the thunder on the day of judgement shook the very foundations of the city, and a rain such as the rain that flooded the world in forty days and forty nights began to pour from the heavens above the earth and then escape down through chasms and crevices in torrents and streams upon us below. The waters so released put out the fires of Phlegethon and I could walk through it without any difficulty.

As I walked I heard this voice say: You have overcome the most treacherous beast of all, the beast with many names but one aim. Go forth in peace and may your children go with you.

Asphodel
meadows, in the valley of that which is not reduced to ashes

I looked up at the sky. My beating star had completed three full circles, and then some again.

It would seem that my greatest battle was going to be with time, yet I had not the slightest idea as to what it meant or why it went the way it did and how to go about controlling it or making the most of it. The obvious answer was that it did not go anywhere or do anything, but that I was going through it, gradually unravelling and unveiling it as I went along. This wasn't much comfort, nor any help either.

There was only one thing for it: keep on doing whatever I could do, tackle what came my way the best I could, and let time or whatever else take care of itself. If ransom had to be paid to get a hostage back, then ransom had to be paid to get a hostage back. Whether or not that led to more kidnappings in the future was not in my hands. In my hands was this life, *now*, and it was my duty to this life *now* that mattered. I could not equate doing the right thing with doing nothing. That would be abandoning hope and relinquishing faith in the future, and nothing could possibly be worse than that, except abandoning a life that was in my hands; and, lower down the scale, running away from an adventure or an escapade that it was my lot to experience; or refusing to eat a jacketed potato.

So, meadows of that which is not reduced to ashes after the fires of Phlegethon, here I come. Hit me with whatever you have got, and I shall hit back with whatever I have got.

Behind me the Phlegethon disappeared from view, once

again in torrential floods of fire. In front of me the valley opened out to reveal itself. Fields and fields of asphodels, limitless when it came to numbers, sadly limited in variety: nothing like my flaming and vibrant asphodel, but pale green funerary flowers upon greenish pale funereal stems rising out of the earth like the undead of the plant world. Here and there bunches of dry shrubs and groups of dreary poplars served not so much to relieve the monotony as to underscore it.

Once I had gone deeper inland, though, it turned out to be not too bad a place. There was quite a pleasant little lake not far from where I had first stood, around which grew hosts of white narcissi. Birds and animals of various species abounded, giving the whole area a simple but wholesome aura. The people were friendly, though somewhat bored and boring. They lived in small huts, mostly made from dried asphodel stems, but some were made of mud taken from the banks of the lakes, of which I was told there were quite a few. All in all, if the people somehow learnt to perk up a bit and not look so downcast – and, dare I say, dead – life there could not only be easy-going and reasonably comfortable, which it was, but also enjoyable, even delightful, in a subdued sort of a way. With a little initiative, collective will and concerted effort it would be no bad place to spend the rest of the days of one's death.

I made friends with a sad-eyed, pensive-looking man of about twenty-five called Marcus. He had been a Roman soldier and was killed between what are now Rochester and Gravesend in the south of England during the Roman invasion of Britain under Claudius some time in the early forties. Apparently black soldiers and fighters were highly prized then, and he thought I came from a superior race, closer to the gods, even though most of the newly dead held a somewhat different point of view. I wasn't a true black, I told him, true blacks are Africans and I was merely an Indian. A black Indian was neither here nor there and not the same thing at all. He nodded wisely at this, though I had a feeling he didn't quite follow, a feeling reinforced by his remark that I had perhaps died of a severe blow to the head. It was quite a pastime there, guessing how each newcomer had met his or her end, especially in the case of those still young. He had been killed by his commanding officer for refusing to obey a command, a rude command. The irony of it was that he had been quite willing to be persuaded, but the language of persuasion was never used and his initial refusal, only decent, was taken as his final refusal. Dashed unfair, he thought.

When I asked Marcus why most people here showed no sign of life and carried on in that humdrum, half-dead manner, he took me to one side and said that there was a reason for it, a very good reason. Then he walked away. I had virtually to beg him before he told me of the rumours that a god, or rather *the* God, the One and Only True God, lived somewhere beyond the red lake of sacrifice, and that all the enterprising and exciting souls went over to serve Him in return for great and wonderful rewards. Those left behind just did not have it in them to make the extra effort needed, or were simply content to remain as they were. He himself didn't try for he was still bitter over his death and refused to do anything to make it worthwhile since he had not deserved it in the first place.

But you know me. A bit of anima animus, a sprinkling of Sigmund over a helping of Carl, a few quotes from Shree Ramnath, a lot of coaxing and cajoling . . . and we were on our way to look for this One True God and to partake of His wonders.

Getting to the red lake of sacrifice was simple, it was virtually next door. Marcus was surprised that he had been living dead close to it for so long without realising it. The sacrifice required was the sacrifice of no return. That came easy to Marcus: because he had no particular urge to be anywhere, it did not matter where he was. It posed a problem for me. Apparently in my case a simple oath by the waters of the lake was not enough. I had to leave my asphodel behind, planting it next to the bank amongst a cluster of white narcissi.

It was Marcus's turn to persuade me. He had left everything (?) to come with me, so surely I could leave behind a silly flower. The whole valley was full of asphodels, and if I was so fond of one, surely we would find one that was as bright as that one! In fact he had seen one like that not too long ago, this side of the red lake. As for the other side, why, that was overgrown with flaming asphodels, if even *half* the stories were to be credited. He needn't have tried so hard. I would have given anything to come face to face in death with the One True God – no holds barred, no games, no funny stories.

I planted my asphodel by the lake among a cluster of narcissi. A sharp pain hit my heart and my beating star missed a beat, but it was too late by then to have second thoughts, for the lake and everything close to it vanished in a flash and we were in the presence of the One True God.

I wouldn't have believed it. In fact, I didn't believe it. If She (yes, She, unmistakably) was the One True God then I was the One True Man.

However, if I did not believe her (not Her) to be the One True God then I was in a minority of one, by the looks of it. There was a surging sea of humankind between where she stood and where we were, and already a surging sea of humankind behind us, even though we had got there just that instant. I have said 'we' and 'us' here, but you know what is interesting? It wasn't we and us any more, but back to good old I and me. There was no sign of Marcus anywhere.

She seemed to rise from that surging sea of humankind like some latterday Aphrodite cum a primordial Statue of Liberty, towering above one and all, the faces of those closest to her not even reaching up to her toes, her head, shoulders and massive breasts tearing through the roof of the Underworld and manifesting themselves in their hypnotic glory up above in the world of the living. In fact, the majority of the ever increasing crowd surrounding her were falling from up there rather than crossing the red lake.

There was an epidemic of struggle going on around her ankles, calves and knees; the number of those crawling up her thighs was comparatively smaller; those actually entering the gigantic opening between the thighs, criss-crossed as it was with a round mesh of ropey yet slime-ridden and slippery pubic hair, was smaller still, much smaller.

Those with access to the sacred labial gates kept them well oiled and helped each other fight off the upstarts trying to force their way up and in. A similar struggle was going on round the back of her legs and thighs as people tried to get in via the back door, but I couldn't see that from where I stood. Her legs were soaked with sweat and urine, and of those with nothing but bare hand and knees to climb with, more were slipping and sliding downwards with each renewed effort than going up. Many were on some kind of a tenuous ladder, the rungs of which kept coming apart under the weight of relentlessly struggling men and women – mostly men, the women were generally lower down, goading them with electric prods and poisoned javelin tips, or encouraging them with words of love and fury and songs of war and grandeur, deserting them if they fell and looking around for others to undertake the perilous journey upwards. Young children getting younger by the minute were joining in, and a scene of such strife as never was forecast by any pundit or prophet in any doomsday scenario was in full swing. Every now and then *she* urinated and defecated, the torrential piss and the avalanche of shit drowning and burying alive hosts and hosts of aspirants; others, though bone-drenched and turd-shocked, managed to survive and continued their climb with redoubled efforts.

Another struggle, the deadliest of all, was in progress between those who entered through the vaginal gates and those who chose the anal door. Once inside, they all supped and laughed and lived together as one, enjoying the luxuries and pleasures of life – from open or secretive ownership of the great treasures of great art, to the open or secretive ownership of countries, presidents and carphones. Sycophantic and parasitical individuals and organisations were supported in a never-ending mutually agreeable display of opulent grandeur. But on the outside there was this bitter show of animosity between the two groups, alike in all respects except their chosen route. Only minions of both sides suffered, but they were dispensable.

The stench of their apertural abode was almighty, or would have been were it not kept under control by the use of the most exclusive of perfumes. Also, an excess of food and drink deadened the senses enough to make the sticky repulsion of the endlessly stretchable grotto more than bearable. Designer clothing, designer decor and designer media-image-building completed their triumph.

I wanted to get away from it all, but knew that I could not. Strangely, I was so repelled by the vile filthiness of it all that it ended up by becoming fascinating beyond measure. I even stopped bemoaning the self-inflicted tragedy and grotesque folly of my relinquishing the flaming asphodel and with it my right to flight. So forging ahead I began to relish this ultimate degradation of the pride of creation.

To my surprise the crowd parted before me like the waters for Moses, and whereas others were having to fight for every centimetre of the way, I bounded onwards with such ease that soon I was at the god's feet, and then, as if by magic, up and away between those stately thighs. The labial gates quivered invitingly. When I continued to remain outside, crowned men in purple robes and with ringed fingers and bedizened women in outfits that shall remain nameless and priceless beckoned to me with promises of diamonds, private planes, guaranteed tickets for the Centre Court at Wimbledon, unlimited supplies of champagne and regular appearances with Wogan, not to mention fifty different kinds of soap powder.

I began tugging at one of the rough and ropy hairs and, to my great surprise, managed to uproot it. I began weaving a net.

What do you think you are doing? said Marcus, suddenly appearing from nowhere.

Making a net.

What will you do with a net? There are no fish up here. If you like fishing you can own your very own lake, lakes, your own rivers if you like. All you have to do is walk through those gates. I can help you with everything else, but I cannot make you walk in, not unless –

But I don't want to walk in, nor do I want to fish. Not for fish, anyway, I –

But why then . . .

If only you'll let me finish, I said, which was a bit of a cheek since I had not let him finish once, I am making this net to fish for people. I will put this round as many as I can, then toss them down, away and safe from the . . . the clutches of this One True God of yours.

You mean, you mean . . . actually *fish*, like in, like . . . only literally . . . His once sad eyes acquired a glint, first a gentle one, then sharper and brighter. A mischievous smile forced the corners of his mouth upwards, and a giggle forced itself out of his fleshy lips, a giggle which turned into a rip-roaring, thigh-slapping bout of laughter.

I don't know what he was laughing at. I was never more serious in my life.

But to Marcus it was no end of a joke. He laughed and laughed, until his very appearance began to change. Before my very eyes he started to metamorphose. Fishing, people, using the very hair from . . . He couldn't go on, and burst into another raucous laugh which got higher and higher in tone. All this while he continued changing shape and form until he became once again the woman I had seen in the cave between Cocytus and Phlegethon – the woman with the familiar face. Suddenly it came to me who she reminded me of. Tracy, our Trevor's wife and our Terry's mum.

I know I shouldn't be do-gooding like that mealy-mouthed, hymen-infested, tight-holed Artemis, but I cannot let this pass without reward. No one has made me laugh like this in centuries. Let god nor mortal accuse Hecate of not having a sense of humour. I have enough for three.

With this, still laughing hysterically, she held out her hand, and in it lay my flaming asphodel. I picked it up hastily, lest she change her mind as she had her appearance.

You may not have overcome the most obvious and the most powerful of beasts, but you did not let it overcome you either, she said. Go, and I beat Artemis at her own game by giving you your time back as well, which is more than what she can do. With that she was gone.

I found myself in Erebus, in front of the Palace of Hades itself.

My star was still three and some cycles gone, no further on than when I had entered the meadows of asphodel.

Erebus
the palace of hades

I was facing the unseen, the unseeing, the unseeable. It was overwhelming beyond possibility.

A feeling of frothy elation ran riot in my blood. Something very special was going to happen to me here, of that there was no doubt in my heart. But with the excitement came a generous helping of apprehension. Whatever awaited me, I hoped I would be able to resist the temptations it offered. Must remember to heed Athena's warning this time. I had just had a very lucky escape, thanks to the maligned Hecate; I could not afford to make another mistake without ruining everything.

My first rush towards my destination proved frustrating, somewhat like my attempts to get to the tiny tent with the open and fluttering flap within which I had left my Belinda on that fated night oh so many years ago. No matter how much I walked, the Palace seemed to retain its distance.

I also began to dread the thought of meeting Cerberus. Perhaps I should have done so all along, but up until then I had been so absorbed in the dangers immediately surrounding me that I hadn't had time to think about impending perils. Although I now had doubts that Cerberus was 'the triple-faced' against whom Athena had warned me, and believed that her words more likely referred to my now old friend Hecate, he was still not to be taken lightly. Evil though he was to shades, his attitude to living mortals was far from polite. I was not even sure whether I was one or the other. Would he be satisfied with just tormenting me a wee bit, or would I simply petrify at the sight of him and that would be that and no more? As Charon had reminded me, I had neither the Lyre of Orpheus nor the might of Herakles; nor indeed the sop of the Sibyl of Cumae. Would he drool over me and his very saliva be the death of me? What would it be like for me to die now, again? Would it be again, or just the first time?

There was no point in worrying, not that it stopped me worrying. Does it ever? The point was to plan a strategy. I decided on one: if I couldn't get to the Palace, the Palace would have to come to me.

I stopped rushing, took seven deep breaths, lowered myself on to the ground and assumed the lotus position, asphodel in lap. I was waiting, not meditating, but who was to know? Not even I, for before I realised it I had stopped worrying, which meant I was meditating not waiting.

When I stood up I was in this banquet hall inside the Palace and a great feast of food and wine was in progress.

I need not sketch the scene for you, you must have often seen it before, either on the big screen or the small, or in your dreams. Scantily clad slaves, mainly female, serving what passed for food of all sorts of revolting varieties in dishes of gold and silver to the accompaniment of acceptably pleasant music, and pouring champagne out of glasses or down throats, and so on and so forth. The setting was rich and sickening, the usual. If this was Athena's idea of a temptation difficult for me to resist then she had an even lower opinion of me than I had.

Mind you, since it was obviously being organised by that daughter of strife, the eldest of Zeus, the banished one, Ate – she could be seen running hither and thither ensuring the smooth progress of the feast and approaching guests every minute or two to ask if everything was all right – there was bound to be some nastiness behind it all. But I couldn't have cared less.

However, I was hungry, not having eaten since my last dinner with the children. In fact, I was very hungry, ravenously hungry, you might say.

Would you care to change before dinner, Sir? asked a

dark-eyed brunette with the most astonishingly shaped breasts, like mangoes from Benares. They even smelt like mangoes. My hunger seemed to grow by leaps and bounds.

Would I not be allowed to eat if I were not suitably attired? I looked around. Everyone was dressed in a manner designed to make one of two statements: I am *so* rich; or, I have such exquisite taste in clothes. Some even aspired for both. But I couldn't have cared less.

However I was hungry, not having eaten since my last dinner with the children.

The brunette with the dark eyes and breasts like mangoes from Benares repeated her question: Would you like to change before dinner, Sir? There is a princely wardrobe with a selection of clothes down the hall, if you would care to come with me, I am sure we can find something that would suit you. I am sure we will, she added, and smiled, but without opening her mouth. For a moment I had this shock run through my toes. Could she be Belinda, playing me up? She did look a lot like her, just slightly blanched; her skin was the colour of the skin of almonds. Smelt like almonds too. I looked into her eyes again, like the eyes of a cow from Delhi. Too good to be true. Besides, Belinda was one hundred per cent the magic of Africa. This girl was the lure of India, and fake at that.

No thank you, I said, I am fine as I am.

Boy, was I hungry.

She looked a little disappointed but did not pursue the matter. In that case, would you care to select a seat, Sir. There is plenty of room. How about there, by the window facing the gardens, one of the best seats in the hall. She smiled again, this time widely. Scintillating teeth bared themselves momentarily, then disappeared within generous lips like a rhino's vulva. I was about to be steered towards the seat facing the gardens when I saw a man's head on a silver platter, well done (overdone I would have said) and with a mango stuffed in its mouth. I nearly threw up. Slightly better than seeing a pig's head like that, but still, not my glass of water. I was so thirsty, suddenly.

A cold, controlled voice, the sort reserved to deal with

troublemakers, invaded my ears. Is there anything I can do to help? The breasts of Ate insinuated themselves between me and the breasts of the girl with breasts like mangoes from Benares. The breasts of Ate were like melons from Naples. Could these extraordinary pairs be the temptation Athena had in mind? Perhaps, but you know my problem . . . I couldn't feel anything stirring, except in the mind.

Before I could say anything her eyes rested on my asphodel and with a completely changed voice she cooed, I am *sooo* sorry, come with me, please. Then turning round to the other girl she whispered angrily: Wrong banquet, fool.

I was sure I had not moved a step, but we were in this other banqueting hall. Or had the same hall changed character, guests and food?

Food. Everything to bring a herbivore down to his knees. Not basic, though: the most rare and unusual vegetarian dishes, from nut roast to spiced seaweeds and herbs of the most delicate flavour.

In honour of Daniel, smiled Ate. But of course.

The guests were no longer kings or princesses or money barons. There were no presidents and ministers, no rulers of the world, whether of style or pop, fizz, rock or vox; no pillars of the Stock Exchange, no players in the game of big monopoly, no lords of the commodity markets. Just plainly dressed men and women having heated discussions or an intellectual tête-à-tête in various sections of the room over a drink of barley water, or a glass of red wine and a simple, but *so* simple, repast.

The philosophically unassimilated tradition of critical theory as most eloquently expressed in *Dialectic of Enlightenment* met its challengers in one corner; the popular paranoia in all its uncomprehending absurdity surrounding Jürgen H's blindly pragmatised thought along with ultra post-modern bourgeois ticket thinking psychology and identitarianism in the cold light of the fascist dawn were also having a hard time.

In another part of the room the presence of a radical absence which served as the fundamental condition of possibility (Immanuel) of Western consciousness was being analysed, along with the complexity of the relational power-system and the asensory, aseptic hint of death in its constant yet ever-receding horizons.

If Virgil was a splendid failure did it affect the content of a civilisation based on bad infinity, Hegel or no Hegel? And how did the *Aeneid* become the precursor of the founding impulses of the American empire? And what happens when metaphysics runs into civilisation?

Finding all that intellectual diarrhoea a bit hard to take on top of all that regalement, albeit sans blood and flesh, I moved a little further on. There I was hit a solid blow on the heart with the cold steel of fear.

At the far end of the hall, next to one of the many ornate pillars topped by the heads of Cerberus, sat Jason, huddled up like a half empty sack of hay, head bent forward, a shirt spread out in front of him with a sheet of paper upon it saying 'Hungry and Homeless'. I had heard of swinging Phaedra, but this was too much. Not the manner of death but the manner of life!

My heart went out to him, as did I. Rushing up to where he sat I lifted him up by the shoulders only to realise he was not Jason, just a blond boy. His eyes were pale brown. He seemed close to death, just a handful of bones, as light as a paper bag. His young skin hung loose over cheeks that met within his face. His lips were dry and cracked, his mouth open, his chin hanging down like a dead weight.

Just what do you think you are doing, young man, said a very old man who was relaxing upon a table close to where the boy had crumpled back again. Come and sit beside us, you might learn something to your advantage, and to the advantage of this unfortunate youth.

It was the last phrase which calmed me down and I joined the circle of four other men who sat round the table.

Pray continue Fred. The very old man turned to one of the four.

I have nothing more to add to what I have already said. Of course, I am not against compassion, but compassion for this youth can only mean one of two things: pity or patronage. Both would demean his fundamental dignity, both would dishonour his natural life force. That can't be right, even were

I to accept your criticism of me as being elitist in my view of the human animal, contemptuous of the common herd.

And you, Jean, what is your verdict?

I believe that the tragic vision of abstract power is the essence of our times. And to understand that you have to accept the four great refusals of classical sociology, and its victims, such as this poor unfortunate boy. The first is a devalorisation of the social; second, a rejection of the naturalistic discourse of the historical; third, a refusal of dialectical reason – a semiological reduction of the exchange system of the structural law of value is much to be preferred; and finally, a rupture with normalising, and hence with the accumulative conception of power. Offering charity to this boy would hinder that rupture and be tantamount to the abuse of power, normalising it and rendering it accumulative.

Exactly! said the third man. The four-tier rejection of values: Christian, secular, herd, and post-Socratic Greek, as proposed by Fred, ties in quite well with the four refusals suggested by Jean, except the third of Jean conforms with the fourth of Fred, and the fourth with the third.

I disagree, the fourth interrupted. The principle of super-abundant life has to be respected at all costs. As you well know, when Karl spoke of the fetishism of commodities not too long ago, he was merely referring to the fact that the commodity-form is no more than a modern and material formulation of a more ancient metaphysical principle. This nucleus of the capitalist cycle of exchange is morphologically identical to the Christian trinity, provided you see the trinity as the fundamental meta-physical code for the operation of the will to will. Equally, the Christian expression of the will to power uses God as a reality-effect, a circuit of grace like the circuit of capital. Both lead to abstract, disembodied power. Whether machines are the sex organs of the world, or a source of dead power, the commodity-form is not antinomic but trinitarian: dead labour, dead capital, and cynical power. I believe the boy should be left alone.

But I thought you disagreed with the others? remarked the very old man.

I do. I disagree with their ratiocination. I concur with the conclusion.

It was my turn to speak. I spoke: I agree with the last gentleman here. I too am a great trinitarian. Since before I learnt to read and write. Broom the fluffy, Broom the spiky, and the Shit Bucket. In the meantime, while you chew on that, here is something to keep you entertained.

I got up, picked up a plate of pasta shells filled with spinach and garnished with pickled radishes, knelt beside the boy, fed him a spoonful and waited for him to gobble it up and ask for more.

Eeeyyuk! He spat it out in my face. I hate pasta shells and bloody spinach. Get lost! And take your fucking black hands off me.

I had fallen into the trap of temptation after all.

Did this mean that that was that? I should hang up my hat and lie down flat?

Perhaps no, for my asphodel, which I had left on the table as I got up to take the food to the boy, was still there. I dashed back to pick it up, afraid that it might vanish before my eyes or slip through my fingers into some dark abyss. But it was still there, still fresh and still alight.

Within a single breath the boy turned into a strong young bull and disappeared into an alcove behind the two pillars directly in front of me; but not before he had looked me straight in the eyes, winked, and mouthed: Thank you.

My hunger was sated and my thirst quenched without having taken a morsel of food or a sip of water.

The very old man said: Remember, young man, the perfect being cannot be omniscient *and* immutable.

Are you telling me that I have just witnessed perfection.

You disappoint me, young man. If immutability is incompatible with omniscience for perfection, which it is, it cannot but imply the reverse proposition. If a perfect being is a perfect being it knows everything, and if it knows everything it knows what time it is. And if it knows what time it is, it changes along with the time, which makes it mutable, which means it is not a perfect being for the simple reason that it is a perfect being. Hence there can be no perfection. But of course there are objections to this line of reasoning, and objections to the objections. Would you like me to elaborate?

Thanks, but no thanks. Some other time maybe. Actually, I am trying to find out what I am doing here. Can you help me with that instead?

Certainly, young man. Walk straight ahead but look anywhere except where you are going or to your right or to your left or to your feet or up to the world of the living.

I started walking straight ahead, determined not to yield to the temptation to look straight ahead or this way or that way – not even a teeny-weeny glance or a little peek to see where my foot would fall or what my face might hit.

I heard the roar of waterfalls about to descend upon me, and the echo of my footfalls as if mountains were enveloping me, and rumblings beneath my feet as if the ground was about to split open any second. Oh, just look at my new kitchen, said Persephone. Save me, please save me, screamed the distressed voice of a nymph. Turn around and walk back, ordered the terrible voice of a terrorist-maker, or I'll blow your head off. Oh, just look at my new tiara, said Persephone. No, cried an unborn child. No, no, no, please don't, no, no, no. Shake hands on it and the shares of United Holdings are yours for half the price of tomorrow, offered a voice just broken. Oh, just look at my new bathroom, said Persephone. Oh look at all our wrongs, moaned a pygmy and a pig and an abo in unison. Oh look at all our rights, crowed Elizabeth and Robert and Germaine in separate voices.

I carried on walking straight ahead without looking where I was going or to my right or to my left or to my feet or up to the world of the living. It was very hard indeed, I can tell you that. At least in the beginning. Once I learnt how to look inwards, though, it was simple. I just kept my eyes inwards.

The dreaded happened. I put a foot wrong, slipped and fell. I must have been on the edge of a precipice for I kept falling and falling and falling until I came to rest on something hard.

It was a bench in a court. I could tell without looking. However, since I was no longer walking straight ahead, or in any direction, I thought it would be safe to look around.

The judges were sitting on the dais in front of me: Aeacus, Rhadamantus and Minos, sons of Zeus and arbiters of the fate of pale humans. Nemesis hovered above and behind them, the snakes entwining her body hissing impatiently.

Will the defendants please rise, rose the cultivated voice of the clerk.

I stood up.

No one paid the slightest attention to me, all eyes were on a table to my left, between me and the judges. There, next to a tall, gracefully dressed woman – Artemis if I was not wrong – stood Jason, Hagar and Sal.

Screams and scuffles broke out all across the huge courtroom, the size of a modest sports arena, as I ran towards the children shouting, Jason, Hagar, Sal! Jason, Hagar, Sal! Jason, Jason . . . A fledgling pigeon fell in my path and I would surely have trodden on it had not Artemis rushed over and pulled me to one side.

What followed was utter pandemonium. I was held in the vicious grip of two stalwart security guards as Artemis and Hecate (with a different face) went over to the judges and a special conference was hastily arranged. Cameras clicked all around us and reporters and TV crews jumped over each other's bodies to get a close shot or an interview. A blanket was put over my head and I was forced out, kicking away and screaming with all my strength.

After a short walk during which I could hear several doors open and shut, I was sat on a chair and my hands tied behind the back of it.

The blanket was removed from my head.

In front of me, across a table, stood my children; behind them, Artemis and two security guards; two guards stood behind me.

Suddenly I lost all voice. I had thought of a million things I would say to my children if ever I saw them again. I couldn't speak a word. Tears began to trickle down my cheeks, my lips quivered soundlessly, distorting my ugly features and making them uglier still. My body shook in spasms. And of all the things in the world that I could have wished for at the time, I wished that my hands were free so that I could cover my face.

The children started crying as well. It wasn't easy for them, certainly not for Jason, who thought of himself as a hard-boiled grown-up man and not as a child at all.

When the haze and mist of tears and shame cleared a little, Artemis and the guards had gone, my hands were free and I was alone with the children.

Sal came up to me, tied a strangely glowing yellow ribbon round my left wrist and said: This is for something you have always wanted, Dad, this is for Death.

Hagar came up to me, tied a brilliantly shiny red ribbon next to the yellow and said: This is for something you have always wanted, Dad, this is for Beauty.

Jason came up to me, tied a radiant green ribbon on my right wrist and said: This is for something you will always have, Dad, this is for Immortality.

Then all three of them faded away, like a scene from a science fiction movie.

I had not been able to give them anything.

I had nothing to give them.

Even my asphodel had been lost somewhere in the scuffle.

I hadn't even said hallo.

† † †

I don't know what beast I was supposed to have overcome there, but I must have been successful for I found myself at the border checkpoint between Erebus and the territories this side of the river of no birds. My ribbons were on my wrists, my asphodel was down the front of my shirt.

My beating star was short of completing four cycles.

I had crossed five loops of the Styx. Not bad going.

If only the children were with me.

But then, I had to remember that other people had children too.

I wished I could have been happy.

I would have been, if only I wasn't so sad.

Aornis
the river of no birds

USCIT? asked the wry-looking immigration officer. Not far
behind him stood a number of heavily armed policemen and
heavily armed soldiers.

That question was in answer to my request for entry to
the Aornis country. I wasn't sure what he had said, perhaps
because he was speaking through this intricately entwined net
of electrified wire that rose like a wall on the Erebus/Aornis
border and stretched right up to the skies, then over and across
to the far bank of the river itself, to the Aornis/Tartarus
frontier. Sounded like 'Use it?'

Use what? I said, more than a little mystified.

It, anything, everything. Use it, shove it up your ass and
leave it for friends to find it, wipe your shit with it and flush
it down the toilet, dump it on a tip, like your lot do with
everything else. Or, if you don't like *Use it*, how about *You
zit*? You zit on the face of mankind. Or, as some purists would
have it, *You sit*, as in: You sit, you stand, you live, you die, you
get fucked. I decide, and I do the fucking. That is what you
USCITs do, don't you? Fuck one and all. But I don't care, so
you can do what you like. Not that *you* will have much of a
say in it, though you could inform the Bureau. But I do not
care, not any more. I am being sent to Tartary as it is. Can't
do any worse to me. I wouldn't have been here today if my
replacement hadn't been poorly. So, here goes: You zit, Use
it, or the official You sit. Take your pick, USCIT.

My face registered utter blank. If he hadn't ascribed all those
powers to USCITs, from his contemptuous tones I might

have thought he was talking of black people. Colour might have had something to do with it, but that was obviously not the crucial issue.

You really do not know what I am talking about, do you? he said with some surprise in his manner, this time rolling his 'r's and 'l's and drawling in a fake American accent.

Oh, you mean an American? I said, light dawning in my eyes. I probably had traces of a lingering American accent. But I still didn't understand half of what he was implying.

What do you mean, American? Canadians are Americans, as are Argentinians, Brazilians, Mexicans, Peruvians, Columbians . . . You don't own *both* the continents, do you? I mean, you might, you might own the world, effectively do; but there is still a distinction, however nominal. What you mean is the *United States of America*. U.S.CIT: United States Citizen. You zit, Use it, or him or her, or them. You sit, you stand, you live, you die, I rule the world! Get it, dumbo?

He clearly did not like Americans, I mean citizens of the United States. He was right, though. At least in his geo-political comments.

No, I am not an Americ . . . not a USCI . . . not a citizen of the United States, I said, thinking he would be pleased to hear that.

Instead he became even more shirty. If you are not a USCIT (he said it the official way this time, which sounds most like You sit) you may have no right to enter. Niggers are allowed entry, and that grudgingly, only if they happen to be USCITs, or nationals of US protectorates, Australians but not Abos, New Zealanders, pariahs inclusive, and Japanese. No other nationalities allowed in here, mate, regardless of colour, they say, but we know what *that* means. Except in the case of USCITs and protectorate nationals.

I am from England, I said hopefully. Colour had become the crucial issue.

Why didn't you say so in the beginning? he said peevishly.

How could I have, that was the first chance I'd got.

You should have said so earlier, he repeated. You can be allowed, then. Britain's a prot, along with Europe, and Saudi

Arabia and UAE. I said prots are allowed, didn't I? His ill humour continued to mount instead of abating.

But I was too relieved to mind. My eyes scanned the electrified net to look for a point of entry.

He made no attempt to guide me, just kept looking at me.

Well then? He spoke after a short silence, more annoyed than ever. Well then, where is the passport?

My brain burst through my cranium.

How in Hell was I going to get my passport down here? I hardly ever had a proper one up there.

I didn't think you'd need passports here, was all I could think of saying.

You didn't need passports up there until well into the billion billionth year of creation. People came and went on the Lord's good earth as they were meant to be. But things change, time moves on, new regulations come into force. The law has to be obeyed.

Law, the arch enemy of humankind and of all that is wholesome and good – with apologies to Marcus Tullius C – was rearing its prickled prick up again. And time! No refuge from it, is there? No more in the modern post-death culture than in the death of post-modern culture.

Along with the fear of being pipped so close to the post, a feeling of having been unfairly treated began to creep up on me. And you know how destructive that can be. After all, I thought, I acquitted myself well in Erebus – must have, otherwise I wouldn't be here – despite the unimaginable pain and delight of seeing my children again, followed by the unimaginable delight and pain of the meeting and the parting again. I should have been allowed free access to Aornis – that was the promise, or so I understood it, and that was the way it had worked so far, without all this interrogation, and now this impossible demand for a passport!

I realised later on that for all moral purposes I had already been transported into Aornis and that what took place there was part of my trial, but at the time it was difficult to see it that way.

I am sorry, I do not have a passport.

I am not sorry I cannot let you in.

I almost stooped to pleading, but prevented myself before the first please could escape my lips.

All right, if that is the case, I'll turn back and take my chances. If you can't break the rules or change the laws, then I suppose you can't break the rules and change the laws.

I felt better as soon as I had made and announced that decision. Perhaps that is what I should have done all alone. Perhaps my mission in Erebus was not complete, that was why I had not been transported straight into Aornis country. Perhaps I was destined to see more of Jason and Hagar and Sal. And even if not, anything was better than standing there and arguing with that pompous prat. For all his anti-American rhetoric, I bet if I had been a white American, he would be sucking on my toes without taking my shoes off. Anyway, who wants to go to a country where even birds are kept out by a vicious electrical netting? Not me.

I had just turned round when he called me back and said in a different, much nicer voice: Just hold on, I have a quiz here: eight questions, three concern wisdom and hence ignorance, five about some countries on earth. I have been out of there for so long I do not know much of what is going on any more. The other day I was talking about East Pakistan to a friend and he told me it didn't exist as such any more, that it was now Bangla Desh. If you can help me answer all eight questions, I can win a two-week holiday in Asphodel. In return, I'll let you enter.

I was suspicious. I thought you were condemned to Tartarus, I said to the man. How come you'll be allowed a fortnight's holiday?

You are not here to be my accuser or my judge. If you want to get in, I am giving you a chance to do so. If not, farewell and goodbye.

He'd got me there. Just when I had talked myself into believing that returning to Erebus was a hot idea, this. Worth a try. Who knows, I might not be able to do the quiz, which would settle the issue. It would be foolish to pass up the chance.

I nodded agreement. He passed me a sordid piece of paper,

a grubby, much handled photocopy of what might have been
a page from a book. It contained five questions on one side.

SECTION A

1. Which is the country of the covenanting God?
2. Which is the country of honour?
3. Which is the land of one meaning?
4. Which is the beloved country?
5. Which is the hated country?

Is this some kind of a joke, I said. For if it is, I do not find
it funny.

No joke, I assure you.

I still didn't trust him. I am sure he must have known the
answers, anybody would. But I gave my answers: South
Africa, South Africa, South Africa, South Africa, South
Africa.

He gave me a look, then said, Turn the page over.

The other side had three questions.

SECTION B

1. What is the womb called that mothers the foetus of
   ignorance to adulthood?
2. Which is the organ from which ignorance is born fully
   grown?
3. Whose is the seed that fathers ignorance?

I gave my answers: The womb which mothers ignorance
is called the human mind. The organ which gives birth
to ignorance is the human mouth. The seed that fathers
ignorance is the seed of human knowledge.

One final question, said the immigration officer after what
I would call an unnecessarily long pause: What does not exist
but lives eternally; has no eyes but sees the invisible; has no
tongue but speaks the truth; is nescient but defies ignorance.

The human heart as a metaphor, I replied.

Come on in, he said, rather reluctantly. You possess a

527

wisdom that prevents the beast of ignorance from overpowering you.

As I entered the territories of Aornis, I saw that I was leaving the territories of Aornis. The relief was overwhelming, for great and unbearable is the desolation of a place without the flutter of wings.

He was right about the beast of ignorance, but perhaps not in the way he meant it, though it would not have occurred to me if he hadn't mentioned it.

There would be no mistaking the last two beasts that awaited me in Tartarus and Lethe. Anger and apathy, the terrible twins: one inciting, the other blocking. Nothing covert or mysterious or many-faceted about them, even if they were many-layered. They were to spring at me from all angles upon my penetration of their respective haunts.

As the oppressive netting of Aornis drifted out of sight I looked up and saw that my beating star had completed five revolutions. Almost one and a quarter in the last few minutes . . .

Tartarus
the wages of sin

Deafening cries of silence tore through my ears. They were
human and yet not human. A seething disquietude began to
rise from somewhere deep within my entrails and spread
through my entire being.

No visitors today, said a harsh voice, a hard face and sharp
eyes. No visitors for another . . . The eyes saw the asphodel in
my hand and the ribbons on my wrists, the voice disappeared
and the face somersaulted. When the voice returned it was the
voice of a low-ranking civil servant in panic; when the face
was back in place it was the face of a low-ranking civil servant
in panic. The eyes were humble and held low. We were not
expecting you today, Sir, otherwise I would have arranged
for a reception committee . . . I do apologise, I really cannot
imagine what could have happened to the memo, I really
can't. He stopped as another thought occurred to him, a
thought which sent him reeling back a step or two, I-i-is
i-i-it a surprise inspection, Sir? Is it? We were only inspected
the other day, last week, in fact, last month. Everything was
found in order: the food of good quality; medical facilities of
high standard; grounds and gymnasium well equipped; the
library well stocked; the television licensed and in working
order; why, the Chief HMI personally congratulated the
Governor on the smartness and efficiency of all the officers
and staff . . . He finally ran out of words. My silence was
demolishing him more than any reprimand would have.
His crawling was annoying me more than any rudeness
would have.

Would you like a nice cup of tea, Sir? I will put the kettle on, immediately. His desperation forced him to that last refuge of troubled souls. I must admit it worked. We both felt slightly calmer and a little reassured at the very mention of a kettle.

Where would you like to start? Unfortunately the Governor is unavailable today, he had to see his . . . dentist today. I mean, he didn't have to, but it was an emergency. Left molar. Rotting away, all black and holey, he had to . . . My interest in the man's rotting left molar was negligible, and it showed. Where would you like to start, Sir? He repeated, pouring tea out into a cup of delicate china, pale blue and pale rose. Would you care to inspect the kitchen first, or the playground, or the medical rooms?

I think I would like to start with the inmates.

The inmates! His voice assumed the semblance of a high-pitched scream, the fine china cup clattered between his fingers, dropped out of his hand and fell with a muted crash on the blue and white lino of the kitchen floor.

The inmates! screamed another shocked voice to my right.

The inmates! The inmates! The inmates! an ill-formed chorus of voices began to blast out from all corners of Tartary. The inmates! The inmates! The inmates!

Yes, the inmates, I repeated.

But no one has ever asked to see the inmates, not for . . . for . . . a hundred great years, nearly, came the first voice. Or so I have been given to believe. Well before my –

Well, it's high time someone paid them a visit then, isn't it? I was surprised at the note of austere authority that had crept into my voice. After all, all your facilities, medical, sporting and otherwise, are meant for their benefit, aren't they?

Oh yes, of course, but no one has ever –

I think we had better not waste any more of your precious time. I'll have my tea when I am through. Just point me in the right direction and I will wander around. You needn't bother –

But they are dangerous criminals in there, some of them very dangerous. You cannot go in there. Not without prior security arrangements. We cannot guarantee your safety in these circum –

You do not have to guarantee my safety. I can look after myself. Criminals have never frightened me, I am one myself, it is the other lot who scare me.

I made towards the corridors and cells of the inmates' section. I knew exactly which way to go, I have no idea how. Heavily locked steel doors automatically opened at the sound of my footsteps to allow me access to their long-held secrets.

I was back on earth.

In all of earth in all of time rather than in a part of the earth at a given time.

And I was so angry.

My heart burned with the fire of anger until my meat was roasted and my skin aflame.

No wonder the poor shall always be with us.

Because they deliberately and wilfully and criminally refused to enter the mainstream of the honest, hard-working members of the community. The cussed bloody-mindedness of the shitty ones to stay shitty, cosseted within the shit valley of any free and thriving society – witness Harlem, next to Fifth Avenue – had always been known, recognised, asserted and maintained by the assholes who produced that shit in the first place. But to see that self-evident truth visibly and inviolably demonstrated in the excremental, implosive, disaccumulative cycle of post-mortem power where nihilism is both antithetical to *and* the condition of historical emancipation, both within *and* beyond the expanding dimensions of post-experiential history, on earth as in Hades, in the wake of the fourth limousine, as beneath its spinning wheels – this was like having red-hot pokers work their way into the eyes of the soul. In the circumstances clearly those who had been fucked in the world above were continuing to be fucked in the world below. Once a fuckee, always a fuckee.

Yes, the poor shall always be with us.

More than that: they shall multiply, as proved by the steady rise in the number of their live births, not only in the third-class world, but in the great and wonderful United States of America. Would they never learn how to roll a condom on, or know the days of the week well enough to be able to cope with the pill, or have their wombs scraped out? Of course they would not. And the bloody socialists would make matters worse by providing facilities which served to reduce the number of necessary deaths at a time when political pragmatism demanded culling – through economic policies, of course, no overt violence, not unless the Will Absolute is challenged. Then watch out Muammar, look out Leopoldo, honest and corrupt alike.

And here they were, the trod-upons, as they were up above. Only worse, for there was no death any more to present even the misplaced possibility of escape and refuge.

The hungry were suffering eternal pangs of hunger, and those in pain were going through pain everlasting.

Mother was being raped in every corner of every field and Auntie Neelum was straddled by a group of sturdy coppers all at once and turn by turn. Aunt Verna was scraping and scrimping and doing without to be able to afford a good broom in good working order so she could clear up other people's shit, weeping snotty tears all the while over her barren womb. And Father was if-only-ing away with every bout of coughing his bloodied lungs out.

I was so angry, so very very angry. Angry, just angry.

Yes, the poor shall always be with us.

And so will those who study them, gold in their pockets and hearts of gold – metallic, cold, hard and sold on the open market – in order to alleviate their suffering in an intelligent, scientific manner – by trying to teach them the value of self-reliance and the value of making the best of their abilities and the value of good, honest hard work – so they can be worthwhile citizens of democratic meritocracies. But no revolution, for revolutions begin with compassion.

We can bury our heads down to our butt-cracks in the Gospel according to Mark or Marx, then raise the selfsame butt-cracks to the skies and fart to the tune of *We shall overcome one day, we shall overcome* till kingdom come, but we never shall. That 'one day' will never see light.

I was so angry, so very very angry. Angry, just angry.

And in my anger I crazed over and ran amok. But even as I crazed over and ran amok I knew that that was exactly what I should not be doing – that if I had any hope of getting out of there it lay in restraint, I had to *control* my anger, rise above it, and walk away from there. When I did that I would hear a voice saying, You have overpowered the beast of anger, and I would be transported to the banks of the Lethe. If I gave way to my anger I would be condemning myself and my children and the children of other people to eternal damnation. But there was no way I could control myself or the rage that swelled up and rose from within me like a continent of fire out of an ocean of oil.

In maniacal fury I seized a knife from one of the guards who was sharpening stakes and a lathi from a policeman who was polishing his lathi and a machine-gun from a Marine who was walking by, and ran amid the multitudes of the sick and the hungry and the cold and began beating them around the heads with the lathi and stabbing them in the hearts with the knife and machine-gunning them in the guts. I stomped on a starving kid here and jumped upon a pregnant woman there as I rained bullets in all directions.

Die, bastards, die! I screamed. In Heaven's name, in the name of all that is decent and good and worthwhile, die, die, die! Die, scum, die! Die, die, die, in the name of your Lord and creator who loves you dearly and gave His only begotten son to die on the cross so that you might have life eternal. Now you have life eternal. Get rid of it. Die. Die, die, die, die sinners die.

Have the grace to die.

How foolish of me, I hear you say, for they were dead already. But you should have seen them. They lived, even as you and I do. They lived, and breathed and felt pain and fear and hunger and cold. And they screamed, if only the screams of silence that tore through my ears when I first set foot on black Tartarus.

Die bastards, die. Die. Die. Die.

I went up to Mother and knifed the breasts that fed me the milk-poison of life. Die, die, stupid woman, die. For God's sake die. Die before they take your shame and drain your blood and chop your bits off and hang you upside down. Die, die, die. Rest in peace. But she would not die, she just looked at me. A flicker of recognition crossed her pain-glazed eyes, her lips trembled and she smiled. He is born at last, she said, turning to look at Umrao. But Umrao was being butchered so she could not reply. She was not dead, though; Umrao was not. Neither was Mother. No matter how deep my dagger dug into her yielding flesh, she would not die. She would not die.

Die, stupid man, die. I took an abandoned machete to Father. Die, die, die, I shouted as I hacked away at his emaciated flesh, cutting through the brittle bones, die, die, die. Rest in peace. Die, die, die. If only I could, he said wordlessly, if only I could, my beautiful son. If only . . . if only . . . Beautiful! He must have gone blind in his old age.

I couldn't even get close to Belinda's burning body because of the flames.

I raised my machine-gun again and started blasting away at her, and at the multitudes of the shitty ones.

Die, die, die, die, die, die, die, die, die . . . I chanted until I was utterly exhausted, until every ounce of energy was drained so absolutely out of me that I fell limp and lifeless by the banks of Lethe.

Lethe
the river of forgetfulness and a pool of memories

The banks of Lethe!

In my rampant madness I must have fought my way out of Tartarus.

But it did not seem to matter.

Even had I known that what I had been through was no more than a fractional rehearsal of one scene from a many-act drama in which I was to play a central role in the near future, it still would not have mattered.

As I lay flat on my back drinking the intoxicating mist of forgetfulness that rose out of the wonderfully drowsy waters I could look straight up at my beating star for it was practically on top of me. It was just completing its sixth revolution. One more revolution to go, with two loops of the Styx to cross.

But it didn't matter.

There was a slumberous cypress behind me next to some sleepy-eyed narcissi. I managed to raise myself up slightly in order to lean against the tree and adopt a more comfortable position.

I could ask for nothing more.

If this wasn't Heaven, I couldn't have cared less what or where it was.

My recent rage, which had ended up as a sort of dull pain in the middle of my forehead, began to spread itself out again, gradually transforming itself in the process into a weary sensation of sensuous pleasure as it weaved its sinuous way through the atoms of my blood, capturing my head, my heart and my feet with its warm and indolent generosity.

My eyes became the focus of possible dreams, an impish grin stretched my lips from corner to corner, my head rolled to one side and I let myself be taken over by a force whose very strength was gentleness and whose gentleness was music, the music of the gentle flowing waters of the river of forgetfulness.

Just when I was ceasing to be, hoping to experience in the end of strife the end of life, and in the end of life the end of pain, and in the end of pain the cessation of hope, and in the cessation of hope the death of strife; and upon the culmination of that cycle, the end of activity and movement, whether of mind or limb or fluids, I felt a tear come to my eye.

It felt strange. Strange because it was superfluous and unnecessary. I was not unhappy. Far from it. Nothing was troubling me. Far from it. I was more content, more rested, more resolved than I ever remember being in my entire life.

Why the teardrop then?

It was hot and burning, too.

It was followed by another, and then another, until an unstoppable flow of inexplicable tears began to well up into my eyes, and then trickle down my cheeks and my nose – my head being tilted – and on to the ground to my left.

Soon there was a regular pool beside me. I opened my eyes and looked in – not consciously, it just happened. My eyes turned, and there below, in front of me, was this pool of tears. My tears.

I stifled a scream and my body jumped, electrified.

For there in that pool I could see reflected my entire life, which the waters of the Lethe had so successfully obliterated.

I could see Jason calling out to me, and I could see Sal looking at me with that uncomprehending look that came into his eyes whenever he saw me, not being really sure who I was or what a father was. I could see the angelic beauty of Belinda and hear her rare and honeyed laughter as she put her arms round Hagar and told her silly stories of her great big fool of a father. And there was my own father. To think that I had spent years searching for him among the treacherous trees round the basin of the Ganges when he had been here all along, in the pool of my own tears. And there, not far behind, was Shakti. I nearly mistook her for Mother. She really was like Mother. Somehow it had never occurred to me before how very like Mother she was. And I do not mean because she was older than me. Not at all. She was like Mother because she had a certain inner strength which no amount of life and living could take away from her. I would have given anything to see her again. I wouldn't have minded if she sat beside a pond of ice-cold tea. But if she did, what had I to offer her now, now that I couldn't even . . . But Shane didn't care. He still liked me, even if I couldn't, even when I could but didn't, which was worse. Yes, Shakti would be happy to see me, I was suddenly quite sure of that. But how could she see me if I lay here, more dying than dead, more dead than dying? After all, Shakti was the only living person left on earth whom I loved but did not destroy. Or perhaps I did. But not as disastrously as I destroyed Jennifer. Jennifer, poor, poor Jennifer, I took her whole world and turned it to ashes and dust. If only there was something I could do to make up for it, to make up for a tiny part of it! But how could I, if I lay here, more dying than dead, more dead than dying?

Yes, I would have to make an effort to get out of here.

But the waters of the forgetfulness wouldn't let me go.

All right then, I might as well just stay here and forget about it all.

But the pool of memories wouldn't let me be.

I let them fight it out.

A powerful battle began between the two, causing untold floods and storms in which I was swept first one way and then another until I thought my very being would be liquidised and intermingled between the two, between memory and forgetfulness, between caring and not caring, in such a way that both would lose their substance and their worth, their very raison d'être.

Just then I heard a flapping of failing wings and a wounded pigeon fell not far from my feet. I rushed towards it not knowing what I could do to help. The pigeon flew away, hooting like an owl, and that instant I realised that in jumping towards it I had jumped the waters of Lethe.

Elysium
the palace of styx and the crossroads of truth

The Blessed Fields, at last.

But before I finally left the sacred waters of Lethe I took one breath of its aromatic vapours, just enough to minimise the pain of memories invoked by Tartarus. I couldn't face this final arena of my challenges in death while so heavily laden with the aftermath of the challenges of life.

Even in the golden light of Elysium's eternal dawn my personal star was clearly visible. No more than half a turn to go before my allotted seven!

However, the Behemoth tamed, all seven beasts successfully despatched, I was more hopeful than I had dared to be up until then. The gods had favoured me so far and I had this lightness of foot which suggested that nothing could go wrong now. The colour and music of a flight of birds affirmed my optimism. All I had to do was find the Palace of Styx, not be guiled by it and by those who walked in it, not leave it through the pillars I entered it, get to the Crossroads of Truth and take the wrong road. Nothing could be simpler. Well, a few things perhaps, but so what. I had been through worse.

I ran my fingers through my hair, checked that my magic ribbons were properly displayed on my wrists, stuck my asphodel in the button-hole of my shirt so that the stem went inside while the blazing flower stuck its head proudly out, almost tickling my chin. I wanted to look my best in this land of eternal spring and everlasting bliss, in this abode of the great ones of the world.

To my right, surrounded by sprawling tropical gardens and

natural lakes and not-so-natural swimming pools, stood the magnificent residences of Ferdinand Marcos. However, their splendour paled before the twin marble-domed palaces of Papa and Baby Duvalier: the smaller, baby dome marked the acres of Papa D, while the large dome, the papa dome, announced the villas of Baby D. Behind them loomed the ranches and beach houses of Anastasio and other Somozas. The Shah of Iran's palace was only a short flight away. Special Marine squads flew over these properties in Army choppers keeping a constant guard on the life and welfare of the dignitaries within. Somewhat to the left a multi-national architectural venture was in progress in anticipation of the arrival of a certain Mr P. Pot. However the comparatively modest Château Noriega had been abandoned half way through due to irreconcilable differences between the parties of the first party.

I wasn't interested in any of them. I wanted the palace of the great queen herself.

I didn't have long to wait. The septagonal palace with seven pillars of silver supporting the seven arcades that made up the seven façades of the severely imposing building sprang into view with the awesomeness of a sleek and many-legged prehistoric sea monster raising its centuries old bulk above centuries old waters to cast a wearily critical eye upon the new world and its new ways.

It was the construction of the palace which provided me with the clues regarding entry and exit.

The frontage was wedge shaped, with two sets of seven pillars converging like the angular bow of a ship, the second twin set of seven pillars fanned out a little, the third twin set turned inwards, and the final, single set blocked it all off with a straight cut across, forming the unusual aft of this cruiser of a building. All the pillars were set in identical arcades.

The best way to enter would be through the final flat arcade. It was situationally different from all the others, and if I went in through it I could come safely out of any of the other six, whereas if I went in through any of the others I would have to come out of the one that cut across, and that alone: clearly much more difficult than having a choice of six exits. It was easy to see which was which from the outside, but from the inside they would all look the same.

I walked in unannounced and unchecked, after making a slight detour past Zia Cottage.

So far it couldn't have been easier.

As to being guiled by the palace, I felt safe enough. Whatever my failings, and there are bullock-cartloads with some to spare, being guiled by the pretensions of wealth and luxury is not one of them. I had still to be wary of being guiled by those inside the palace. But once again, the beloved offspring of the lady of the house – Bia, Cratos, Zelus and Nike – represented attributes for which I had little time and no affection. They ignored me as naturally as I did them. Indeed, none of the august guards in there seemed to take the slightest bit of notice of me, which was just as well for if they had been curious I would have been hard put to explain my presence.

An anxious hand grasped me by the elbow as an excited whisper caught my ear: Cyrus, Cyrus, I am so glad to see you! I turned to see Edwina's thin face looking up at me with a joy that I would never have thought possible on anyone's face at the sight of mere me, least of all Edwina's. I was not exactly the hot favourite brother. Strangely, my face reflected her joy. At least one member of the family had made the big time. How come you are here? I regretted saying it the moment I said it. The words had a none too polite implication, as if someone like her had no right to be there. I tried to explain but she silenced me. I know, I know, and you are right. I and many like me are brought here to work as servants. For some it is better than being in Tartarus, for some it is worse. We are sent back whenever it suits their purpose. But listen, don't worry about me. Nothing can be done about me any more. But *you* still have a chance. Remember, no matter what happens, beware . . . She froze, as did her words. I turned to see who or what she had seen. It was Shakti, carrying a small baby in her arms!

Shakti . . . I nearly choked on the word. To think I had been thinking so much of her lately. Shakti, I repeated, not knowing what, out of all the things I wanted to say to her,

I should say first. The obvious and the present came to my rescue. Shakti, I said again, come here and meet my . . . I turned to introduce Edwina, but she was gone.

You come here, Cyrus, and meet your son, said Shakti, pointing to the baby in her arms.

My son? My son! But how, he is only, what, a month old? I haven't seen you in years.

He died at birth, as I did. Perhaps I was too old to have –

But with all modern medical facilities? How, how . . .

Medicine is not God. She came and stood next to me, almost touching me, almost but not quite. Time passes slowly out here, she said. Then looking at the child, she added softly, Takes after my mother. The baby was blue-eyed and bright blond. She may have thought I would find it hard to believe he was my son. But that helped to convince me. After all, Jason was blond and blue-eyed and he was my son, or perhaps even my father.

Here, would you like to hold it? She raised the baby up towards me. We happened to be standing in one of those open-air quadrangles you find within palaces of old, with flowerbeds and garden seats, fountains and statues, time and timelessness.

As I stretched out my hands to hold the child in my arms I could see my beating star. It was moving with great speed and was within an arm's length of ending its last revolution. Didn't worry me in the least. What better way to spend my life, or death, than here, in the island of the blessed, with Shakti, my first love, and my son, my first child?

Just then I saw something else, something so startling that I froze in my motion towards my son. And as I froze, so did my star.

What I had seen was myself.

Out there, straight in front of me, behind Shakti and the baby, stood I, looking at my self.

It was only when he, the other I, raised a rustic flute to his lips that I realised that he wasn't me at all, but Krishna, the lord and lover, the black one and the wise one.

As his lips touched the flute and its magic notes began to reverberate in the atmosphere, Shakti's whole body started to tremble. It quivered and shook and shook and quivered until it re-assembled itself in the shape of Hecate, absorbing the baby within its own being.

Lord Krishna began to dance as he played the flute, and I danced too. Together we danced out of the palace, I can't even remember through which exit, seemed not to matter at all, until we were at the Crossroads of Truth.

There I had to take the wrong road. That was easy, for wrong is the opposite of right.

Lord Krishna kept playing the flute to charm my star into stillness while I took the road leading left and found myself well enough to be tried for the murders of Jason, Hagar and Sal, along with sundry other offences, in Her Majesty's Court down in good old England.

Part VII
RIDING THE WHEEL AND FLYING THE TANGENT

December 24

This morning I woke up to find the asphodel by my side, the ribbons on my wrists. I had not seen them since I was last in Elysium. I had almost begun to believe that my journey through Hades was no more than a nightmare of delirium on a hospital bed. But here they were. It could only mean one thing: time to go, to continue on, to fulfil the prophecy, to meet my destiny. Christmas Eve. Nine days before the New Year. Nine days before my thirty-sixth birthday. Three years since the children's deaths, the final three years come to an end. Eastern Europe was coming to an end, too. Would it go on as well? No visitors allowed tomorrow or the day after. Must get word to Adam or to Father O'Neil to be here on the first of January.

December 25

Newscasters enthusing over thousands killed and widespread butchery in Rumania, but despondent that only a couple of hundred bodies could be found in hospitals and streets. Remember my first Christmas. Remember the tinkling of hundreds and hundreds of glass bangles, in the vendor's straw basket, on Mother's wrists right up to the elbows, on Aunt Verna's wrists, on Auntie Neelum's wrists, along the streets. Remember the crackle of washed and starched saris, the smell of the red and green dye on the one Mother wrapped round herself, cuddling me close to her body for warmth. Remember the look of worry on Father's drawn face on the way to church. The debts of the previous Christmas were still unpaid. Great Grandmother smiled each time our eyes met. It was a good feeling. Remember the fragrance of henna on Umrao's snow-white body, now spotted and starred with the red glow of henna related patterns. Remember the church bells, remember falling asleep when the organ played, remember crying when the priest started. Remember Junior twisting my parts.

December 26

Antonio disappeared last night. Some talk of ghosting, others say he slit his wrists. He did so every Christmas, but was more than usually successful this time. Now fighting for his death in some hospital in Hastings. Great and wonderful news, Nicolai and Elena executed. Emancipation of Eastern Europe mercifully complete.

December 27

Saw Father and Jason playing cards by the riverside, Indianised Bridge. May have been a dream. Lively debate after tea on the relative merits of summary trials and instantaneous executions versus prolonged trials and life imprisonments. Tempted to speak. Confirmation that both Adam and Father O'Neil will be visiting on the morning of the first of the New Year.

December 28

Saw a cow from my window this morning. May have been an illusion for it was not a British cow, not clean and fat and sleek and birdless like Aornis, but covered in patchy earth and manifestations of minute life, happy that crows were pecking at her skin, cleaning her up as they fed themselves; but not too happy at the flies which kept invading her ass – the angry flicking of her tail testified to that. Or perhaps not, perhaps it was a joyous flicking of the tail. Reminded me of Aunt Verna. Saw her taking a bath by the handpump once, kept kicking at the flies with jerky wrists.

December 29

Barry and George angry with me for not cleaning up the library properly and for tearing pages out of the Bible for rolling cigarettes. They know I do not smoke but believe I sell them in order to raise money for publicising my book. I do not think they really believe it, but they say they really believe it. If I was out I would be appearing on Wogan, they said, that was how scum got treated these days, better than those who deserved better. But as long as they were there they would see to it that justice was done. Stripped and locked in the experimental pink cell with walls that do not quite reach the ceiling and a catflap in the middle of the door. I was to remain there as a treat and a special privilege right through to New Year's Eve. Hagar and Sal came to see me. Told me Jason could not come because he was playing cards with Father. It was a bit embarrassing as I had no clothes on, but they didn't seem to mind. Besides, it is amazing how much you can hide by just sitting right.

December 30

The pink cell is quite soothing, but I am let out a day early – do not know why – just as I was beginning to make friends with a tiny black spot on the wall opposite me. It had this little trick of enlarging itself and assuming all sorts of different shapes when I shut my eyes or set my back to it; but the instant I turned round, or opened my eyes if they were closed, it reduced itself to the size of a full stop on the wall. We had great fun playing. On one occasion I nearly caught it dancing around in the form of Mae West, but it collapsed before I could lay my hands on it.

December 31

Eastern Europe set to embrace multi-party democracy in the coming year. Hope and pray the United States follows soon.

Repeat of the double birthday celebrations and no snags this time; nothing gone wrong, no drugs, no fire, no deaths. What a wonderful way to see the old year and the old life out. Prepared for what has to be done. There can be no escape. Just as Jason, no matter how different from me, was my son, for I chose him to be my son as he chose me to be his father, even though I was far from perfect, so He who had chosen me was my Father, whether or not He was perfect. I had to accept His will, whatever it entailed, and however many routes and however many worlds – Eastern, Inner, Western, Under or Prison – it took to reach me. Time to give up the struggle had arrived, as had time to embrace the struggle. Time to acknowledge my Father at last as I had acknowledged my son at first.

January 1

Allowed out of my cell at breakfast time and stand leaning against the balcony.

A marvellously black man with crisp hair and crisp eyes tries to push past me. I extend my hand and hold him by the eye. What are you here for? I ask. Robbed a bank of some money, didn't I. He raises his hunched shoulders and tries to defy with his body the discomfort of his heart.

Blessed are you for you did not rob another human being of his dignity or a nation of its heritage.

A few more prisoners move closer, astonished at the sight of someone fraternising with me and keen to get a bit of the action if a fight is in the offing.

I killed my wife, says a pale young man, stabbed her till she was dead, then stabbed her again. She wouldn't wake up. His face was full of annoyed surprise at the wife who wouldn't wake up. I topped a man, says a cheerful-looking redhead pushing the pale young man aside, what you going to do about it?

Blessed are you for you do not let millions die because it suits you to do nothing or because it would set a precedent or because it is good for the arms trade.

Oy wha'? says a voice from behind me.

Don't let that nonce get any nearer, says the cheerful redhead pointing to the Oy wha'. He goes about putting his bloody prick into young lads' hands.

Blessed is he for he did not put a bloody gun in their hands.

† † †

In the silence that follows I bless all who gather round. When I have touched them all I say: I am now ready to go to my Father who is your Father. Bless me, as I bless you all.

† † †

Taken back into my cell to await Father O'Neil and Adam. While I am waiting, I kneel and pray to my Father in Heaven for the forgiveness of my sins, and for the courage to bear what I have to bear.

The time for the desecration of my body and the sacrifice of my blood is at hand.

For the rest, bear witness!

EPIPHENOMENA
ecumenic, ecclesiastic, realpolitik

Since I wrote the Foreword to *Zoetrope* and while the manuscript has been undergoing the process of editorial scrutiny, some unexplained occurrences have allegedly taken place to which I must now draw the reader's attention.

The body of Cyrus is rumoured to have escaped from wherever it was stored and to be stalking the British countryside. Indeed, the world. In fact it was seen in Moscow at the opening of the first McDonald's in Russia, holding a doubleburger in its left hand, crying its eyes out and saying, *The end of the world is nigh, more than nigh, it is upon us.* And as proof it raised the doubleburger high before waving it about in the face of a young Muscovite, whether male or female beneath those clothes, it was difficult to ascertain.

In Britain itself it is supposed to have appeared during several church services of all denominations, each time tripping up the vicar or minister or priest just as he was on his way to the lectern to deliver his homily. In one or two cases it is alleged to have forced reverend men of the cloth to uncloth themselves and perform the act of mooning while facing (away from) the congregation.

On one occasion it reportedly turned up formally dressed at a Monday Club dinner given especially in honour of a

moderately well known lady with moderately well known
and well tolerated views. Not only that, it asked the lady
concerned for a dance after dinner, to which she is said
to have acquiesced, not knowing who it was with whom
she stepped up the pace and pleased to have made a rare
black conquest. It was only half way through the samba that
she was informed, by a discreet whisper in the ear, hearing
which she so forgot herself that she uttered a few ill chosen
words in her normal rather than trade voice, or perhaps I
should say in her trade rather than trained voice.

BURIAL
ecce homo!

The rumours of Cyrus's body turning up here there and everywhere have forced the government to publicly lay it to rest in the hope that the rumours will meet the same fate soon thereafter.

The actual place of burial was kept a secret from all barring a few, myself and Father O'Neil among them; but the funeral itself was well publicised, and many photographs as well as a video showing the body of Cyrus encased securely in a simple but hardy coffin, and then the same being lowered six feet under, were released for the benefit of the press, the television and the public. By a pure coincidence this happened to happen exactly seven months after his disappearance from the prison cell, just as forecast by Cyrus. Had the authorities realised this earlier on they would have waited, but by the time it was pointed out to them, announcing a postponement would have caused a spate of rumours worse than those likely to arise as a result of the accuracy of his prediction, which with any luck could go unnoticed and unremarked.

However, everything did not go as smoothly and uneventfully as expected.

Just after the last shovelful of sod was cast, and the legend-free headstone set in place, and we were about to leave, a scroll appeared upon the stone which to our collective horror read, *Ecce Homo!* To some it was Greek but Father O'Neil assured them it was Latin. Not just that, the asphodel and the three ribbons, which were believed to be safely in the hands of scientists in a secret and heavily guarded laboratory somewhere in the Highlands, suddenly appeared, the ribbons going round the headstone and the flower laying itself upon the body of the grave.

It was decided to leave well alone and a hasty retreat was considered the best option. None of this was of course revealed to the public or the press, and I do so now at some risk to myself.

AFTERWORD

Nine days after the burial, I couldn't not go to Cyrus's grave. Would he rise? No matter how ridiculous the idea, I had to be there. I wanted Father O'Neil to come with me, but he said it would be perpetuating a blasphemy and he wanted no part of it. For all his concern for Cyrus, I have a feeling that he secretly regarded him as someone who had seriously gone astray and needed saving from Satan and all his works more than from anything else.

I lost my way.

My navigation is not the best in the world as it is, and I had only been there once, and that driven up and back by a taciturn Inspector in a car with heavily tinted glass all around. Having to drive myself I lost all sense of direction. Landmarks which I thought I remembered were either not there at all, or led elsewhere. In fact, if it hadn't been for what I can only assume was the beating star of Cyrus and its guidance I would not have reached my destination.

It was dark by the time I got there, and as I stood by the grave it looked so unremarkable and ordinary – there was no sign of the ribbons or the asphodel, nor any scroll upon the stone – that I began to feel a little foolish and wondered why I had taken the trouble to come. I did like Cyrus very much, even admired him. He had that rare combination of naivety and audacity, innocence and corruption, ignorance

563

and knowledge, which I would have dearly liked to possess myself. But still, he was gone. And my publishers were very much here. Not that I am complaining, on the contrary, but I had a deadline to meet: a much extended – as in much married – deadline. Perhaps I should have been at home working away on my latest effort in collaboration with my equal and superior, my word processor. Equal in status, superior in intellect, much stronger in willpower. It did what it wanted to do, and no amount of coaxing or cajoling or button-pushing would make it do aught else. Indeed, button-pushing sent it wild, making a cipher of what little I had managed to produce.

I was about to turn and go when the night split and out of its womb burst forth the head of the sun. And it shone. And it shone upon a desolation at the dead centre of which stood I, Adam Zameenzad, man, son of earth.

And the desolation was the dead centre of a dance of war going on all around it.

And the dance of war was the cause of the circle of desolation at the dead centre of which stood I, Adam Zameenzad, man, son of earth.

And the circle was an ever-widening circle, which if the dance of war continued would encompass the circle of life of the very planet itself, making it a circle of death, and all within it as desolate as the desolation now within its epicentre, in the centre of which stood I, Adam Zameenzad, man, son of earth.

Cyrus was dancing the strongest dance of the attack, Shiva's dance of death, beauty and immortality. Ribbons of Death, Beauty and Immortality glistened blindingly on his wrists in the unnatural light of the midnight sun. The talismanic asphodel blazed away, its flames protecting his black breast from all evil with the blessed union of Agni and Rartri.

As his vigorous feet pounded the earth with the strength

of madness they destroyed all fields and all that grew in them, and all things living fell beneath their raging fury.

Next to him danced Jason. His thin legs moved up and down like mechanical pistons as he kept pace, step by step, with his unnatural father while at the same time wielding a chainsaw and cutting through all trees that came his way, whether young as the morning or older than gods.

Sal followed him, too young to care about the niceties of form and grace, frolicking about in the free and wild manner of a happy child on a sunny day out. In his tiny fingers he held a tiny vial, tiny but with an inexhaustible supply of concentrated poison. This he poured into all the seas and all the rivers and all the lakes and all the waters of the earth. And as he did so, all creatures of all the seas and all the rivers and all the lakes and all the waters of the earth came to die at his feet, from whales the size of ships to beings the eye could not see.

Hagar was by his side. Her step was light and gentle, and she sang as she danced. Her song had no words, just a voice, and as they heard her voice all the birds in the air and all manner of fowl and pheasants and all winged creatures, with or without flight, and their young, precocial or altricial, turned into stone and rained down upon the earth below with a heavy rain of stones, unless they already happened to be on earth when the song hit their ears, in which case they lay as stones on the earth where a moment ago they breathed as beings of delight.

Belinda started singing along with her daughter, though her song had words instead of just a voice, and a staccato, drum-like beat rather than a plaintive melody. Yet curiously both the songs blended musically to provide a rousing anthem for the crowds that followed.

Behind them were crowds and crowds of dancers and singers, and drummers and pipers, those still alive outnumbering the dead, some of them so sick or so hungry or so fleshless you wouldn't have thought them capable of standing up without a crutch. But here they were, dancing and singing and chanting and drumming with the unashamed abandon of the lost with nothing left to lose; though many were content merely to spread methane into the atmosphere, along with herds of cows and rhinos and hippopotami, some of which was used to set alight any fields and forests which survived the feet of Cyrus or the chainsaw of Jason.

Tommo and Net danced wildly and joyfully, selling 'old needles for new' for the price of a diseased fuck. They were giving the same away free and freely to the old and the weary, or whoever asked.

Men were liberating themselves by burning condoms, women by hurling away the pills; though many piled their pills and dumped their condoms on to the ever-distending condom and pill mountains, and danced the ritualised dance of fertility round and round them while mating indiscriminately with lusty howls of delight and praying for more and more live births.

Some of the crowd were clamouring for an instant nuclear war, clapping rhythmically to the cries of: *Push the button, push the button, push the button NOW! Push the button, push the button, push the button NOW! Push the button, push the button, push the button NOW!*

The onslaught against the war dancers was being led by the Woman, the Beast and the Leviathan, who were doing all they could to prevent the disaster and destruction which seemed to be so rapidly engulfing the planet and threatening the lifestyles to which they had been accustomed.

Their minions in their millions were planting new trees and rushing around trying to stop the destruction of the existing ones. To win over people, especially the young and the fit, they were throwing incentives about in the form of gold and silver nuggets, with very encouraging and favourable results indeed. They also acquired the services of renowned pipers, sons and daughters of a much-loved Auntie known to the world as Beeb and fathered by repeated fucks at garden parties and party conferences by someone so important that his name is always printed in capital letters, someone called VOA. These pipers played the most marvellous tunes which lured thousands and thousands of young hopefuls from all over the world to their ranks. The four limousines played their part, and with tremendous success. Invitations to democracy by the white limousine increased the numbers of the faithful with devilish speed, while justice and peacemaking by the black and scarlet limousine caused heavy casualties among the opposition. The pale limousine hit back by dragging its wheels and sending on its companion ahead of itself to torment the living along with the dead and dying.

Ms Footsei was on all fours, servicing a Mr D. Jones orally while being taken from behind by the ever up and always coming Nikkei. As a reward she was given the power to offer digitally indexed fucks, as practised by heavily testicled bulls and thickly pricked bears – inequitably shared and unequivocally addictive – to the eager youths and youthesses of the new age, thus swelling the body-politic of the City lickers and drying up the recruiting potential of the dancing army of Cyrus. Every asshole was privatised and every cunthole was thrown open to market forces, in order to attract more dicks, not to mention Toms and Harriets, and more capital and more investment and hence a younger and more enthusiastic clientele. This further limited the appeal of the less sophisticated and more socially orientated group campaigners of the other side.

However, despite great desertions, especially by the young and the fit and the able, and the shortage of new aspirants to the ancient art, Cyrus and his team of dancers continued their dance eternal.

No matter how many trees you plant, more can be cut down.

Besides, death needs no time to grow.

The ozone hole will swallow up all the other holes. The greenhouse effect will end up browning the Greens and the Blues and the no-longer Reds. Or else all will merge into the cold white of cold ice and melt into nothingness, nothingness which is the mother of all things.

Nothing and no one could now stop the Dance of Shiva, as danced by Cyrus Cyrus.

The dark Man with the donkey looked on, a prayer in his eyes. God was screaming away with hysterical laughter; Yahweh welled up with righteous wrath; Allah was outraged.

Brahma was calm as ever.

One Kalpa ends, another begins. The end of yesterday's dinosaurs was not the end of the world, nor would the dying of tomorrow's dinosaurs be the death of life. The universe will go on, so will the Dance of Shiva, as danced by Cyrus Cyrus. Or somebody else.